EVIL CAVERNS

Raymond suddenly became aware of an evil odor. With a shiver, he recognized it as the smell of human decay.

John sniffed and his eyes took on a speculative cast. "Funny, I didn't notice that smell before." He shrugged. "Let's go. I'm anxious to look at that inner chamber." He led the way into the gloomiest section of the tunnel. The temperature here was at least ten degrees lower and damp slime lined the passage walls. The feeling of evil was almost palpable, a swirling invisible cloud that enveloped them as they made their way deeper and deeper into the underworld.

"It's right there," John breathed. He gestured to the utterly forbidding blackness beyond the arch. Neither the light of his flashlight nor the glow of Hunt's hissing torch seemed to penetrate that awful void.

Hunt stepped into the chamber, his light illuminating the hideous contents of the deep, hollow depression which stretched away from them into the shadows of the opposite wall.

"Good God, man!" Raymond could not stifle his gasp of shock. All three of them stared aghast, horrified at what lay in the pit.

"John," Hunt found his voice with difficulty, "do you think that it was . . . was . . ."

But John could not answer, though his jaws worked soundlessly. His face was twisted into a horrible mask of hate. He laughed hideously, insanely, with a voice bearing no resemblance whatever to his own, freezing the blood of his two frantic companions.

Transfixed in horror they watched him come forward, his disfigured face now a greenish cast, his hands reaching out to them with the promise of death, and worse. And then, when he had almost reached them, his foot slipped on the edge of the depression and he was gone, tumbling down into the hungry darkness . . .

THE ULTIMATE IN SPINE-TINGLING TERROR
FROM ZEBRA BOOKS!

TOY CEMETERY (2228, $3.95)
by William W. Johnstone

A young man is the inheritor of a magnificent doll collection. But an ancient, unspeakable evil lurks behind the vacant eyes and painted-on smiles of his deadly toys!

SMOKE (2255, $3.95)
by Ruby Jean Jensen

Seven-year-old Ellen was sure it was Aladdin's lamp that she had found at the local garage sale. And no power on earth would be able to stop the hideous terror unleashed when she rubbed the magic lamp to make the genie appear!

WITCH CHILD (2230, $3.95)
by Elizabeth Lloyd

The gruesome spectacle of Goody Glover's witch trial and hanging haunted the dreams of young Rachel Gray. But the dawn brought Rachel no relief when the terrified girl discovered that her innocent soul had been taken over by the malevolent sorceress' vengeful spirit!

HORROR MANSION (2210, $3.95)
by J.N. Williamson

It was a deadly roller coaster ride through a carnival of terror when a group of unsuspecting souls crossed the threshold into the old Minnifield place. For all those who entered its grisly chamber of horrors would never again be allowed to leave—not even in death!

NIGHT WHISPER (2092, $3.95)
by Patricia Wallace

Twenty-six years have passed since Paige Brown lost her parents in the bizarre Tranquility Murders. Now Paige has returned to her home town to discover that the bloody nightmare is far from over . . . it has only just begun!

SLEEP TIGHT (2121, $3.95)
by Matthew J. Costello

A rash of mysterious disappearances terrorized the citizens of Harley, New York. But the worst was yet to come. For the Tall Man had entered young Noah's dreams—to steal the little boy's soul and feed on his innocence!

Available wherever paperbacks are sold, or order direct from the Publisher. Send cover price plus 50¢ per copy for mailing and handling to Zebra Books, Dept. 2380, 475 Park Avenue South, New York, N.Y. 10016. Residents of New York, New Jersey and Pennsylvania must include sales tax. DO NOT SEND CASH.

THE UNBLESSED

PAUL RICHARDS

ZEBRA BOOKS
KENSINGTON PUBLISHING CORP.

ZEBRA BOOKS

are published by

KENSINGTON PUBLISHING CORP.
475 Park Avenue South
New York, N.Y. 10016

Second printing: June, 1988

Printed in the United States of America

Author's Foreword

The religious and historical background against which this story takes place is factual. The Anansi Demon described in Part One, and upon which the Anthrada Devil is based, is widely feared by a number of tribes in central Zaire.

According to legend, the Anansi actually did journey to America at least once, in the hold of a slave ship, during the early part of the eighteenth century.

The hero Niyikang referred to in the Ostium inscription at the beginning of the book was an actual person whose exploits have been handed down from generation to generation through the oral tradition of middle and northern Africa.

All linguistic and cultural details of Africa and the Americas are authentic, as are the references to the Sudan excavation. The various psychic phenomena described in the book have their counterparts in actual human experience.

ONE
Sudan, North Africa
January 4, 1970

The two visitors stood for some moments, oblivious to the horror that awaited them, examining the inscription in the stone by the light of their torches. They stood shivering in the desert night air just inside the entrance to a stone passageway leading into the mountainside.

"Do you recognize these characters, Dan?" the senior of the two men, Dr. Mason Raymond, asked his companion.

Daniel Hunt frowned as he tried to decipher the lines that seemed to dance in the flickering torch-light. "Mmmm. No, Doctor. Some of the hieroglyphs seem similar to those at the northern site, but . . ." He was interrupted by the beam of a flashlight shining out at them from deeper in the mountain. Both men turned to look in the direction from which a third man was approaching.

"Doctor Raymond?" a faceless voice asked from behind the advancing glow.

"Yes." Raymond peered at the silhouette. "Is that you, John?"

"Yes, yes of course." John reached them, striding

into the limited light of the torches, and set his flashlight on a rock shelf. He stretched out his hand and pumped Doctor Raymond's vigorously. "Thank you for coming so quickly. Its very good to have you here." He looked out beyond the overhang of the tunnel entrance and seemed to realize for the first time that it was the middle of the night. "They must have directed you up from the camp."

"Yes." Raymond turned to his companion. "John, meet Dan Hunt, our senior Egyptologist at the Cairo office. Dan, this is John Garfield, who is in charge of the Ostium dig." The two men shook hands. John Garfield was just over six feet tall, his thin, foreboding features rendered almost cadavorous in the yellowish light. Smudges of dirt streaked every part of his body, and Dan Hunt felt a momentary impulse to wipe his hand on his khaki trousers after Garfield released it.

John looked back at Doctor Raymond. "I suppose you must be wondering what prompted my urgent telegram?"

"I caught the first flight from London and rendezvoused with Dan here in West Semna this afternoon." Raymond turned away from the inscription on the stone wall. "What is it, John? What's so remarkable about this site?" Doctor Raymond was the director of the London Archaeological Society, the organization that had sponsored the Ostium dig.

John picked up his flashlight, switched it on, and led the two other men deeper into the passage. "As you know Doctor, we found a fragment of a pottery map in the diggings forty miles east of Mirgissa, near the Egyptian border." Garfield was speaking for Dan

Hunt's benefit. "Very little was left of the outer structure of the temple, and we found the exact spot mainly by luck. The rubble you saw as you made your way up from the desert floor was buried under nearly thirty feet of loose rock. It is all that remains of the part of the temple that was originally above ground. This passageway, you see, was once part of the main building which extended out into the canyon." John stumbled slightly as he came to a point where the passage had been sealed by a massive wall of earth and rock. A small tunnel, just large enough to accommodate a man, had been burrowed through the obstruction.

John resumed speaking as he aimed his torch into the smaller passage. "Indications are that this passage was buried deliberately by those who tore down the outer temple."

"Tore down?" Dan Hunt echoed.

"Yes. The damage we've seen here can hardly be the result of natural conditions. The place was deliberately destroyed."

"How long ago?" Raymond asked. He noticed that his voice echoed strangely in the almost total darkness around them.

"As of now, we don't have an exact date. However, geological evidence, carbon fourteen analysis, and," he continued pointedly, "certain references in the inscription there," the man nodded back toward the wall with the carved symbols, "lead us to estimate that this find dates from the late Neolithic Period, perhaps originating three thousand five hundred years ago."

Doctor Raymond nodded. "That would make this

by far the earliest intact remains of the Nagada culture."

John looked around. He had dropped to all fours and was preparing to make his way into the breach in the seal. He coughed in the dust that he stirred up. "Yes, Doctor. The earliest by almost a thousand years."

"You mentioned the inscription." Daniel Hunt spoke softly. He was an understated man; thorough and competent. "Have you translated it already? I didn't recognize some of the characters."

John had already disappeared into the tunnel. His voice echoed back to them. "We've just completed a tentative translation. I'll have copies of it for you tomorrow."

Raymond, and Hunt, who had had the presence of mind to grab one of the torches before he had followed Garfield into the passage, bent down and crawled after their guide, who had vanished. As they made their way down the surprisingly long tunnel, Hunt noticed an electrical cable and called ahead. "Don't the lights work yet?"

"They won't be hooked up until tomorrow." John had come out on the other side and begun to shine his light about, stabbing into the pitch darkness with its beam. Raymond emerged, stood, and began to brush the dirt from his jacket. His head followed the random swings of the flashlight beam and he whistled in amazement. They stood at one end of an enormous underground chamber, cathedrallike in size and decor. The dusty floor beneath their feet was of polished marble, scuffled here and there with the tracks Garfield and his people had left during the

10

forty-eight hours since the tunnel had been opened.

"My word!" Doctor Raymond exclaimed as Hunt climbed out of the tunnel and stood up beside him. The Egyptologist was too stunned to speak as he saw the chamber for the first time. His torch illuminated the scene more thoroughly than Garfield's flashlight. In the center of the vaultlike room, just barely visible across the vast distance, was a black oblong—an altar.

"According to the inscriptions on the walls in here, this is the heart of what was once a temple of Anthrada, one of the early demon-gods of the period." John Garfield talked casually, seemingly oblivious to the magnificence of the chamber, the enormity of the find.

"I don't recall Anthrada," Doctor Raymond said.

"One of the Anthracidies entities," Hunt muttered, never taking his eyes off the spectacle before them. He was conscious of a sense of brooding menace in the chill damp air.

"Oh, yes." Raymond took a step over to stand beside John. "I had no idea the Anthracidies cults were so strong. There's never been much hard evidence that they even existed in fact."

John grinned. He knew this find would put him at the top of his profession. "Well, we've got some damned hard evidence now. The inscription at the entrance tells the story of a hero called Niyikang, who came to the devil's temple and drove him out."

"Is it the same Niyikang of mid-African folklore?" Hunt asked. "Part man, part god."

John nodded. "Very probably. According to the story told in the inscription, the demon Anthrada

11

had a pretty tight grip on the native population around here at the time. Anthrada's chief priest, a fellow called Cymonatha, ran things for well over a hundred years. Supposedly, this priest was granted immortality in exchange for being Anthrada's guardian. And the priest had tremendous authority."

"Was it he who instigated the building of the temple?" Hunt asked.

"Apparently. Quite an achievement this far down into the Sudan. But there's an interesting twist to this form of devil worship." Garfield grimaced at a swirl of dust in the air. "According to the inscriptions, the people here seem to have regarded Anthrada as a living creature, rather than a spirit. They speak of feeding and tending it. It's supposed to have been very powerful in terms of magic. Not only was it supposed to have consumed human beings physically, but legend has it that the demon was capable of possessing people at will, taking over their minds." He began to walk toward the altar. "A neat trick." He paused and set his hand upon the flat tabletop of the altar. "And here, the inscriptions say, they carried out ceremonial human sacrifices."

Garfield paused as Raymond and Hunt caught up with him, each man trying to see everything at once. Raymond gestured to Daniel Hunt, and they knelt down beside the altar, examining the dusty remnants of a human skeleton.

"According to the writing at the entranceway, these are the bones of the high priest, Cymonatha, the man who supposedly lived for centuries."

"How did he die?" Raymond asked. Both visitors knew better than to touch anything.

"Well, the story is that this superman Niyikang was invulnerable to the power of the Anthrada. One day he got annoyed enough at what was going on in the valley that he charged in here and wiped out the entire priesthood singlehandedly, including Cymonatha. The inscription mentions specifically that in order to kill the high priest he had to use a special weapon, blessed by the various gods in some sacred ritual. As you can see, it must have worked." His grin took on a death's-head cast in the uncertain light. As professionals, they all knew how wildly stories of religious combat were embellished.

Raymond pointed to something with the tip of a pen. "Bit of a metal blade lodged in the breastbone. There goes the supernatural weapon idea."

"Science wins out again," John chuckled. "We shall have plenty of time to puzzle out the details, gentlemen. Let's press ahead."

Hunt looked up at him in amazement. "You mean there's more?" For no reason he could pinpoint, he felt decidedly uneasy about penetrating any deeper into the depths of the temple.

"What you've seen so far is merely, shall we say, an appetizer." John led them across to the far end of the chamber where several more tunnellike passageways led farther underground.

"Where do these other passageways go?" Hunt asked as he followed Garfield down the center one.

"Oh, to tell you the truth, we don't know where all of them lead yet. We haven't had time to explore, really. There must be miles of tunnels."

Raymond and Hunt exchanged glances as they continued. The passages here were of hard-packed dirt, in contrast to the rock passageway that had led them to the chamber from the surface.

"We are heading for the heart of the honeycomb," John said as he led the way through the rough, irregular passage. Raymond looked at the strange scuff marks on the floor, worn into it thousands of years earlier, and wondered what on earth could have made them. John continued, "The inscription says that after Niyikang destroyed the priesthood, he dared to violate the so-called 'inner ways.' According to the legend, he searched until he came to some sort of inner chamber; I think the inscription refers to it as a 'lair.' Interesting choice of word. Anyway, it was in this innermost chamber that the demon Anthrada was actually supposed to have resided. Niyikang supposedly confronted it there and somehow destroyed it, or drove it out. The inscription is vague on this point." He stopped at a point where the passage forked into diverging tunnels. "At any rate, he turned around and marched out of here and the local population was evidently delighted to tear down the outer temple and bury the entire site." He paused as Raymond and Hunt caught up with him. "The last words of the inscription are intended as a warning against breaking the seal and entering the underground part of the structure, which they apparently were incapable of destroying. It reads: 'Do not awake the evil which rests within.'"

"Have you found this 'inner chamber'?" Doctor Raymond asked.

"I think so. I had just located a space so enormous I couldn't see across it with just my flashlight. I was coming up for one of the torches when I ran into you.

14

That's where we're heading now, back to the chamber I found. On the way out I'll show you other things. Unbelievable things. One long passage I stumbled across this morning is filled with the remains of literally thousands of people, piled like so much garbage.''

"Does that account for the smell?" Hunt sniffed several times, and Raymond became aware of the subtle trace of an evil effluvium. With a shiver he recognized it as the smell of human decay. It was not strong, but definitely present.

"Partially." John sniffed and his eyes took on a speculative cast. "Funny. I didn't notice that smell before." He shrugged. "Let's go. I'm anxious to get another look at that inner chamber." He led the way into the gloomiest section of tunnel they had yet encountered. The temperature here was at least ten degrees below what it had been in the altar chamber, and damp slime lined the passage walls. The feeling of evil was almost palpable, a swirling invisible cloud that enveloped them as they made their way deeper and deeper into the underworld. Raymond, who had stood in the darkness of a thousand ancient tombs in his career, wondered to himself how John Garfield could have had the phenomenal courage to venture down here alone, in the dead of night, knowing what this place had once been.

"We're almost there," John breathed, quickening his pace unconsciously. They came to a point where the rock walls curved to form a natural archway. Here John stopped, barely concealing his impatience, and waited for the others to join him. "It's right in there." He gestured to the utterly forbidding blackness beyond the arch. Neither the light of his flashlight nor the glow of Hunt's hissing torch seemed to penetrate that awful void.

"You have to watch out. There's a ledge of some kind a few feet beyond the archway. I almost went over when I was here before. That's why I went back for the torch before exploring farther." The excitement of discovery shone from him like rays of light. He turned from them and stepped across the threshold, shining his flashlight ahead like a conquerer's sword. Raymond followed, his eyes straining to make out the shapes of the objects the tiny spot of illumination revealed as it crossed the opposite wall of the chamber, hundreds of feet away.

"I remember now an inscription I saw once in the ancient city of Hieroconpolis, written during the time of King Zoser. It referred to a demon Anthrada. I . . ." But Doctor Raymond never finished his sentence, for at that moment Hunt stepped into the chamber behind him and the light of the torch in the Egyptologist's hand flooded into the great cavern like water into a bowl, illuminating the hideous contents of the deep, hollow depression which stretched away from them into the shadows of the opposite wall.

"Good God, man!" Raymond could not stifle his gasp of shock. All three of them stared aghast, horrified at what lay in the pit.

"John," Hunt found his voice with difficulty, "do you think that it was . . . was . . ."

But John could not answer, though his jaws worked soundlessly. The look of hopeful excitement was gone, as though it had never been. His face was

16

twisted into a horrible mask of hate. He laughed hideously, insanely, with a voice bearing no resemblance whatever to his own, a voice that froze the blood rushing frantically through the veins of his two companions.

Transfixed, frozen in unimaginable horror, they watched him come forward, his disfigured face now a greenish cast, his hands reaching out to them with the promise of death, and worse. And then, when he had almost reached them, his foot slipped on the edge of the depression and he was gone, tumbling down into the crevice, his flashlight flying into the hungry darkness.

For a long moment they could not move. Then, Doctor Raymond slowly bent down and picked up a crumbled copy of the translation to the entrance inscription that had fallen from Garfield's pocket as he disappeared.

"We'll seal it off," he said, looking down at the remains of what had once occupied the cavern. "No one must know of this for the time being. Not until we know more." In a state of shock and horror he held up the papers as though to read. "It has been dead for three thousand years." His voice came back to him as a strange, distorted echo from across the vast expanse of the cavern. "Yet still its evil lingers to possess a man, to drive him mad." He looked at Hunt with the wide, terrified eyes of a horse hearing the chill wind whistle through its own ears. "What if there were more such creatures?" Hunt looked at him and said nothing. "Imagine," Raymond went on, looking back down into the pit. "Imagine the power it must have had back then. Who, what sort of man

17

could have stood here and looked into it, conquered it?"

"We shall never know," Hunt said.

"No. No, perhaps not. But we've got to try and find out." They turned and began the cold, frightening journey back to the outer world, huddled together within their tiny sphere of light, trying not to look too closely into the blackness all around them.

ZAIRE, CENTRAL AFRICA
Eleven days later

The moon was well up when Christopher Arthur Collin strode the length of the river village for the third time that night. It should have been a night of celebration, an evening of dedication to a bottle of good scotch or a deck of cards, for today he had completed the tedious project that had brought him to Africa nearly three months earlier. His finished product was an article detailing the incredible market in illegally obtained ivory. The slaughter of elephants supposedly protected in game preserves had become big business, and poachers operated almost openly, selling their contraband tusks through a network of smugglers to investors and speculators all over the world. Ivory, Collin had discovered, was considered an excellent form of insurance against the possible collapse of the dollar. It had been an unusual project for Collin, who normally concentrated his efforts as a freelance investigative journalist on American politics. But the story had interested him when his partner, Terry McPhearson, first brought it to his attention because it seemed to exemplify the current state of a world torn by the mortal conflict between economics, politics, and nature.

But tonight he was in no mood to celebrate. His fiery, animated eyes were focused unseeing on the surrounding rain forest, and his lean weathered features were set in an expression of concerned indecision. The Sedgewick hunting expedition, some of the members of which had provided him with invaluable aid in his work, had failed to return on schedule from the deep forest. He was deeply troubled by this, and by what he had recently learned about the area into which they had ventured.

The Levi's-clad American paused in the dirt street and stared at the reflection of the three-quarter moon in the river. Then he moved with some resolution down the street in the direction of the government center, a wooden structure surrounded on both sides by grass huts. He strode up the wooden steps and into the foyer, asking for a native ranger whose tribal name was Lianga, but who invariably referred to himself as "Smith" to Europeans. The officer of the watch informed him that Smith was quartered in a room upstairs whenever he was assigned to duty at the headquarters in Gundji, which was the native name for the river village.

Collin climbed the steps to the second floor, trod the simple but tasteful carpeting of the hall to the third door on the left, on which had been painted simply "Smith." He knocked once.

"You may enter." Smith's deep voice carried easily

through the wood paneling.

Collin eased the knob and stepped into Smith's room. A large picture window would provide an unbelievably beautiful view of the river in the daylight. Beside it stood a simple bed.

Smith himself, a handsome well-muscled African, sat in an old but obviously very comfortable armchair. A reading lamp burned above his head and in his hand was a thick volume, *Plutarch's Lives*. On the dresser rested a washbowl half-full of water, and next to it a well-worn desk stood, across which were scattered a few papers and envelopes.

Collin nodded at the book. "Heavy stuff."

"Have you read Plutarch?" Smith asked, allowing the book to rest face down on his stomach.

"As a matter of fact, yes, I have."

"I fear that not many people do anymore. A pity. There is so much to be learned from the study of what has gone on before."

"I quite agree."

"But," Smth smiled, "you have not come here to discuss literature, I fear."

"I wish I had." Collin shook his head. "Mind if I sit down?"

"Forgive my lack of hospitality, Christopher. I am afraid that my thoughts are still far in the past." He watched as Collin seated himself in the desk chair. "Would you like a drink? I have just been indulging in an excellent aged whiskey that I acquired before returning here from England some years ago."

Collin smiled. "Don't mind if I do." He reached across to accept the scotch that Smith poured into an ordinary water glass and handed across. "Is that where you got your education? In England, I mean?"

Smith leaned back in his chair. "Partly." He seemed to contemplate his answer. "What you think of as an education, yes. There, and in the United States. I once spent four years studying in New York City. Have you been there?"

"Briefly, a time or two."

"But to be honest with you, the part of my education that I value most I received . . . out there." He gestured with his head in the direction of the rain forest. "Does that surprise you?"

Collin sipped his scotch. "Not at all."

"From anyone else, I would not believe that." A moment of silence followed. "It is said among my tribe, the Ngbandi, 'All that we have, we get from the forest.'"

"I'm here to ask your help," Collin said at last.

"In what regard, Christopher? As a friend, or in my official capacity?"

"Both."

"Go on."

"Perhaps you are aware that Lord Sedgewick and his people have not returned. They were due back Tuesday afternoon."

"As a matter of fact, I did not check today into the status of that expedition."

"Then you're not worried about them?"

"You mistake me, Christopher. I didn't trouble to check into the matter of their return because I already *know* they won't be back."

Collin was taken aback. "How?"

"The people here speak about you, Christopher.

Do you know what they say?'' Smith smiled warmly. "They say that you are a good man, for a white visitor. That you have a feeling for the jungle here, for the people. I agree with them, for once. But,'' the smile faded rapidly, "there are things about the Anansi Shaktowi land that are not for the ears of any white. Not just because we are fond of keeping our secrets. It is for your sake that we do not tell what we know. Why should we trouble your sleep with something you can neither live with nor understand? We, we of the jungle, know. It is in our blood to accept these things as part of the jungle, and therefore part of life. Christopher, take my word and do not press your inquiries any further.'' He chuckled at the look of surprise in Collin's face. "Yes, I am aware of the evening you spent yesterday at the government center. Word spreads among us when the Anansi land, or Spider God is discussed by the whites.'' He shrugged indifferently. "With regard to Sedgewick and his hunting party, I am not responsible. I warned them against journeying into the Anansi land. They are victims of their own greed and stupidity.''

Collin had listened throughout with eyebrows upraised. Slowly he shook his head. "Smith, I'm going in tomorrow. Somebody has to.''

The black man's usual impassivity gave way to an expression of real concern.

"I'm not doing it out of curiosity,'' Collin went on, "although I am curious. I don't want to invade your people's privacy, and I definitely don't want to go looking for trouble. But those people are my country-men, and I can't let them go in and vanish without doing something about it."

"Alas, I fear I understand you." He lifted his hands in a sad gesture. "You plan to undertake this escapade alone?"

"No. McPhearson has agreed to go."

"McPhearson is not a bad man. But, once in the jungle, for all intents and purposes you will still be alone. McPhearson does not know the jungle."

"And then there's you."

"Yes," Smith said quietly. "And then there's me." He stared out the window in thought for a few moments. "Is there nothing I can say that will dissuade you?"

"I'm afraid not. We leave at first light."

Smith set his book, still face down, on the desk beside him and slowly rose from his armchair. "Grant me one favor, friend Christopher. Get McPhearson and come with me now. When you have seen what I have to show you, if you still want to go into the Spirit land, I will accompany you."

"Fair enough." The two men drained their scotch in unison and left, pausing only long enough for Smith to strap on his pistol belt.

They traveled by jeep for almost an hour along what Collin would have sworn was a virtually impassable road, unfit even for foot travel. But Smith seemed to have no difficulty negotiating the dangerous turns and overgrown passes, even though one headlight on the jeep was broken.

Collin's watch registered the time as 10:38 P.M. when they pulled into sight of a row of huts with corresponding campfires.

The ride in the open jeep had been extremely bumpy, noisy, and cold, and conversation was kept to a minimum. Collin and McPhearson had no idea where the young African ranger was taking them as they disembarked from the vehicle.

"Where are we?" Collin voiced the inevitable question as they made their way up the gentle grade toward the huts.

"We are on the outskirts of the Ngbandi village." His hushed voice was almost a whisper.

"You grew up here?" Collin asked. He looked at the open fires, the racks of fresh meat and the earthen jars and tried to equate them with the man he had just seen absorbed in a copy of *Plutarch's Lives*.

"Not here. When I was a boy, we lived much deeper in the forest. The people have since moved here to be nearer the river and the trade it provides."

They walked in silence along what proved to be a main path leading past the row of huts. The few people tending the fires and attending to various chores invariably stopped their activities and watched quietly as the three men made their way deep into the settlement.

Smith brought them to a halt before a larger hut set off by itself. Before the open entrance, a pole had been implanted in the earth. In the dim light it was impossible to be certain, but Collin and McPhearson believed that it had been painted in a variety of shapes and colors. Indistinguishable objects dangled from the top of the spearlike shaft.

"This is the home of the spiritual and political leader, the chief of this community," Smith said solemnly. "Say nothing and do nothing unless I specifically instruct you."

Smith called out softly in his native tongue. He waited in silence for a moment, fidgeting slightly. He glanced once at Collin, as though uncertain of what to do next, then his call was answered from within. A faint glow shone out from the doorway as a lamp was lit inside. Then Smith crouched slightly to avoid the low doorway and stepped into the hut.

As they waited alone in the dark, McPhearson leaned across and whispered into Collin's ear.

"What in the world do you make of all this?"

Collin had given McPhearson only the briefest explanation when he and Smith had burst in upon the sleeping man earlier that night.

Collin merely shrugged and whispered back, "I'll tell you all about it later."

Terry McPhearson, a burly man of fifty, seemed about to ask another question when they both heard a hissing invitation to enter and saw an upraised black hand reach through the doorway and beckon them inside.

In the dim light provided by an earthen-bowl lamp in the center of the hut, the chief, or "spiritual leader," sitting upon a wooden three-legged stool, looked up at the two white visitors.

Smith had seated himself crosslegged on the other side of the lamp, and he now motioned for Collin and McPhearson to do the same.

When they had complied, the spiritual leader looked them over carefully. He turned to Smith and a brief conversation ensued, during which it was impossible to determine anything at all by the expressionless faces of the two individuals.

McPhearson vowed silently to himself that he would never indulge in a poker game with either of the two gentlemen.

The black man with whom Smith communicated was absolutely bald and his black skull glistened in the lamplight. The stern face could have been that of a man of any age between thirty-five and sixty-five. His body was not trim, but it was definitely not fat. He wore a skirt of braided grass, and an animal hide over his shoulders. Apart from these, his only clothing consisted of bracelets, necklaces, and a variety of other ornaments. Whether they were ceremonial or personal art, it was impossible for the Americans to say.

His attitude and gestures were those of a man accustomed to authority, and the deference which the normally indifferent Smith displayed to him reinforced the impression.

After a few moments of conversation, Smith turned slightly and gestured to Terry. He spoke a few more words, ending the sentence with the name McPhearson. Plainly this was an introduction. He repeated this with Collin, gesturing and speaking the name Christopher.

When this was done, the older native solemnly bowed to each of them, then looked to Smith, who indicated the spiritual leader with a sweeping hand and pronounced the name "Luba."

Collin and McPhearson in their turns bowed as Luba had done, then waited patiently as the two black men again entered into a discussion.

There came a pause as the chief appeared to be taking some weighty matter under consideration.

Then he nodded once, spoke a few more words of Swahili, then rose to his feet effortlessly. Smith quickly followed suit, indicating that the others should stand also. When all three were on their feet, the chief led the way outside.

They moved away from the heart of the village rather than toward it, and stopped before a long hut even more isolated than the chief's had been. To McPhearson, this one seemed dilapidated compared with the other structures he had seen. The embers of a nearly dead fire burned directly before the entrance and a sleeping figure huddled near the fire ring.

The chief kicked out, none too gently, and hissed what could only be a reproach. When the first blow did not bring results quickly enough, his bare foot lashed out again.

The unfortunate sleeper raised himself up on two skinny arms and looked around for a heartbeat, apparently slightly dazed. Then with remarkable suddenness he seemed to collect his wits and threw off the woolen covering under which he had slumbered and jumped guiltily to his feet.

Collin was shocked to see that it was an old woman who stood before them. She wore only a woven skirt like that of the chief, and her sagging breasts hung almost to her navel. Her skin was uniformly shrivelled and lined all over her body, and her face seemed to have a death's-head cast to it.

Collin surmised that she was supposed to have been awake and going about some duty or other, for she launched into what was unmistakably a long-winded excuse.

Luba dismissed the matter in midsentence with an

impatient wave of his hand and barked out a terse command. The woman turned at once and disappeared into the hut.

She reappeared after a few minutes with another woman who appeared to be even older and more weather-worn than herself. Between them they supported the hunched figure of an old man whom they guided to the fire. He wore only a short loincloth and looked to be almost comatose by the sluggish manner in which he moved.

The first old woman carefully helped the old man to sit crosslegged before the fire while the second laboriously bent down and added more wood. She stirred the embers and wheezingly blew air into them until the new wood burst into flames.

As the flames grew, and the light they cast illuminated the face of the old man, McPhearson could not refrain from uttering a sharp curse, bitten off in mid-word. The few wisps of hair that were all that was left on the scabbed, scarred skull seemed to writhe like hydras in the air currents generated by the fire. The dancing pattern of shadows served only to accentuate the shrunken folds and lines of skin that seemed etched into his face.

A drop of spittle ran down from one corner of his mouth and the labored breathing came in short asthmatic gasps. Plainly the man was very close to death, very old, and very ill-treated by fortune. But these things had passed almost unnoticed by the Americans, for the sight that had drawn the oath from an otherwise stouthearted McPhearson was that of the horribly disfigured eyes of the unfortunate wretch. The skin ringing each of the sockets had been burned and mutilated to the point that it no longer bore any resemblance to human flesh. It was a kind of dull gray in color, nothing was left of eyebrows or lashes, and the eyes themselves had somehow been burnt out completely, as though red-hot pokers had been thrust ruthlessly into his sockets and held there.

As the light from the flames danced upon the old man's twisted features, seemingly trying to gain admittance into those agonized sockets, Collin and McPhearson caught only fleeting glimpses of carbonized scar tissue.

Chief Luba seated himself to one side of the old man and nodded to Smith.

"Sit down." Smith's voice sounded remote. Collin and McPhearson complied and the two old women knelt on the other side of the old man. One of them held a clay cup to his lips. Steam rose lazily from whatever was contained in it. The old man appeared to sniff the aroma, then he leaned forward with the help of the other old woman in attendance. He sipped a drop or two and swallowed only with great effort. He tried again and spilled far more of the liquid down his face and sunken chest than he managed to get into his mouth.

"This is Hasha," Smith said grimly. "He has been to the Anansi land. Over ten years ago, when my tribe still lived in the deep jungle, two young men, brothers, went hunting in the heart of what is now the Nkundo Reserve. Their path took them across the eastern foot of Anansi Mountain. As you realize," Smith continued, his voice mechanically cool and even, "the mountain range to the west is forbidden to us. It has been for generations. But game was especially scarce that year because of a drought that had plagued the area for several preceding seasons.

"So they hunted closer to the Devil Land than has been the custom. They succeeded in taking some small game and were headed home when they reached a bluff looking down at the point where the slope of the east side of the mountain reaches the valley below.

"Imagine their astonishment to see Hasha staggering blindly out of the jungle, crying out like a crazy man. He tripped and crawled deliriously. But always he kept moving, and always to the east, away from the Anansi land. Then, to their even greater amazement, they saw this blind man confronted by a lioness that had evidently been stalking him for some time. Sickness and helplessness is very quickly sensed in the jungle, and the lioness moved in for the kill while the hunters watched helplessly from the bluff.

"But the animal did not kill. It crept close to Hasha, and it raised its head slightly, as cats often do when they test the scent of prospective prey. And then, to the amazement of my tribesmen, the cat turned and bolted for the brush.

"The hunters caught up with Hasha in the clearing where the cat left him. His strength had given out and he was barely crawling.

"When they saw what had been done to him, one of the men drew his knife then and there. If this seems harsh to you, remember that the law of the jungle still prevails here, and a blind man in the jungle has no hope. Perhaps it would have been a merciful thing. But the hunter's brother stayed his hand before the stroke. Hasha had been mumbling in his delirium, and by the few words they could understand they realized that this was a matter for the attention of Chief Luba."

Smith paused to take a deep breath before continuing. He showed a slight reluctance as he fought the conditioning that forbade the disclosure of tribal lore to outsiders. "You see, Christopher and Mr. McPhearson, oral tradition has preserved memories of other men with such wounds. Anansi Mountain is forbidden. My own father, as a boy, described to me a body he once saw brought back from the deep rain forest. It bore the same disfigurements as poor Hasha.

"But in all our tradition, there is no recollection of anyone surviving to testify about what had been done to him in the Anansi land. And for us there was a need to know, even though there was a great fear of having anything to do with the Spider God. So they didn't kill Hasha. Instead, one stayed guard over Hasha and the other ran to the village to bring back the chief.

"By the time Chief Luba reached Hasha, he was unconscious. Still, though, he spoke enough in his sleep for the chief to realize what might be gained by preserving the life of this unfortunate man." Smith glanced at the tribal leader with respect. "Another man in his position might have ordered Hasha destroyed at once. There is a widespread belief, not unfounded in actual occurrences, that the curse of the Anansi, or Spider Demon, can be called down upon a person just by speaking or even only thinking about it. Actual contact with a thing or a man who has been in the presence of the demon is regarded as a risky

31

business indeed. He took the risk of helping Hasha, though, and I believe that this was in his mind. He realized that somehow this man had been to the heart of Shaktowi land. Not only that, Hasha had suffered the gravest mistreatment, and presumably the full ill-will of the Spider Demon that we have called by the name of Anansi. Still, he survived and even escaped. My people would reason that such a man had the favor of some powerful ancient god. This was the rationale by which the chief could preserve Hasha and possibly learn the truth. Still, Hasha was kept apart from the tribe, and no one but these two old women, who are priestesses, is allowed to talk to him. They have their own protections from the curse. Hasha is fed and sheltered by the tribe, with everyone contributing, and as long as he stays alive, Hasha in turn is regarded as contributing to the welfare of the tribe. He has become a sort of living amulet." Smith smiled.

"There is no way I can make you understand the complexities of sympathetic and symbolic magic, gentlemen. But it is enough if you can visualize Hasha here as a spiritual representation of the humans in the tribe, all in a general way subject to the afflictions of this devil-god, but he has survived. It is thought that his continued survival demonstrates to the spirit world a pattern they will hopefully emulate with regard to all the humans of the tribe. It is the same sort of principle by which a young wife plants and nurtures various seeds and plants in sacred ground in order to ensure her own fertility. A common thing among so-called primitive people the world over."

Smith paused and Collin was aware of the depth and quality of respect he felt for this calm black man who could integrate two such completely different worlds within himself and still maintain such a remarkable objectivity about each.

McPhearson spoke for the first time. He had not taken his eyes from the old blind man's face throughout Smith's monologue. Terry's face was noticeably pale. "What a thoroughly unbelievable story." It was plain that he did not doubt a word of it.

"Do you know why the lioness didn't attack him?" Collin asked.

"As you can well imagine," Smith's eyes shone in the fire, "there were a number of religious theories put forth to account for that. My own personal belief is that the scent of whatever did that to the old man was still heavy on him. It was an unfamiliar and threatening scent, and the cat was scared off." The ranger shrugged. "That is as good an explanation as any."

"Were you in the village when all this happened?" McPhearson asked. His voice broke in midsentence.

"No. I was away on my first year of schooling at a missionary school at Budjala. But I know the two brothers who first found Hasha, and I have repeated to you the story they told me firsthand."

"What was it like?" Collin asked with a sober glance at the swaying, silent figure with the tortured face. "Did he tell you what happened?"

Smith's mouth stretched in a grim line. "Yes. He has testified amply of what he saw. But it is a facet of his position here in the village, a religious mandate, that only *he* can tell the story. In private on very, very rare occasions, Hasha has been called upon to relate to the spiritual leaders of other tribes the details of what happened to him. Though I have heard him do this, I am not permitted to speak of it here and now. You are the first outsiders who have seen him, with the exception of a missionary doctor who happened into the village some years ago and came upon Hasha unexpectedly. The doctor was not told the truth. He examined Hasha and did contribute a fact which has significance in light of the story you are about to hear."

"Why are we being told the truth?" McPhearson asked.

Smith looked around very solemnly. "I have taken upon myself responsibility for your behavior here, and for your continued silence. In fact, from the point of view of the tribe, I have taken responsibility for your souls, since they reckon a serious risk of your losing them through what we are doing. If you speak later of what you are seeing and hearing now and the tribe learns of it, there will be very serious consequences not only for you, but also for me. I have done this," he swung and stared into the fire, "to save his life." He nodded in Collin's direction. The muted crackle of the fire was the only sound for several seconds.

"I have told you that I can't speak Hasha's story from my own memory, or in my own words. But since you don't understand Ngbgandi-Sango, the language of the people here, the chief has consented to allow me to translate the story as Hasha tells it. Indeed, it is a night for the breaking of many traditions." Smith turned and nodded to Chief Luba, who leaned across and spoke a muted command to the blind man who stared with his sightless eyes into the fire.

Hasha shook his head slowly, as though clearing dazed thoughts. Even this movement seemed to cause him pain for he let out a pathetic, animallike whimper. Then, in a voice so strained and soft that they could barely hear the sounds at all, he forced out what sounded like words, a few at a time. His wheezing breaths and occasional choking seemed to fight with the efforts of his larynx to produce sounds.

"So, so I tell it again . . ." Smith began translating. He had to lean over slightly to catch the words.

"Second season . . . second season of great disease . . . tribe starving . . . starving . . . children dying . . . so we," Smith shook his head, "try, no, move . . . move to new land. Ten men, good men go hunt . . . Anansi land . . ."

The old man spoke with no outward emotion. Whatever terrible feelings the memories may have held for him must have long since been washed away by the lethargy of his life, by the insanity that had gripped him, or by the constant retellings. He spoke as one would replay a record already heard many times.

"Game good . . . very good . . . zebra, okapi, monkeys, all show no fear. We kill . . . take much skin . . . happy men. Then, my friend, Shanaib, Shanaib grow strange . . . strange face . . . say nothing . . . walk off alone into jungle . . . into jungle. We try to stop, he strike, kill two . . . then go. One by one others also go strange . . . follow into jungle . . . great fear."

35

The old man let out several feeble shouts and motioned with his hands as though to push something away.

"Great fear . . . great fear . . . great fear . . ." Hasha repeated the phrase like a litany, his hands moving in agitation. "Hasha and friend last ones left . . . last ones . . . only ones. Leave meat . . . leave meat and run to escape . . . then devil come . . . here," the old man put a hand to his forehead. "It live here . . . in head . . . know thoughts . . . laugh at Hasha's thoughts . . . fear greater than tiger . . . devil make Hasha's feet move back . . . not escape. Devil make Hasha's hands be still, feet move back into jungle. Devil say Hasha and friends be devil's meat . . . devil's meat. Hasha scream in head to gods . . . devil laugh . . . say no gods. Devil make Hasha walk, walk, walk through jungle. See cats . . . but cats no attack Hasha. Devil make Hasha walk through briar . . . feet cut. Devil laugh. Devil make Hasha make water. Devil laugh in head . . ."

The old man's head began tilting from side to side in a pattern which repeated to no apparent purpose.

"Walk, walk to high mountain . . . great fear, great fear, sun going down. Walk to big cave . . . see friends ahead . . . all walking to cave . . . men stand guard there. No move . . . no talk . . . no life in faces. Just stand. We walk down, down into dark . . . walk forever in dark. Down . . . down. See nothing. Cold . . . smell death . . . big smell death . . . long time dead. Then begin see light . . . bigger . . . bigger . . . bigger. Devil laugh . . . say we die soon . . . hear in head, not with ears. Then we enter big cave . . . big cave . . . flat floor . . . cavern . . . there devil be . . ."

The old man paused, and as frightening as his story was, it was even more frightening to see the old man swing his head around as though he could clearly see the men who sat in stunned silence.

"Hasha see devil then . . ." The old man spoke more slowly, the way a judge might pronounce a death sentence on a convicted man. "Devil see Hasha. Devil laugh. Say Hasha ugly. Devil have many faces. Sometimes spider . . . change . . . lion . . . wolf . . . fanged demon. Many Hasha cannot name. Great fear, great great great fear. Bodies . . . man bodies all around . . . bones . . . mountains of bones . . . skulls . . . some animal bodies. Devil big . . . big . . . big. Hear sound of fire . . . see no fire. Walls glow . . . many colors. Some men there . . . live . . . live but not move. Stand still like guards . . . wait, wait. We walk up. Stand in line against wall."

Smith's emotionless voice was somehow more unnerving to Collin than a more animated account would have been. But the intensity in the air was growing with each passing word. McPhearson found himself holding his breath.

"First man, Shanaib. Shanaib walk slow to front of devil. Devil one giant spider. Devil laugh. Two of devil's men come . . . hold Shanaib. Shanaib scream, struggle . . . cannot get away. Devil enjoy struggle. Devil let him struggle. Devil laugh. Devil become something else. Hasha has no name. Devil become no more spider . . . no eyes . . . giant . . . like mountain. Hands reach out . . . no fingers . . . grab Shanaib's head . . . hands push into eyes . . . smoke comes . . . burns. Hands push deeper . . . deeper.

Shanaib scream . . . beg . . . hands push deeper . . . more smoke . . . blood run. Shanaib scream . . . long time . . . fear. Hasha try to look away. Devil laugh. Say no looking away. Devil make watch. Say soon me. Then, after long time Shanaib become still . . . dead. Devil's men say nothing. Carry away and drop in bones . . ."

The impassive faces of the old women at Hasha's side said that they had heard the story many times. One of them held the cup up to Hasha's lips and again he tried to drink. He launched into a fit of choking and coughing which lasted at least a minute. Collin and McPhearson exchanged glances.

The old woman raised the cup again but the old man pushed it away feebly and continued. "One by one . . . one by one . . . one by one . . . great fear . . . great fear . . . great fear. All die . . . all die . . . all die. Me last one. It make Hasha walk. Hasha try smash Hasha's head against wall. Devil laugh. Devil say dead head no good. Devil laugh. Devil make Hasha walk close where others die. Devil's men come . . . hold Hasha . . . hold Hasha's arms. Then devil let Hasha move. Hasha struggle. Hasha fight . . . but Hasha can't be free. Help . . . too tight . . . devil men . . . too strong. Hasha smell devil . . . smell bad . . . very bad. Arms come out . . . feel arms grab head . . . fire . . . Hasha scream . . . feel hands push eyes . . . burning . . . push slow. Hasha no see again. Devil laugh and laugh in head. Devil say he drink blood . . . brain. He made me feel pain everywhere . . . arm hurts . . . legs . . . groin . . . pain everywhere. Smell blood boil . . ."

Collin's hands were clenched into fists so tightly

that he drew blood from the palms.

"Then devil scream mad . . . very mad. Throw me from him to ground. Scream and scream. Scream at devil's men to take Hasha away . . . thing in Hasha's head poison to devil . . . it curse me . . . it laugh . . . say blind man in jungle die quick . . . fear . . . great fear to be blind. Hasha feel hands of devil's men. They drag . . . pain . . . pain. Hasha remember nothing . . . maybe sun . . . trees . . . but memory far away. Hasha wake up here . . . stay here . . . stay here. Now Hasha still feel devil's thoughts sometimes . . . but devil forgot Hasha. Hasha know devil come through sky . . . like white man. Hasha know it can take any man . . . man helpless. Hasha know brains food to devil. Devil cannot think far from cave. Wait for man to come close enough . . . keep some men alive to work. Devil know thoughts. Devil's meat, devil's meat, devil's meat . . ."

The old man let out a cry and shuddered, sobbing as he repeated "Devil's meat" again and again. He was still repeating it when, at a nod from Chief Luba, the two old women gently eased him to a standing position and led him back into the hut.

As the words of the old man faded in the night, Smith spoke again. "I told you that the missionary doctor had examined Hasha. He claimed that Hasha has all the symptoms of a benign tumor in his brain." Smith did not need to elaborate. They were all thinking of the "poison thing in his head" that had made the old man unsuitable as "Devil's meat."

A long moment of silence followed, during which the Americans made no comment. Then, McPhearson turned to Collin with raised eyebrows and shaking hands. "A delusion, do you think? Was he driven mad by what was done to him?"

Collin made no answer. He turned inquiringly to Smith.

"Well, gentlemen," Smith said with a bitter smile, "delusion or no, mad or no. Something did that to him. And that something is still out there, whatever it is."

"Maybe it's time someone found out," Collin said softly. He was thinking of the unfortunate men in Lord Sedgewick's overdue expedition.

McPhearson and Smith exchanged horrified glances as Collin poked at the fire with a sharp stick.

TWO
London, England
January 15, 1970

Dr. Mason Raymond glanced tiredly at his watch as a gentle knock came at his massive oak door. It was 11:27 P.M. He rubbed his forehead in a futile attempt to ease the pain of overworking.

Dr. Raymond had not slept well in the weeks that had passed since that terrible night he had spent at the excavation at Ostium, the night his young associate had died so horribly. Mason knew he would never sleep well again.

With a sigh, he eased the wire-rimmed spectacles from the crook of his nose and set them down beside a nameplate on his desk bearing the words "Mason William Raymond, Ph.D. Director, London Archaeological Society."

"Come in."

The door opened, flooding the room momentarily with the relatively bright light of the hallway beyond. A young woman stepped through the doorway and eased it closed behind her. She was a pleasant-faced woman with a good figure, not above five feet, six inches in height. Her hair was blond and neat, and she wore a long-sleeved safari shirt and khaki trousers. In her arms was a large bundle of bulging manila folders.

"I have them, Doctor," she said. "I'm sorry it took so long."

"That's quite all right, Samantha." The old doctor swiveled his chair around, forcing a smile to his tired face. "Set them right here, will you?" He indicated a general section of cluttered desk space to his right.

"We had to send over to Brentwood's archives for some of these," she said, setting the folders down and picking up a single sheet of typing paper. She scanned it as she continued. "Our own library had originals of four different versions, each from a different period. But none of them were Badarian. I found records of at least six other manuscripts, and references to as many more."

She sat down tiredly on the edge of the desk. "So far, we have secured copies of eight of them, and fragments of three others." She rifled through the manila folders. "Only two are complete, though." She pulled one folder out of the stack, then continued to shuffle through the papers, holding the one she had extracted under her chin. "Here it is. The first one dates from the seventh century B.C., and was found intact in a cave in northern Manchuria. It was inscribed on clay tablets."

As she talked, the doctor leaned back in his chair, one arm of his glasses held up thoughtfully against his mouth. He stared off into space, a frown of concentration on his face.

"The other is Egyptian, dating from the seventeenth dynasty. It was found in the third dynasty tomb of Phara Zoser in eighteen eighty-seven by Jean Phillip

42

Lauer, the famous Egyptologist." She looked up briefly. "It was never translated."

"Why?"

"They had thousands of inscriptions, they never got around to this one. Only after Lauer's death did the curator of the Cairo Museum commission the Berlin Conservatory to undertake its complete translation, along with literally hundreds of other papyrus and stone inscriptions found in the lower region of the Nile Delta. Most of these were relatively unspectacular, and most dealt with details of Egyptian religious and superstitious beliefs."

"So," Raymond turned to face her, reaching out for the folders she still held in her hand, "these are the two completed versions, eh?" He began to leaf through the papers contained within.

"Doctor?" she began, almost tentatively.

"Yes?" The doctor glanced up at her briefly, then back to the folder on the desk, his attention already completely captured by the writing. "What is it, Samantha?" With a visible effort, he forced his eyes from the pages and turned them to the girl with the same kindly, nearly paternal smile he had given her at her first entrance.

"That . . . legend. I'd never heard of it before last week, and I thought I was familiar with most of the significant documents associated with North African antiquity."

"You are, Samantha, you are indeed. A more competent research associate I have never had in all these twenty-five years." He looked down at the papers before him with a look which bordered on actual fear. "No, these have never been thought to be significant in the past. At least not by our culture. They are almost virtually unknown by the world at large, and unremembered even by most of my, uh, colleagues."

"Isn't it a religious manifest of some type?"

Dr. Raymond took a long breath. "Mmmmm. In a way, yes. A number of modern cults are based on it and it has been used as a religious blueprint in some medieval cultures. But actually, it's much more. It is, in effect, a collection of accounts from different cultures and different periods that have been rather loosely grouped together and presented as records of factual occurrences."

"Sounds a little like the Dead Sea Scrolls—the Old Testament."

The doctor pursed his lips, as though he found the comparison unsettling. He finally nodded his head with apparent reluctance.

"Yes. It is vaguely similar in some ways." With acceptance of this thought, his mind began to present him with the deeper implications of this correlation. He began to chew on the arm of his glasses and Samantha recognized this as a sign that he had made one of his intuitive leaps, linking apparently disjunct bits and pieces of information. This ability to see subtle relationships and parallels was his own special genius. She could see that her comment had somehow inspired him to view this current strange project from some new and different angle.

"Doctor? Doctor Raymond?"

"Yes, Samantha?" She still had only his partial attention.

"What is it that is so interesting now about these

obscure legends?" She put the single sheet of paper on the desk in front of him. "Is it connected with the Ostium excavation?"

He looked at her with an odd, unreadable expression. "Why do you ask that?"

"Well, since John died . . . well, you've been . . . different. We've all been worried about you."

"Ahh, dear Sam. There isn't a reason in the world to be worried about me." He paused to put fingertips to temples in a rubbing gesture which belied his words. "As a matter of fact, though, you are half right. This is related to the Ostium project."

"Why have you never let me go there? And since we're on the subject, why have so few of the staff been sent? And why are they all so tight-lipped when they come back?"

"Dear, dear," the doctor chuckled gently, sombrely.

"Something is wrong there, isn't that so?"

The doctor nodded slowly. "Yes, Samantha. That's so."

"And it's related in some way to that dreadful book, isn't it?"

Again the older man nodded. "Possibly. Probably."

"Why haven't you told me about it?"

"To spare you, my dear. To spare you. There was no need for you to know."

"How many of the others really know what is going on?"

"A few, only a very few."

"Tell me." She leaned forward earnestly. "What does that thing mean?" She gestured to the open folder. Across the top of the page, exposed to the ruthless light of the desk lamp, were typed large capitalized letters.

DOCUMENT # 4236 .755A
a14 BROOKHURST COLLECTION

THE BOOK OF THE ANTHRACIDIES

Nichola translation, #904
completed December, 1910.

A photograph of the original clay tablets could be seen in the folder beside the typed page.

"I don't know yet. Honestly."

"You'll need my help," she said reaching out to rest a hand affectionately on his arm. "I'll be more use to you if I know the truth. Please tell me. What happened at Ostium?"

The doctor set his glasses down on the table and yawned into the palms of his hands, rubbing his face as he did so. Then he rested his elbows on the surface before him and tried to think.

"I'll tell you this much," he said at last. "We've stumbled on something that may be of dreadful, critical importance. And until we know more, absolute secrecy is vital. There must be no hint to the world at large that there is anything significant amid the rubble of the Ostium temple." He paused and leaned back in his chair, conscious of the weight of years that had settled upon his tired frame over the last few months. "Get me a cup of coffee, if you would, my dear. And I'll tell you as much as I dare about what happened."

She made the trip to the coffeepot down the hall and back in less than a minute.

"Now," she said. "What happened at Ostium?

"Well," Dr. Raymond took a tentative sip of the steaming liquid in his cup and set it on the desk. He was staring off into the shadows. When he spoke it was in a hushed, contemplative tone. "We may have opened a Pandora's box." He would give her only a tiny fragment of the truth.

In late afternoon, Smith, Collin and McPhearson made camp, which consisted of a small fire and three one-man tents with mosquito netting. Smith studied a map and concluded that they had traversed less than ten miles of jungle that day. As a campsite, they had selected a small clearing beside a rare rock formation of flaking granite. Smith climbed to the top and took sightings of various landmarks to pinpoint their position.

Each of the three carried a Springfield 30.06 hunting rifle and spare ammunition, as well as thirty-eight caliber Smith and Wesson revolvers. In addition, each had a compass, field glasses, water, and a walkie-talkie that Smith had procured from the ranger station.

Smith carried one additional item which the others did not. As they were preparing the night before to depart from the native village where they had heard Hasha's tale, one of the old women had approached Smith and taken him aside. The two engaged in a short, hushed conversation. Then from around her own wrinkled neck, she lifted a leather cord, from which was suspended a shiny metal medallion about the size of an American quarter. This she placed around Smith's neck. She kissed him once on the cheek, muttered a few words in the village tongue and turned to shuffle away.

Smith's surprise had been evident on his face as he lifted the medallion so that he could examine the pattern inscribed upon it. But the solemnity of the occasion was such that Collin had delayed questioning the tall African.

That night, as the three sat around their small fire and discussed plans for the coming day's search, Terry McPhearson brought up the matter of the strange gift.

Smith lifted it from against his chest and held it so that the others could view it in the firelight.

"What is it?" McPhearson asked, leaning forward and squinting slightly to distinguish the pattern.

"A charm. A protection of sorts. The woman who gave it to me is called Yolana. She has owned this most of her life. It belonged to her mother before her, and her grandmother before that. You see, Yolana is what you might call a priestess of the tribe. And the office is hereditary, passing from mother to daughter. Since in their official capacity, they must deal with thoughts, and sometimes items, relating to the Anansi, they need protection from the curse; ways to avoid demonic possession, which has been known to happen to the unwary or the unfortunate. This is Yolana's primary protection. She has worn it every day of her life since her mother put it around her neck over fifty years ago."

"Where did it come from?" Collin asked. He glanced up from the walkie-talkie he was repairing with a small screwdriver.

"Believe it or not, gentlemen," Smith grinned, "it was forged here in the deep jungle generations ago."

"I had no idea that the tribes here had developed any degree of skill at metallurgy," McPhearson remarked.

"No, it's not widely known," Smith agreed. He took a sip of scotch from the metal flagon he had carried in his pack and handed it to Collin. "Recently, a team of archaeologists from Harvard University in the United States discovered the remains of several forges in the jungle a few hundred miles from here. Much to their amazement, they found that the forges had been constructed to produce relatively high-grade tempered steel in many ways comparable to modern steel. And this was done several thousand years ago."

"Was it at such a forge that the medallion was made?" Collin asked. He grimaced as he made an adjustment on the walkie-talkie.

"Mmmmmm. To tell you the truth, I don't know." Smith rubbed the medallion with his thumb and scrutinized it closely. "This appears to be made of some rust-resistant metal. Perhaps it contains silver." He shrugged and dropped it to his chest again. "I myself have never seen such a forge."

"Why did the old woman give it to you?" McPhearson asked.

"She told me," Smith answered with an absent gaze into the jungle around them, "that her mother had come to her in her dreams the night before and told her that I would come. Yolana's mother told her of my plans to enter the Anansi land, and commanded her to bequeath the medallion to me. She said it was the will of the spirits that I be protected. Dreams are heeded carefully by the Mondo-Nkundo people."

"But how could she have known?" Terry asked. "That was a full day before we had even decided to go ourselves."

Smith nodded. "Yes."

"It must have been a tremendous sacrifice for Yolana to give that up," Collin remarked quietly, nodding in the direction of the metal disk. "According to her lifelong beliefs, she has put her own soul in mortal danger."

"Yes, a great sacrifice," Smith echoed distantly. "I tried to protest. And she told me that it was her special place in the pattern of all things to give me her medallion. She said it was the reason she had been born, lived, suffered. She told me there was a purpose beyond what we could see in this time." He smiled. "I could hardly refuse. Besides, this symbol is one of the most powerful in the lore of the tribe. And in this land," he glanced around at the shadows, "I will take all the assistance I can get. Further," he smiled, "there is an old saying of my people, 'Mayele ma nwasi maleki mondele.' It means 'the cunning of a woman surpasses even that of a white man.'"

McPhearson, ignoring Smith's humor, took a long swig from the flagon of scotch he had just been handed by Collin. "You believe in it then, the power of the medallion?"

Smith looked long and coolly into McPhearson's eyes. "Yolana believed very strongly in its power, as her mother and grandmother had before her. And belief in itself is a kind of power, or protection." Smith clasped the circle of metal once again. "Those women have dealt daily with realities that aren't even hinted at in your world. They have seen things that would haunt the dreams and perhaps destroy the sanity of most others. Something has kept them safe. Yes, I believe in it. And I think, for as long as I do, it will work for me as it did for them." He quickly changed the subject and regained his composure. "I didn't realize you had a technical background, Chris." He nodded at the dismantled walkie-talkie in Collin's hands.

"It's his hobby," McPhearson spoke up. "Gadget happy. In his spare time he builds televisions from scratch." Terry grinned.

"Seriously," Collin said, "I studied electronic engineering in college." He flashed an ironic smile. "A fine preparation for a journalistic career." He flipped a switch and the device began to hiss. Collin turned it off. "Well, that's fixed." He headed for his sleeping bag.

The following morning, Collin, who had stood the last watch, gently shook McPhearson and Smith awake before there was more than the faintest suggestion of light on the eastern horizon. The three men broke camp with the swiftness of people who distrust the shadows around them and fear to remain too long in any one spot.

By sunup, they had located the place where Sedgewick and his party must have spent their first night in Shaktowi land. Sedgewick's people had not been as tidy as the rescue party; bits of refuse cluttered the

51

area and the remains of several meals lay scattered where the men had left them.

Collin and McPhearson continually relied on Smith's judgement, and Smith went to some length to instruct the Americans in basic forest survival, pointing out edible plants, dangerous insects, and hidden dangers such as possible quicksand, bad footing, the hidden lairs of carnivorous beasts. He seemed to harbor a continuing fear that the three would somehow get separated, and so he constantly pointed out landmarks, even though, as he remarked several times with sarcastic amusement, a blind, deaf, and dumb man would have no difficulty following the trail left by Sedgewick's people.

Throughout the remainder of the day, they penetrated farther into the Anansi land, making far better time in the relatively thin jungle and flat landscape.

They were over thirty miles into the Shaktowi land when they came upon Sedgewick's second campsite in a clearing scarcely fifteen feet across, directly in the path of an old and well-used game trail. The tracks of a cat were clearly visible both entering and leaving the clearing. Smith sniffed the air.

"There is water nearby. Probably somewhere beyond." He gestured in the direction in which the tracks led.

The sun was just touching the horizon; night was falling. Smith looked at it for a moment, appearing totally unimpressed by its splendor, then swung in a slow circle, surveying the surrounding area through three hundred and sixty degrees. "Set up camp here." he said. "So far there is nothing sinister indicated in the signs." He gestured to the footprints in the game trail.

Collin and McPhearson had seated themselves on convenient rocks, too tired to comment. They rose wearily and commenced to obey Smith's command.

"For safety's sake," Smith went on, "I'm going to scout a few yards down the trail. We don't want any surprises in the middle of the night. None that prudence can avoid, anyway."

"Don't go far," Collin warned.

Smith moved carefully down the trail, not dignifying Collin's warning with a reply.

The white men had long since set up the three simple tents and ignited the small fire in Sedgewick's makeshift firepit when Smith returned. He carried something dull-white and roughly spherical in his hand. He set this object to one side, and seated himself on a rock beside the fire. Then he unslung his rifle and set it carefully beside him.

"What did you find?" McPhearson asked. He was tearing pieces off a chunk of dried meat in his hand.

Collin, who was busy repacking his backpack, looked over and noticed the unusually grim expression on Smith's face. He pushed his pack aside and moved over to join the other two at the fireside.

Smith was rubbing his chin with his hand in a contemplative fashion. "Mac, Christopher," Smith had finally gotten around to calling McPhearson by his nickname, "you know how the tracks have looked up to now." He picked up a twig and drew illustrations in the dust. "There has been a certain casualness in the path each man has taken. Sometimes the trails cross, sometimes they are parallel, and sometimes single file. And I have shown you how to know

53

the pace of the man you are tracking. Whether he walks or runs, is fresh or tired. All these things should vary over the course of the day. And they have."

He paused for a moment, as though not sure how to go on. "But up ahead, the tracks seem different to me. The change is subtle, but it is there. As they proceeded away from this clearing, each man took the same way, as though they walked single file. And the pace is unnaturally constant, as though they never slowed to survey the footing ahead, never stopped to take their bearings. And normally, men just don't follow each other's steps that closely. Not even in thick jungle."

"Trouble then?" It was Collin who asked.

"Perhaps. Perhaps not. There may have been some reason why they would have been unusually careful. Perhaps the tracker, Chaka, grew nervous. Though he has never heard the details of Hasha's story, he knows a little of what lies here. Perhaps when he found this," Smith picked up the white object he had brought with him into camp, and the others could see that it was a human skull, "he may have cautioned the others to follow him very closely and carefully. Still, I don't like it. We should be on our guard more than ever."

"Where did you find that thing?" Mac asked.

"Just ahead. Down the game trail, there's a fairly large stream. Beside it, I found the remains of a hunting camp. Very old. A few rotted fragments of spears and hunting tools, a few animal bones, a few misplaced stones. Chaka, the tracker, had found it, too."

Collin and McPhearson exchanged measured looks. They were all thinking of Hasha's story.

"Could that have been Hasha's camp?" McPhearson's face was as impassive as the ranger's.

"It's impossible to say." Smith sighed in frustration. "It could be." Smith looked away momentarily. "There is something else. Something I have hesitated to mention until now. It sounds like a cliché, but throughout the day I have had the strong sensation that we are being watched. Normally, were either of you to come to me with that statement, I would tell you that it would be astonishing if we didn't think we were being watched after the psychological buildup we have all been subjected to. Our imaginations have been given all the justification they need for a diversity of uneasy feelings. Nevertheless, even knowing this, I have found myself growing increasingly jumpy all day, increasingly convinced that something has followed us, observed us, since we started out this morning."

McPhearson looked to Collin. "And you?"

Collin nodded.

"That makes it unanimous," McPhearson said. "I feel like I did in Korea." He shook his head.

"You were a soldier in the Korean conflict?" Smith asked.

"Yes, First Marines."

"Mmmmm. Sometime I should very much like to question you about your experiences, if you don't mind talking about it. I'm an amateur historian."

McPhearson laughed. "After your telling us about all this," he gestured toward the darkening jungle around them, "I owe you one."

Smith pulled his flagon of scotch from his shirt, uncapped it, and handed it to McPhearson. "I find the presence of a blooded soldier somewhat reassuring."

"That was a long time ago." McPhearson took a drink. "And I'm afraid I've had no experience at all at killing demons."

Smith shifted to a position of greater comfort. "It may be far too late to worry about such things, but I suggest that we try to curtail any direct thought or discussion about the Shaktowi. If the lore is true, such thinking can actually call its attention to us. My people say 'the dog you do not feed will not hear your call.'"

"If it *is* a demon." Collin spoke up for the first time. "I've come up with some alternate theories to explain what's out here."

"Such as?" Smith inquired.

"A particularly hostile and cunning tribe indigenous to this area called the Leopard-men. They capture unwary travelers and subject them to the kind of unspeakable savage tortures Hasha went through. Supposedly they can transform themselves into leopards at will. I have heard they even sacrifice members of their families in the process. Perhaps they do it under a cloak of religious symbolism, planting the seeds of what might be Hasha's delusions about the demons."

"Plausible. Highly plausible. The Zande, who also inhabit this forest to the north, call the Spider God 'Tula.' Perhaps they foster this madness," Smith commented thoughtfully. "I know of the Leopard-men. But how do you explain the high incidence of demoniac possession among my people?"

"I don't really have to. Manifestations that have been termed possession have occurred in nearly every culture and at every period in history. In fact they are particularly common among African and South American tribes, as I'm sure you know. Here," Collin hesitated, "the very hysteria of the religious feeling about the Anansi could set off possession reactions. Don't get me wrong. I'm no expert in these things. I've just been thinking of plausible alternative explanations. We'll be better off if we are prepared for whatever happens."

"Agreed," said Smith.

"Nevertheless," McPhearson broke in, "Smith's suggestion about limiting our thoughts and words with regard to this Shaktowi seems a sensible precaution to me. I've seen enough," he nodded at the skull resting in the sand, "to believe that anything is possible."

There was a long pause as full darkness seemed to settle in all around them. Then, McPhearson spoke.

"You know, boys, I've been thinkin' a lot about my wife."

"Why didn't you bring her to Africa with you?" Collin asked, recalling that Terry's wife had accompanied them on several prior business trips.

"She didn't want to come. She's been here before, and she felt like staying home this year."

"No trouble between you, I hope?"

"No," Mac laughed softly, "nothing like that." He turned to Smith in a vaguely awkward attempt to compensate for having briefly excluded him from the conversation. "You married?"

"Once." Smith's face retained its usual impassivity.

"What happened?"

"She died."

"Oh," was all Mac could say.

"And you, Christopher?" Smith asked quietly.

Collin shook his head. "No. Never been married, myself. I'm engaged though. She's home—in the States."

Collin looked from one man to the other. Both faces bore the same sober expression of longing. "Hey," he said, "why don't you get some sleep." Collin picked up his rifle and headed for a rock beside the fire. He wrapped a blanket around his shoulders and sipped from a metal coffee cup. "I'll take the first watch."

Smith turned to McPhearson in a rare expression of humor and asked, "Do you think we can trust him?"

McPhearson shrugged. "He's not much, but he's all we've got."

The two moved to their respective tents, crawled in, and closed the mosquito netting over their faces. Collin noted that despite their joking casualness each of them had pulled their rifles in with them.

Collin pushed the button that illuminated the face of his watch. 9:14 already. His guard lasted till midnight. He leaned across and added a few more pieces of wood to the small fire.

Stars were visible by the millions in the sky above his head. It seemed to him that he could see far more stars in the African night sky than he had ever seen before in his life. Even the deserts in the American southwest could not match the display above him now. He took a few minutes trying to pick out constellations before remembering that most of those that can be seen from the Southern Hemisphere are entirely different from the ones to which he had grown accustomed all his life. He gave up, and for a time contented himself with inventing his own constellations.

By 10:30, the eerie feeling of being watched, which had abated when they had first set up camp in the clearing, returned at full force, and Collin found himself staring for long periods into the shadows of the jungle around him. The night abounded with life, as the nocturnal creatures that had lain in hiding throughout the daylight hours were about the business of survival. The wide variety of sounds they made echoed in a strange and frightening fashion. These things did not trouble the American, for he had grown accustomed to the normal night sounds of the forest on his previous outings with Smith. He was troubled instead by the impression of things unheard and unseen, which seemed to hover at the edge of his perception. Smith had said it: They were being watched.

Collin found himself replaying the story Hasha had told two nights before, despite Smith's precautions against doing so. Here, alone and in the middle of a hostile terrain of evil reputation, it was easy to credit Hasha's account with far more reliability than the American would have preferred. The skull and abandoned hunting camp ahead, although far from conclusive proof, at least supplied disturbing substantiation.

Suddenly, the fire crackled loudly and unexpectedly, causing Collin to jump in alarm. He laughed mirthlessly at himself and settled down again, determined to thrust his grim musings from his mind.

In order to keep himself awake and alert, he rose, clicked off the safety on the bolt of his rifle, and quietly walked a circuit of the clearing, observing that his companions were sleeping comfortably. He stared into the blackness of the rain forest around them and couldn't help but wonder at his own motives for subjecting himself to the dangers ahead, whether real or imagined.

He acknowledged his concern for the welfare of those they tracked. Beyond that, he realized that a part of him was deeply enjoying this incredible escapade; tracking endangered men in a trackless waste, and he realized that he would not go back now even if the dangers ahead were much more tangible.

Collin completed his circuit and sat down again on the warm rock. The furtive watcher he sensed beyond the outer limits of the firelight was still there, but having now come to terms with his own motivations, it did not seem to bother him as much. He passed the remainder of his time on watch by carefully cleaning and loading the small Nikon camera he had packed with him, an activity, he realized with a sardonic smile, that was his personal equivalent of whistling in the dark.

With fifteen minutes remaining till midnight, when he was scheduled to awaken McPhearson, he noticed that his countryman was stirring uncomfortably in his tent, muttering in his sleep. Unquestionably, Terry was having a particularly disturbing nightmare. Collin gingerly stepped over to him and lifted the mosquito netting. He watched the troubled McPhearson for a moment, and decided to wake him early, so that the sleeping man's mumbled cries would not arouse Smith.

"Hey, buddy." Collin shook Mac's shoulder gently. "You okay?" He shook him again and Mac came to himself.

"My time so soon?" McPhearson groaned. He rolled over and tried to read his watch without success.

Collin chuckled softly. "You were having a nightmare. I woke you up a little early; thought I'd spare you the climax."

"Was I? I don't remember." Mac rubbed the side of his face. "I could use a shave."

"Well, you could always borrow Smith's straight razor."

"Ha! I'd be dead in ten minutes if I tried to use that goddamned thing of his. Here, take this will you?" McPhearson handed Collin his rifle and crawled laboriously out of his tent.

McPhearson took a deep breath of the chill night air, then wrapped his arms about himself to keep warm.

"Here." Collin handed him the blanket and his rifle, then settled into his own tent. "You know, Mac? I don't know why we bothered bringing three of these fucking tents. Only two of us ever sleep at the same time."

Mac laughed quietly. "Yeah. But what if we get separated for any reason?"

"Oh yeah," Collin responded sheepishly.

"How's it been going up here?" McPhearson asked, looking around into the shadows.

"Just fine." Collin yawned. "Quiet as a tomb."

McPhearson shook his head in exasperation. "Brilliant choice of words. Brilliant."

"Sorry." Collin put his head upon his pack and closed the netting. "Good night."

"Good night yourself."

Collin was asleep in a matter of minutes, and McPhearson was left, as Collin had been before him, to face the fears that his own subconscious conjured up to populate the dark jungle. As Collin had done, he cogitated briefly on the events that had led up to this unsettling night of this strange, bizzare quest. Then, as his tension built, he thrust his speculations from his mind, also as Collin had done.

More to pass time than because he really wanted it, McPhearson brewed up another canteen cup of coffee, cursing at one point when he burned his hand on the hot handle. Then he sat sipping the steaming liquid and thinking of his wife and family. If only the kids could see dear old dad now, he thought. He found himself wishing his sons were with him. They were good boys, young and strong. A trip like this would make men of them. McPhearson looked around at the shadows of the jungle and found himself changing his mind. No, maybe it was for the best that the boys had gone to summer school this year and missed the trip.

He looked suspiciously into the forest and wondered what it would be like to die here, so far from home and those he loved. He wondered if death were the complete end of everything—total oblivion. He tried to imagine it and failed.

There was a feeling in these jungle nights that seemed to induce such introspective contemplation, Mac thought. There seemed to be a kind of communion with the gigantic mechanism of the universe, powers and processes imponderable—a sense of the infinite. Yes, that was it. Infinity. It was here, it seemed to stretch all around him, beckoning.

He nodded in satisfaction at having put a label to the sensation that had been haunting him, and bent over to pick up his coffee cup. The night wasn't going to be so bad, he thought. Why, in just a few more hours he'd awaken Smith and get in three more hours of sleep before dawn. He began to imagine pleasant things to dream about.

With the suddenness of a striking cat, it was on him, taking his mind in a stranglehold from which there could be no escape. The coffee cup which he had drawn up to within an inch or two of his lips dropped from his now immovable hand, spilling the burning liquid across his right shin.

Mac tried to open his lips and cry out, more in disbelieving surprise than in pain or fear. But he couldn't move, not so much as a muscle, not even to the batting of an eyelid.

And then, from within the depths of his own soul he heard a dreadfully sinister laugh, a laugh that could have come from the devil himself, and he felt his body and mind freeze in unimaginable horror. He tried unsuccessfully to cry out a warning as he watched his hand move outward and down of its own volition, pick up the rifle leaning next to him and cast it away into the jungle. In a split second, McPhearson had been transported from a peaceful fireside to the very limits of sanity, where he teetered on the threshold, waiting helplessly for the tiny shove that would send him careening into the abyss of madness forever. And through it all, there was only one thought in his paralyzed, violated brain. *Hasha had been telling the truth.*

The firelight faded as the flames suddenly faltered and struggled for life, as though something was sucking all the energy from the surrounding atmosphere, damping out all light and warmth. In the dancing shadows of the nearly extinguished flames, McPhearson's body was jerkily raised to its feet, his unbelieving eyes bugging out in terror. His right foot came out slowly and shakily to be followed by the left. With each movement the shaking and struggling subsided, until, as McPhearson bent down over the entrance to Smith's tiny tent, his movements appeared relatively smooth and controlled.

With grotesquely exaggerated caution, McPhearson's hands reached out and eased the mosquito netting away from the sleeping African. He pulled the blanket from the man's chest and stood for a moment looking down at the small medallion sparkling in the dim firelight. An inhuman snarl came to McPhearson's lips, and a small trail of spittle ran down his chin.

McPhearson's other hand found the hunting knife at his belt and eased it from its sheath. Slowly, the hand with the knife moved forward until the point almost touched the side of Smith's neck, just below his left ear. Then, the blade turned and looped itself under the leather strap which supported the medallion. With a smooth stroke of the blade, the leather string parted. Slowly the knife was withdrawn, and McPhearson's free hand reached down and gingerly lifted the medallion from the black man's chest. He pulled it free, trailing the severed string, and threw it contemptuously to the ground. His distorted lips twisted into a travesty of a smile as McPhearson stood up and turned toward the jungle. He had not even walked beyond the circle of firelight, in the direction of the stream beyond, when the now unprotected Smith began to stir in his sleep, awakening from a troubled sleep to a nightmare that was only beginning.

A grinning skull sat on a table in Mason Raymond's office. Except for a greater quantity of books, papers, and pictures, and the addition of a small metal circlet which might have been a bracelet of some kind, the office appeared exactly as it did on the night of the fifteenth. Dr. Raymond wore a cardigan sweater and was absorbed in reading from one of the manila folders. As he read, sweat beaded noticeably upon his creased forehead. Uncharacteristically, he mumbled to himself as he read.

> And such was the fate of the unfortunates upon whom the curse of the undead descended, that in the dead of night they would lose themselves to the Prince of the Outer Dark, and the terrors of demoniac possession would hold them forever. And the demon that would come to inhabit the body of the victim could not be cast out, save by certain rituals known only to those priests of the

Cybil, who by words and actions preserved from antiquity, were sometimes successful in driving Satan from the body of the possessed, but more often succeeded only in calling upon themselves the wrath of the succubus. And those who succeeded in exorcising the Dark Ones were often murdered with ceremonial knives in the dead of night by members of the Anansi, or Spider Cult; voluntary worshipers of the devil. And afterward their blood was drunk by all members of this dark fellowship that was, in earlier times, very widespread among the civilized nations. Herewith is a description of both the rites followed by those who would drive the spirit from the body of a human victim, and of the ceremony by which the cult members would consume the blood of these brave priests.

Dr. Raymond read on, feeling the icy fingers of death running up and down his spine. The skull on the table behind him seemed to have shifted position slightly, staring now toward the shrouded window in the opposite wall. It was 2:40 A.M. by Raymond's wristwatch.

January, 1970

Collin awoke slowly to the sound of a muted buzzing in his ears, as though a swarm of mosquitos hovered about his head. As he came to his senses, he found himself shivering violently in a surprisingly bitter, almost glacial cold that seemed to penetrate his tent, blanket, and clothing as though they didn't exist.

He opened his eyes and looked around to find the cause of the buzzing but could see nothing in the dim glow of the embers.

The American sat up abruptly, realizing that Mac was nowhere in his field of vision. And, as he looked again, he saw that the fire was fluctuating strangely, as though its supply of oxygen was being partially interrupted and it was being suffocated.

It took his sleep-dulled mind several seconds to realize that the flaring and dying of the fire coincided exactly with regular fluctuations in the intensity of the sound he seemed to be hearing. He found the sound increasingly irritating, and put his hands over his ears in a vain effort to shut it out.

From beneath his pack, he grabbed his revolver and stepped up out of the tent. In a matter of seconds, he established that both Smith and McPhearson had disappeared completely. He quickly turned and retrieved his rifle from the tent, switching the safety off and sticking his pistol in his belt. Then he made a careful inspection of the camp.

The fallen coffee cup beside the rock where Mac had been seated hinted darkly of evil tidings. Collin went down on one knee to pick it up, noting that the spilled coffee beside it on the ground was still steaming. Whatever had happened to draw McPhearson and Smith away must have occurred within a very short time indeed.

Even more disturbing was the discovery of Smith's rifle and pistol, both still in the tent. Collin simply could not imagine Smith straying into the jungle without his weapons, or the flashlight that still rested beside the entrance to the tent. The white man bent and picked it up, switching it on and off to test the batteries.

He could not possibly conceive of both Smith and McPhearson leaving the camp without awakening him.

Further investigation revealed that Mac's flashlight also rested untouched beside the fire. Collin clicked on Smith's light and painstakingly examined the ground in the clearing. The fresh tracks of both men were plainly visible and seemed to indicate that they had simply got up and walked off in the direction of the stream ahead.

Collin studied them more closely and noted that Mac seemed to have risen and walked first to Smith's tent, perhaps to awaken him, before moving into the jungle. Then Smith had apparently followed, as his tracks crossed McPhearson's path and erased them where both men had stepped in the same spots.

Collin walked the perimeter of the clearing, and though he was meticulous in his examination, he could find no indication that anything, man or beast, had set foot in the camp. As he was completing his circle, the flashlight caught a reflective surface at the edge of the jungle, and Collin, with his rifle ready and trigger finger tightening, stepped cautiously into the brush.

The man was profoundly disturbed to find McPhearson's rifle lying in a thicket. The jungle surrounding it was unmarked. No tracks, no broken branches. The weapon had unmistakably been thrown there. Collin retrieved it, careful to keep his eyes on the territory around him.

His heart rate was fantastically high, and his limbs were shaking uncontrollably. Then he realized he was still cold, bitterly so. His fingers had grown so stiff with the chill that he feared he would be unable to operate the bolt action of his rifle should the need for action arise. Switching his rifle to his right hand, he held his left out close to the struggling flames, only to draw back his hand in fear. With his flesh almost touching the dancing thread of flame he had felt no heat at all from the fire!

At that moment, the buzzing in his ears reached a crescendo and ceased abruptly. As it did so, the fire flared to life again, flames shooting up three or four feet above the ground and then subsiding to a normal level. Collin was terrified as he had never been in his life.

The abnormal cold seemed to seep away, and as it did so Collin was aware that the jungle was unnaturally quiet. The normal night sounds were completely absent, and all he could hear was the rasp of his hushed breathing and the insistent crackling of the fire. Collin added more wood and sat down on the rock, trying to calm himself and make sense of what he had observed.

He had initially restrained himself from striking out in the jungle after his friends, realizing that blind action of that kind could be the rankest folly. In the moonless night, with only the narrow game trail to follow, he could be lost in a matter of minutes, and further, he would be one man alone at the mercy of whatever dangers stalked the night beyond the ring of fire.

Christopher had clung at first to the hope that

there was some rational explanation for the sudden departure of his friends, and though he was not a religious man, he found himself mumbling a prayer that they would return to the camp of their own accord, and he would be spared the terrible decision he now faced. But the evidence of some inscrutable form of foul play was all too clear, and as he sat upon the stone he made himself face the fact that there was little doubt his friends had somehow fallen into the hands of the enemy, whatever it might be.

Collin cursed himself suddenly, remembering the walkie-talkies they all carried at their belts against the possibility of becoming separated. He grabbed his and turned it on, switching the callup signal that would register as a beep from the twin units his friends carried. The callup signal would only sound if the units were carried in the standby mode, and Collin recalled that they all turned off their transceivers when in camp. So, unless one of them turned on his set, the signal would be useless.

Still, the lone man sat for several minutes pushing the callup switch and listening tensely for a reply.

He finally gave up and returned the radio to his belt, then checked his wristwatch. 12:52 A.M. It had now been seven minutes and thirty seconds since he had awakened. Collin was amazed that so much could have happened in such a short time. He felt as though he had sat waiting and thinking for hours, trying to signal his friends.

The coffee spill was completely dried up now, with no sign of moisture visible at all when he turned the beam of Smith's flashlight on the spot where the spill had been.

He tried to consider his alternatives rationally. It was still nearly six hours till daylight, and he knew he couldn't wait that long for his friends to return. He knew that if they were in danger, his chances of helping them decreased dramatically with every passing minute. On the other hand, he realized his chances of tracking them through the night were slim, and he appreciated the extreme dangers involved in traversing the jungle in the dark, alone and poorly qualified as he was. This far from human habitation, nocturnal predators made the search he now contemplated a dangerous proposition, even disregarding the imponderable element of the Anansi curse.

Collin stood up. There was no point debating the risks, he knew. With every passing minute they could be getting farther ahead, deeper into trouble. And there was no question of remaining in the relative safety of the camp.

Collin took from his pack what he thought he'd need: compass, canteen, and some dried meat in case he was unable to find his way back to the camp. He strapped on his pistol belt and transferred his Smith and Wesson from his waistband to his holster. After a moment's thought, he also took up Smith's pistol belt and slung it around his shoulders, stuffing his pockets with extra rifle and pistol ammunition. He debated bringing along an extra flashlight, and decided against it. He did not want to be loaded down with too much gear, not knowing what kind of skulking he might be forced to attempt. But he compromised by unscrewing McPhearson's light and extracting the batteries. He did not want to be caught

71

alone in the jungle without a light. He stuck them in his jacket pocket and turned to survey the campsite in search of any necessary item he might have forgotten.

As he did so, he noticed something he had not seen before, possibly due to the peculiar behavior of the fire. As he turned his head, Collin caught the glint of a small metal object lying on the ground beside Smith's tent. He knelt down and picked it up, noting with surprise that it was the medallion the old village woman had given to the ranger. His eyes widened as he examined the leather cord that accompanied it. The strap had been neatly and cleanly severed by a very sharp edge; almost certainly a knife.

He clutched the medal tightly in his fist and grimaced at the thoughts that rushed into his brain with this discovery. He turned three hundred and sixty degrees, staring into the jungle. He could see nothing, but he knew by now that that had no meaning.

Resolutely, he stood up, thrust the medallion into the pocket of his bush pants and buttoned the flap. Before leaving the clearing, he gathered up one more item of equipment: his Nikon camera. Whatever had happened or was happening to his friends, whatever was out there waiting in the jungle, Collin was sure of one thing. He wanted a picture of it.

Fortunately, the two missing men had followed the game trail leading out of the clearing, the same path followed days earlier by Sedgewick's people, so Collin had no difficulty following. The trail ran at a slight upward incline for several hundred yards and Collin followed it at the fastest pace he dared, pausing at intervals to switch on his carefully hooded flashlight and check for Smith and McPhearson's tracks.

It was terrifying, moving blindly through the haunted jungle, expecting at any moment to meet up with whatever it was that had spirited away his friends.

In the unnatural quiet, the young man's footfalls seemed thunderously loud, even though he did his best to move silently. The fourth time he stopped to check the trail he fancied he could hear the sound of running water somewhere ahead. The stream Smith had mentioned, beyond doubt. He quickened his pace slightly, aware that the combination of the stream and the darkness might be sufficient to frustrate his limited tracking skill.

He burst from a thick patch of jungle and came into sight of the water, which was wider than he had expected, perhaps fifteen feet across. Collin could see the reflection of the stars in the water, but in the darkness it was impossible to tell how deep it was, or even how fast the water was flowing. Almost simultaneously, he heard the even crunch of footfalls, approaching from the jungle beyond the opposite bank. They were the footsteps of men making no effort whatsoever to conceal their presence.

Collin dropped behind a bit of brush and leveled his rifle in the direction of the approaching footsteps. His eyes, which had by now grown accustomed to the extremely low light level, could just barely distinguish two black silhouettes detach themselves from the jungle and walk evenly down the bank toward the water.

Sight and sound seemed to slip slightly out of sync with each other in a peculiar illusion caused by the darkness and the echo pattern of the terrain as the shadows splashed into the water with the same even, unconcerned strides. Collin waited until he judged that both figures were approximately in the middle of the stream and then he turned on his flashlight, centering the beam into the faces of those in the water. He was careful to hold the flashlight at arm's length from his body so that he would have an even chance of escaping any shot fired at the source of the light.

"Hold it right there," Collin called in a low and menacing tone. "I have you covered, and I won't hesitate to fire, believe me."

The splashing progress ceased abruptly and as it did, Collin's eyes adjusted themselves to the new glare of the flashlight, which seemed as blinding as the sun by contrast to the pitch darkness it penetrated.

There, illuminated in the circle of light stood Smith and McPhearson, eyes compressed to slits, trying to see beyond the shining white beam. They both appeared unharmed, relaxed to a degree, though they had frozen in response to Collin's warning.

"Thank God!" Collin exclaimed, allowing his pent-up anxiety to escape in a long sigh of relief. His finger eased off the trigger of his rifle and he got up, grabbing his flashlight as he did so. "It's okay," he called, "come on ahead. It's me, Chris."

Collin trained the light on the water in front of the men as they resumed their progress across the stream.

As they reached the other side, Collin stepped to the bank to meet them. "Holy shit," he whispered, still wary of the jungle, "you boys sure gave me a scare. Why the hell didn't you—" His voice trailed off as he realized for the first time that something was wrong. They were close enough now to reach out and touch him, yet neither of his friends had spoken. Out of courtesy, he had avoided shining the light in their faces, but now he did, only to be shocked at the expressionless set of the muscles and horrified by their eyes, which were filled with what he suddenly realized were expressions of sheer terror.

"What," he stammered, "what's wrong?" But the awful truth began to dawn on him too late. Smith's strong right arm reached out to grab the American by the neck and pull him even closer. Through his shock, some part of Collin's mind registered awareness that the buzzing had resumed at full strength in his ears, like a whole swarm of hornets nesting in his head. His eyes were now within inches of Smith's contorted face. He watched as the black man's jaw twitched and worked in an almost spastic fashion. Then, slowly the words rasped out in a deep distorted voice which bore no resemblance to Smith's own.

"Who are you, animal filth?" It was the voice of hell and it chilled Collin to the center of his being. "What are you and where do you come from that I don't hear your miserable thoughts?"

Collin was far too deep in shock to answer. He shook his head from side to side, trying to awaken himself from the nightmare but it went on. Smith laughed deeply and mockingly; a laugh Collin would remember till his last breath. Then, with one hand, he lifted the white man off the ground by his neck and shook him violently, as though Collin were nothing but a child's doll.

The buzzing, which Collin now realized originated inside his head rather than in his ears, had reached an intensity that brought with it physical pain. In addition, Smith's grip on his throat had not loosened as he continued his violent shaking, and it was effectively cutting off Collin's breath. He was growing dizzy and disoriented. He knew now what it would feel like to be hanged.

Abruptly both the shaking and the buzzing ceased, and Smith threw the American contemptuously to the ground. Collin fought for the last dregs of consciousness, gasping in lungfuls of air as he lay upon his stomach helplessly.

He heard approaching footsteps, then cried out in agony as he was kicked in the ribs hard enough to be flopped over onto his back. Smith's face appeared in his field of view against the stars as the African bent over to look at Collin. The expression on the black face was not Smith's, Collin saw. In fact, even the eyes, which before had reflected terror within, belonged to someone or something other than the man Collin had known. He made himself accept the impossible fact: This was not Smith.

From somewhere to one side, a light clicked on to shine into Collin's eyes. McPhearson had evidently retrieved the flashlight Collin had dropped when Smith had grabbed him. Then he began a painstakingly thorough examination of the cranial region of the forehead. Not only did Smith look with great care, but he ran his chilled fingers all across the American's skull, combing through his hair. Collin shrank from that icy touch as he would the hands of death.

After what seemed an eternity, Smith gave up the examination and allowed Collin's head to fall back to the ground with a dull thud that sent the world swimming round again. When Collin's vision cleared, he could see Smith still looking down at him, a faintly puzzled expression on his malicious features. Whatever he had been looking for, he evidently had not found. A look of distaste replaced the bewilderment and Smith straightened his back and stood up, moving out of Collin's sight.

The American laboriously raised himself on his elbows, terrified of what might happen next, and wanting to keep his eyes on the two figures before him. The light was still in his eyes, McPhearson had followed his face with the beam. But beyond it he could see both of the men standing side by side and looking down at him.

"Who are you?" Collin rasped out painfully. "What do you want?" His voice cracked.

Instead of answering, they took a short step backward, as though any further contact with the prone man would bring with it some foul contamination. Both faces bore the same expression of supreme disgust.

Wordlessly, McPhearson handed the light to Smith, and so smoothly was this transfer effected that the beam did not waver for a second from Collin's face.

"Well, speak up, damn you!" Collin's voice was

nearly a shriek, he was on the verge of hysteria. Then he saw McPhearson reach for the holster at his side and pull forth his handgun. Collin watched silently, the calm acceptance of inevitable, impending death settling on him like a cloak. He grimaced as the pistol was lined up carefully between his eyes. He saw the finger twitch spastically on the trigger and was aware of an interplay of expressions across McPhearson's face. The jaws worked as Smith's had, and a voice emerged in a halting fashion, as though each sound was a struggle of immense magnitude. "I'm sorry . . . Chris. . . ."

Collin stared into the eyes with new horror. Unmistakably, it was Mac's voice coming from that twisted face.

In an instant all trace of McPhearson was gone from the face as it smiled with the old demonic presence once again in full control. In a flash of insight, Collin perceived that the display had been a deliberate, cruel tactic designed to terrify him.

This time the finger tightened upon the trigger of the Smith and Wesson with complete confidence. In what was more of a reflex action than any deliberate ploy, Collin's right foot kicked up just at the instant that the gun went off, catching the butt of the pistol with force enough to deflect the shot up several feet.

With the strength of fear he kicked out again, this time sending McPhearson crashing back into the water of the stream behind him. Collin rolled over and narrowly avoided being crushed under Smith's charging body, which struck the ground where Collin had lain only a second earlier.

In an instant, Collin was on his feet and running

south along the bank. Hope sprang into his heart as he did not hear the footsteps that meant immediate pursuit. But that hope was almost immediately extinguished as the glow of the flashlight found his body and shots began to ring out. One, two, three shots, and on the third he went down hard and fast, splashing in spectacular fashion into the water. First came the feeling of falling, then the disorientation of striking the water and finally the feel of the current whisking him along. Collin was conscious, but he did not know whether he had actually been hit, or whether he had caught his foot on some unseen protrusion and simply fallen. He was in pain, confused, and in shock, of that he could be certain.

He made a feeble effort to submerge himself under the water as it carried him downstream, though the stream was not more than three feet deep. He found himself bumping his face and chest against the bottom.

When his agonized lungs could hold out no longer, he managed to flop around onto his back and ease his face up out of the water. He tried with only marginal success to control his fevered gasping for air, afraid that the sound would bring the others down on him.

He half expected to hear the sound of another shot as the fire in his chest eased, but moments passed and the crackle of gunfire never came. He was still allowing the current to sweep him southward, but he had no idea how far he may have gone from Smith and McPhearson.

His question was answered as he caught sight of the beam of the flashlight back upstream. As he watched, the light was trained back and forth across the water a good fifty feet from his present position. He muttered a prayer of thanksgiving, inhaled a deep breath and then submerged himself, swimming as far and as fast as he could downstream. Twice more, he rose for air, and twice more he dove beneath the shielding water, taking no chances of being sighted, even though the odds of that occurring were remote indeed. Then, when he looked back upstream and couldn't see even the faintest sign of any light, he made his way to the bank slowly, and carefully crawled out to lie exhausted among a pile of driftwood. For as long as he could stay awake he lay unmoving, watching and listening, straining his senses for anything that would indicate that he had been followed. But he could hear only the sounds of the jungle night, and he knew that these sounds were his friends. It was their absence now that he dreaded, and at times with the passing of a mosquito or other insect, his heart stopped in unbelievable terror for fear he was hearing the horrible buzzing that heralded the presence of the enemy.

After a time, his exhaustion overtook him, and he slept a deep dreamless sleep, unstirring until the first light of morning began to invade the jungle.

Collin roused from his sleep during the twilight before true dawn and was first conscious of an almost overwhelming thirst. He tried to get up and move the few feet necessary to reach the stream and immediately became aware of the injuries he had sustained during the previous night. He forced himself to ignore the pain, in his side where he had been kicked, and in his neck, which felt as if it might have been broken. At least he had not been shot.

He sprawled out prone at the water's edge and drank his fill of the refreshing liquid. Then, he stuck his aching head under the water to try and ease the torment behind his eyes and in his skull.

When he felt his thoughts begin to clear, he withdrew into the jungle for cover and ate some of the dried meat he had brought along.

Oddly enough, in view of his vivid recollection of abject terror from the night before, he felt little or no fear this morning. Assuredly, a part of him, that part whose function it was to advocate self-preservation, screamed continually at him to run from this accursed jungle as fast as possible. But he had no difficulty bottling this up in some out-of-the-way portion of his subconscious and ignoring it. The questions that occupied his thoughts upon awakening had nothing to do with self-preservation.

During his sleep a profound change had come about in the American. There was no longer any doubt in his mind regarding the accuracy of Hasha's story. He accepted its truth now in the same way as he accepted the presence of the sun in the sky. There was something in this jungle. Something real. But whatever the legends and superstitions surrounding it, it was fallible. Collin's survival proved that.

And Collin apparently was immune to whatever strange influence it appeared to exert over everyone else. Not only could he not be taken over as the others had been, but his escape under the water indicated that he might be able to move through the jungle undetected by the thing. He remembered the question that had been of such great concern to it the night before. "Where do you come from that I don't hear your thoughts?"

It seemed worth the gamble to him to assume his surmises regarding the meaning of that exchange last night were correct. If they were, he might have a faint chance of rescuing his friends. He didn't believe for a minute that, were their positions reversed, they would abandon him to the demon, or whatever it was. And he had no intention of abandoning them.

Collin had given almost no serious thought to trying to go back to civilization for reinforcements. If Hasha's story were to be relied upon, time now was extremely short. Collin looked at his watch, which fortunately was waterproof.

5:47 A.M. They had several hours on him now. If action were to be taken at all, he realized it must be immediate.

His clothing had dried while he slept, but he checked his pistol to see if it was still operational. The cylinder turned freely and the double action mechanism operated smoothly. There was some chance that the ammunition had been ruined by the water, but it was not likely. There was no way to check without attracting unwanted attention, so Collin decided to take his chances and hope for the best.

He skillfully made his way back upstream to the fateful spot where he had almost lost his life the night before.

He was relieved to see tracks leading from the

stream indicating that the two men had set out for whatever lay at the end of the game trail. The tracks were at least several hours old; the mud from their stream crossing had nearly dried out. Collin intended to follow them. In the daylight, it would be easier to do so without exposing himself to ambush. And if his surmises were correct, he would not be expected.

Before leaving the stream, he searched the west bank and found his rifle, right where he had dropped it when Smith had grabbed him. He was overjoyed to find it. The ammunition it contained had not been wet and so it was completely reliable.

The process of following the trail was nerve-racking and tedious. All the while Collin was torn between his fear that he would be too late to save his friends, and his fear of being sighted or ambushed.

For all his precautions, Collin saw and heard absolutely no sign of anything threatening or unnatural. He came upon the entrance to the cave so suddenly and unexpectedly that he nearly stumbled into the open, in full view of the two black African natives who stood as still as statues at either side of the entrance.

Collin made his way to the top of a small embankment to observe the open ground around the cave entrance. Four hours had passed since he had awoke that morning; it was nearing ten-thirty and his fear that he was too late was growing stronger with each heartbeat.

But he forced himself to examine the cave entrance and try to think slowly and logically. The cave itself was a jagged vertical gap in the side of a cliff which rose perhaps a hundred feet above the jungle floor. The ground leading into it had been packed into a path by long usage, and the jungle seemed to refuse to grow in a rough semicircle perhaps twenty feet in all directions from the yawning mouth of the cave.

The men who stood with such unnatural stillness at either side of the entrance appeared to be guards. They wore very little clothing, even though a cold mist hung over the jungle that morning and Collin was shivering in his jungle khakis. Their loincloths generally resembled the clothing of the natives in Smith's village, and there was nothing about their persons by which Collin could get any specific ideas of their origin.

He noticed that they never looked to the right or left, and in fact, seemed oblivious of their surroundings. But he did not doubt that they were stationed there for a purpose, and he knew it would be unforgivable folly to presume that the men he watched would be any less effective than Smith and McPhearson had been the night before.

Collin retraced his path into the jungle for a few yards and began collecting baseball-sized rocks. He found perhaps half a dozen, and stuffed them into his jacket as he moved. Next, he worked his way around to the edge of the jungle on the extreme west edge of the cliff face, directly to the right of the entrance and perhaps thirty feet from the man guarding the right side of the cave entrance. With extreme care, he began to cast the stones into the jungle on the opposite side of the open space, achieving a very satisfactory rustling of the vegetation in the jungle beside the man guarding the west side of the entrance. The noise caused by his third rock seemed to arouse a response. The men turned their heads, focusing attention in the general direction of the point of impact. Collin threw another rock and achieved the best effect of all as it struck a tree branch and rattled its way to the ground. The guards began moving then, slowly but with determined and confident purpose, to investigate the disturbance. Collin threw his last two stones for good measure and edged his way along, the cliff face to his back, disappearing into the entrance of the cave before the two guards had even reached the edge of the jungle. Had either of them turned around, the American would have been in full view.

Even a few steps inside the mouth of the cave there seemed to be no light at all, and Collin flattened himself back against the slimy wall to wait for his eyes to adjust to the darkness. He had no lantern or flashlight. McPhearson had taken his, and he wouldn't have used one even if he could. When he felt he could distinguish varying degrees of shadow, he continued in with his rifle held out in front of him. Fear was a physical sensation, a taste in his mouth and a crawling in his stomach, but he continued on, one step at a time as the cave led downward, first gradually and then more steeply.

Fortunately the floor of the cave was relatively flat and smooth, so that Collin had no trouble with his footing. But the stench that began to reach up at him was so repulsive that he almost puked with every breath he took, and his imagination populated the darkness with swirling, hideous shapes waiting just beyond the limits of his rifle barrel to sweep in upon him.

Once, Collin heard footsteps coming up from below. In terror, he flattened himself against the wall and waited as what sounded like two men tramped evenly past him.

By the echoes of their footsteps, Collin judged the dimensions of the passage to be not more than fifteen feet from wall to wall. He could have reached out and touched the men as they walked by. He was suddenly struck by the thought that McPhearson and Smith might have just walked past him. He hesitated for a moment and then moved on down into the cave, reasoning that in all likelihood the ascending individuals had been dispatched as reinforcements for the guards, who might still be engaged in a fruitless search for the source of the diversionary sounds Collin had generated.

After several minutes, Collin began to see a faint light ahead. Slowly it grew larger until he could distinguish an end to the downward tunnel. It was not the even white light of day. Rather, it was a soft glow of pastel colors, of which orange and red predominated, although blue and green could also be distinguished. They shone with a pulsating, vaguely phosphorescent sort of glow which reminded Collin of the glowing of a firefly or of the light caused by a ship's wake as it plows through flourescent waters.

As he moved toward the light, the stench grew ever more powerful. It was indeed the smell of dead and decomposing animal matter, and seemed to contain in addition every foul smell Collin had ever encountered. Resolutely he closed his mind to it, concentrating on making as little sound as possible while he approached the cavern from which the light emanated. He flattened his back once more against the wall and edged the remaining few feet to the entrance to the cavern. Very slowly, he pushed his head out from the wall and looked inside.

THREE
Zaire, Central
Africa
January 18, 1970

No medieval fantasy of hell could begin to match the scene which confronted the man as he gazed for the first time into the lair of that thing the natives called Anansi, the Spider God. The cavern which stretched before him was at least several hundred feet from wall to wall, and roughly square in shape. The overhanging earth above was very high off the floor, giving a cathedrallike dimension to the place, and the floor was so smooth and packed that it obviously had been fashioned by some artificial means, although as far as Collin could discern the floor consisted of the same dirt and rock of which the walls of the cavern were composed.

The light which dimly lit the interior emanated from sections of the walls upon which appeared to cling lichenlike clusters glowing in various colors. Collin thought he saw one of these spots crawl slowly across a wall from one cluster to another, and this reinforced his impression that these were living things and not deposits of phosphorescent minerals.

Enormous piles of remains, most of them reduced

to nothing but bones, littered the floor. Most of those that were recognizable to Collin were human, although he caught occasional glimpses of animals. In one corner he thought he saw the familiar coat of a black leopard huddled in death along with the decaying bodies of other animals, but he could not be sure.

In the very center of this tangled mass of stinking decay, occupying nearly a fourth of the total floor space, Collin could clearly see the demon whose intelligence he had confronted the night before. It was like looking into the sun: a mass of glowing bioluminescence so blindingly brilliant that he could not make out the true form of its body. The rays of multicolored light played on the walls of the cavern, shifting in hue as though with the play of emotions being experienced by the demon. Though he could not clearly discern the thing's characteristics, Collin could see that it was very large, towering at least fifteen feet from the floor of the cavern.

As the man watched, it appeared to expand and contract slightly, as though breathing. But he could not tell if the being possessed any active physical organs. Collin held up his hand against the glare, like a man trying to see something silhouetted against a very bright searchlight, but to no effect.

Collin remembered the deadly "hands" Hasha had spoken of. There were no appendages of any kind protruding from the mass of light.

Lined up helter-skelter along the wall to Collin's right, perhaps thirty feet away, a motley collection of human beings stood at inhuman attention, their eyes fixed straight ahead. All of them appeared to be dressed in the same jungle clothing as the two guards had worn, and though Collin scanned the line of perhaps thirty individuals with care, he could find none wearing the European clothing of either Sedgewick's people or Smith and McPhearson. He could see in that wall another opening, however, which led deeper into the ground.

He turned his attention to the north wall, which was the one to his left. Here were three or four more of what Hasha had termed the "Devil's men" and more piles of bones and corpses. Collin's breath caught in his throat as he caught sight of a number of freshly killed men lying among one of the piles of bones. They all wore the jungle dress of the European hunting parties and Collin scanned desperately for some clue as to the identity of the unfortunate victims. They were perhaps thirty to forty feet away and in a particularly dimly lit area, but Collin finally decided that what he viewed were the remains of Sedgewick's people, and not of McPhearson and Smith. Sedgewick's jungle Jim helmet lay in a pool of blood alongside the bodies, and Collin was able to distinguish six different sets of arms and legs in the tangled heap. That accounted for Sedgewick's entire entourage, excepting only the tracker, Chaka, and though Collin looked for him, he could remember nothing about the African's apparel distinctive enough to identify his corpse among the hundreds of nameless dead.

Collin had been concealed in the entrance to the cavern for several minutes and had seen no sign of any activity either on the part of the creature or any of the men who were apparently its unwilling servants.

He had been forming a rather distinct impression that perhaps it was in a state similar to human sleep. Collin thought to himself that he would hate to see the thing roused to full fury.

In the absence of movement in the cavern, Collin dared to stick his head out into the cavern and look up and down the face of the wall that harbored its entrance. This wall, he could now see, was not as smooth and featureless as the others. Its irregular surface contained numerous natural alcoves, some deep enough that Collin could not see their back walls and therefore could not be sure if they were depressions in the rough wall or entrances to more passages. He looked first to his left, seeing bone piles or human beings, but when he turned his head to look to the right he immediately caught sight of Smith and McPhearson, standing as expressionless and still as the others.

With the first wave of relief still washing over him, the American began to plan. He could see that his rifle and revolvers were pitifully inadequate to attack the gigantic mass of light in the center of the cavern. He had no idea what might constitute a vital organ on the monstrous abomination, if any existed. He knew that the way to proceed would be to bring back some high explosive, like dynamite, and blow the thing to dust, and the cavern with it.

But Collin also knew that by the time he could get out of the jungle and return with high explosives, Smith and McPhearson would long be dead. He began to consider ways to get them out of the cavern. Even if both men could somehow be rendered unconscious, Collin realized that he could not carry them both up that long passage. Especially not when he would undoubtedly have to fight his way out. Thoughtfully, he reached his hand into his pants pocket and drew out the medallion. With Smith freed, the two of them might have a chance of getting McPhearson out. He began to tie the loose ends of the leather string of the medallion together, thinking that if he could get it over Smith's head. . . .

It was a pitiful longshot, he realized. Essentially he was betting his life on this little speck of jungle magic that he would have laughed at just a week ago. Even if he could get Smith free, the odds against their getting out alive were remote.

Collin was still searching for a better plan when the room began to come alive. Gradually, more and more of the creature's body began to take on that bizarre sparkle, and the rate of its "breathing" began to increase. Collin was conscious of a faint hum in the air, and the level of light coming from the walls of the cave increased substantially. He had pulled back in at the first sign of this change, taking his friends from his line of sight. But he could still see the creature as two of the creature's servants came to stand before it. They stood within two feet of what passed for the front of the ever brighter mass of quivering light, which appeared now to be flowing slightly back and forth into various shapes and patterns. Collin had no doubt that the thing had come to a state of wakefulness.

After a few moments, the two Africans turned and walked woodenly in the direction of the wall that harbored Collin's tunnel. For an instant he feared that they were coming after him, and he raised his rifle in preparation for a fight to the death. Instead, they moved out of his line of sight and reappeared with another black African between them.

Collin was shocked to see that it was Chaka, the tracker for Sedgewick's hunting party. He wanted to move forward and rescue the man, but caution, and the absence of any meaningful plan prevented him. Collin had no choice but to watch, gripping his rifle tightly and helplessly as the two men marched Chaka toward the spot where they themselves had stood seconds earlier. About midway across the bloody, bone-strewn floor Chaka was released from whatever compulsion had held him enthralled and he began to struggle furiously, screaming with the most mindless and nerve-shattering terror Collin had ever heard. He reminded himself that Chaka had undoubtedly witnessed the deaths of everyone else in his party and knew exactly what to expect. Indeed, he had apparently been given plenty of time to dwell on it, a refinement of torture that gave Collin renewed and redoubled hatred for the hideous monstrosity that now seemed to wait so greedily. It seemed to Collin that the substance of the creature was reaching and stretching in a grotesque gesture of welcome to the screaming victim being dragged to the spot where death waited.

Collin became aware of something new going on. Shapes seemed to fill the air above and before the creature. They were fleeting, barely discernable ghosts that faded in and out of view.

Collin thought he could see a devilish face for a few

seconds, to be replaced by the form of a strange many-headed creature that could not possibly have ever walked the surface of this world. Others came and went for a few seconds, some familiar and some unknown. Gargoyles, unicorns, and sea serpents. But superimposed over them all was the image of a giant spider. Collin found that when he shook his head and concentrated on seeing clearly, he was able to block the images out, and he began to understand that the beast was somehow manufacturing terrifying illusions for the benefit of its victim and the future victims who were being forced to watch. Apparently this terrorizing was a part of the feeding process of the thing. But whatever had protected Collin from its possession and detection apparently also protected him from the full force of its illusions.

They had dragged Chaka right up to the creature by this time, and his screaming was all the more frenzied for that proximity. Collin was glad he could not understand the language in which Chaka yelled so desperately.

The men on either side of the struggling man held him with iron-hard grips so that for all his frantic efforts he did not make any headway at all toward escape. The devil's man on the right side of Chaka reached around and grabbed him by the hair on the back of his head. With a cruelly vicious jerk, he pulled Chaka's head around to face the creature and now Collin, in horror, saw the beginnings of ten-taclelike appendages grow from out of the feature-less mass. They writhed like reaching fingers, growing ever closer to the agonized, insane tracker.

So, these were the "hands" of Hasha's account. The shock of what he was seeing held Collin rooted to the spot, motionless. Farther and farther the tentacles reached with Chaka watching in unbelievable, insane panic. Then came the instant when the tendrils first made contact with his face. There came, clearly carrying above the screaming of the victim, the sound of burning flesh, and Collin could see clouds of smoke and steam rise from the two spots on Chaka's cheek and forehead where the devil's touch first found him.

The screams told of more than unimaginable fear now. There was the edge of agony in those cries, cries that came from a soul no longer human. And Collin, in his own sympathetic agony of helplessness raised his rifle and sighted in on the back of Chaka's skull. The tendrils had thickened now and circled to half embrace Chaka's skull. Parts of the tendrils then folded back, in the manner of two thumbs, and began to press themselves into the wretched man's eyes. A new and even louder sound of boiling blood carried across the cavern, and dense clouds of smoke and steam rose clearly above the frightening scene. Collin could smell it now, though he would have sworn that his sense of smell had been destroyed by exposure to the stench of the cavern. It was the smell of burning human flesh. And all the while, Chaka writhed in agony, still screaming.

Collin's finger tightened on the trigger and for a second, he almost fired, unable to endure witnessing the worst torture he could ever conceive.

But he knew if he pulled that trigger, he would be

dooming his friends to the same fate. It was already too late for Chaka. However great his agony, it would soon be over and there was no saving him. But Collin could still try to rescue Smith and McPhearson. He lowered his rifle and put his hands over his ears, trying to shut out the intolerable screaming long enough to think. He shut his eyes tightly, oblivious of the danger inherent in the act.

But he could not shut it out. The screams still rang in his head, and the image of the doomed tortured victim seemed imprinted forever on the insides of his eyelids.

The screams were fading now, as Collin took his hands from his eyes. A choked gurgle and then silence, except for a sickening sucking sound that persisted for a few seconds, until it too died away. When Collin looked again, the tendrils, ends hideously stained, were withdrawing into the body of the thing. In seconds, they were completely gone, leaving no sign of where they had emerged.

The attendants were already dragging Chaka's lifeless body over to join the others of Sedgewick's expedition. Collin realized that he had run out of time when the two dropped the corpse on the ground and began to walk with the same emotionless gait in the direction of Smith and McPhearson's section of the wall.

Collin gathered the medallion into the palm of his right hand and took up his rifle. He watched, preparing himself as the two attendants marched across his limited field of vision and then he calmly stepped into the open, bringing up the rifle to textbook firing position.

They were going for McPhearson first, he could see. And they almost reached him, standing there like a stone sculpture of a man beside the motionless form of Smith. His friends' backs were against the wall waiting with outward patience for what was soon to come.

The first of the attendants to arrive had just reached out to take McPhearson's arm when Collin's first shot exploded his head. The blast of the thirty-aught-six-caliber cartridge going off in the enclosed space was literally deafening, so Collin did not even hear his second shot, which, being more hasty, caught the second attendant in the chest. He worked the bolt action of his rifle and turned to face the line of men against the south wall, perhaps sixty feet away. His appearance had been a total surprise, and there was a moment of hesitation before anything moved in the hellish lair of the demonic creature.

Collin was already running across the thirty feet of open floor to Smith and McPhearson before the devil's men began to move toward him. They did not seem in a great hurry, and Collin understood why when he saw McPhearson begin to draw the revolver that still hung from his waist. Collin dodged just as McPhearson fired and heard the bullet ricochet off the wall behind him. He saw McPhearson pull the trigger a second time and braced for the impact that was sure to come.

But this time, nothing happened. McPhearson's pistol was out of ammunition. Collin all the while continued running toward Smith, trying to get close enough to bring the medallion into contact with his flesh. But he was still ten feet away from McPhearson, an inhuman scowl upon his features, when he threw the now useless weapon. It struck Collin a glancing blow to the side of the head, which knocked him off balance and dazed him slightly.

The devil's men, who had crossed roughly half the distance by this time, broke into a shuffling run, and Collin turned to bring his rifle to bear on the first of them.

They kept coming as he shot down the first three, they had no regard at all for personal safety. Collin's rifle was out of ammunition, and they were upon him before he had time to reload it, or even to draw either of the two pistols he carried. Collin fought them off for a time, bringing down three with the butt of his rifle. But there were still over twenty of them, and they overpowered him by the sheer force of numbers. They quickly subdued him, displaying with the grips of their hands upon his upper arms the same iron strength Smith had demonstrated the night before.

Sick with despair and dazed by the blows of these inhumanly strong zombielike creatures, Collin was impassive as he was roughly swung around, not to confront the thing itself, but the form of Smith.

"You!" Smith spat in disgust. The buzzing had returned to full force in Collin's head, even above the ringing in his ears from the blast of the rifle shots.

The creature looking through Smith's eyes laughed its chilling, hellish laugh.

Collin could say nothing. His thoughts were on

the medallion concealed in the palm of his clenched right fist.

"You are even worse than these other slime, for you appear to have no mind at all for me to deal with. You are less than nothing. *Nothing!*" It roared, and then laughed derisively. "And for you, an especially unpleasant death. But first, you can watch these things die ahead of you." Smith's body gestured to McPhearson, and two of the devil's men stepped from the surrounding pack and took his arms.

Collin's stomach churned and he fought against retching from pure animal fear as he watched them march McPhearson across the floor. When they had reached the halfway point, in accordance with the pattern used on poor Chaka, McPhearson was released from his invisible bonds and began to struggle insanely, crying out curses and oathes, followed by entreaties and prayers.

"Collin, Smith, you've got to help me! You've got to. Oh, dear God, please do something, stop this!"

Finally, Terry McPhearson broke down and sobbed, crying uncontrollably as he crossed the last few feet to the creature. From the haze in the air, Collin knew that he was being subjected to the same hallucinations that had been paraded for Chaka.

Collin tried to shut out the horror of what was happening as he looked around at Smith. The alien, animating force had apparently been partially withdrawn as the creature began working itself into a feeding frenzy, for Collin could see the look of terror in Smith's eyes that signaled that Smith's personality still had partial access to the outside world. All of the men surrounding Collin were absolutely immobile, as the creature's attention was diverted. But Collin could feel no weakening of the viselike grips on his upper arms.

Smith, on the other hand, was standing free, not more than two feet away from Collin. The American tried to catch Smith's eye, but it was apparent that he was being forced to observe the torture and murder of poor McPhearson, who still sobbed uncontrollably, begging in pitiful degradation to the monstrosity he faced.

Collin swung his head for a split second's glance at Mac, and saw with growing horror that the tendrils were beginning to emerge, writhing in anticipation as they moved in the direction of Mac's face. He looked again over to Smith and knew that the time had come to play his only card.

From a state of inaction, Collin instantaneously launched himself directly at Smith, throwing the men on either side of him off balance and bringing all three of them down on Smith's unmoving body. Though the devil's men fell with Collin, they did not release their grips even to protect themselves as they hit the ground. But Collin had landed squarely on top of Smith, and in the seconds before he was roughly dragged to his feet, he had managed to lodge the medallion in the ranger's shirt so that it rested between his clothing and the skin of his chest.

Swiftly coming to life, the men who held Collin captive pulled him to a standing position and one of them aimed a backhand blow that nearly knocked him out. He swung his head from side to side trying to clear his vision and then tried to focus on Mc-Phearson who had renewed his pleading. "Collin . . . Chris, you've got to help me . . . please . . . oh, please, God, help me!"

Collin could see that the reaching tendrils had almost stretched far enough to touch the writhing man.

With the seconds ticking away, Collin swung his head down to look at Smith, who still lay where he had fallen.

"Smith, Smith," he yelled urgently. "I brought the medallion. Can you hear me? Listen to me, damn you. I brought the medallion the old woman gave you. . . ." He was shouting the words as fast as his throat and mouth could form them. "I put it in your shirt just now. Feel it there, against your skin. God-dammit, man. Feel it there. You said it can protect you if you believe in it. Well, it can! They had to cut it off you before they could get you. . . . Smith, Smith, listen to me!!" Collin tried to say more, but the man to his right let loose a powerful punch to the side of his head and Collin hung semiconscious in the grip of his captors.

But he had said enough, for Smith dazedly shook his head, then put his hand to the spot beneath his shirt where the medallion rested. The touch seemed to spread strength and purpose through him, for he launched instantly into action, pulling the leather and metal charm from beneath his shirt and slipping it over his head with the speed and desperation of a drowning man clutching a lifeline.

Just as the ranger completed this action, Collin

could hear the sound of blood and flesh searing, accompanied by a scream of unendurable pain from McPhearson.

Smith sprang up off his back with the speed of a caged cat running for escape. He pounced, not for the two men holding Collin between them, but for the pistols on Collin's belts. He pulled them free, one in each hand, and instantly pointed them into the faces of Collin's captors, firing point-blank.

Collin would have fallen with them had not Smith caught him. The rugged African supported the white man with one hand and with the other he slapped him vigorously across the face. "Wake up, wake up."

Within a heartbeat, Collin had roused enough to stand on his own, and Smith began to fire at the nearest of the devil's men, who had begun to move toward them. The actions of the devil's men were sluggish now, as the creature's attention was still devoted to feeding, so Smith had time to drag Collin back against the wall beside the passage from which Collin had first observed the cavern.

"Here," Smith handed Collin one of the pistols, "reload this."

Collin accepted it and came to full alertness. "Oh, my God!" He had looked across to see McPhearson's head being grasped by the weaving tendrils, and the thumbs begin their agonizing pressure into his friend's eye sockets.

At least a dozen of the devil's men were still on their feet, and they were moving purposefully in the space between the creature with its struggling prey and the two invaders.

Smith had already launched himself into an all-out effort to cross the cavern. He moved much more quickly than the advancing men, but there were too many to avoid them all. One of them grabbed at Smith's jacket, and Smith turned with wild, insane rage to shoot him down. Three more went the same way, but as two attendants approached Smith in tandem, he fired his pistol again only to discover that he was out of ammunition. He threw the gun into the face of one of the men, then drew his knife and forced it under the ribcage of the other. Still, he had barely covered half the distance between Collin and McPhearson, and more of the devil's men stood to block his way. These, Collin could see, carried long-bladed knives, and one of them seemed to hold a pistollike weapon of a type the American had never seen before.

Smith crouched, obviously preparing to charge the line of armed men in a fight to the death. But Collin, who had seen scores of armed men emerging from the passage in the opposite wall, realized that they could not possibly win against such numbers. He ran across the distance that separated him from the ranger, grasped the back of his jacket and spun him around.

"Smith . . . Smith! It's hopeless. Come on, we've got to get out of here." Collin gestured to the opposite wall where men literally flooded out onto the floor of the cavern. Smith seemed to be in the grip of battle fever, and for an instant he seemed not even to recognize Collin.

"But," Smith stammered in rage, "we can't leave him to die there . . . we can't leave him!"

Collin turned to where McPhearson shrieked out his life in the awful embrace of the devil thing. The tendrils had burned far into his eye sockets now. Too far, Collin knew. Even if they could reach him somehow, it would not be in time. His screams of agony tore into Collin's soul. McPhearson was his best friend.

Without hesitation, Collin raised the pistol in his hand, sighted it carefully on the back of McPhearson's immobilized head, and pulled the trigger.

He fired once more, despite the fact that McPhearson had slumped lifelessly in the arms that supported him, and he might have fired a third time had not Smith taken his arm and said, "Christopher, we may need that bullet."

Collin looked around through eyes clouded with fears of grief and rage at the lines of men advancing on them. They were noticeably more active and faster on their feet, as the demon turned its full attention to them.

"You're right." Collin looked around. Two of the possessed advanced from the direction of the passageway out. Collin shot them both and then turned to hand Smith a clip of thirty-aught-six ammunition. "Grab the rifle on the floor there; it's the fastest thing to reload."

Smith nodded, ran over and scooped the weapon off the ground. In a smooth motion, he opened the bolt, rammed the cartridges in place and closed the bolt again. "Let's get out of here!" he shouted. As one, the men turned and ran for the tunnel. As if this were a signal, the devil's men broke into a charge after them. Collin paused at the tunnel entrance to fire the last round in his cylinder into the massive body of the creature. But there was no noticeable effect either on it or on the zombies that had now covered three quarters of the distance across the cavern floor.

From the darkness of the tunnel, Smith called, "Hurry!"

Collin turned and ran for his life to join his friend; together they bolted for the surface.

"There are four men, that I know of, up ahead," Collin gasped out as they ran through the darkness.

"Do you have a light," Smith asked, not breaking stride.

"No."

Over the noise of their own rapid footsteps and breathing, Collin could hear nothing with his tortured ears. But without warning Smith fired his rifle directly up the tunnel ahead into the pitch darkness. In the muzzle flash which illuminated the tunnel for a split second, Collin could see that two men had been running down the passage directly toward them and that Smith's bullet had passed cleanly through the first and brought down the second as well.

Neither of them paused for a second as they ran up over the still twitching bodies.

"Something's wrong," Collin muttered. "We should be seeing daylight by now."

Smith made no reply, but he increased his already breakneck pace so that Collin was strained to the limit of his endurance to keep up with him.

Collin strained his eyes ahead for some trace of

light and finally thought he saw a faint lightening of the shadows ahead. At that instant, they burst from the tunnel into the open and Collin realized why he had seen ho light. It was already full night. He had passed the full day in that hellhole below. The American tripped on a rock he could not see and went down, and as he did so felt the swish of a blade passing over his head, in the space he would have occupied had he not fallen.

Smith turned and shot the man with the blade who had nearly succeeded in ambushing Collin. But he had no time to work the bolt action of his rifle in preparation for a second shot when the dead man's teammate appeared and swung his jungle sword downward at Smith's head.

Smith raised his rifle and intercepted the blow once, twice, three times. Then Smith tripped as he backstepped and went down, losing his hold on the rifle as he did so.

The sword-wielding native stood over Smith and raised his blade high, but Collin got him before he could start his downstroke, ramming his hunting knife into the possessed man's heart from behind.

As Smith rose swiftly to his feet, Collin picked up the rifle, worked the bolt and panted, "Come on."

They ran full tilt into the jungle in the general direction from which Collin had come that morning, not stopping, though they cut themselves severely on the rocks and vegetation that neither could see, until they were so deep in the trackless jungle that nothing could get at them without betraying itself in the brush.

They hid in the bowl of a dead tree for a few minutes, catching their breath. Then, without having spoken a word, the two of them set out slowly, carefully, using all of Smith's jungle skill to leave no trace of a trail behind them.

When they reached the stream, several hours later, they came out onto a point on the bank a considerable distance north of the point where their original trail had crossed it.

"Which way now?" Collin asked breathlessly.

Smith paused, also taking in air in great lungfuls, and stared up at the stars. "If we go to the east, back the way we originally came, we will inevitably have to fall back upon our old trail. Not a wise thing for prey seeking to elude the hunter."

"What other ways are there?"

Smith looked down at the stream flowing at his feet. It came from the north and headed down to the lowlands of the south. "That way, perhaps ten miles, the Anansi land ends. There is a ranger station in the valley beyond."

"Can we make it?"

"I don't know. It will mean crossing Sedgewick's old trail about a mile downstream."

"You mean the place where . . ."

"Yes. That place." Smith's voice was grave.

Collin scowled, considering the options. "There is an ancient superstition to the effect that running water presents an impediment to evil spirits. Maybe, we wouldn't be bad off taking to the water." He was thinking of his success in eluding the demon the night before.

"In places, the water runs deep enough to offer good concealment," Smith agreed. "And farther down it may be deep enough that we could swim comfortably. You do swim, don't you?"

"Yes."

Without another word, Smith splashed out into the water and headed downstream, finding himself immersed up to his waist, and began moving with a minimum of noise.

Collin joined him, holding his pistol and ammunition out of the water. Smith once again carried the rifle, and Collin had long since reloaded his handgun.

Fifteen minutes later, they reached the point where Sedgewick's trail crossed the stream and they paused, waiting and watching for a few minutes. Hearing nothing suspicious, and reassured by the presence of the normal jungle night sounds, they immersed themselves completely in the water, swimming along the bottom of the stream to a point well below the ill-fated crossing where Collin had escaped from Smith and McPhearson the night before. They had been forced to get their firearms wet, but as soon as they were out of sight of the crossing they paused to shake all the water from the guns and ammunition.

From then on, pausing only for brief periods of rest, they traveled the rest of the night, during which they eventually stumbled out of the water and traveled by land along the stream's muddy bank.

By dawn, they had reached the valley Smith had spoken of, and breathed easier knowing they were out of the accursed land. It was 8:36 A.M. by Collin's watch when they stumbled, exhausted, into the small, isolated ranger station and collapsed before the astonished faces of the men on duty there, falling into deep oblivion without uttering even a word of explanation.

Five days after their miraculous escape from the hell's pit, Collin and Smith returned to the lair of the Spider God. They had made their approach by night and held up in hiding within sight of the cave entrance to wait for daylight. Collin had brought a complete set of camera equipment with the intention of obtaining photographic records of the cavern before blowing it up, and he was adjusting these as he lay side by side with Smith. His watch showed the time as 4:45 A.M. Just a few minutes before twilight. Smith was watching the cave entrance with unfailing vigilance.

"Just a few minutes, now," Collin whispered.

Smith nodded, and Collin began to pack the camera apparatus into the straps that held it ready against his chest.

Smith picked up his submachine gun and checked the chamber. Just as he did so, a rumble started from deep under the ground. It grew in intensity and then ceased abruptly. In the predawn illumination that had crept in over the sky from the east, the men could see dust and smoke belching from the cave entrance, which that night had been left unguarded, at least to outward appearances.

"What is it?" Collin asked. "Earthquake?"

Smith shook his head. "No. I have heard such

things in the diamond mining camps to the south. Underground explosion, perhaps."

They turned their gazes to the cave entrance. When the dust began to settle, they could see the gaping hole in the earth had been completely filled by tons and tons of rock that had collapsed from the cliff above. On the hillside above, they could see the ground collapse suddenly in several spots, settling down as much as twenty feet, as though an underground fissure had just opened, swallowing soil into it.

"Looks like it's caved in all the way along," Collin said. "Why, do you think?"

Before Smith could answer, both men gasped in wonder as a brightly glowing object, a large, C-47 cargo plane glinting in the morning sunlight rose above the level of the surrounding mountains and headed north-northwest. Clearly it had taken off from a hidden airstrip in the valley beyond the next hill. In the distance they heard a whirring noise that accompanied its flight. Both men stood up to get a better view, shading their eyes with upraised arms.

Higher and higher it rose, taking a northerly heading, until it disappeared into the early morning clouds and was lost to sight.

"Shit!" Collin exclaimed bitterly.

Smith's expression was even more bitter than Collin's had been.

"It's gotten away from us," Collin murmured in disbelief. "God in heaven. Now it could be anywhere. Anywhere on this earth. How are we ever going to find it?"

Smith turned and slung his machine pistol on his

back. "Well, Christopher, there is one man who may know where the Shaktowi is going." He picked up a pack of high explosives.

"Who is that?"

"Hasha."

"Oh." The two of them gathered their supplies and made their way toward the rising sun.

FOUR
Denver, Colorado
February 21, 1970

A feeling of brooding menace pervaded the basement room that was roughly square, and perhaps thirty feet on a side. Debris that had obviously taken up most of the floorspace until very recently was now piled up against the walls, almost to the dirty, moldy ceiling leaving most of the floorspace in the center of the room free. A large five-pointed star had been traced in soot and ashes on the floor, and at each point of the star large blood red candles in elaborate silver stands had been placed. These were lit, and provided most of the light to the scene.

In the center of this pentagram stood an altar, which was also illuminated by candlelight. In the center of the altar lay the freshly killed body of some small animal. To one side of this was a gold ceremonial chalice. At the other was a large, gilt-bound book, resting open in a wooden stand designed for this purpose. On the far side of the altar, positioned as though it were, itself, the object of worship, sat a full-length mirror, set in a highly ornate wooden frame.

Standing at the altar, just setting down a bloodstained silver dagger, was a man. He was over six feet tall, with dark, latin good looks and a well-muscled upper body. The skin on the narrow face was without blemish of any kind, and his upper lip supported a small, neatly trimmed mustache. His eyes were very deep set, almost impossible to see in the limited light. The man's name was Maximillian Grey.

Grey mumbled unintelligible words while reading from the book at his left. As he did so, he scooped a fingerful of powder from a bowl and added it to the chalice at his right. Another pinch of this powder he then tossed expertly into the candleflame, where it exploded into a flash of brilliant orange and sent up a dark cloud that hovered darkly over the altar.

The man spoke more words, some of them audible. "Nexus, obligaturs ferensious chilo . . . beregerentus verus cortuburutu." As he spoke, his right hand grasped the chalice, exposing to view a very large gold ring sporting a red stone that flashed with a fire of its own, independent of the candles that lept into even greater ecstasy.

With the chalice at his lips, he paused, and the room was filled suddenly with the sound of distant chanting, chanting with a slow, ponderous rhythm that rocked even the dancing candle flames. The voices, as though from another world, were low in pitch, and sinister.

With a smile of pure evil, Grey tilted the cup back and drank the blood mixture contained therein, draining it dry in one smooth gesture and throwing the empty vessel away from him, out into the center of the pentagram.

At that instant, a flash of fire rose in a column from

the spot where the cup fell, and the chanting rose to a fever pitch. From nowhere a wind came whistling through the tomblike basement, rustling the pages of the book, swirling through Grey's black hair like the caressing fingers of a lover. In his eyes was a look of mad ecstasy, of evil triumph. He raised his arms, the flowing red robe that draped his body spreading out like the wings of some monstrous bat.

"Aaaaaaah." He breathed a deep sigh, as though air had not entered his lungs in a thousand generations.

Grey turned then, away from the center of the star on the floor, back to face the altar, and the mirror beyond it. Up until this moment, the mirror had faithfully reflected his own image. But now, the figure staring down at him bore no resemblance whatever to the red-clothed Satan-worshipper.

The form in the mirror was humanoid but not human, clothed in a featureless, long gray robe that shimmered in an almost luminescent fashion. Its hairless skull featured a cranium somewhat larger than a human head, and the ears were pointed. Its eyes were cold and sunk deep into the skull, with ashen eyebrows arching at an unnaturally steep angle far up into the forehead. The mouth was a cruel slit, smiling a smile of unbelievable malevolence.

Grey breathed in rapture, falling down to his knees in supplication. "All my life I have searched for you, believed in you. And now you have come at last."

The figure in the mirror smiled even more broadly, betraying the points of fanglike teeth on his lower lip.

"Yes, faithful servant, I have come." The thing in the mirror spoke for the first time. Its voice was a hollow rasp containing within it the cries of a thousand tortured victims. It smiled down at the man on his knees below. "Are you ready to receive your master?"

Grey spread his arms, "Yes, great one, Master of the Outer Darkness. I bequeath to thee my body, my soul, my self."

A chill wind again rushed from the shadows, and the smoke from the candles gathered to swirl, obscuring the mirror and the man for a few seconds.

This subsided. The candles were now burned almost to the quick and they fought for life. The mirror again reflected the handsome features of the man kneeling below in the red ceremonial robe. But as Grey rose slowly to his feet and turned to face the altar, the eyes that stared out of the well-formed skull were no longer those of Maximillian Grey. They were those of the thing in the mirror. After an absence of ages, the Guardian had returned to Earth.

LOS ANGELES, CALIFORNIA
November 1

The telephone was ringing insistently, and Christopher Collin dragged himself from the depths of his haunted dreams to the dreary reality of his third-floor apartment.

He reached up from under the covers and grabbed for the telephone, only to knock it off the cluttered nightstand onto the floor. Collin leaned over the edge of the bed and clutched the receiver.

"Hello," he mumbled.

"Hello. Is this Mr. Collins?"

"Collin. Yes."

"This is Mrs. Swenson calling. We wanted to let you know that your equipment is ready. He finished it up last night."

"Oh, uh . . ." He sat up in bed and rubbed his head, trying to wake up. "That's great, wonderful." His voice was barely working. "When can I pick them up?"

"Today, if you like. We'll have them ready for you." Her voice was warm and friendly; her usual manner.

Collin looked at his wristwatch and swore to himself. It was nearly 11:00 A.M.

"Ummm, I could be there about four-thirty. Would that be too late?"

"Oh, no, that would be fine. You sound a little under the weather, Mr. Collin."

"Oh, no," he laughed softly. "Just a little laryngitis."

"Well, I certainly hope it's nothing serious. Try hot tea, with lemon, honey, and a little rum. It never fails for us."

"Thank you, I certainly will."

"See you this afternoon then."

"Yes. Thank you very much. And thank your husband."

"I will. Good-bye, Mr. Collin."

"Good-bye." Collin picked up the phone and set it on the nightstand, hanging up the receiver as he did

116

so. He groaned to himself and swung his legs over the side of the bed, which was of the day-bed variety, doubling as a sofa when not in use for sleeping in his bachelor apartment. He reached over, picked up several dirty glasses with the remains of drinks from the previous several evenings still sloshing in the bottoms, and headed for the kitchen sink, which was piled high with dirty dishes.

He made his way into the bathroom and turned on the cold water in his shower. He stuck his head under the icy flow for nearly half a minute, then he grabbed a stained towel from the rack and walked back into the main room. He parted the drapes and pulled the frayed cord on the venetian blinds, pausing to dry his face and hair absently as he stared down into the street.

The cars crawled by to the accompaniment of occasional honking horns and angry shouts, and a steady flow of pedestrians passed by on the sidewalk below. They were all oblivious to the man looking down on them, and though Collin examined the dirty street scene with care, he could see no sign that he was under surveillance.

Wrapping the towel about his waist, he made his way back to the kitchen and opened the door of his tiny ancient refrigerator. There was very little to be found, but this did not seem to concern him as he extracted a pitcher which contained a thick light-colored liquid. He set the pitcher onto an electric blender that sat on the counter and pushed the button that brought the device to life. It roared and squealed as the liquid in the pitcher swirled from the half-full position into a whirlpool that obscured the entire interior. After a few seconds, he took his finger from the button and the sound died away. He lifted the pitcher from the blender and poured a glassful of the liquid for himself.

Collin mentally braced himself, then tossed off the faintly unpleasant mixture in one long gulp, immediately refilling the glass with water and tossing that down after. The liquid was a homemade diet supplement, a mixture of brewer's yeast, eggs, lecithin, salad oil, bone meal, and bananas, along with a few additional unlikely ingredients. He had gotten the recipe from an Adele Davis nutrition book, and drank a glass of the stuff every morning in place of a normal breakfast in order to assure that he was properly nourished for the day, regardless of whether he was able to get balanced meals.

He set the glass down on the counter and then crossed to the door, which was the only way into or out of the apartment, short of the window, three stories from the street level. Collin checked the lock and chain that secured the door, and the thread he had taped between a point on the doorknob and the door itself in order to see if anyone had turned the handle during the night. It was intact and he turned to examine the apartment, which was a considerable step down from what he had come home to from Africa nearly eight months ago. The threadbare carpet and peeling paint accorded well with the place's location: the middle of a low-rent section of downtown Los Angeles. And even with the drapes and venetian blinds open, light never seemed to penetrate very far into the dingy atmosphere, giving the place a claustrophobic, almost cavelike quality that Collin found profoundly disturbing. Yet this lifestyle was necessary in view of his current situation.

All of one wall was taken up by a giant map of the United States, into which hundreds of pins had been positioned, with plastic heads of every conceivable color. A desk sat directly beneath this map, and its top was strewn with literally hundreds of papers, a reading lamp, a few pens and pencils, and a large clear plastic box with yet more colored pins.

Cardboard boxes lined the wall on either side of the desk, all crammed to the brim with newspaper articles, magazines, and official government correspondences. And by the door were several very large stacks of old newspapers.

On the only other wall space had been hung a large cork bulletin board, which was covered on every inch of its surface with newspaper clippings, each having one thing in common with all the others. Every clipping related to mysterious disappearances somewhere in the United States within the last eight months.

To Collin, the place looked exactly as it had when he had finally drifted off to sleep in the early hours of the morning. Despite his almost habitual fatigue, sleep always came hard for the man, and he not infrequently fell asleep only to wake up screaming from dimly remembered nightmares.

Briefly, the young man contemplated running a few miles to shake off his lethargic state. He glanced down at the worn running shoes beside the sofa-bed and then realized that he had no time today. With a sigh, he took his watch off, though it was waterproof, and threw it on the bed before heading for the shower. Fifteen minutes later, he was showered, shaved, and dressed in old jeans and a workshirt.

Before leaving the apartment, he picked up his revolver, the same one he had carried in the Anansi caves back in Africa and had shipped to the United States by Smith through the Ranger's Office. He stuck it in his waistband and covered it with a denim waistcoat.

He stepped outside, looking up and down the hallway to see if he was observed, and then carefully locked his door. Then he made his way down the hallway and out the back way: He didn't like his comings and goings to be noted by the landlady who occupied an office in the lobby during business hours.

The walk to the post office, which he made every morning, was less than two blocks. He climbed the steps and entered the section of the station devoted to post office boxes and walked down the aisle to one in the very deepest recess of the labyrinth.

He bent down and opened box number 901609. It was crammed full to the point of overflowing. It was always crammed full. He reached in and extracted the mail, not stopping to sort through it.

He closed the box and made his way quickly outside, where he purchased a cup of coffee at a small stand and seated himself on a bus stop bench.

Here, he began flipping quickly through his mail, paying no attention to the numerous official-looking envelopes from police and sheriff's departments in various parts of the country. He came upon a large manila packet from the Nick Olsen Private Detective

Agency, and set this to one side. He also came upon two other letters that he set aside, both of these obviously addressed by feminine hands and personal in nature, and then he came upon a flimsy blue envelope upon which had been stamped "Special Delivery" and "Priority Mail." It was postmarked Capetown, South Africa. Collin didn't bother to look at the name on the return address. It was different every time, although the South African letters were always from the same person.

He tore open the seal and extracted a letter and several smaller pieces of paper. He looked at them, noting with a sigh of heartfelt relief that one contained a money order made out to him and drawn on the First Bank of South Africa in the amount of $500. Now he would be able to pay his rent for another month and cover some of the more pressing personal bills.

He unfolded the letter and began to read.

"Van Helsing," the letter began, "hope this check is sufficient. Will send more next month. Met with grandfather last night. Impressions strong that Goliath relocated to position gleaned from memories of Drol party. Earlier belief regarding United States as target area reconfirmed.

"One additional clue: Grandfather mentioned old wooden structure—three stories high, perhaps more. Description suggests structure perhaps hotel."

Collin leaned back and thought for a few seconds before reading on. "Van Helsing" was Smith's highly literary code name for Collin, Van Helsing being the name of the vampire hunter in Bram Stoker's *Dracula*. "Goliath" was their code word for the Anansi. "Grandfather" meant Hasha. "Drol" which was "lord" spelled backward referred to Sedgewick's people.

Collin returned to the letter. "Currently preparing complete report on all tribal lore regarding current subject. Will forward soon. Please send update on recent progress. Regards, Wood."

"Wood" was apparently the name Smith had chosen for himself this week. Collin laughed bitterly. A progress report would take very little time to prepare. In the eight months since he and Smith had last seen each other in Africa, he had spent every day searching, collecting information, chasing across the country following leads that invariably turned out to be false, and all the time he was burning up what remained of his savings while generating no income. Gradually, to subsidize his search, he had sold off his portable property, including a fine Porche, stereo equipment, most of his cameras and photographic supplies, and even his few family heirlooms.

Smith had wanted to come to the United States with him, but had been forced to remain behind in order to remain in contact with Hasha, the poor dying blind man whose face had been so horribly disfigured by the Spider God. Hasha seemed to retain a tenuous, one-sided psychic link with the monstrous thing, a link that had so far given them their only concrete leads. The old tribesman had provided them with half a dozen vague clues as to the current whereabouts of the Anansi, but the unfortunate African appeared to receive impressions only at intervals, and his ability to communicate with the people around him was so diminished by his experiences that most of Smith's sessions with Hasha were totally fruitless.

But gradually, over time, Smith had been able to infer a number of important things. Their very first session with Hasha had strongly indicated that the destination of the fleeing Shaktowi had been America. Subsequent sessions after Collin's departure for the United States had only confirmed this. In addition, Hasha had once sputtered forth a sporadic description of countryside that included the observation "midway between two oceans." From that point, Collin had concentrated his research on the middle states, although he had not limited it to them. On one occasion, Hasha had described what appeared to be a steam shovel, though he had certainly never seen one and almost certainly never heard of one in his life. And once, Hasha had awoke screaming from a comalike condition, crying out that the thing was at that instant feeding on some unfortunate soul, a soul it had pulled in from the surrounding countryside.

This most recent reference to an old wood building was their most specific one to date, but it was still little to go on. Two months ago, Hasha had come through with his most vital contribution. Hasha had mumbled, almost unintelligibly according to Smith, something to the effect that the Anansi demon had selected its destination from the minds of one of the men in the European hunting party of Lord Sedgewick.

And it was this clue that had given Collin the basis of his most concentrated research. He had, since his return to the United States, been gathering all available data on missing persons from throughout the country. He subscribed to every major newspaper and news magazine, and in addition had approached most federal and local law-enforcement agencies looking for information on the pretext that he was writing a major investigative report on the phenomenon of missing persons in America. His already well-established journalistic reputation made this a highly viable cover story, and he had received a considerable amount of cooperation. Reports had poured in for months from many sources, and every night he patiently went through them, singling out those that would possibly relate to the activities of the Shaktowi and marking the locations of these on the map.

At first, he had been astounded at the number of people who simply vanished each week, and at the wide variety of peculiar circumstances under which people disappear. Family men, teenagers, housewives, even elderly persons from convalescent homes and priests and clergymen, all are known to drop from sight on a fairly regular basis. Going through the maze of reports was a time-consuming job, and for the first few months he had hired a secretary from Kelly Girl to do most of the sorting and filing. But his money had run out, and for the last few months, he had been staying up at night and doing it himself.

It was after receiving an urgent wire from Smith informing him of Hasha's statement that the Anansi Spider God had gleaned its destination from the mind of one of those in Sedgewick's expedition that Collin had begun a program of cross-references.

He had begun a process of painstaking research

into the lives of each man in Sedgewick's crew, pulling out localities of significance in their pasts and referencing them against the reports of missing persons he had already located on the map.

He had a simple code. There were four kinds of disappearances he isolated and marked on the map. Those marked with the red pins were those that had occurred under the most suspicious or bizarre circumstances and therefore were most likely to have been caused by the Anansi. Orange, yellow, and white, respectively delineated the locales of disappearances or abductions of descending likelihood. Collin had assigned a different colored pin to the lives of each of the six men in Sedgewick's team. Black was for Sedgewick himself, who though English had spent a significant part of his life in the United States. Blue was for McPhearson, who though not technically a member of Sedgewick's team, may have been lumped together with them in the mind of the Anansi. Carlson was purple, Briason gold. Carter was pink and Witherspoon green.

Within a few weeks, Collin himself had been able to ferret out most of the significant locations from the lives of the various individuals. Places of birth, schools, hometowns, residences, were all matters of public record. But none of these locations had matched with localities of significant disappearances, and Collin had been forced to turn to private investigators to delve more deeply into the men's pasts.

He had hired a different agency for each of the victims whose lives he was investigating. Secrecy was a passion for Collin. He was dealing with an intelligence that could literally pick information from the minds of those around him, and this fact made it impossible for him to confide in anyone at all. Only Smith, protected by the medallion and thousands of miles of ocean, shared his quest, and contact between the two of them was kept to a minimum, so that Collin had come to feel completely alone.

In the minds of his friends and relatives, who knew only that something had happened to him in Africa when his friend McPhearson had disappeared under mysterious circumstances, Collin seemed to have undergone a severe personality change. He was reclusive, obsessed with his new project, and reckless in his apparently impulsive spending habits. He had curtailed all social activities and now contacted his family and friends only with unexplained requests for loans of large amounts for vague purposes. And such were the friendships that he had built all his life that most of his friends had come across with support.

Preliminary reports had come in on all the men from the various detective bureaus, and comprehensive reports on a number of them. Once, Collin matched up a small midwestern town where Carlson had spent a summer as a firefighter with a number of mysterious disappearances. Collin took off in his broken-down Mustang to investigate, only to be present when the mutilated bodies of six people, two men and four women, were found in the bottom of a gully, the victims of a deranged mass murderer.

The report he had received today from the Nick Olsen Agency would be a detailed dossier on the life of one James Briason; deceased. Tonight, Collin would be up late sticking gold pins into the map. In his dreams sometimes, the map took the form of a giant doll of the Spider God, and Collin himself was clothed in the woven skirt of an African witch doctor. In the dream, he was sticking the colored pins into the map-doll in the fashion of a voodoo practicioner, trying to find a vulnerable spot as he could hear the real Anansi demon struggling up the hallway toward the door to his room. More and more pins would go into the map as he desperately raced against time, and closer and closer would come the sound of creeping in the hallway. And then, he would look over at the door, which would bulge inward as though collapsing under terrible pressure, and the bulging surface of the door would suddenly sprout those horrible, blood stained tendrils that would grow and grow. And again he would hear the horrible, nerve-shattering sucking sound, like air being pulled into the hose of a vacuum cleaner.

Still, with sweating hands, he would struggle to get the pins into the map and would hear the enraged roar of the thing as the pinpricks hurt it. And then his hands would get too slippery to hold the pins, and try as he might, he succeeded only in dropping them. The dream always ended the same way. He would turn suddenly to find the weaving tendrils right in front of his face. Then, he would awake screaming in the darkness, reaching for his pistol by reflex action, ready to use it on himself if his dream should turn out to be real after all.

Collin took a few seconds to glance over the other letters he had received and set aside. Both were from Sandra, his fiancée, and both said, in effect, the same thing. He put them aside sadly. She was asking him, tenderly and sadly, if he wanted to break their engagement. She still loved him and always would, but his recent behavior seemed to indicate that he no longer wanted her. Nothing could have been farther from the truth. It was tearing him apart to shun her, but he was desperately afraid of involving her in his terrible work. He had not seen her for weeks now, and there was no way to explain that he trusted no one any longer, to explain that no one, no matter how well intentioned, could hide their thoughts from his enemy.

He hid behind his story of being devoted to his book and determined to spend every minute on it. But this excuse had grown threadbare over the months during which he had so patiently avoided his friends. Collin continually reminded himself that nearly everyone who knew him well also had known Terry McPhearson. And the Shaktowi could, according to Hasha, know about them and keep their thoughts under surveillance of its own. It did not seem likely, but it was possible. Anything was possible. And Collin knew that he had developed an intense paranoid attitude toward everyone and everything, and the pressure of this, more than any other factor, wore at him continually.

Collin tied all the mail into a bundle, which he secured with a rubber band. Then he got up and made his way down the street to where his car—a rather battered old Mustang—waited tiredly at the curb. It was burgandy colored and the rust along the bottom of the fenders was therefore somewhat less visible than it might otherwise have been. A parking ticket flapped in the breeze on his windshield.

With a scowl, Collin grabbed it and glanced down. He had only been able to find a spot yesterday evening in a two hour parking zone and had slept far too late this morning to move the car in time. He tore the ticket up and threw it down the sewer drain. The faded black and yellow license plates on the Mustang were not his own. He had procured them in the dead of the night from a derelict car rusting in a junkyard on Seventh Street. He wanted nothing to give clues of his address or identity when he was out on the trail of the demon. So the ticket would never be connected with him.

Collin got behind the wheel and turned the key in the ignition. The engine roared to life with far more vigor than the appearance of the car would have indicated. Collin kept the vehicle in as near to perfect mechanical condition as his abilities would allow, realizing that reliable transportation could save his life at a critical moment.

It was a short drive down Olympic Boulevard to a withered building sporting large broken windows on which had been rather crudely painted the words "Karate" and "World Karate Federation." Collin parked on the street in front of the building, ignoring the hostile glances he attracted from two young Mexican men loitering on the corner. He stepped from the car and opened the trunk, extracting his black gear bag. With this in hand, he closed his trunk, unobtrusively checked to be sure his car was securely locked, and strode into the building, ignoring the uncomplimentary remarks, made in Spanish, which seemed to be directed at him by the people on the corner. It was a typical day in this part of town.

A clock on the wall showed 11:55 as he made his way down the hall toward the locker room. A young Oriental girl at the reception desk looked up and smiled at him as he walked by. "Hi, Chris."

"Hello Leia." He smiled, not breaking his hurried stride. "Is the Sinsi here yet?"

"Yes. You're a little late today."

"Yeah, dammit. I gotta hurry."

"Have a good workout."

He made his way to the locker, checked to see that the room was deserted, and transferred his pistol into his gear bag. Not that concealed weapons were particularly unusual at the Karate school. Many of the students carried them. But there was no reason to be indiscreet.

He dressed quickly in shorts and light rubber-soled shoes, leaving his *ghi* in the locker. The white cloth outfit was to be worn when he joined the regular one o'clock class. For his private lessons with the master he often wore only his tennis shoes, tee shirt and light shorts.

He ran out into the training room to find his instructor waiting, warming up in his agile, catlike manner. Collin bowed low. "Hello, Sinsi, I'm sorry I'm late."

The Sinsi bowed in return and said nothing. He was Japanese, perhaps forty years old, with a face that could be the sternest, most inflexible Collin had ever seen, or the most warm and compassionate. He was the greatest living exponent of his particular style of self-defense, and Collin had sought him out almost immediately upon his arrival in Los Angeles eight months earlier. With the exception of a few courses in self-defense in college, Collin had had little or no experience with the martial arts. But he had launched an immediate investigation to determine who was the best local instructor in the street-fighting style, and he had come into the school one day to seek private instruction from the head teacher, Mr. Hidatachi Mishiori.

Today, as always, Mishiori wore a white karate *ghi* with his well-worn and faded black belt, in which Japanese figures had been sewn in gold thread.

"Warm up," he told Collin, and the American immediately went into his regular loosening-up routine, which involved a wide variety of bending and stretching exercises for every part of the body. He did modified jumping jacks, long swinging kicks to loosen the leg muscles, and various contortionist splits, which never failed to agonize.

"Enough," grunted Mishiori. "Practice basic training. First punching. Kibidotch stance ready. Three punch, one face, two stomach. Start slow. Eeeech, ni, san . . ."

And so the lesson began as Michiori spent the first ten minutes on standard warm-up practice of the various punches, kicks, and maneuvers that were the basic components of karate.

Collin was sweating freely after just having performed several hundred kicks. "Enough," Mishiori said. "Natural stance, relax." Collin had come to an upright position, his feet shoulder width apart, his fists clenched at his sides.

"You must always remember, all power come from stomach. Never lose connection with shoulders, stomach." Mishiori illustrated by slapping hard on the various parts of Collin's body to which he referred. "Shoulders too high—still rely too much on arm muscles. When punching, initiate movement from stomach, arm muscles relaxed. Then at moment of impact, focus sharply. Eeeech." Mishiori demonstrated a punch in slow motion. "All muscles tense for one split second," the man walked in a slow circle around the motionless Collin, "then after first technique, relax again, ready to start next technique. Understand?"

Collin nodded, still breathless.

"This very important. You work with punching board later."

Collin nodded.

"One other thing. Stance still too high. Keep longer, lower stance." He demonstrated. "Make front stance. Hoi!"

Collin immediately assumed front stance, with one leg forward and the other back, and his fist held protectively before him.

"See, you too high." He pushed Collin painfully. "No balance, no connection. Easy to knock over, see."

He hit the American hard in the stomach, breaking his stance. Collin nodded and quickly resumed his previous position.

"Today, we work on sparring. Purpose, you recall, develop timing. Very important. You must learn to sense your opponent's rhythm and then break it." He held up his thumb and forefinger, opening and closing them in illustration of rhythm, and then suddenly, in between the strokes, he brought them sharply together.

"Today, we try reaction training."

Collin nodded. They had done it many times before.

"Sparring stance." Collin assumed a crouching, modified front stance with his hands open and held out before him, protecting his face and stomach.

Mishiori stood at ease in front of him. "I make threatening move, you strike—here." He patted his stomach. "You strike hard. Always strike hard."

Collin nodded. They stood in silence facing each other, Collin trembling slightly as his muscles remained poised to react to the slightest move the master might make.

Mishiori focused, as though to initiate a technique, and Collin struck, as hard and as fast as he could.

"No good," Mishiori commented mildly, unaffected by Collin's punch. "Relax, learn to trust sixth sense, it will tell you when punch comes. Try again."

When the hour was up, Mishiori called a halt to the timing training. "Last exercises," he said. "Kicks. Two front, two roundhouse, two side snap, two side thrust, two back. One count, all motions. *Keeyi* on last kick. Full speed, full power. Ready, Eeeech. Ni. . . . San. . . ."

Collin went through the extremely laborious combination two hundred times. A few months ago, he could not have done twenty. When they were done, they bowed to each other and walked off the smooth hardwood floor, signifying the end of instruction.

"Sinsi," Collin approached him, addressing him by the instructor's title, "I will be unable to make the regular class today. Something important has come up."

His instructor looked at him impassively. "You self-train tonight. Work on Kata."

"Yes, Sinsi." Collin bowed again, and left quickly. He showered and changed as fast as he could, knowing that if he were to reach the Swensons' shop by four-thirty he would have to leave at once. It was seventy-five miles south of Los Angeles.

He greeted his classmates, who had all arrived and were preparing for their forthcoming session, then stepped out the door and onto the sidewalk.

He dropped his gear bag and began running down the street when he caught sight of two Mexican men, the same two who had tried to provoke him as he went into the dojo, trying to break into his car. They were working with a coat hanger on the driver's side. One of them looked up and saw him coming. He nudged his companion and instead of running away, the two men moved around the car to meet the single running man.

As he drew within a few feet of them, they were smiling sarcastically. "That you car, man?" one of them asked, jerking a thumb at Collin's Mustang.

"Yes, it is," Collin answered. At the same instant, he struck out at the nearer of them, catching him neatly on the point of the chin and knocking him back several feet. Before the downed man's friend could do more than register an astonished look, Collin had rounded on him with a swift kick to the groin, which he followed up with a punch to the face that put the second man on the sidewalk, unconscious alongside his partner. The entire episode had occurred in a matter of seconds. Collin turned to see several of his classmates running down to him, one of them carrying his gear bag.

"Chris, are you all right?" asked a young black man who was a fellow student.

"Yes. I'm fine Isaac." He reached out and took his bag. "Thanks." He turned to see Mishiori standing in the door of the school, half a block away. He was looking at the scene with an inscrutable expression in his eye.

A crowd was beginning to gather, mostly comprised of students from the school. Conversation was an excited buzz as witnesses began to describe the chain of events. Someone was examining the two unconscious men.

"They'll be okay," he said. "They're just out of it."

Collin looked around at the crowd. "Anybody know who they are?"

No one answered, so he crossed to the men and extracted their wallets. There were a few dollar bills in each, but Collin ignored them, looking instead for identification. Neither had drivers' licenses, but they had green cards from which he copied their names and addresses on a scrap of paper. If, in the future, anything happened to his car while he was in class, he would know where to go to settle accounts.

"Want me to call the police?" asked the young man who had examined the two men.

"No," he said, looking down at them with distaste. "We're even. He walked around to his car and climbed inside. "I'll see you tomorrow," he called to his friends in the crowd. Then he drove off down Olympic, headed for the freeway, never to see any of

135

them again.

Traffic was not heavy on the southbound lanes of Interstate 5, and Collin made good time as he covered the seventy some miles to his next destination—the combination shop and home of one of the world's foremost gunsmiths.

Armand Swenson's shop was located north of Escondido in an isolated and incredibly beautiful section of southern California. His house was large and tastefully decorated, with an adjoining shop wherein the master gunsmith carried out his trade.

And it was here that Collin first met him, standing at a bench and filing lines on the front strap of a pistol frame. Swenson was a powerfully built man, and bulky, with short fat fingers and a protruding belly that testified to his fondness for beer and good food.

He spoke with his own particular whistling style, and liked to imitate the accents of other nationalities, particularly the Swedish of his ancestors, and he seemed to enjoy talking as he worked, though he carried out complex metalworking operations that Collin would have thought would require a man's full attention.

Mrs. Swenson's phone call had come in the middle of the ninth week since Collin had left his hand-picked forty-five automatic pistols with the ingenious craftsman, and he was extremely anxious to get them back into his possession. He found Armand in the shop, in the same clothes and the same posture as when he had first visited him.

"All done, huh?" Collin asked as he shook hands.

"And a beautiful job, as well, my friend." He

leaned forward and in a hushed voice designed to keep his wife from hearing in the kitchen he asked, "In time, I hope."

Collin nodded. "Yes. Thank God."

"Here they are." Swenson led the way around the back of the shop and out to his car. He unlocked the trunk and fished around among what might have been twenty guns to select Collin's. He dug out some targets also, showing marks he had apparently scored.

"I took these out on the range this morning," Swenson remarked. "Great group, huh?"

Collin glanced at them, and found them as amazing as those he had been shown on his last visit.

"Great," he echoed. His guns were now of dull silver finish, hard chromed, he knew. The standard military sights had been removed and in their place larger Smith and Wesson sights had been installed. The trigger guard had been squared off and the front of it, as well as the front strap, had been checkered with twenty lines to the inch. The hammer spur of his standard auto had been modified, and he knew both guns had been made fully accurate. The feed ramps, along which the cartridges slid up into the barrel, had been polished, and enlarged, and ambidextrous safetys had been installed in place of the standard ones.

"They're beautiful," Collin said. "Is there anything special I should know about care and feeding?"

Swenson grinned. "Just don't fire more than half a million rounds through them between checkups, and don't immerse them in sea water for periods in excess of a year at a time."

Collin had paid in advance, so now he asked, "Were there any additional expenses?"

"Nope. Heard you did well in the Oceanside combat pistol shoot last month. You going again next week?"

"Probably. I'm gonna try these out."

"Maybe I'll see you there."

"I'll be looking forward to it." Collin put the pistols in his waistband. "Thank you, Armand. Thank you very much." He shook his hand and headed for his car.

"You're welcome to stay for dinner if you want," Armand called after him.

"I'll have to take a rain check. I've got to be back in Los Angeles by eight. Thanks very much though. I'll see you next week."

"You bet." Armand waved casually and turned his attention to the weapons in his trunk.

As Collin pulled away from the Swensons', he reflected upon the rest of the day's activities. He was still contemplating ninety minutes later when he pulled into a parking lot in front of the Neuropsychology building on the campus of the University of California in Los Angeles.

It was 7:45, and dark as he got out of his car and made his way into the reception area of the building. A handful of people had gathered there, and Collin joined them.

They sat in a circle with the lights off, holding hands in the manner of a traditional séance, except that there was no table. On the floor in the center of a circle stood a microphone stand, from which a cable

138

ran to a cassette tape recorder under one of the chairs.

There were twelve people present that night, which was about average. In the six months since Collin had been attending the informal gatherings he had sometimes seen as many as twenty-two people, which made the activities very difficult to manage, but often there were as few as six or seven people. Tonight, there was only one newcomer, with all the rest veterans of at least several sessions. That, Collin reflected, was probably a good thing, but he had found that it was impossible to predict how well any given session was going to go.

The group was extremely loosely organized. Regular meetings were held every Wednesday night at eight in this basement classroom at UCLA, and they were open to anyone who wanted to attend. They were free, no one took your name, and no demands of any kind were made on anybody.

The purpose of the gatherings was simple: People attended in order to improve their personal extra-sensory perception by participating in various group exercises designed for this purpose.

The sessions were run quite scientifically by two UCLA faculty members, a team of psychics who had achieved national recognition and who were frequently called in to assist various law-enforcement groups in the solving of particularly difficult crimes. The initiator of the group, which had been conducting regular meetings for over six years, was a short, dark-haired man of about thirty-five years of age whose name was Jerry Sherman. He was small boned and delicate featured, and had a particularly sharp wit and outgoing personality.

Collin had been extremely impressed by the man's psychic gifts from the very first session. Jerry's specialty was in gathering medical or diagnostic impressions, although his gift was by no means limited to this area, and he could perform highly detailed diagnoses of individual ailments with unbelievable accuracy, using technical terminology regarding anatomy and diseases to describe what he perceived in cases of special interest. Collin had seen him turn to people around the circle and say, "Your foot's asleep," or, "You had asparagus for dinner, I can taste it," only to have the individual so addressed confess that this was indeed the case, and shake their heads in amazement.

Jerry's ESP had been with him since early childhood, and had developed to the extent that he exerted influences upon objects in his environment: He had learned when riding or driving a car to be careful not to think about the battery, as this could result in the car's engine failing.

Larry Smith, on the other hand, had shown no outward signs of possessing any degree of ESP when he first began attending Jerry's group meetings over five years ago, but it was a testimony to the effectiveness of the sessions that he had since developed his mental abilities into a tool useful enough to enter into his current casual partnership with Jerry. Collin had noted that Larry's perceptions could be very accurate, though they were more sporadic than Jerry's, and he observed that Larry's insights often had to do with visual images, or objects seen with the mind's eye, as contrasted with Jerry's physical-sympathetic symptoms.

Tonight, the group was engaged in its most common experiment, which involved selecting one individual as a "sender," with the others around the circle acting as receivers. The sender, often a newcomer to the group, was instructed to select someone they knew particularly well, over the age of sixteen, still living, whom no other person in the room had ever met. The sender, having made his selection, would wait until the lights were off and the group had gone through a mental relaxation exercise, then would state the name and sex of the person about whom they were thinking.

The sender then was to think idly about the person, concentrating generally about him instead of trying to send specific items of information.

The remainder of the group then went into a kind of stream-of-consciousness state, in which everyone was free to spontaneously contribute any flashes or impressions that might surface in their minds. Often the insights would come in such a steady stream that it would be difficult to find an opening in the communal commentary to jump into. Any and all sorts of information would be apt to come up; physical characteristics, various geographic locations associated with the person being focused upon, events from that person's life, ages, other people's names who were associated with the subject person. In addition, information could often surface in the sessions about the sender as well as the subject, though the sender would not be thinking specifically about himself.

After a given period of time, Jerry would call a halt to the proceedings, turn on the lights, and rewind the cassette.

He would hand the remote on-off switch to the sender and have him replay the recording, stopping the tape at every point where someone had made a significant comment.

Collin had seen sessions where nearly every comment was accurate. Other nights, the success rate was down as low as thirty percent. In the course of his own participation, he had at first tried to imitate those around him, trying with little success to come up with physical characteristics or visual images of the test subjects. But he quickly learned that whatever ability he possessed lay in different directions, and he developed a definite talent for perceiving facts about the personality or mental state of the subjects. He was able to rattle off insights about the person's attitudes on various subjects, their fears, their emotions. Where everyone else seemed to see the physical person, Collin learned to look for the "soul" or "mind" of the man or woman who was the object of the transmission.

Tonight, the sessions went particularly well, and Jerry stopped the proceedings after the second one with an announcement.

"We are going to try something new tonight," he said. "We weren't certain that we were going to, I wasn't expecting anything great, you know, because of the full moon, but everyone seems hot, so, hell, we may as well. Do you all remember the story of the English and American hunting safari that disappeared without a trace in South Africa last year?"

Everyone nodded and an excited buzz of conversation on the subject began. Collin could feel icy fingers crawling up his spine.

"Well," Jerry went on, "Larry and I have been approached by the family of the leader of the party, Lord Percy Sedgewick, to see if we can determine what happened to him and his people by psychic means."

Collin froze. Everyone in the group had heard of the great mystery by now, the African taboo land had received nearly as much publicity during the last eight months as had the Bermuda triangle during its heyday. The entire group was very anxious to proceed.

No one present had any idea of Collin's connection with the mystery. The young man's mind raced. He had joined the group in an effort to understand extrasensory perception, and to develop his own to whatever extent possible, looking for tools and weapons in his war with the Anansi demon. Also, he sought to understand the reasons for his apparent immunity to the deadly powers of the thing—so far with no success at all.

He had subtly approached both Jerry and Larry on the subject of mind blocks, but the science of parapsychology was still in its infant stage, they could offer only speculation as to why some minds are susceptible to extrasensory stimuli and some do not seem to be.

The last thing he intended to do, in the group or outside of it, was to meet the Anansi on its own home ground. The idea of a mental quest to locate the thing was so absurdly risky, so completely repulsive that it sickened him on the spot. To match mental powers with the Shaktowi creature could bring only one thing . . . disaster.

Collin opened his mouth to protest, then snapped it shut again. At all costs, he must not blow his cover. There was no reasonable excuse he could offer to prevent the group's going ahead with the session other than to tell them at least a fragment of the truth, and that was out of the question.

"Melissa," Jerry said, "would you mind bringing me that box from the table there. It contains some personal items that belonged to Sedgewick." The attractive brunet got up to comply. "Larry, if you'll get the recorder ready, I'll explain to them how we are going to do this."

Melissa returned with the cardboard box and handed it to Jerry. She took her place, which happened to be in the chair to Collin's right, then turned as she seated herself, noticing that all the blood had drained from Collin's face.

"Are you all right, Chris?" she asked. "You're pale as a ghost."

Collin looked over at her and forced a smile. "Oh, yes, thanks, Melissa."

"You're sure?"

"Absolutely. I'm a bit tired, but that's all. Thanks for your concern, but really I'm okay."

"Well." She turned away, unconvinced. "This should be interesting," she said, changing the subject.

Collin put his hands under his legs so she would not notice them trembling. "Yes, it could be." He felt sick.

"Now with these objects," Larry was saying as he pulled a variety of items from the cardboard box, "we are going to try something called psychometry." He set upon the floor in the center of the circle a gold watch, a ring with several large stones of types unknown to Collin, a burgundy ascot, and a pair of patent leather shoes.

"All of these things were Lord Sedgewick's personal property, and all of them, at one time or another, were worn close to his skin." Larry turned and set the box outside of the circle.

"What we are going to do," Jerry took up the story, "is undergo our usual relaxation interval, with the lights off, and then pass the objects around the circle. Keep holding hands with the people on either side of you unless you are actually handling one of the objects. When you do get to touch and examine them, open your mind to any impressions at all that they may inspire in you. We have no one here who actually knew Lord Percy, and so you can think of these objects as taking the place of the sender we normally employ in our sessions."

"Are there any questions?" Larry asked.

"I have one." The man who spoke up was one of the regulars, Philip Dexter. He was a very massive individual, well over six feet tall and ruggedly muscled. He had a full black beard that obscured most of his features and a deep rumbling voice to match. Collin had marked him down as an especially intelligent and cool-witted individual, the type that would be useful to have around during times of trouble.

"How are we going to know if anything we come up with here is accurate?" Dexter went on.

Jerry shrugged and smiled. "We don't really. But I

have a physical description of Sedgewick, along with details of the area in which he disappeared, so that we *can* cross-reference some basic details to see if we are getting anything that seems at all valid."

"What, specifically, are we looking for?" Melissa asked.

"You should know by now, Melissa, that we can't narrow the focus down in our sessions to any specific points. We've got to open our minds to any information that may come through. But what we are hoping to come up with are clues as to what really happened to Sedgewick's group, where they are now, and whether they are in fact still alive."

"That brings up the final point," Larry spoke up. "Sedgewick may be dead. If he is, what we are doing here will amount to a séance, basically. We've tried that kind of thing before, and the results can be pretty strange, let me tell you. So if anyone here doesn't feel comfortable with that possibility, it might be better that you do not participate. And, please, be ready to break the circle at any time, should things suddenly get . . . out of hand."

"Right." Jerry nodded emphatically.

"Well?" Larry looked around the circle. Nobody said a word.

"Let's begin then." He nodded to the newcomer, a young, bookish looking woman with horn-rimmed glasses who happened to be sitting closest to the door. "Would you get the lights, please?"

"Sure." She got up and accommodated him, plunging the room into a deep darkness broken only by a faint light coming in from under the massive door.

They went through five minutes of relaxation exercises, holding hands in the circle just as they had done earlier.

"I'm passing around the watch now," Larry spoke up, handing it to Jerry.

"I'm getting an impression," Jerry said at once, rubbing the watch between the fingers of his left hand. "I see a rather tall man, perhaps thirty-two or thirty-three years old. Dark hair, neatly combed. He's dressed in one of those jungle jackets you see in the old movies. At some point in his life, he had acute appendicitis. He had it removed, but it feels as though there might have been complications. Also, I'm getting pain in the face and forehead region, now intense pain in the eyes, as though he were looking into some blinding light."

He handed the watch along and someone from across the circle spoke up, "I see a woman called Marge, or Marjorie."

"Ships, I see ships," Melissa broke in.

"He had a passion for martinis," someone whom Collin did not recognize said, and Christopher realized that this was perfectly true.

The watch came around to Collin and he hurriedly passed it along to the next person, making no attempt to participate in the experiment.

The comments were coming at a steady pace now.

"I see a sadness in him. . . ."

"He was having trouble with his wife. . . ." someone else added. That also was true.

"I see a cat," Larry spoke up. "A gigantic black one, maybe like a black panther. It's got really bright red eyes, and its face looks almost demonic,

147

you know?''

Collin had jumped visibly in his seat at the mention of the cat.

"I'm getting fear, as though he was scared of something . . . really scared.'' The voice was unquestionably the giant Philip Dexter's.

"I'm seeing colors . . . colors fluctuating. . . .''

"There's an enclosed room . . . he's in a dark space. . . .''

"Snakes . . .'' Melissa whispered beside him, "snakes wriggling closer and closer.'' Her voice was edged with fear.

"Someone named somethingspoon . . . weather . . . weatherspoon?''

Collin's hands were like ice, and they were trembling now so that the others could not possibly fail to notice, but no one said anything. Weatherspoon was as close as it had to be to Witherspoon. But that meant little. The names of the party had been printed in most of the major papers.

"Definitely something wrong related to the eyes. . . .'' Jerry spoke again.

"Snakes getting closer still,'' Melissa continued.

The shoes were passed through Collin's hands.

"Pain in the upper arms. . . .'' Jerry again.

"Starting to see things,'' someone else contributed, "like reruns of an old horror movie. Demons, trolls, monsters flipping in and out of view.''

Nobody appeared to notice the gradual chill creeping into the room.

"Death,'' someone else said. "Dead bodies, looks like pictures of the extermination camps of World War Two.''

"Snakes getting closer. . . ."

"See something in the sky now, bright like a star, except it's moving . . . like an airplane, maybe. . . ."

"Getting a hot pain now, in spots on his forehead and cheeks, as though someone had splashed acid on his face. . . ." Jerry spoke emphatically, apparently reacting to the empathetic pain.

"Snakes. . . ."

It was absolutely freezing in the room, and Collin realized suddenly that the reason no one had noticed his own hands shaking was that everyone else was also trembling with the cold. Collin was growing more fearful each second.

"Colors glowing, getting brighter, brighter. . . ."

"Weaving . . . snakes . . . no . . . I can see them now . . . not snakes . . . tentacles perhaps. . . ." Melissa was clenching his hands so tightly that Collin thought she would break his fingers.

"More pain in the upper cranial areas, spreading across the face. . . ."

"I still see the cat . . . keep getting this repeating image. . . ."

"Tentacles, weaving . . . getting closer. . . ."

"There's a stuffy, enclosed feeling . . . like a cave or a tunnel. . . ." Phil Dexter again.

"I can see—" Melissa began again, but suddenly her voice broke and her body tensed convulsively. Her back arched and she continued to speak, but this time in a heavy masculine voice, a voice Collin had last heard months ago in South Africa. It was a voice he never had expected to hear again, the voice of a dead man. It was the voice of Percy Sedgewick. "No, no, go back . . . you must stop this. . . ."

The voice was pleading desperately, and the girl's hands were gesticulating emphatically up and down with the words.

"You've got to stop this . . . you don't know what you're doing. . . ."

"Getting pain . . . more pain . . . much worse now. . . ." Jerry cut in as though nothing had happened. He seemed oblivious. "Definitely something about the eyes. . . ." he continued.

"You must stop, *stop*," Melissa stammered in Sedgewick's tone. Collin was horrified.

"Still see a cat. . . ."

"Tunnel. . . ."

"Intense burning in the cranial region," Jerry continued, "as though he exper—"

Collin had just decided to break the circle, was on the verge of jumping up and turning on the lights when the air was torn to pieces by a scream of unendurable agony that lasted for second after heartrending second. Collin could tell by the direction that the scream was from Jerry, though he could never have associated such a sound with the small, delicate man. In that instant, Collin was aware of something else. Something infinitely worse than the sound of any scream. The buzzing was back in his head, just as he had heard it on the other side of the world.

"My eyes, *my eyes*," Jerry was screaming. From the sounds, Collin knew he was rolling about on the floor, screaming over and over and pleading for help. Then, in the midst of it all, as everyone sat too stunned to take any action, a roar burst forth from Melissa's throat. It was deep, demonic, far far louder than anything Collin had ever heard produced by a human throat.

Cries of fear burst from the people around him as he bounced up, knocking his chair back from under him and tearing his hands from the viselike grips of the terrified man on his right and the comatose Melissa on his left.

He had no recollection of bulldozing his way through the various invisible obstacles between himself and the lightswitch by the door, but he found his hand groping on the wall, locating the switch and turning it, bathing the room in a pale light that sputtered and flared, just as the campfire had done in a distant jungle on the night that the Shaktowi had taken Smith and McPhearson.

The scene was ghastly. Melissa was sitting in her chair, her head rotated back on her neck farther than human anatomy normally allowed. Her head was tilted so far back that she was actually looking behind herself, her writhing face upside down with respect to the floor. Her entire body was trembling with exceeding violence, her feet tapping on the tile floor as fast as a drumroll.

But no one in the group was looking at her. No one, indeed, had even noticed her. They all sat in stunned terror looking down into the center of the circle where Jerry rolled over and over, back and forth in agony, screaming and holding his hands over his eyes. Smoke and steam rose from between his fingers, and blood flowed freely down his face, literally soaking the carpet and splattering all over the horrified spectators. In between the shouts of pain could be heard a terrible sizzling sound, like that of frying meat, and beneath that, a strange, gurgling, sucking sound.

The newcomer in the horn-rimmed glasses who had shut off the lights began to scream hysterically, then collapsed in her seat. Collin jumped forward, knocking the unconscious girl aside and leapt into the center of the circle. Phil Dexter was already on his feet, the first of the others to rise, and he moved forward to join Collin as they tried to help the squirming, agonized man.

Melissa had collapsed, unconscious, and slipped to the floor, and Joan Armatidge, a young kindergarten teacher, jumped up, screaming, and fled from the room, shock and panic written all over her face.

Larry, Jerry's partner, moved instinctively to the remaining members of the group, who still sat frozen in horror in their chairs, still gripping each others hands as though their lives depended on it, and physically pulled their interlocked fingers apart, all the time screaming, *"Break for God's sake. Break!!!"*

Collin had just gathered Jerry in his arms, subduing his struggles as gently as possible when the buzzing in his head reached a climax and then was gone. At that instant, the flourescent lights above finally flickered to full power. The blood that was everywhere seemed an unnaturally bright red.

An alarm was ringing somewhere in the building. Someone had had the sense to trip the fire alarm, and Collin could hear the sound of running footsteps in the hall. He could also hear the sounds of people puking and wretching in various parts of the room. Collin looked down at the bloody figure he cradled in his arms. The poor man was semiconscious, in deep and dangerous shock, and his violent struggles had finally ended.

Collin and Philip Dexter gently eased Jerry's bloody hands away from his eyes and looked at the wounds.

"Oh, my God!" The janitors had just come bursting into the room. They looked down for all of two seconds, then fled from the room, their hands held up to their mouths.

Phil Dexter, too, turned away briefly and returned seconds later, bits of puke stuck in his beard.

He looked at Collin, who was ministering to the hollow, burned eye sockets as carefully and thoroughly as he could. Christopher did not feel at all sick. That would come later, he knew. He looked down at the mutilated man and swore eternal revenge for the thousandth time.

"What the fuck happened?" Dexter's face registered his uncomprehending horror.

Larry came up to them and knelt beside his friend, his eyes wild with panic, shock, and hysteria.

"My God, we've got to help him!"

"There's nothing we can do," Collin said bitterly. "We can only keep him still and as comfortable as possible until help comes." He dabbed at the blood to see if the hemorrhaging would continue.

"Oh, God, Jerry, Jerry," Larry sobbed, his hands on his partner's arm.

Collin gestured to Dexter with his head. "Get him out of here, for God's sake."

Dexter eased Larry up and led him from the room, which was now alive with the sound of crying, incomprehensible yammering, and running footsteps as someone entered the room. Over it all clamored the sound of the alarm, and Collin was astonished to note that the pulse of the siren seemed to match exactly the throb of blood in his temple.

"I'm a doctor, let me through," said the man who had just arrived. He got down on his knees beside Collin and pulled the makeshift bandage away. He was in his shirtsleeves, balding, perhaps forty.

"Dear God in heaven!" he gasped. He took Jerry's pulse and shook his head. "We've got to get him into the emergency room at once!"

"The emergency room?" Collin's brow wrinkled.

"You damn blithering idiot!" said the doctor. "The building next door just happens to be the university hospital! We could carry him up to the emergency room in a minute and a half."

"Shouldn't we wait for help to—"

The doctor shook his head. "No time. We'll have to carry him. Very, very gently." As he talked, he swabbed the blood away, examining the horrible disfigurement on Jerry's forehead. "How did this happen?"

"I don't know, Doctor."

"It was dark." Dexter had just returned, and some of the color had come back into his face. "We were having one of our regular sessions, just as we do every week. Suddenly he just started screaming."

The doctor made no comment. He turned to Collin and noticed the blood that literally covered his torso. "You all right?"

"Yes." Collin looked down at himself. "It's his blood." He looked over at Melissa, still lying on the floor and being inexpertly tended by what appeared to be some students who must have come in response

154

to the commotion.

"She may need help, though. I heard her scream."

"If you could call it a scream," Dexter said with a visible shudder.

"I'll take a quick look," the doctor said, his professional calm returning. "You two get him up. You," he gestured to Collin, "take his shoulders, you take his ankles. And for heaven's sake, be extremely gentle."

By the time Collin and Dexter had lifted Jerry from the floor, the doctor was back from his look at Melissa.

"Shock," he said. "She'll keep until more help gets here. "Let's get him up."

The three of them began to move out of the room and down the hall, screaming for people to clear out of the way in front of them. They hurried as fast as they dared down the hall, turned right and walked down another hall until they came to the elevator, which was fortunately just opening. The doctor shouted at the occupants to get out as quickly as possible and they piled in, pressing the button for the first floor. During the few seconds it took for the machine to lift them to the first floor, the doctor took Jerry's pulse again.

"Mmmmmm. Holding steady. What in the world could have done that to him?" he asked, obviously not expecting an answer. "I've never seen anything even remotely like it."

The door opened and they made their way into the hallway leading to the passage that interconnected the neuropsychology building to the university hospital. The words "Emergency Room" had been painted in red letters on the wall with an arrow pointing the way.

As they moved, Collin could hear the sounds of approaching sirens, and doors slamming in the parking lot.

Within seconds, he and Dexter set the poor victim down on the operating table in the confines of the emergency room. Immediately, the staff took over, joining with the doctor who had first accompanied Jerry up from the classroom.

A nurse came up to the two bloody men. "Are you injured?"

They shook their heads, looking at each other grimly.

"Then you must leave at once," she said, indicating the door. "Someone out in the hall can help you get cleaned up." She was gone before they could say a word.

"Well, let's go," said Dexter. He still could not seem to take his eyes from Jerry.

In the hall, they were directed to a washroom where they could get themselves cleaned up. They scrubbed their faces and arms, then stripped off their shirts and deposited them in sealable bags provided for that purpose.

"Incredible," Dexter kept saying. "What do you think happened?"

"I have no idea." Collin shook his head.

"Whatever it was, it was still happening when the lights came back on. Say . . ." a look of enlightenment came over him, "that was you who hit the lights, wasn't it?" He rubbed his chin whiskers with his fingers. "I always thought of myself as a quick thinker when the chips are down. But you sure had me beat. I got to hand it to you."

"I'm just deathly afraid of the dark," Collin said. It was the kind of joke people make when they have just been subjected to terrible pressure.

Dexter laughed shortly.

"You've got nothing to be ashamed of," Collin said. "You kept your head pretty damn well yourself."

"I was in the war," he said, wiping the water drops from his beard with his arm. "Saw plenty. Never got sick, though. Not until tonight." He turned to Collin. "What in the *world* could have done that to him? Could it have been one of us?"

Collin appeared to think for a second. "No. Remember? When I hit the lights, everyone else was still in the circle, all holding hands. All except poor Jerry. And, like you said, whatever was happening to him, it was still going on when the lights came on."

"Yeah." He looked into the distance. "Did you see that steam coming from his eyes? Fuck." He shook his head. "That's the last time I ever come to one of these things."

It was midnight by the time Collin arrived at his apartment. He and Dexter, along with those few of the other eyewitnesses who were coherent enough to talk, had gone through a tedious interview process with the police. They had returned to the classroom where the session had been held and described in vivid detail everything that had happened leading up to the accident.

The police had immediately impounded the tape, which had been running throughout the ill-fated session. And in the presence of the witnesses, the detective lieutenant in charge of the investigation played through enough of it to verify that the tape was a faithful record of what had occurred.

Then they had dismissed everyone not in need of medical help, with the notification that they would probably be called in for further questioning within the next few days.

Collin made his usual inspection of the apartment before crossing to the refrigerator. He picked up a small bottle of Chivas Regal from on top of it and poured himself a generous quantity. He did not add water or ice—he always drank it straight and at room temperature.

Collin crossed to the sofa and sat down, opening the paper bag in which he had carried his pistols in from the car. He breathed a prayer of thanks that he had not worn one into the meeting that evening, as he had been tempted to do.

Although he had had an incredibly long and arduous day, he was far too wound up to sleep, so he spent some time examining his pistols, fitting them into the holsters he had long since purchased for them—one a belt holster and one a shoulder rig. He patiently loaded his spare magazines with factory ball ammunition and set his equipment on the night-stand beside his bed.

Still not tired, though it was by now 1:30 A.M., he turned his attention to his mail, seating himself at his desk in front of the wall map and singling out the report he had received that day from the Nick Olsen Private Detective Agency.

He slit the manila envelope with a letter opener

and extracted a thick plastic bound notebook, which bore the title "James Briason" in neatly typed letters across the front.

Collin took a long deep breath as he tried to rid himself of the mental images that flashed across his consciousness of the horrible scenes he had witnessed that evening. He forced himself to concentrate as he scanned the first page of the report, which contained a synopsis list of the important dates and places in the life of the unfortunate James Briason. As one part of his mind mechanically read over the neatly typed columns, some other portion of his awareness was given over to dealing with the shock of the night's events, and to struggling with the feelings of guilt he suffered for not having made some effort to stop the session before it had begun. He realized that, despite the fact that he could never have imagined that any of the group members had been in physical danger, he would never rid himself of the responsibility he felt. Depressed, he debated phoning Sandra, his fiancée, but decided against it.

The taste of defeat and despair was in his mouth, and he was reaching for his glass of scotch when his eye returned of its own accord to an obscure name and date, hidden and insignificant among the rest. "Melville, Montana — 1961, spent summer with grandparents."

Melville, he thought. It sounded oddly familiar. He could not be certain with the hundreds of places he had marked on his map as the sights of peculiar disappearances, but there was something promising about the sound.

He put the scotch down, untasted, and reached for

one of the gold headed pins that stood for significant places in the life of Briason. He rose from his chair and leaned toward the map, which faced him on the wall above the desk. In the dim light, he had to strain slightly to read the small print on the pin-bristled map, so he ran his hand up and down the state of Montana. There was only one red pin, which stood for a disappearance under the most suspicious of circumstances. It protruded from the paper on a spot in the northeasternmost corner of the state, and Collin bent it out of the way in order to read the name of the community to which it referred. He moved his face even closer to make out the word and felt his heart begin to beat rapidly. Melville.

His hand shook as he fitted Briason's gold pin alongside the red one.

Seconds later, he was frantically flipping through his files of newspaper clippings, which had been referenced by state and city, till he pulled out a thin manila folder titled "Melville, Montana."

There were just a few clippings from some obscure country papers, written in the rather unsophisticated style of country journalism typical of small midwestern communities. A bus load of people had vanished several months ago while traveling over a country road during a thunderstorm. The bus itself had been found in a thicket miles from its appointed route, as had the driver, dead from what were described as "unknown causes." But no trace of the thirty-some passengers known to have been aboard was ever found.

The folder contained a few smaller clippings

chronicling the details of the ensuing investigation, which appeared to be an exercise in futility. The final item in the folder was a clipping from the *National Enquirer*. It was a brief column devoted to describing in highly sensationalistic terms, a supposedly haunted hotel on the outskirts of the little community of just over twelve hundred people. An *Enquirer* investigative reporter passing through the town had heard stories of mysterious and supernatural activities in the old structure, activities that had hastened its abandonment a few months before and he had interviewed some of the locals who claimed to have seen or heard mysterious things on the grounds. The last lines of the brief story were of special interest to Collin:

> The elderly owner of the now abandoned property, who swears she would rather die than set foot in the stately structure, insists that in several cases, guests checked into the hotel only to disappear without a trace during the night. These claims, initially ascribed to senility on the part of Mrs. Van Esson, who is now in her late seventies, are being investigated by the *Enquirer* staff. In the meantime, the weary traveler through the sleepy town of Melville, Montana, would be wise to bypass the dilapidated old hotel in favor of the modern Holiday Inn on Route 76.

He took the folder over to his desk and laid it down beside the detective's report on James Briason. With a shaking hand he began to draft a wire to Smith in South Africa. It read simply: "Possible pay dirt. Prepare to come America. Get all possible details from grandfather. Await further word. Regards,

Van Helsing."

Tonight he would study the details of Briason's file, and pore over the news clippings until he knew them by heart. In the morning, he would make copies of them and leave the originals in a safe deposit box for which Smith already had a key.

He glanced at his watch; 2:50 A.M. He debated with himself as to whether he was tired enough to try to sleep but was sharply interrupted in his deliberation by a gentle knock at the door. Instantly, one of his pistols was in his hand and the desk lamp was off. He had heard no footsteps on the hardwood floor of the hall, and he had no idea at all who or what might await him in the hall outside.

"Who is it?" Collin asked from his position behind the door. His ear was pressed hard against it, but still he could hear nothing.

"Mr. Collin? I'm very sorry to disturb you at this hour. My name is Mason Raymond." The voice was cultured; the tone gentle.

"Just a minute." Collin draped a dirty towel over his automatic and opened the door against the latched security chain, peering out at the figure in the hall. His visitor was a fairly nondescript man of middle years. He was heavyset, about six feet tall, had dark hair and a dark complexion. He was wearing a tweed overcoat and in one hand he carried a hat of a cut often seen on the streets of New York City. There was an aura of intelligence, of honesty about the neatly groomed man. Though his shoes were mud-splattered, as though he had walked a fair distance in the recent past, his clothing was clean, his hair

162

in place.

"Do I know you?"

The stranger hesitated, then smiled. "Not personally, no. Though I have written to you several times in the last few months."

"Written?" Collin's eyes narrowed suspiciously. "What's your name again?"

"Raymond. Dr. Mason Raymond."

Collin racked his memory and had to admit that there was something vaguely familiar about the name.

"You have to excuse me, Dr., uh, Raymond," Collin said with a marked lack of cordiality. "But at this hour, I'm afraid I'm having a little difficulty remembering."

Raymond smiled apologetically. "You see, I'm the man who wrote to you about setting up a possible collaboration. I'm working on a similar comprehensive investigation of the increasing missing person phenomenon in this country, and time and again I have come across evidence of your work. I'm working on a grant from the government, and I thought we might both benefit from a little mutual cooperation."

Collin recalled some letters to that effect that he had read and hurriedly discarded.

"How did you get my home address? All my correspondence is handled through a post office box."

"Like yourself, I am an investigative reporter. I have read your previous works, and have considerable respect for you as a journalist. So I was willing to go to some lengths to see you."

Collin was profoundly disturbed that he had been

traced with such apparent ease. He reached up to slide the safety chain loose and open the door. "Won't you please come in, Dr. Raymond, and forgive the mess." Collin had to know at once whether his uninvited guest was as he seemed. If he was not, Collin vowed, the man would not leave this room alive.

He stood aside as Raymond moved easily into the darkened room. Collin clicked on the light and said, "Please sit down. Can I offer you a drink?" Without appearing to, he watched Raymond's every move. As the man made his way to Collin's only armchair, Collin noted that the mysterious Dr. Raymond walked soundlessly, like a cat.

"No, thank you. I am really very sorry to disturb you at this hour. I realize it must be a terrible imposition. But you see my time here in L.A. is severely limited. In fact, I've got to catch a flight out in just a few hours."

"Where to?"

"East."

Collin seated himself in his dilapidated desk chair.

Raymond sighed. "When I received no answer to my letters, I began to wonder if you were receiving them at all. And, I must admit, I became more than a little curious about you. You seemed to be going to extraordinary lengths to keep yourself at arm's length from your own investigation."

Collin nodded, both outwardly for Mason Raymond's benefit and inwardly to himself. That last rang true. Curiosity is the stock in trade of a good journalist.

"What brought you to L.A., Dr. Raymond? Surely not curiosity about me."

"I confess," Raymond raised his hands in an embarrassed shrug, "there were other matters that brought me to this city this evening. Not very pleasant ones, I'm afraid. Quite a curious thing, actually. It's all over the wire services. A psychic got himself injured tonight, seriously and hideously injured, while trying by psychometry to determine the fate or whereabouts of the ill-fated Sedgewick hunting expedition in Africa. The ones that were lost last year."

Collin's finger tightened on the trigger of the gun he still held concealed in his right hand, as he felt the icy fingers of death play up and down his spine. His mind was racing.

Was this some peculiar game of cat and mouse? Did Raymond know of Collin's presence in Africa, of his participation in the group session at UCLA? Was he now merely watching for the younger man's reactions? The thought crossed Collin's mind that this Mason Raymond, if that were his real name, might be a member of some law-enforcement agency. If so, the situation was even more complex: To shoot such a man could bring about his own arrest and effectively remove him from the gameboard forever.

These thoughts played through Collin's mind in a fraction of a second. He prayed that his face showed no signs of his thoughts or of his reaction to the mention of the terrible events of the evening. Collin was afraid that his eyes were betraying him, and he inwardly cursed them for not being better liars.

"So, your investigation is government sponsored?" He tried to make the question sound innocent.

"Yes, an offshoot of the Congressional Subcommittee on Crime and Violence." Mason Raymond's words came easily, as though it was an explanation he had made time and again in the course of his work. Collin had never heard of such a committee. But there were so many organizations on Capitol Hill.

Dr. Raymond looked pointedly around the small apartment with eyes that appeared casual, and yet that Collin was certain missed nothing. One searching sweep at the piles of cardboard file boxes in the corner, the bulletin board littered with newspaper clippings, the desk liberally strewn with papers, including the folder and file relating to Briason that Collin had not had time to conceal, and the older man made no effort to reexamine them. Obviously he had seen all he needed to assess the scope and resources of Chris's one-man operation. But when his eyes came to the map on the wall, Raymond's hand came up and he scratched his chin reflectively, giving the multicolored, bristled document a thorough examination.

"Mmmmmm." He rose, and to Collin's consternation walked across the room as soundlessly as a feline, and leaned forward to examine the map closely.

"You've obviously progressed quite far in your research, Mr. Collin."

Collin rose, unobtrusively tucking his pistol into concealment in his waistband, and crossed nervously to the desk.

"Nothing, I'm sure, compared with what you've been able to do with the resources of a Congressional Subcommittee at your disposal. Actually, as I'm sure you've noticed, I'm self-financed, operating with no outside help and no real budget." His words sounded unconvincing even to himself. "Actually, I'm getting ready to give it up."

"I'm really very disappointed to hear that. It's clear that a tremendous amount of work has gone into this." His eyes had never strayed from the map, and Collin was growing increasingly desperate to get the stranger away from it.

"Yes, but things just aren't coming together as I had hoped they would." Collin shrugged.

"Perhaps," Raymond said, "if that is the case, you might benefit as much as myself from a collaboration of some sort."

"What would you be getting out of it?" Collin was growing increasingly desperate to get Mason Raymond's attention off that map, which now, though coded in the language of the colored pins, contained his most valuable secret. The thought had flashed with lightning swiftness into his brain: *Perhaps this Raymond has a photographic memory!*

"Mmmm." At last the calm-mannered man turned his gaze from the map. "You underrate your own talent, Mr. Collin. Such persistence, such determined inquiry! Do you imagine that these traits are common among my staff of government employees? Organization has its benefits, of course. But there are some things that require individual creative genius to accomplish."

Chris ignored the implied compliment, tried to lift his scotch casually to his lips and noticed that his hand was trembling very slightly. For a second, his eyes flew from his own hand to Raymond's piercing blue eyes, and their gazes locked. Collin was sure that Mason Raymond had seen his instantaneous betrayal of nerves. The man made no comment, no reaction, and Collin could read nothing in the depths of those piercing orbs.

Raymond broke the spell, glanced down at the inexpensive wristwatch on his arm. "Mmmmm. It's getting quite late. I'm afraid I must be going." Strange, Collin thought. He must have seen what he came here to see.

"I hope you'll consider my proposition, Mr. Collin. I'm quite certain that there is a great deal we could do for each other. A very great deal." The emphasis on the last words was inexplicable to the younger man. It seemed almost as if Raymond were trying to convey by inflection a message he was reluctant to put directly into words.

"I'll think it over," Collin responded, and realized at once that his mind was a dull thing indeed by comparison with that of the razor sharp brain with which he fenced. He had failed to assess his unwelcome guest, had failed to take the lead in the conversation, had failed to prevent this stranger from invading his only fortress and freely examining his private records. Balancing this against the obvious fact that the stranger had accomplished whatever mission he had set out to accomplish, and had betrayed nothing, Collin felt himself the novice that he most certainly was at this deadly game of nerves and wit. "Where can I reach you?" he asked as Raymond moved toward the door.

"Forgive me." Mason dug into his coat pocket. "My card. You can always reach me through this number."

Collin accepted the card and glanced at it for a second. It was plain white, of expensive paper, containing only the name Dr. Mason Raymond embossed with gold letters, and beneath that the phone number (800) 351-4476. An eight hundred number, and no address. Collin smiled wryly to himself. He was not the only one who took pains to cover his tracks.

"Again, please forgive my intrusion at this ungodly hour. I simply had to see you while I was in town." Collin held the door for him as Raymond moved soundlessly into the hall. Once there, he turned back and for the first time the twinkle in his eye dimmed and his voice grew serious. "Should you need help in your investigation for any reason . . . hmmmm, or should you, shall we say, encounter a situation in which you need the support or assistance of a larger organization, call me any time, day or night. In an investigation of this type, one can find oneself dealing with, hmmmmm, imponderable elements."

Collin nodded from the doorway as Raymond began to move down the hall.

"Oh, one last thing, Mr. Collin," the visitor was hardly more than a black shadow beneath the pitifully inadequate bulb that illuminated the hallway, "I understand you happened to be in Africa las[t] year at the same time that the unfortunate Sedgewick group was lost. It must have been quite exciting."

Collin felt as though a knife had been thrust into his ribs. He opened his mouth, tried to speak, then took a deep breath. "I was in the area, yes."

"I should very much like to speak with you about it, sometime. Fascinating mystery. Fascinating. Till we meet again, Mr. Collin." He raised his hand to the brim of his hat, which he had set upon his head as he talked, in a kind of half-salute.

"Good night, Dr. Raymond." Collin might have said more, but he choked it off. Any word now might be a betrayal. He was walking blindly in unknown territory. He watched the stranger out of sight then gently closed the door and locked it with exceeding care. Then he pulled his pistol from his waistband and toyed with it idly as he leaned against the door, trying unsuccessfully to fathom the underlying truth about who or what Mason Raymond might represent.

Collin doused the light, then crossed to the window and looked down at the street three stories below in time to see the stranger emerge from the front door and walk gently down the street toward Wilshire Boulevard. The overcoated form turned a corner and vanished from the glow of the only street-light on the block.

Collin lowered the shade and crossed to the desk, picking up his glass of scotch. There would be no sleep tonight, tired as he was. For the next few hours, he would pack, and with first light he would be off for the airport to catch the earliest available flight to

Montana. He was in the grip of a feeling of terrible urgency, the root of which he could not understand. But he was oddly certain that the appearance of Mason Raymond on the very night of the discovery of the most promising lead in nine months of intensive effort was in no way attributable to coincidence.

No moon shone that night.

FIVE
Melville, Montana
November 2, 1970

Overhead, the thinnest sliver of moon was becoming visible as the sun sank beneath the horizon, silhouetting a disheveled three-story structure. It was an old hotel, situated at the top of a rolling hill covered with more brush than trees. The terrain consisted of these gentle slopes for as far as the eye could see.

The stars were beginning to appear, and they twinkled down on a blue Ford sedan that pulled up to the drive and stopped next to several other cars that were parked off to the left side of the building.

Collin emerged, wearing a slightly tattered sport jacket and corduroy trousers, both of which were considerably wrinkled. He stretched his arms and legs briefly, then walked back to the trunk and opened it. After extracting a small briefcase and a battered suitcase, he slammed the lid with somewhat more force than seemed to be called for, and headed for the three wooden steps that led to the main entrance of the building.

He passed a sign on one of the pillars supporting the leaning eaves. "Melville Hotel" was painted on the sign in faded, pealing paint, and over this had been crudely tacked a paper sign bearing the words "Hotel Earth." Beneath this were several other signs, among them the cryptic message, "Under New Management." With barely a glance at the signs Collin stalked tiredly into the lobby.

Collin walked up to the hotel front desk, an ancient mahogany bar that bore the marks of countless carelessly discarded cigarettes and wet glasses. He put his luggage down and, seeing no one around, rang the bell several times.

After a few seconds, a very old and unpleasant looking woman emerged from a door in the rear of the clerk's station. Her dried out gray hair was dirty and pulled into a loose bun on her wrinkled head. She wore a dirty cotton dress that hung upon her like a parachute and old-fashioned nylons were on her flabby legs, the type that reach up to a point just below the knee, leaving the unsightly top seams in plain view.

"What'll it be, mister?" she asked, totally uninterested. She was chewing, or more properly "gumming" gum. She had no teeth.

"I'd like a room, please."

Her beady eyes looked him up and down. "You alone?"

Collin stared back just as frankly. "Yes."

"How long you stayin'?"

"Not sure." Collin smiled in a futile attempt at cordiality. "Couple of days, maybe."

She stared at him for a second or two longer, then turned to the pigeonhole keyrack behind her and studied it for a moment. "Third floor okay? I've got a

vacancy on the second, but that's more expensive."
She looked pointedly at his frayed sport jacket.

"The third floor will be fine."

She swung the register around to him. "Sign here."

Collin began to sign the name "Nathaniel Jacobs" in bold strokes, then froze partway through, for another name on the register had caught his eye. Up near the top of the page, just three lines above the line upon which Collin was making his mark, the neat careful signature of Dr. Mason Raymond lept off the page at him. He looked at the check-in time: 3:15 P.M.

Improvising, he glanced up at the crone, who was now paying very close attention to his every move. "Uh, I'm due to meet someone here—he may have checked in already. His name is Raymond, Dr. Raymond."

She glanced down at the register. "Yea, Mr. Jacobs." She ran her finger up the names and found Raymond's signature. "Just a couplea' hours ago." She gave him a key.

"What room is he in?"

She turned around slowly. "One-oh-four."

"One-oh-four," Collin repeated "Thanks."

"He's not in," the hag continued.

"What?"

"Dr. Raymond," she said, hitching at the ill-fitting bra jutting from the parachute dress. "He went out shortly after he checked in. Said he had business in town."

"Hmmm," Collin grunted speculatively. "Thanks."

She did not offer to summon a bellhop, and Collin did not ask for one. He gathered his own bags and headed for the stairs, distrusting the elevator.

It was after eleven o'clock that evening when Collin emerged from his small single room. He had felt so exhausted that the prospect of a few hours' sleep was irresistible. Moreover, his plans were best carried out during the dead of night.

Wearing a black leather jacket and blue jeans, he stepped from the door marked "311" and shut it as quietly as possible. Only one dim light illuminated the hallway, but its glow was sufficient to assure Collin that he was alone and unobserved. The main stairway was down the hall to his right but he turned to the left and stealthily moved to a door at its end. Letters on the door spelled "Stairs." He tried the knob and found the door open, then eased the heavy panel door inward and stepped inside, taking care to close the thing silently. If the illumination in the third-floor hall had been poor, the lighting conditions in the narrow stairwell were unsafe.

Collin made his way as carefully as possible to the second-floor landing, passed the access door without a pause, and continued down to the first floor.

The stairway led down to the east end of one of the hotel's several lobbies. In its prime, the lobby must have been luxurious to the point of ostentation, but now the upholstery of the chairs and sofas was faded, dirty, and worn away in spots. The heavy satin drapes were impregnated with dust, which clouded the air as Collin brushed against them.

There was no sign of anyone at the desk, and only a

couple of redneck-looking characters with bulging briefcases were sitting in the lobby, earnestly involved in a game of checkers. They didn't so much as glance his way when Collin crossed the far side of the lobby, passed the vacant clerk's desk, and headed down the hall past the elevator in the direction of room 104.

He reached the door he sought, identical in every way to the other doors that lined the straight hall except for the number. Looking up and down to see that he was unobserved, he rapped softly but firmly several times.

Though he listened carefully, he could detect no sound of movement on the other side of the door. He rapped again, this time more loudly. Nothing.

Again looking up and down the hall and observing nothing, he reached into his jeans and came out with a silver object that bore some resemblance to a jackknife. He reached with his thumb and folded out a steel projection. It was roughly cylindrical and had a gentle curve over the last third of its length. Two months ago he had paid an aged locksmith on Wilcox Street in Hollywood fifty dollars to teach him the ins and outs of lockpicking. Within seconds, he proved his fifty dollars well spent; the door opened soundlessly.

Collin shut the door. A lamp by the threshold had been left on.

Raymond's single room was substantially nicer than the tacky accommodations Collin had been offered. Apparently the older man had made a more favorable impression. A large comfortable looking double bed stood majestically against the opposite wall. Above it hung a beautiful tapestry in which a serene looking deer stood at the side of a mountain stream.

A marble washbasin and Edwardian desk stood on the wall adjacent to the bed, and a dresser was placed against the wall to Collin's left. An open door beside the dresser gave access to a small bathroom and the remaining wall space was given over to closets, of which there were several, all standing open. A few suits had been hastily hung in one of them. Two suitcases stood in the other. On the table by the bed a leather bound briefcase rested.

After first making certain that the room was indeed empty, Collin began to search Raymond's luggage. The first thing he attacked was the briefcase. It was locked, and Collin had considerably more difficulty with the two catch locks than he had with the hotel door. Eventually, however, he got them open.

The inside of the briefcase was as neatly organized and arranged as its owner had been. A calculator rested in a leather pocket obviously designed especially for this purpose. A checkbook drawn on the Bank of London rested beside the calculator, as well as a passport identifying the bearer as one Dr. Mason Winston Raymond, III. It gave his age as fifty-seven, his place of birth Bangor, Maine. Its mottled pages bore the customs stamps of England, France, Germany, Italy, Czechoslovakia, and a score of Middle Eastern and North African countries. Collin could find no indication in the passport that the enigmatic gentleman had been to any of the South African nations, however. Beside the passport were a number of rather old books. Collin's eyes widened when he surveyed the titles. The first was entitled, *The Search for the Historical Dracula; A Biography of Vlad the Impaler*. Beside that was a treatise on the druidic culture, and then several books on demonology and witchcraft in general. One of them was very old, bearing the inscription *Occult Religions of the Mediterranian*. Beneath these books, which Collin put aside on the bed he sat on, rested a clear plastic binder with several sheets of paper inside. Collin picked it up and read its title:

> List of Travelers Reported Missing Since February, 1970, Whose Planned Routes Included the Section of Interstate Highway 76, Which Extends from Melville, Montana, to Willow Falls, Montana.

There followed a list of at least forty names, some including entire families, of people that had disappeared en route through this area during the last nine months.

Collin was simply staggered as he read over the list of names. At first he could not believe that so many disappearances could possibly have gone unconnected. But then he glanced at the two left hand columns listing the various points of origin and destinations of the unfortunate people listed. They came from cities scattered up and down the Midwest, and their destinations varied by thousands of miles. He could begin to understand how difficult it would be for already overworked law-enforcement agencies, flooded with disappearances all over the country, to assemble this kind of information.

But then, Collin asked himself, how in the world

178

did Raymond come up with this? He put it aside. Beneath a piece of cardboard was a copy of the very same *Enquirer* article that had first put Collin on the trail of this hotel. He set this aside in turn and unsnapped the upper section of the briefcase, exposing those papers stored in the folding compartments in the lid of the case. There was nothing in this section of special interest to him, although he noted a number of letters addressed to various archaeological societies on subjects that were of a nature technical enough that Collin could not assess them.

He replaced everything in the briefcase in exactly the order he had found it in, then turned to the suitcases in the closet.

He picked up the largest first, and set it on the bed. Less than thirty seconds were required to master the extremely simple lock mechanisms on this larger suitcase. But though Collin went carefully through every stitch of expensive, immaculately cleaned and folded clothing, he could find nothing of interest at all. He came across another archaeological book, detailing excavations in North Africa, and a spare pen-and-pencil set. Disappointed, he examined the case itself for hidden compartments, and ruefully admitted that there were none.

After closing the suitcase and relocking it, he exchanged it for its smaller cousin. They were both of the Royal Traveler trademark, the manufacturer whose ads featured their luggage being bashed and battered by gorillas and remaining intact.

That same gorilla, with the little tool the man now held in his hand, could have opened the case in a minute and a half. He smiled to himself; the locks opened with ridiculous ease.

The contents of this suitcase were somewhat more incriminating. On top of a thick layer of clothes was a bundled kit of tools, containing a small but remarkably brilliant flashlight that Collin tried out wistfully, thinking what a splendid addition it would make to his own equipment, and a variety of screwdrivers and wrenches. His eyes widened as he came upon a small packet that he at first didn't recognize and then realized with some chagrin that it was a lock picking kit that made his little tool look like a child's toy. He could not imagine the uses for which most of the little implements had been designed, but they had been made with the precision of a surgeon's scalpel, and they reflected the ambient light with dazzling brilliance.

Beneath this kit were two items he found less explicable. One was a wooden mallet, the other a short oak torch with a sharp point at one end. He put these aside.

Most of the clothes in the pile were black. A plastic pullover with pockets in the front and a hood attached was one of the first things he saw. Also to be found were black turtleneck shirts and sweaters, black leather gloves, and several pairs of dark canvas pants, almost of military cut.

The significance of these items was not lost on Collin. Raymond was a skulker. And a far better equipped one than Collin himself. Beneath these clothes were a pair of sneakers, which had inevitably been spray painted black.

The only remaining item in the case was a small

shaving kit, which apart from the normal shaving gear, toothbrush, and shampoo, contained only a couple of vials of prescription pills for the relief of minor arthritic pain, according to their labels. Collin shook the bottles, holding them up to the light. There were a lot of pills in them. He didn't bother to uncap the bottles. One pill looked the same as another, so far as he was concerned. They could be cyanide or aspirin.

He was about to repack the case when it occurred to him to check again for a hidden pocket. This time, his effort was rewarded. On the bottom, through the cardboard lining, he could feel the bulge of something that had apparently been placed between the inner lining of the case and its external plastic shell. Collin tried for several seconds to determine how the clever doctor had gained access to this little nook in the suitcase. Finally he gave up, already apprehensive that Raymond might appear at any moment. Collin hesitated less than a second before taking his four-inch knife to the lining.

The first thing to come into his hand through the slit in the lining was a 380 caliber Barreta automatic pistol. This was followed by two spare magazines, and a small box of cartridges, thirty-eight special caliber. Presumably, Collin thought, spare ammunition for another gun he was at this very moment carrying. He placed the firearm and ammo on the bed and reached deeper into the lining.

His fingers came out with two manila envelopes. He opened one and extracted the large bundle of soiled papers it contained. On top of the stack, held together with a very large paper clip, was a slip of paper with Collin's complete name and address. Under this, hastily scribbled, was the address of UCLA, where the nightmare had occurred last night.

Beneath this scrap was an abused bunch of manuscript paper, soiled and torn in spots. It had been stapled together in the upper left hand corner. In the upper center of the first page had been typed "Translation: Ostium Inscription" in the unmistakable script of a government typewriter. Below this was the date, "January 4, 1970." Collin scanned the first few lines. "In the beginning, Cymonatha, drinker of blood and high priest of the Shara Cult came forth to the people of the village Giami where dwelt our king, and spoke in words of fire, with a face twisted into hideous shapes, threatening to call down the forces of Thanta [hell] upon our children if we did not forsake the labor in the fields and journey to the mountains to serve the demon Anthrada. . . ."

Increasingly disturbed, Collin read the entire translation, which detailed the growth and eventual destruction of the reign of a monster very strongly resembling the thing he had faced in the African cave. In the translation the thing was called Anthrada. Though he searched his memory, he had never heard the name before.

He examined another clipping, an outline of a Central Africa epic legend about a mysterious man named Lianja. This caught his attention because Lianja was also Smith's tribal name.

The legend came from the Mondo-Nkundo peoples, which Smith's tribe was a part of. It documented the adventures of Lianja, supposedly the son of the god of death, as he underwent many uncanny adventures, meeting and conquering weird creatures in the rain forest.

A penciled note in the margin read "Anansi—Spider God who came to America with the slaves." "Anansi" was the name Smith's people had given to the demon in the cave.

With a hand that shook slightly, he replaced the papers in the envelope from which they had come. Suddenly, he had the strong sensation that he had been there long enough. It was time to leave, and quickly.

But there was one more envelope, and he mastered his irrational reaction as he straightened the tiny arms of the brass clip that held the envelope's flap closed.

He pulled out a bundle of papers, and beneath them some photographs. He quickly scanned the titles of the manuscripts. They all were reports on various excavations, containing within them translations of various inscriptions, as well as descriptions of artifacts discovered. Collin noted that the excavations referred to were scattered over half the earth, and pertained to periods ranging from medieval to four thousand years ago.

But he spent no time reading any of the reports. Instead, he flipped directly back to the photographs. These were all black and white eight-by-tens. The first one resembled many other archaeological pictures he had seen; the lighting arranged for maximum detail rather than any esthetic consideration. It gave the photos a tendency to appear stark. The photo showed a section of ground at the base of a barren mountain. A few trucks and workmen could be seen in the foreground, and in the center of the picture was a gaping tunnel mouth, surrounded by tumbled stone blocks. A large section of the mountain had apparently been dug away to reveal this cave mouth and its accompanying ruins.

The second photo showed the inside of the tunnel, just beyond the entrance. A portal that had once been erected there, effectively blocking entrance to whatever was beyond, had been pierced in one corner, making a hole large enough for a man to climb inside. Several electrical cables had been strung through this opening. Beside it, a very long and detailed inscription had been laboriously cut into the rock and plaster. Collin associated this with the translation he had first come across, in the other envelope. The next several photos showed a progression of passageways, which had been cleared of the debris placed within the first ten or twenty feet in order to seal it. Beyond this was yet another sealed portal, with another inscription. This, too, had been opened in one corner. The next picture was a close-up of the second inscription. A few notes had been penciled in the margin of the photo. The few words there convinced Collin that this was indeed the original version of the story he had just read from the other envelope.

The next few photos were various views of an immense cavern, the walls of which had been finished in some kind of smooth stone. Heaps of objects that appeared to be human remains littered the floor, and thick dust was everywhere, broken only occasionally by the tracks of recent visitors.

In the center of the great room was a black altar on

a raised marble platform. Something unidentifiable still rested upon it.

There was a close-up in one of the photos of the pile of bones that lay at the foot of the altar. Unquestionably, they were human remains. A small black arrow had been printed on the picture pointing to a splintered, half-burned wooden spike lying among the bones. It reminded Collin of the one he had found in Raymond's luggage.

Several more photos documented a passage that led deeper into the heart of the mountain. This was tunnel-shaped, made of very hard and firm earth, which held only the barest suggestion of footprints. A string of electric lights ran partway along, but they did not extend past the first few frames. Presumably, work on the lights had not progressed beyond a certain point, or else it had been discontinued for some reason.

Collin paid particular attention to the last few photographs. They showed a point where the tunnel ran into an arched natural portal, beyond which was a ledge. Dr. Raymond stood there, crunched down, indicating scuffle marks in the dust at several points. A pile of loose papers lay upon the floor to one side of him.

Collin flipped to the last two shots, holding them side by side. His heart literally stopped in his chest, for the scene was a huge bowl-shaped depression, obviously lit by some sort of high-powered flash unit, because the light penetrated to the end, which must have been a hundred feet away.

Enormous piles of decayed bones were everywhere. They were recognizably human, the eyeless skulls plainly visible among the mountains of remains. Some of the piles stretched almost all the way to the ceiling of the cavern, casting long shadows. In the foreground lay a mangled human corpse clad in a pair of light trousers and a digger's jacket. Collin could plainly see bloodstains about his head and shoulders.

In the center of this hellhole was a jet black shapeless mass, resembling to some degree cooled volcanic rock that was smooth and crystalline, frozen in bizarre peaks and valleys.

Collin had seen such a nightmarish scene before. In a cave in Zaire, Africa.

"Ah, Mr. Collin," a soft voice whispered from somewhere behind him. "I hadn't expected to see you again quite so soon."

Collin froze in an instant of paralyzing shock. Had his life depended on quick reactions that moment, it would have been forfeit.

Slowly, he lowered the photographs onto the bed and turned around.

"Doctor Raymond, I presume."

"Yes," Raymond smiled, lowering the revolver in his hand and easing his door closed. "But, unfortunately, you do not seem to be Dr. Livingston."

Collin felt nauseated. "I've just been looking through your family album." He gestured toward the pictures and the mutilated suitcase.

Raymond's left eyebrow was raised. "So I see."

"Where were those photos taken?"

Raymond listened at the door for a few seconds, still not taking his eyes off Collin. "A small canyon called Ostium about twenty miles north of West

Semna. That's a small town in the Sudan. Interesting place. Nothing grows there. I mean nothing. Not weeds, not cactus. Nothing. Nobody has been able to figure out why." He gestured with his pistol casually. "Sit down if you want." He released his breath, relaxing the tension that had gripped him at finding an intruder in his room. "You don't look well."

Collin moved to the desk chair and sat down heavily, mopping the sweat from his forehead as he did so. It had begun to drip into his eyes. "You don't seem all that surprised to see me."

"I suppose I'm not." He gestured toward the photographs. "You know what that is, don't you?" It was more a statement than a question.

Collin looked long and hard into Raymond's piercing blue eyes. He nodded, looking downward and resting his head in his hand, between thumb and forefingers. He rubbed his forehead in a gesture of emotional trauma long suppressed.

"Why did you visit me last night?" Collin asked after a moment of mutual silence.

"To find out why you were investigating missing persons. As I told you, I kept running across your inquiries. When I found out, quite by accident, that you had been in Africa when the Sedgewick expedition disappeared—well, the arm of coincidence doesn't stretch that far." He looked again at the photographs. "I wanted to find out if you were looking for the same thing I am. And if so, how close you were to finding it."

"Am I?"

"What?"

"Looking for the same thing you are?"

Raymond's look became level, measuring. "I think we both know the answer to that question, Mr. Collin."

Collin returned the doctor's gaze. "What's your interest in all this, Doctor?"

Raymond hesitated, then put his pistol down and lit a cigarette from a pack on the table. His hands were shaking slightly. "Simple. Fear." He smiled and Collin could see the fear in his eyes for a fleeting instant. A moment of nonverbal communication passed between the two men. With that single word, Raymond had struck a sympathetic chord in the younger man. In a fundamental way, separate entirely from any words, logic, or even thought, they now understood each other.

Raymond put his match in an ashtray on the desk and turned away from Collin, gazing absently into the mirror above the dresser.

"You see, I was the director of the institution that sponsored that dig," he nodded in the general direction of the bed, "the one at which those photos were taken. I had never been there, but the night the seal was broken I received an urgent call in my office in London. I flew out early the next morning.

"One of my brightest assistants was in charge. Young, brilliant, utterly responsible. At midnight, with a copy of the translation of that inscription in his hands, he led myself and two colleagues into the temple."

"I read the inscription," Collin interjected.

"I surmised that you had," Raymond responded absently. "When we got to the . . . the inner chamber, a physical change came over him. He went mad, completely mad. I've never seen anything like it. He was like a man—"

"Possessed?" Collin finished for him.

"Yes." Raymond gave him a sharp glance. The retelling had visibly affected him. He took another puff of his cigarette and continued. "I used my authority to have the place sealed off, allowing no one near but myself and my immediate staff. For the next few months we studied the place as thoroughly as possible without arousing the interest of the press."

"Why the secrecy?"

"Have you read the ancient collection of documents loosely referred to as the 'Book of the Anthracidies'?"

Collin shook his head. "Never heard of it."

"The Ostium inscription confirms a number of statements made in those documents. And the 'Book of the Anthracidies' makes mention of other incidents throughout a long period and in a variety of locations far removed from one another, which closely resemble the events described in the Ostium stone." Raymond turned for a moment to face Collin. "Do you know . . . well, obviously you cannot . . . that the ritual of Roman Catholic exorcism is derived largely from the 'Book of the Anthracidies,' which has existed in one form or another since several thousand years before the birth of Christ?"

Collin shook his head. He was beginning to grasp the enormity of the forces he was dealing with.

"You see," Raymond was pouring himself a drink

of whiskey from a flask that reminded Collin of the one Terry McPhearson had carried, "I had to consider seriously the possibility that a creature such as the one that occupied that cavern three thousand years ago at Ostium could actually exist in secret somewhere today." He tossed off his drink in one gulp. "It occurred to me that it would be very wise to make a determination on this point before making the discovery public. I had no way of knowing the extent to which such a being might have secretly insinuated itself into the world political structure."

Collin nodded, wondering whether he, had he found himself in Raymond's position, would have had the presence of mind to take these steps. He doubted it.

"How did you track it to this point?"

Raymond shrugged. "Roughly by the same process as you." He smiled. "It was somewhat easier for me, though. I had the services of a staff, and a rather sophisticated computer."

Collin smiled in turn, wearily. "I can see where that might have helped some."

Raymond sat down on the bed. "I have told you my story, now I feel entitled to know yours. What did you see in Africa?"

Collin's face grew very grim: "Before I say anything to you, I must warn you that what you are doing is very, very dangerous." He shook his head. "Without protection—"

Raymond raised a hand to silence Collin. Without a word, he extended his right arm and pulled back his sleeve. A wide metal bracelet covered his forearm. It was very dark, very simple. Collin had never seen anything like it. "In the course of our excavations, we found this near the entrance. It had apparently been dropped there for some reason. It is an amulet, and it was worn by the man Nyakang, who is described in the inscription as the one who eventually killed the Anthrada, which is what the thing was called. This amulet is referred to several times in the 'Book of the Anthracidies.' I believe it protected him. I believe it protects me."

Collin remembered Smith's metal medallion. "Yes. That's possible."

Raymond leaned closer. "You have seen something like this before; seen it work?"

Collin half shook his head, "Not precisely like it. But I have seen the principle in operation."

The doctor was desperate to know more. "You must tell me. . . ."

Collin had just opened his mouth to launch into his terrible narrative—the first time in the long months since the incredible nightmare had begun that he would breathe a word to another living soul besides Smith.

"I have seen the thing," he began solemnly.

"You have actually *see* it?" Raymond's normally iron control dropped, and his eyes widened in disbelief.

"In Africa, I—"

At that moment, a terrible piercing scream ripped the fabric of the night. It went on and on, for second after nerve-shattering second. Then, just as suddenly, it was gone.

Before the last echo of that agonized scream faded into the heavy folds of the night, both Collin and

Raymond were halfway up the wide main staircase leading to the second floor. As they almost reached the top of the flight, running headlong, a figure shrouded in a black cloak charged out of the semi-darkness of the hall and careened straight into the two charging men.

The black-clad figure brushed the two out of its path as easily as if they did not exist at all. They were thrown against opposite walls of the staircase with force enough to drive the air from their lungs. Collin tumbled almost to the very bottom of the stairs and was forced to lie helpless until he recovered his wind.

The figure with whom they had collided took no notice of them, not pausing for an instant in his headlong flight toward the ground floor.

Collin caught a glimpse of a very white face, capped by dark hair. That was all.

Lying on the steps, he saw the form disappear through a door at the back of the lobby marked, "Employees Only."

There were no other guests in the lobby at that moment, although only seconds later a crowd began to form of pajama- and nightgown-clad men and women. Collin was fairly sure that he was the only one who had seen where the escaping man had fled.

Still gasping, he regaineᵈ his feet and climbed to where Raymond was just struggling to get up.

"Who the hell was that?" The doctor was clutching his side and wincing in pain.

"I don't know." He pointed with his chin. "Let's see what happened." They mustered what strength they could and ran limpingly up to the second floor and down the hall.

A door was open almost at the far end and two or three concerned people were milling about, chattering excitedly. Collin shoved his way through them and entered the room.

A middle-aged man was standing just inside holding a young, bookish-looking woman against him very tightly. "There, there, miss," he was saying, patting her back consolingly, a sick look on his face. The young woman was sobbing and shaking intensely, obviously both hysterical and in shock.

Collin looked at the bed. Another young woman lay in it, the covers pulled down to her waist, revealing naked, shapely breasts. Her head was tilted over at a sharp angle and she lay very still.

At a distance of ten feet, Collin could see a bloody, two-inch long cut at the base of her throat. He could not believe it. She was as white as the sheet she lay upon.

Raymond crossed to the bed and checked for a pulse. He looked over at Collin and shook his head.

Collin crossed over to where the hysterical girl had taken to blindly pounding her fists into the chest of the man who was trying to comfort her. Collin reached over and grasped her sharply by the shoulders and jerked her out of the grasp of the older man. He seemed only too happy to be relieved of his unpleasant task, although he plainly disapproved of Collin's roughness.

"Miss, miss." Collin shook her. She continued to struggle until Collin raised his arm and struck her a backhanded blow across the side of the face. She wilted like a dying flower, and Collin sat her down on the nearby desk chair. Raymond came over with a glass of water and a handkerchief, which he soaked and draped over the semiconscious girl's forehead.

"Miss." Collin slapped her face more gently, again and again, trying to arouse her.

"Stop that, young man!" An outraged elderly woman in a red satin dressing gown had reached out to grab Collin's shoulder with a remarkably steady grip. Collin simply ignored her, urgently trying to revive the girl in his arms.

Raymond had just disengaged the elderly woman, gently but firmly escorting her out of the room, as the signs of renewed life began to appear in the young girl. Abruptly, she leaned over, eyes opening rapidly, and puked all over the floor, violently, retching over and over until there was nothing left in her stomach to choke up. Even then the dry heaves continued. Finally, she stopped, and trembling hands accepted the glass of water Raymond held out to her. The elderly woman had returned with someone else, presumably her husband, and they were wiping the puke from the girl's face with a handtowel they must have gotten from the bathroom.

"Miss, tell me what happened." Collin was supporting her by a firm grip on her shoulders.

"My sister . . . I just came in to borrow something from my sister. . . . I'm in the next room, you see. He was bending over her . . . and she wasn't moving . . . and when he turned I could see his face. . . ." She put her hands to her face, as though to shut the vision out of her eyes. "It was horrible! Horrible!"

She broke out into fresh sobs, and Collin handed her over to the old woman, saying, "Better get her out of here."

The old woman scowled at him and began to ease the poor young girl out into the hall.

Collin looked at the corpse on the bed, which Raymond was examining. "It seems there's a facet to all this that I wasn't even aware of," Collin remarked bleakly. He always spoke in exaggeratedly peaceful, conversational tones when he was under pressure.

Raymond looked over at him. "I was afraid of something like this." Their eyes met. "It's in the book."

Collin bit his lip, considering. He crossed to within a foot of Raymond and whispered, "I saw where he went. Let's go."

Raymond nodded. They left the mutilated corpse to the other guests and dashed out of the room, heading down the stairs in the path the mysterious form had taken only minutes earlier.

At the bottom of the stairs they paused, breathless. "Wait." Raymond panted. "Let me go get my kit."

Collin nodded. "Right." He stood catching his breath for a few seconds, watching the steady stream of frightened people tentatively ascending the stairs.

At the desk, he could overhear an elderly gentleman on the phone to the police.

"You've got to come right away," he was saying. "There's been a killing—a terrible murder." His voice was unnaturally high and loud, and it cracked with fear.

Raymond was at his side, breathing fast. "I got it. Now," he turned to face the younger man, "which way?"

"Come on." Collin led the way to the small door marked "Employees Only" at the far side of the lobby. He looked around, but could not see anyone in the agitated group of badly scared people who was capable of taking the slightest interest in them.

In an instant, they were through the door, which led directly onto a very narrow flight of creaking wooden stairs.

Both men had pocket flashlights, which they turned on. Collin pulled his forty-five from under his leather jacket, switching off the safety as he did so.

Raymond's revolver was in his hand, the hammer cocked. Together they started down.

"This leads to the cellar—a combination wine cellar and storage place, which also houses the furnace," Raymond whispered as they descended.

"How do you know?" Collin whispered back.

"I spent a good part of the day in City Hall, looking at the plans to this building," Raymond answered.

Collin mentally chided himself for not having thought of such an obvious strategy himself. "Are there any other ways out?"

"Other than the coal chute, which is normally impassable, none."

"Then he still has to be down here."

They looked at each other, the beams of their lights playing up and down the dank, moldy walls.

At the bottom, a row of racks holding the inevitable dust- and cobweb-covered wine bottles stretched out into the shadows. There appeared to be several rows of them, leading into a more open storage space beyond.

"We'd better separate," Collin said, playing his light along the shadows. You stay here and guard the exit. I'll go out and drive him toward you. See if you can find a light switch."

Raymond eyed him dubiously. "I don't like the idea of splitting up," he whispered.

"We can't just sit here," Collin hissed. "And we can't just leave the stairs unguarded. Can you imagine this murderer fighting his way through all those frightened tourists up there?" He gestured back the way they had come.

Raymond nodded. "Okay." He swallowed hard.

Collin moved off slowly, his heart pounding and his entire body quivering. He could see the beam of his light shaking in the clouds of dust his feet kicked up.

Slowly, he traversed the first row of bottles. Then he shone his light out into the expanse of open space. At first he could distinguish nothing threatening. Boxes were stacked up helter-skelter against the walls. In a far corner stood the furnace, and just beside it was the enormous coal bin, filled to the brim with black lumps of coal. No doubt about it, the chute was effectively blocked.

As his light swung about, it passed something on the floor and returned. A small five pointed star had been traced on the floor in coal dust, and the lump used to draw it could still be seen slightly off to one side. At the points stood small candles. The hair on Collin's neck stood on end as he saw the little wisps of smoke still rising from the wicks, which must have been burning just seconds earlier.

He turned to his right and had started to head back along the second wine aisle when he thought he could see something red just ahead, partially obscured by the end of the wooden shelf. His grip on the pistol tightened.

At that precise instant, there came a muted swoosh of air from above and behind. Cold, clammy hands, with a grip stronger than steel, grabbed him by the shoulders and literally hurled him through the air, back into the center of the cellar space.

He landed with a dull thud in the center of the pentagram. By a miracle, he still retained both his pistol and his light, and he staggered to his hands and knees.

He tried to call out to Raymond, but he did not have enough air in his lungs to utter more than a wheezing gasp.

But Raymond had been following the steady progress of Collin's light, and had seen it suddenly veer and swing. He heard the thump of his friend hitting the floor.

"Collin! Collin!" Raymond was calling from a distance. "For God's sake! Are you all right?"

But Collin was preoccupied in those seconds swinging his light in the direction from which he had just been launched. His beam swung, searching, then it caught and held him—the black-suited man.

He was tall, very tall, Collin could see. But much thinner than he would have expected, in light of his great strength. His face in the light of the flashlight was a cadaverous blue, and as he raised his arm as though to shield himself somewhat from the light, Collin could see little dribbles of blood still dripping from his grimacing lips.

But it was the eyes that caught and held Collin. All-knowing alien eyes, set in an extremely handsome Latin face.

The man was advancing. One step, two. . . . "Raymond. He's here, I've found him," Collin called, his voice cracking. The man took one more step and Collin began to fire.

One shot, then two, three, and he kept coming, smiling peacefully.

In increasing desperation, Collin fired the remaining five shots in rapid succession directly into the heart of the figure moving toward him.

When it was less than four steps away, the candles at the points of the star burst into flames, seemingly of their own accord.

The man was in the act of raising his arms, preparing to swoop down in violent attack when the candles flared, giving a pitiful dancing illumination to the scene.

Anticipation animated those strangely distorted Latin features. But at the sight of Collin's face, the advancing figure drew back slightly.

The man leaned forward, gazing searchingly into Collin's eyes. The expression on the well-cut dark features contained a mixture of surprise, bewilderment, and consternation. His left hand lifted to caress his chin in an aristocratic expression of contemplation.

Finally, he spoke, no trace of menace in the carefully articulated, softly spoken words. "I have the disturbing feeling that you and I have met before." Collin had never heard such awesome self-assuredness in any human voice. "Why should that be?" he went on in a question obviously addressed to himself. He continued to rub his chin between thumb and forefinger in retrospection, as though he flipped through the files of a memory that stretched back so far that the dust of ages had obscured many things.

"Who are you?" Collin asked.

Still with the puzzled, troubled look, the strange man replied, "I am ice. And you are fire, which must be extinguished."

Collin studied the features, the cold and yet intelligent eyes. "I've never seen you before tonight," he said with absolute conviction.

Raymond had appeared in the circle of light. With no apparent concern, the tall apparition turned to look briefly at the newcomer. Raymond had pulled a small silver cross from his jacket, and held it before him.

The tall man chuckled softly. "The day of such superstitious nonsense is over, Doctor Raymond."

"You know my name."

"It is written there in your eyes." He turned to Collin. "But his?" Again the look of searching.

Raymond lowered the cross, pulled out instead the wooden torch Collin had seen in his luggage. At this, the tall man's dark eyes narrowed slightly in an unmistakably fearful reaction.

"You don't fear the cross," Raymond spoke slowly. "But you dislike the torch, don't you?"

The strange man made no answer. But a look of malice appeared on his face.

"What happens now?" Collin asked. "Do you turn into a bat?"

The aquiline face turned back to Collin and smiled. "The superstitions of past ages are not involved here. I am not a vampire."

"Yet you took the blood of that girl. . . ." Collin began.

"Yes, a barbaric necessity. I drank the blood but I did not suck it hungrily through enlarged canine incisors. It is a thing I must do when I am separated from my . . . primary sources of nourishment."

"And what might those be?" Raymond took a step closer.

All the while, the man had been studying Collin's face with great intentness. Suddenly a light seemed to come on in his mind, and he smiled in satisfaction. "I have it now. I remember you from another time." His eyes narrowed. "I am lucky to have found you now, instead of later on, when it might have been too late." His smile was gentle now. "Have you come back to be my nemesis again? You, Camurious, whose thoughts cannot be read, whose presence cannot be felt, who cannot be made one with the master." The man seemed almost to float above the ground. He began to move closer, and at that moment shots rang out as Raymond emptied his gun into the man, to no effect.

The man turned to glare at Raymond with sudden incredible malevolence. His jaws worked soundlessly in hunger as he advanced on the terrified doctor.

But in one smooth motion Raymond dropped his gun and pulled a lighter from his belt with his other hand.

He lighted the torch, and it blazed into orange flame and Raymond brandished it threateningly into the monster's face, causing him to draw back sharply.

At that instant, Collin sprang, having substituted his knife for the now useless gun. He leapt upon the

201

back of the man-thing, stabbing the knife in again and again, going for the heart.

In an almost theatrical gesture, the towering form swung its arms back, casting Collin off his back as a man would hurl aside a soiled cloak.

Collin hit the floor a few feet away and rolled sideways, losing his knife, but in the meantime Raymond had advanced with the torch and shoved it into the face of the creature.

He made a clawing motion with his hands, trying to reach past the flame to the man behind it. Then the apparition backed away, sneering and spitting with every step.

In the glittering torchlight, he caught sight of the amulet on Raymond's wrist. With a shriek, he swiped again, more violently this time, at the torch, striking it directly on the burning end and almost knocking it out of Raymond's grasp. Collin had meanwhile regained his feet and come to stand just behind Raymond.

"Collin," Raymond's chest was heaving with almost unbearable strain, "reach into my waistband and pull out the sharpened torch stake." Collin complied, lighting the pointed torch and all the time watching the face of the enemy, whose eyes were riveted on the torch stake in Collin's hand.

They were slowly backing him into the corner by the furnace. Twice, he tried to dart past them to the safety of the stairwell, but Raymond was too fast with the torch.

They had almost backed the man against the wall when Collin lit his own torch and spoke breathlessly. "Force him all the way to the wall. I'm going to run it in on him." He held the burning stake out in front of him, preparing to use the force of his lunge to drive it into the breast of the inhuman creature.

But just as he was ready to lunge, the creature threw back its arms and let loose a cry louder than any sound Collin had heard a living thing release. The force of the creature's will paralyzed them for the instant he needed to turn, grab the side of the coal bin and tear it down from the bolts that held it in place on the wall. With a smooth motion the thing ascended the pile of coal now scattered over the floor, ripped the door of the coal chute completely off its hinges, and disappeared into the night.

Collin, dripping with sweat and blood, turned to the man beside him and slowly lowered the burning stake. Both were breathing as though they had just finished a marathon run.

Raymond looked up into the darkness and uttered just two words, "The Guardian." The sound of their own frenzied, frantic breathing echoed in the chill darkness of the basement as the wail of an approaching siren heralded the arrival of the local police.

It was twenty-four hours later in the same basement section of Hotel Earth, where the small pentagram had been crudely drawn on the floor the night before. A much larger, more carefully crafted five-pointed star had been traced. This figure seemed to have been painted with some shiny red liquid. In the center of the pentagram stood a large black altar, identical to the one first seen in the Denver basement wherein Maximillian Grey first contacted the Guardian.

On the altar were the large open book, the candles, and various other utensils. But in the center, in that place where the small dead animal had lain during the previous ceremony, the small butchered body of a human male lay in the stillness of death. Frozen on the contorted facial muscles was a picture of mindless, uncontrollable terror. The throat had been slashed cleanly from ear to ear, and the ceremonial dagger flashed triumphantly from its position of honor on the black altar. A red stain spread slowly beneath it.

The Guardian presided at the altar, standing this time at the far side in the position the mirror had previously occupied. The mirror itself was nowhere in evidence.

A dozen other human forms occupied the basement, arranged in rough lines facing the altar. They, like the fresh corpse upon the altar, were naked, their shed robes lying on the floor about their feet. Recognizable among this group was the old hag whom Collin had met while registering at the hotel. Her unclothed body was hideous. The pendulous breasts sagged uncleanly to her protuberant paunch, the skin of which was ashen gray and flecked with sores and scabs. Other misshapen individuals were to be seen here and there, but none as repellent to the gaze as the hag.

The majority of those present showed no outward sign of the deformity of their souls. They were, for the most part, young and able-bodied men and women, many of whom were physically attractive in the extreme. There was pulsing energy to be felt in the room, an energy resembling sexual excitement. The glow of the candles positioned at the points of the star reflected strangely in their eyes, all of which shone with eager blood lust, religious ecstacy, and apostolic fervor.

The hag came forward in a gesture of humility and supplication to offer the silver ceremonial chalice to the Guardian, whose hand stretched out to accept it. A small runnel of dark red liquid trickled down the side of the cup, and similar stains were visible around the lips of the assembled. Plainly the cup had just been passed from one to another.

The Guardian crossed to the corpse and lifted a large silver bowl from beside the victim's throat. From this he poured a very generous quantity of blood into the chalice.

Like a man with a deep thirst to be quenched, he swept the chalice to his lips and drank it quickly, to the accompaniment of awed murmurs from the crowd. Smiling, he upturned the chalice, to show that every last drop had been consumed.

He turned to his followers, who stood very still amid the swirling smoke whipped to and fro by a great, chill wind originating among the impenetrable shadows.

The Guardian alone among those present was clothed. He raised his arms, spreading the wings of his ceremonial robe as the others imitated him. A vague low chanting filled the basement for a moment in thanks for lust well satisfied.

Setting the chalice down, the Guardian spoke. "My subjects, listen well to the words of your lord and master. All has gone according to his will, and you have earned his favor. In return, he has fulfilled his promise, sending fresh blood for the taking, and watching over all who are his own."

The Guardian paused, looking from one face to another in the group. He conveyed by his benevolent, loving expression the favor of the master.

"The work on the temple in the vally below progresses. But it must go faster, and we who are the Guardians of the great prince must do all we can to bring more and more into the fold. You, Adrienne," he nodded to one of the more voluptuous brunets, "and you Diane, will journey tomorrow to the city of San Francisco, where the master has found two others who are fit to join us."

They nodded, and said nothing. The Guardian continued, "But there is another task that stands now before us, and it is our sacred duty to perform it well and quickly. Last night, two men came among us, to this very room. They are the enemies of the master, if they could they would destroy all that has been so laboriously accomplished. One of them, in particular, must be dealt with at once, for he is an ancient opponent, returned to haunt the sacred places."

He looked significantly around at the disciples, picking up the dagger as he did so. "I charge you all, each and every one, to bend to the task of seeking out and destroying this man and his companion. We have the license plate of the car he drives. We know it was rented in Brawley. You, Gordon, and you, Maria, will go tomorrow. The clerks at the agency will deny you no fact, recollection, or detail, however small. He will have had to show his driver's license. We want his address. Janet, you will go to the airport in Livingston to find out if he flew out of the area." Nodding to two men on the right of the assembly, he continued, "Demetre and Peter, you shall accompany me to the city of Los Angeles. You see," he addressed them all again, "this much we already know of the enemy. He has lived most of his life in that city. It is near there that his family and friends still live, and it is to there that he will probably return. Our lord has searched the memory of a man who is now one with him using the 'dark ritual.' This man knew our enemy well. Thus we know the name of this adversary. It is Collin. Christopher Arthur Collin. Find him, my beloved flock," he said, spreading his arms in the manner of a shepherd. "Find him at once. He must not live to see the next full moon."

As calmly as he had spoken these words, he plunged the dagger into the breast of the corpse on the altar.

LOS ANGELES, One week later.

Collin, Smith, and Raymond sat around a table in a very small room with bare walls and one window. Tiny wires ran in crisscross patterns through the thick glass. Outside this window an illuminated sign on an electronic control console flashed the words: "Faraday Cage Activated."

On the table in front of Raymond was an expended hypodermic syringe and a lump of soiled cotton. A small portable cassette recorder lay on the table to Smith's right, positioned so as to capture every word uttered within the cage.

Raymond was speaking slowly to Collin, who reclined in a state of total relaxation in a heavily padded armchair. His eyes were closed, his breathing very slow and measured.

Raymond said, "All right, Collin, you remember your birth trauma. But I want you to think back even further. Back . . . back in time. Back to a moment before you were born." A short pause, then, "Where are you?"

"Floating . . . black space . . . waiting."

"For what, Chris?"

"Waiting to be born." Collin's voice seemed to come to them across some great distance.

"I want you to go back even further now. Back before conception. Can you understand now Chris? We've done this before. You are now in a time before you were an embryo in your mother's womb."

Collin spoke. "I . . . remember."

"Where are you?"

Collin frowned slightly. "I am in a horse-drawn buggy, moving down a long, straight dirt road. The horse is black, my clothes are black."

"What year is it?" Raymond asked.

"Seventeen-forty-five."

Raymond leaned forward slightly. "We've been to this life before. Do you remember, Collin?"

Collin's brow wrinkled slightly as he concentrated in the hypnotic state. "Yes, I remember."

"Now we are going to go back through many lives, Chris. Back to a time when you were called Camurious. Do you recall it?"

"Yes."

208

"What year is it?"

"A.D. sixty-nine."

"Where are you?"

"I am lying on a beach, just waking up." Collin turned his head as though he felt pain in his neck.

"Why are you on this beach?"

"There has been a shipwreck. Demetrious and I swam for shore during the storm. I can see Demetrious beside me, unconscious. He is breathing."

"Who is Demetrious?" Raymond asked.

"He is my slave. I overcame him in battle on the Byzantine plain. He had killed fourteen of my men. Demetrious was a gallant fighter, so I spared his life. He has been my slave these last five years."

"Were you an army officer?"

"I am Tribune Selicious Camurious, Tribune of the Army, formerly of the Fifteenth Legion. I act upon the commission of Consul Marious Celsus." Collin spoke with cool pride.

"Where were you going when the wreck occurred?" Raymond questioned.

"I am dispatched by Proconsul Vitellios to investigate rumors that Otho, legal Imperial Heir, is being held prisoner in the fortress at Brundusiam by forces of the Pretender, Galba. Also, to investigate rumors of unlawful and barbaric treatment of the men of the Emperor's Tenth Legion by his Royal Bodyguard."

Raymond frowned, considering this. "We are going a little ahead in time. You are meeting with this Otho, who is imprisoned. What do you see?"

"I am in a cell, not more than ten feet square, with a very thick wooden door. There is a single small square window, in which bars are set. I can look out and see the bay beneath, the same bay in which I was shipwrecked."

"Is Otho there?"

"Yes. I have met him before, and I can recognize him now beyond any doubt. The rumors are true. The Imperial Heir is imprisoned here."

"Do you speak with him?"

"Yes."

"What do you discuss?"

"He believes that Galba is possessed by a devil of some kind. He claims his agents have reported to him that this devil lives in a great secret temple somewhere south of Rome. His agents have followed the Pretender to this place of worship. They claim to have seen many unspeakable acts committed in this place."

Smith and Raymond exchanged glances. "Do you believe this?" Raymond asked.

"I have seen the Pretender. He is either mad or possessed, beyond a doubt. And Otho is a man whose judgement is well proven."

"Do you like him?"

"Yes. I now become his man, sworn to his allegiance. He is my Emperor."

"If he is a secret prisoner, how did you get in to see him?"

"With forged Imperial orders, supplied by the Proconsul Governer of the Eastern Provinces."

Raymond paused as Smith turned over the cassette in the tape machine, then set it recording again. "What will you do now?"

Collin did not hesitate for an instant. "Arrange his release."

"With forged documents again?"

"That," Collin smiled, "and the force of arms to back me up."

"We are moving ahead in time, Collin. Otho is free and you have returned to Rome. Where are you, specifically?"

"I am in the Imperial Palace."

"Are you alone?"

"Demetrious is with me."

"Where is Otho?"

"In the barracks of the Imperial Bodyguard, the only troops allowed to be garrisoned inside the city of Rome itself. He is waiting there for me to kill Galba. The troops there are loyal to him. When the news of Galba's death comes, they will carry him through the streets and proclaim him Emperor."

"What time of day is it?"

"Almost midnight."

Smith scribbled a note on a piece of paper and passed it to Raymond, who glanced at it and set it aside.

"How did you gain admittance to the Palace in the middle of the night?"

"I claimed to bear a sealed, confidential, and urgent message from the Proconsul. I do, in fact, carry a document bearing his seal. But the real message is carried in the sheath of my dagger."

"Are you admitted to the presence of the Pretender?"

"Yes, and his attendants are dismissed. We are alone. Demetri waits outside."

"What does the Emperor look like?"

"He has changed much in the last months. He is

thin, pale, his eyes wild. He raves about imagined dangers, enemies everywhere. His hair is thinning, going gray though he has not yet seen his thirty-fifth year."

"What happens next?" Raymond fell into the present tense as Collin had been answering all along.

"I approach and hand him the message. He reads it and finds that it is his death sentence. He stares at me in anger and his eyes seem to shine out red light. Then there comes a buzzing sound, like a swarm of bees in my head. It hurts, but it does not inhibit me. I sense somehow that it is the devil in my head trying to take over me, but for some reason, it cannot. I draw my dagger and step closer. He screams and rages, his face seeming to take many shapes before my eyes, though all these shapes are shadows and indistinct. I am not deceived."

As Collin spoke, he grew more and more excited, his face became flushed and his breathing quickened.

"Does the Emperor say anything?"

Collin was breathing very heavily, his arm holding an imaginary dagger. "Yes."

"What does he say?"

Collin's eyes were opened wide. "He screams, 'Who are you that I cannot possess you like these other worms?!'"

"What happens then?"

Collin frowned. "I stab him in the heart. I stab the man, but not the devil. The devil flees."

"How do you know this?"

"The devil is gone before the man is dead. Galba speaks to me, blessing me for freeing him. He tells me the location of the secret temple of the demon. He tells me that I am the only man whose thoughts the demon cannot hear, the only one whose body and soul cannot be taken by it. I am the only one who can approach without its hearing my footsteps. He lays upon me the task of seeking it out and killing it."

"Does he tell you how this can be done?"

"By fire."

Smith and Raymond again exchanged looks.

Raymond shifted in his chair. "We are going ahead again Collin. To the time when you find the devil."

Collin stirred uneasily. "I am standing in front of it, in a vast cavern beneath the temple. I have crept in alone by cover of night. The sight I see shall never leave my cursed eyes. The remains of so many dead. Oh, unholy night! May the gods take eternal vengeance upon this beast and all who serve it."

"How will you kill it?"

Collin was pale, his features bleak. "I have many skins, all filled with oil. And I have a flint. I will burn it."

"Isn't it too large for you to burn with only the oil you carry on your back?"

"Possibly. It is over thirty feet across. Had I known it was so big perhaps I would have thought of some other way. But that is meat already eaten. I am here, I will do what I have to do."

"What is happening now?"

"I am climbing on an overhanging ledge in the cave. From here, lying on my stomach, I am pouring the oil out over the thing below. I can see it begin to waken. It glows more and more. But still I do not hear the buzzing."

"Are there any of the possessed in the cavern?"

"Yes, but none facing this way. And they do not move about. There, my last skin is empty. But the demon is fully awake now. I can see a figure approaching in the distance. Now I strike the flint. Once, twice, and again. Finally, the torch lights. As I hear the sound of buzzing in my head, the sound that tells me it is trying to make me its own, I whirl the torch about over my head and swing it down onto the oil-covered thing below. It makes a beautiful fire! Oh, how it writhes in agony under the flames. But I must get down, or I will be suffocated by the smoke."

Raymond's voice retained its calm. "What are the possessed doing?"

"I can only just barely see them through the smoke, but I think they have fallen lifeless to the floor. Quickly, I move along the ledge and then jump off into a pile of rotting corpses that cushion my fall. I scramble out and begin my escape, but then I must stop."

"Why?"

"He is blocking my way."

"He?"

"The Guardian."

"What is happening now?"

Collin drew a ragged breath. "The Guardian steps closer and I strike at him with my short sword. But this does not stop him, my blows do not penetrate. One of the possessed, the servants of the demon, has struck me. I grapple with him. By his dress I know he is a centurian from the long lost Drussian Legion. Over and over we roll through the bloody dust, and just when I think he will kill me, I am lucky and escape." Collin was growing increasingly more hysterical.

"The centurian knocks me down," Collin went on, "and comes closer. I am lying on my elbows within a foot of the fire I started when my fingers touch the hilt of my short sword. I turn and pick it up, and realize that it has lain partly in the flame, and the blade is red hot. At that moment, the centurian rushes me and I run him through with the weapon. His blood boils as the blade enters his belly. It is a terrible thing."

"What about the Guardian?"

"He has watched from the tunnel mouth. Now he comes slowly toward me, his face without expression. His arms reach out to take me by the neck. I scream, begin to fall back. Desperately, hopelessly, I plunge the sword into him, and this time he screams." Collin was trembling hysterically. "With blood flowing freely from him, the Guardian falls forward upon me, drawing a dagger from his cloak. No. *No!*" Collin screamed and covered his eyes with his hands.

Raymond made an effort to control his own emotions and spoke on calmly. "What is it? What is happening?"

Collin breathed in gasping sobs. "I take the blade in the ribs as he falls. But I am not yet dead. As I watch, the Guardian's body dies. I feel his spirit withdrawn to someplace else. But I . . . I can feel myself fading. I begin to crawl, inch by inch. Then . . . I can remember nothing more." His face contorted in severe pain.

Collin's eyes were glassy. He stared straight ahead at the blank wall, his face was pale and drained and his breathing was ragged and uneven. Raymond went through the gentle process of returning Collin's awareness to the here and now, then ordered him to sleep deeply and peacefully.

When Collin was stretched out on a cot in one corner, Raymond turned to Smith. "Well, now we know why the Guardian recognized Collin that first night. And also why Collin was not possessed in Africa as you and McPhearson were. He seems to have some type of immunity built into his personality.

Smith raised an eyebrow. "Yes. An immunity that stays with him through different bodies and different lives, if we can believe in such things."

Raymond leaned back tiredly. "Take a look at this." He pushed an aerial photo of Melville, Montana, across the table to Smith. "Here is Hotel Earth. We tracked the Guardian that morning from the point where he left the coal chute. Unlike his mythological counterparts, the Guardian *does* leave tracks. And he does seem to reflect in a mirror." Raymond smiled sardonically. "His trail led down a hillside and into a fenced-off area, which turned out to be a state work camp. We got chased out before we saw what the inmates were working on. But we did glimpse some rather unusual buildings. They were busy excavating and enlarging a tunnel leading into this mountainside. Here it is, see?" He pointed to a spot on the photo.

"Yes." Smith studied the map carefully.

"It turns out to be an abandoned mine shaft,

dating back to the turn of the century when they used to mine silver in this area. There's a stone quarry here," he pointed again, "and this is a heavy-equipment storage area."

"And you think it's the cave?" Smith asked.

"Collin determined that a great many people have been brought into that camp during the last few months that were never sentenced to serve time there by any court in the state. Any *human* court."

"So it's either the cave or the immediate vicinity?"

Raymond gathered up the syringe and placed it in a small case. "We can say that with reasonable certainty."

"Then we must develop a plan that will lead us to the Anansi demon."

Raymond frowned. "Yes. It will not be easy."

Smith pulled a pad and pencil from across the table. "Are you certain this Faraday Cage will protect the privacy of our thoughts?"

Raymond smiled bitterly. "No." A moment of silence followed.

"Let's get on with it, then." Smith reached over and switched off the tape recorder.

Collin paused at the door to his apartment to dig his keys out of his pocket. He glanced at his watch. 4:25 P.M. He had slept for three and a half hours after their hypnoregression session. Collin felt particularly drained after this one, and though he remembered nothing from it he had vague feelings of foreboding and disquiet. In his pocket, he carried a cassette Smith had handed him, along with a solemn look of kind sympathy and the words: "Listen to this when you feel up to it."

The tired young man knew that he definitely did not feel up to it that afternoon. He planned to fix himself some kind of simple meal and perhaps watch television for an hour or two, and then turn in for a good night's sleep.

His key turned easily in the lock and Collin eased the door open. It was good to be home, dingy as the place was. Collin realized that he was a very territorial creature, with a strong need to possess a given amount of space that was his alone.

Just inside the door, he stopped, dumbfounded. His apartment had been ransacked and demolished. All the boxes of files and papers had been emptied out and torn to shreds, the furniture had been broken and piled every which way, the bedclothes had been torn into long strips, the mattress slashed.

The desk had been upended and the great wall map of the United States had been brutally slashed again and again.

Of its own volition the door slid shut behind him and Collin felt something hard, cold, and steely shoved against his back.

From the kitchen shadows, a voice reached out to him, sending shivers up and down his spine. "Please forgive us for making ourselves at home." The gentle, superior voice was soon followed by a familiar figure. The Guardian strode into the main room.

Shocked, Collin made no move to resist as two men closed in on either side of him, grabbing his arms as he had seen McPhearson's grabbed in preparation for being led to the reaching fingers of the demon. They

218

had been waiting against the walls on either side of the door.

The man to Collin's right reached out and extracted his automatic pistol from under the prisoner's leather jacket. The look on Collin's face must have matched his thoughts for the Guardian nodded solemnly. "Yes, you are going to die this day," he said. Then he sat down on the ripped bed and motioned for his minions to force Collin down into the desk chair, which one of them set upright behind him. "But first," the Guardian murmured, "we talk."

SIX
Los Angeles, California
November 9, 1970

The Guardian was dressed immaculately in a black suit. A red kerchief protruded from the chest pocket with a studied negligence. His black shoes were highly polished and reflected Collin's own expression when he looked down at them. He quickly looked away.

The Guardian's helpers were two burly men in shirt-sleeves, both of whom had very short crewcuts and chiseled, cruel features. The light of intelligence did not burn brightly in their eyes, which were brown in the man on the right, blue in the left man. Both carried silenced revolvers. The barrel of one was buried painfully in the back of Collin's neck. All three of them seemed perfectly at home, as the Guardian had said, in the total destruction around them.

They sat in silence for a brief period, during which Collin and the Guardian sat staring at each other. The Guardian was relaxed, calm, casual. He seemed anything but menacing. Collin's face was nearly as pale as the Guardian's with the realization of his plight. But his expression was cold, unmoving. His features might have been chiseled from marble.

Finally, the Guardian leaned back slightly and sighed.

"We had some difficulty tracking you down."

Collin tried to make his own voice sound as steady. "I had some trouble tracking *you* down, as well."

The Guardian smiled. "Touché."

Collin nodded toward the half-empty bottle of Chivas Regal lying on its side on the floor beside the upturned desk. "Help yourself to a drink."

The Guardian smiled. "No, thank you. I never touch it."

"Oh."

A brief moment of awkward silence followed, during which the Guardian fidgeted slightly, looking down at his polished shoes. Collin found himself trying to imagine what it was going to be like to be dead. He had no concrete belief structure to bolster him in this moment. Death to him represented almost certain oblivion. He could not conceive of it, or accept it.

His head was beginning to ache with the pressure of the gun barrel in his neck. His mouth was extremely dry.

The Guardian looked around the room. "From the, uh, debris, I gather that there are at least two others working with you. Possibly more. Dr. Raymond I have met. He is intelligent, very well-informed. But he relies on imperfect safeguards. He can be dealt with. The African I have not yet been introduced to, but his mind is well known to the master. Aggressive, extremely stable, and without the usual human weak points. His shield, that primitive

221

tribal talisman, is somewhat more to be reckoned with than the good doctor's. But he, too, is of relative unimportance. It is your presence in this triumvirate that gives it its power."

"Why?"

The Guardian's eyebrows raised. "I'm afraid even *I* don't know the complete answer to that question. Apparently, your suitability to this conflict extends beyond your immunity to the influences I serve. It is to be speculated that perhaps you have the clandestine support of certain . . . other forces."

"Other forces?" Collin appeared genuinely puzzled. A new element suddenly and unexpectedly inserted into the picture.

"In any case, your imminent removal from the game board renders such speculation academic. What remains to the point is the present whereabouts of your two comrades. As yet, we have been unable to find them."

Collin said nothing.

"Further," the Guardian went on, still in his gentle, sympathetic voice, "I must apprise myself of the details of whatever program of action you have undoubtedly been planning, in the event that we are for some reason unable to stop Smith and Raymond here."

Collin remained absolutely mute. In his mind, he searched for a way to kill himself in order to avoid being forced to talk.

"Lastly," the Guardian leaned forward slightly, "it is important that you tell me who else may be aware of our existence."

Collin shook his head. "Sorry."

The Guardian gestured to the blue-eyed thug at Collin's right. "Demetre."

The sour-faced gunman stepped for a second into the bathroom and emerged with a lit candle, which had obviously been waiting ready for this occasion. He reached out one brawny arm and grabbed Collin's right wrist.

"Fire can be a terrible thing," the Guardian commented sadly. Demetre began to pass the flame back and forth directly under the palm of Collin's hand, which was held tightly by the other thug as to be totally immobile.

"Try not to cry out." The Guardian grimaced slightly, as though the whole business were distasteful to him. "If you do, Peter there will be forced to kill you, and we will have to press ahead without the benefit of your . . . assistance."

"You miserable fucking bastard," Collin hissed out between clenched teeth. Wafting through the air came the now familiar smell of burned flesh.

The look of detached compassion in the eyes of the Guardian did not waver as the torture continued for perhaps a minute more. Collin's body quivered and writhed in the grip of those who held him. Finally, the Guardian motioned for Demetre to withdraw the candle. "Please do not force me to continue to resort to these barbarities. Forcing information from people is an activity foreign to me."

Collin glared at him through tear-filled eyes. "Why not just admit that you enjoy it." His voice cracked but he did not care.

The Guardian shook his head sadly. "You misjudge me. Simply because I hunt and kill for food, you believe I am inherently cruel. You are a meat eater, are you not?''

Collin merely glared.

"It is the lot of all creatures to kill in order to survive. And I do not deny that the activity is fulfilling."

"You rationalize. I have seen what you do. You and that . . . that *thing* you protect. You'll never be able to whitewash that to me!"

The Guardian shrugged. "We kill to survive. But you? Why do you kill us? With your knowledge and immunity, you could live out your life in peace and safety. Anyone else would." The Guardian looked bemused. "Tell me. What is your motivation?"

"Revenge."

The Guardian nodded. "A valid purpose. Noble even. But I see indications of more subtle forces written there in your eyes."

"Very flattering," Collin remarked acidly. He no longer was afraid to die. His only fear was that he could be made to talk. No one could be counted on to hold up under torture indefinitely.

"Accordingly," the Guardian went on, unruffled, "I suspected that persuading you to talk by these primitive means would take up more time and energy than is currently at my disposal." He nodded to Demetre, who set down the candle and turned again to the bathroom. "So I stopped and picked up someone who might prove more persuasive than me."

Demetre emerged from the open bathroom door, leading by the elbow a passive young woman, dressed in a flower print dress. She was a natural blond, with

224

striking blue eyes set in an innocently lovely face. Her figure, though not voluptuous, was very well proportioned. She looked intelligent, sensitive, vulnerable. Her name, as Collin knew all too well, was Sandra, and it was she who had written the sad and sweet letter several weeks ago.

"Your neglected lady friend." The Guardian smiled over at her. She had the blank look of one under the influence of the demonic thing the Guardian serviced. "You were right to separate yourself from your friends and loved ones. To us their thoughts are as easy to read as a child's book. And they are, indeed, a weak point through which we can reach you." Demetre again took Collin's arm. The shock and despair was plain to see in Collin's face. For the first time he erupted in a sudden flurry, struggling futilely to escape the iron grips of the two henchmen.

The man the Guardian had addressed as Peter clubbed him indelicately against the side of the head with his pistol.

The room spun around for an instant, then gradually returned to something approximating stability. His head and hand throbbed painfully, in unison with the fanatic beating of his traumatized heart.

"No," the Guardian said softly. "She will not be raped, beaten, and murdered before your eyes." He paused though, pityingly. "Perhaps you will wish such a fate for her when you know what will happen if you refuse to tell us what we wish to know."

Collin shook his head, wincing at the pain this brought. "Never," he choked out. His voice sounded like the barking of a dog.

"She will be given to the dark one, the master." He looked levelly into Collin's only partially focused eyes. "You have seen the fate of these unfortunates, have you not?"

In answer, Collin's imagination began painting a hideous picture of the innocent Sandra in the grasp of those horrible reaching fingers. He writhed.

"Tell us. Tell us what we need to know, and she will be released. She will remember nothing, there is no reason why we would have to kill her. I will guarantee you immunity, not only for her, but for your entire family. On the other hand, if you do not talk. . . ." A long pause followed.

Finally, Collin again shook his head. "No, I will not bargain with the devil. No matter what the cost."

The Guardian shook his head. "I fear I do not understand you." He gestured and the two men holding Collin jerked him upright.

"It is, in a way, a shame to kill you. We are like the dog and the cat, you and I, fire and ice. Eternal enemies by nature. The cobra and the mongoose, to be pitted against each other by warring forces greater than either of us. This is as it should be. If there were not such as you, there would be no reason for my existence. There would be no need for a Guardian." He gestured to Demetre. "Use your knife, friend Demetre. We will drink the blood."

Complying, the sinister man drew a long, shining blade and moved it slowly toward Collin's exposed throat, as though savoring his fear. When the knife was within a fraction of an inch from his skin, there came the sound of a gentle but firm knocking upon the front door.

"Collin, it's us." Smith's muffled voice came through the thick wood.

Startled, Demetre's head swiveled instantly to look at the source of the sound in an involuntary reaction. By sheer reflex, Collin took advantage of this single instant to bring his leg forward and back in a vicious foot sweep, drawing Demetre's legs out from under him and sending him crashing to the floor. Simultaneously, Collin's left arm arced up, deflecting Peter's silenced revolver, and the shot intended for Collin's heart.

Collin realized that he would have no chance against Peter's superhuman strength, so he reached up, grabbed him by his shirt collar, and deliberately fell over backward, pulling his opponent back over him. He used an upraised foot to guide and launch Peter overhead. The thug crashed heavily into a pile of splintered wood that had once been a coffee table. Collin rolled over from his position on the floor and scooped Demetre's silenced revolver from the spot where it had fallen when its owner had gone down. A quick shot. Peter would not rise again.

The pounding on the door was urgent now, accompanied by Raymond's voice calling out Collin's name.

He looked down at Demetre, who had not yet risen from the floor. Collin could see that he was struggling and writhing, the blade intended for his victim's throat embedded in his stomach. Demetre was not dead, but he was out of action.

Collin whirled to face the black-suited form. He had stood up from the bed, and Collin turned to point the pistol into the Guardian's torso. Collin was shaking in fear.

The Guardian looked calmly from the quivering figure in front of him over to the door, which was now being battered down. He appeared to weigh the amount of time left to him, debating whether he himself had time to take Collin down before the others would have the door open. Indecision was a passing expression on his handsome face as he decided against pressing the attack.

Never taking his eyes from Collin's face, he moved backward to the window, which was open, and climbed out onto the trestle of the fire escape. In an instant, he was gone.

It was only then that Collin looked over to see Sandra's fallen body lying amid the wreckage of his furniture. It was a terrible pity that she had to die here. He was consoled by the knowledge that she had no awareness of this evening's horror, that she experienced no fear and probably felt no pain.

At that instant, the lock finally submitted to the onslaught from without and the door flew open, almost bursting from its hinges. Smith and Raymond exploded into the room, their guns out, then stopped, frozen at the spectacle confronting them.

Smith moved quickly to check the bathroom and kitchen for any hidden enemy while Raymond knelt down beside the dead girl. "Shot in the heart," he murmured, turning to look into Collin's agonized face. "She must have died instantly. Who is she?"

Collin moved over to look down at her, transferring the pistol from his right hand, which was blistered and bleeding, over to his left. "Sandra McAllister. She was my fiancée at one time."

"Oh, God." Raymond shook his head.

"What happened?" Smith had come to help Collin into the chair in which he had so recently been a prisoner.

"He was here." Collin gestured with his chin toward the window. "He got away just as you got the door down." He looked at his friends, then cradled his head in his good hand, on the verge of weeping hysterically. His voice broke as he said, "Had you knocked on that door one second later . . . it would have been too late."

Raymond came over, put a comforting arm around his friend's heaving shoulders. "Collin," he said, "I'm terribly sorry about the girl. Terribly sorry."

Collin looked over briefly at the flower printed dress, the supple legs partially visible. "She was lucky," he said quietly. Tears were beginning to stain his cheeks.

"This one's still alive," Smith said, rolling Demetre over and exposing a great pool of blood. The knife danced in the thug's opened stomach with each labored breath.

Collin seemed to come alive again at the sight of his enemy. He rose from the chair and crossed the floor to kneel at his side. He looked into the wounded man's now terrified eyes. Then, he smiled. A deceptive, friendly, gentle smile. A smile that said: "I'm your friend. I only want to help."

Collin reached over and picked up the candle from the floor where Demetre had left it. It was still burning brightly.

"You are going to die this day," Collin said quietly. "But first, we talk."

ONE WEEK LATER

It was a narrow, cement floored room, garishly lit by a single naked light bulb hanging from the ceiling by a black cord. A sign on one wall read "Demont Rental Storage Units: Rules and Regulations." Beneath it were posted a series of sentences too small to be read from more than a few inches away.

A wooden workbench was positioned against the cement and brick wall, before which Collin and Smith were seated on stools. A portable electric heater sat upon the floor beside them, aimed so that it projected warm air upon their legs.

The bench was crowded with metal devices, equipment for the handloading of ammunition. Rows of shining cartridge cases were set along one end, and large bullet presses and molds took up the bulk of bench surface.

The remaining walls were lined with stacks of crates and sacks, electronic equipment, articles of clothing, all of which were arranged neatly and systematically, as though awaiting the moment when they would be put into calculated service.

Dr. Raymond came suddenly into the field of view from somewhere to the left, carrying a metal tray upon which were a variety of instruments, a Bunsen burner, and a metal bowl.

Smith and Collin watched him without comment

as he set the bowl on the bench and motioned for Collin to extend his arm as he wrapped a rubber tube around it. Raymond inserted a needle into his flesh at a point just below the elbow, and directed a long clear tube to which the needle was attached into the bowl, where a steady stream of deep red blood spurted freely into the container.

When perhaps two inches of the living fluid covered the bottom of the small container, Collin looked over at Raymond.

"That should be enough," he said.

Raymond nodded. "Okay."

The doctor gently removed the needle from Collin's arm, setting a piece of cotton over the tiny needle mark, then he unwrapped the tube.

Meanwhile, Smith set a metal tray, upon which rested dozens of iron pellets, on a stand erected above the Bunsen burner, then took a match and lit the gas flame.

"We'll let them get red hot," Smith said.

Raymond nodded, preoccupied as he set the used needle aside.

Raymond looked at Smith. "Your turn next."

Smith nodded. Collin was busy with a tool hollowing out the interiors of lead bullets on a rack in front of him.

"Heat up this knife blade, will you?" Collin asked. "We'll quench that in the blood, as well.

"Right," Smith responded.

He turned to comply, setting the indicated blade on the plate which held the iron pellets above the flame.

Raymond turned to Collin, handing him a cup

of coffee.

Collin looked over at him wearily. "What do you think the odds are that this process is going to work?"

"I'd say very good," Raymond responded. "Your description under hypnosis of the action sequence leading to the temporary death of the Guardian is fairly definite. The short sword you killed him with was heated red hot in the fire you had started. You first used it to run through a possessed man who was sent against you. The blade was quenched first in his blood. Only then did it actually become capable of wounding the Guardian." He paused thoughtfully. "There are all sorts of precedents for the assigning of strong religious properties to blood."

"Wasn't there an actual person in medieval times who was executed for practicing vampirism?" Smith asked quietly.

"As a matter of fact," Raymond said, "there were many recorded cases. But one of the most famous concerns a noblewoman who killed dozens of her own maidservants over a period of years, drained their blood and actually bathed in it in an effort to attain eternal youth."

"God, that's ghastly."

"Yes. But there are all sorts of other ways in which blood figures into religious ritual actions, some of which are commonplace today. Look at the Roman Catholic Mass, for instance. A large part of the ceremony is concerned with the ceremonial drinking of the blood of Christ, in order to attain eternal life."

Collin and Smith exchanged glances as this thought sank in.

Raymond continued. "But there is a story that

strikes very close to our immediate problem. In ancient Egypt, the legend says, the priest responsible for the forging of metal weapons discovered through some accident that when weapons were used to kill slaves while they were still red hot from the forge, a fantastic strength was somehow magically imparted to the blade. The priest did not understand the concept of tempering. They believed that the spirit of the murdered man somehow entered the weapon, giving it supernatural power. This secret was kept by the priests for centuries. Modern science has assumed that the change in the iron was simply a form of heat treating. And undoubtedly that is at least partially true. But now I wonder if some element or combination of elements of human blood might not react with iron in high temperature conditions to form some type of oxide, or other by-product that is poisonous to the Guardian's metabolic system. Bear in mind his apparent dependence on a regular intake of blood. It is not inconceivable that blood in an altered form could be a systemic poison."

"We may never understand the details," Smith said. "But I agree that there is a high probability that the approach will provide us with at least some defense against the Guardian. In the tradition of my tribe, there is a story of one king Liongo, who could only be killed by a copper needle inserted into his navel."

"The knife I can see. But the bullets?"

"The only way to find out for sure is to try them. But theoretically, by putting an iron core, heated and quenched in blood, in these lead pistol bullets, we should create the same effect achieved by quenching the iron blades. They should be capable of injuring the inhuman creature."

Smith held up the knife blade, now red hot, with a pair of tongs and quickly plunged it into the nearby bowl of blood. It hissed and bubbled, emitting a cloud of acrid smoke and steam that brought wrinkles of disgust to the noses of Collin and Raymond.

Smith withdrew the blade, which was now covered by a black layer of burned blood, and set it aside on the bench. The three bent forward attentively as Smith picked up the plate of iron pellets destined for insertion into the noses of Collin's hollowed out bullets, and plunged these, too, into the living bath.

SEVEN
En flight over Montana
November 20, 1970

Collin looked over irritably at Smith, but did not break the strained silence. His countenance was strained in awful expectation of the events surely to come this night. He had experienced long months of dreadful anticipation, nightmarish speculation about the moment when he would face the unthinkable a second time, and he found the passing hours in flight, hours during which he had nothing to do except consider the immediate future, all but unendurable.

Smith's face betrayed deep concern for other reasons. Before departing for the airport long ago, Mason had leaned over to the young black ranger and spoke slowly and carefully the word "Mayele," a Bantu word meaning "wisdom," one which he would almost certainly never hear by random chance in any conversation in the United States.

The mention of that word had been Smith's cue to fall into a hypnotic state, the details of which had been implanted deep in his subconscious during long hours in a trance induced by Mason Raymond. And what Smith now saw as he leaned over the glowing instruments on the control panel of the aircraft did not accurately reflect the current condition of the plane. The oil pressure gauge in the ranger's mind's eye indicated that the pressure had dropped in the last half hour and was still dropping at an alarming rate. Further, the temperature of the plane's single engine was rising inexplicably, and the fuel level was dropping at an alarming rate. Worse still was the fact that the radio transmitter appeared, to Smith's distorted senses, to have gone out entirely.

The situation, as Smith perceived it, was desperate, and growing more so with each passing minute. Somehow, he seemed to have lost his bearings, and without radio direction-finding equipment he was unable to determine his position with any accuracy, and could not, in the total darkness, get a visual bearing or search out suitable terrain to attempt an emergency landing.

Collin, aware of the anxiety his friend was undoubtedly experiencing, found himself envious. Far better to be concerned about engine trouble in a light plane than to be contemplating a face-to-face meeting with what awaited them both on land. Smith, Collin knew, was utterly unaware of where their flight was really taking them. He was unaware that despite what the instruments seemed to be indicating, the plane was cruising normally and everything was perfectly operational, including the radio. He was even unaware of the presence of his friend in the copilot's seat beside him. In his mind, Smith was alone, flying northward to Canada where he and

Collin were scheduled to rendezvous the following day.

Lastly, the fortunate ranger was unaware that the lights emanating from the ground miles before them came from the sleepy, utterly undistinguished town of Melville, and that a few miles beyond that awaited their unthinkably hideous enemy.

Collin yawned, not out of sleepiness, but as a strange reaction to his extreme nervous tension. He felt his ears pop as Smith eased back slightly on the stick, giving the plane more altitude.

Chris Collin smiled wryly to himself as the ranger leaned forward and put his hand to the choke knob, frowning earnestly as he watched the oil pressure gauge. Manifestly, Smith believed he was sliding the control in or out, but in fact, his hand did not move the choke control even a fraction of an inch.

"F-on-kari!" Smith muttered softly to himself, and Collin supposed he might be cursing in his native tongue.

They were almost directly over Melville now, and Collin looked down briefly, clearly able to distinguish the main features of the settlement in the glow of the streetlights. It was Tuesday night, approaching midnight, and there were almost no lights showing from houses or trade signs. All in the little community were undoubtedly asleep. "We're almost there," Collin thought, and he could see for the first time in the distance a faint bluish glow coming from somewhere in one of the valleys ahead. That was it, he knew. He had seen aerial photos of the terrain at night, and knew what to look for.

There came a faint "beep" from a small black box fastened securely to his belt. Smith appeared not to notice it at all, but Collin tensed involuntarily. The time had come at last. That was Mason's signal that they were approaching the drop zone. In one minute there would come two more "beeps" in quick succession, and then thirty seconds later would come one long tone signal, indicating to them the precise moment they would have to jump. Although Smith did not consciously hear the signal, the tone had penetrated to his subconscious, setting off the next programmed sequence of illusions. He cursed again and gripped the control stick tightly, causing the plane to buck and swerve. He leaned forward, peering intently at the gauges and tapping them. The oil gauge showed the pressure had suddenly dropped to near zero, and the engine temperature soared. Smith made some subtle adjustment he believed would help, and immediately the tone of the engine changed in Collin's ears. Believing he had enriched the fuel mixture, Smith had actually adjusted it to the point that the engine was coughing and sputtering, perilously close to dying altogether. From the ground, if anyone were listening, it would sound like an aircraft in distress.

Smith brought the microphone to his lips and thumbed the button, oblivious to the fact that the transmitter power switch was in the "off" position.

"Mayday, Mayday. This is Cessna two zero foxtrot, over."

He released it, waiting for a response. Then continued, "Mayday, Mayday. If you can hear me this is Cessna two zero foxtrot en route for southern Canada out of Morely Field, Montana. Going down. Going down. Engine trouble. Mayday. Mayday."

Collin once again admired his friend's coolness under extreme pressure. "Mayday, Mayday," Smith tried one last time, then replaced the microphone on its steel clip on the panel.

He reached forward, totally unaware of what he was actually doing, and flipped the autopilot on. As he did so, the two-beep signal sounded on Collin's walkie-talkie. Thirty seconds. Collin looked down and could see nothing.

Smith fumbled behind him and brought around the straps of his parachute pack, which he carefully fastened about himself, a task more difficult than most people would expect in the close confines of the cabin. He reached around and pulled out what he believed to be a reserve chute, and this he attached to his harness in front of him.

Just as the man did so, the long signal sounded loud and clear over the communicator, and Smith unhesitantly sprang the door catch, forcing it outward and away, and exited smoothly from the craft, instantly lost from sight.

Collin lost no time getting his door open, but was a good deal more hesitant in his departure than Smith had been; post hypnotic suggestion was an advantage to a skydiver when jumping at night over enemy territory.

In accordance with their carefully crafted and well rehearsed plan, Chris refrained from pulling his ripcord for thirty fearfully counted seconds. He had jumped, he knew, from an altitude of just over eight thousand feet, and thirty seconds of free fall would bring him almost halfway down. Smith, on the other hand, had been programmed to pull his ripcord immediately upon leaving the Cessna. Collin would be on the ground well in advance of Smith.

There came, for the first time, the crackle of static in the tiny earphone clipped into his right ear. Mason's precise voice came to him from the woods below.

"Turn right, you're almost a thousand yards too far north."

Collin pulled on his right hand toggle and could feel himself shift around. He watched the stars wheel about over his head, beyond the billowing skirts of the chute. Mason was tracking him by a radio beacon, and guiding him to the meadow they had selected as their landing sight. On a different frequency, Collin knew, he would also be guiding Smith, who, however oblivious he would be to Mason's instructions, would be nonetheless obedient to them.

Collin spent most of his time looking down, though he could distinguish nothing below but heavy darkness.

"Come right forty-five degrees," Mason's voice came again. "You're about two thousand feet up."

In anticipation of the coming collision with Mother Earth, Collin forced his feet together, not an easy task with the leg straps of his parachute harness continually pulling them apart. But he knew that he had to keep them together and focus his gaze on the horizon, such as it was, at the moment of impact. Failure to follow these rules would almost certainly be rewarded with a broken leg or other injury.

Mason's voice was with him again. "You're right on target. There's no wind to speak of, so don't worry about having to turn into the wind at the last minute. Smith is three thousand feet above you, will impact a hundred yards to the south of you. You should hit in about fifteen seconds . . . good luck."

Collin forced himself to try not to anticipate the impact, and it seemed to him that Mason had been wrong for once: Minutes seemed to crawl by and still he was floating silently in the blackness. And then, suddenly, dark shadows rushed up at him and he hit the ground with the force of a collision with a moving car. He hit badly and rolled to one side, but seemed uninjured as he gathered the shroud lines of his chute and spilled the air out of it, pulling it to him and rolling it in a bundle in his best paratrooper style. He had made several night jumps in the preceding weeks, but nothing could have prepared him for tonight.

Collin had landed in a grassy, flat landscape, undoubtedly the meadowland immediately north of the cave entrance. He could not see more than a few hundred feet, and could not orient himself precisely with regard to the boundaries of the meadow. He rolled his chute up and dropped it among some convenient brush and shrubs. He did not bother to bury it. If, by morning, there were still any hostile forces around to find it, Collin and his friends would almost certainly be dead, or possibly, worse than dead.

Collin took off to the south, judging his direction from a wrist compass. He reached into his pack and extracted a thin oblong device resembling a small camera. It was an infrared night scope, and with it he had no trouble seeing Smith hit the ground, roll much more smartly than had Collin himself, and recover his parachute.

The black man fumbled at his harness straps, then gave up, apparently unable to unfasten them, and released his chute by means of emergency buckles just in front of his shoulders. That too was according to his post-hypnotic programming. He was unable to shed the harness to which was still attached the supply pack that so closely resembled a reserve chute.

Collin swung the night glasses through a three hundred and sixty degree arc, checking for signs of the enemy. By this time, he was lying on his belly among some brush, at a point scarcely thirty yards from Smith. Collin could see that they were quite close to the edge of the meadow, which was bordered to the south by a thin grove of sycamore trees, most of them at least partially devoid of leaves. Collin could see no signs that any watcher lurked in the surrounding countryside. They had not expected any. Nevertheless, he remained carefully hidden, even from Smith, who was under subconscious directive not to be aware of him.

As the night glasses completed their circle and the ranger came once again into his field of view, Collin saw the usually expressive arms drop suddenly to his side. His head, which had been bent over to look down at a compass, came up slowly. Smith turned calmly and with no hesitancy at all began to walk in a slightly wooden fashion toward the woods to the south, some thirty or forty yards distant.

Chris could not swear to it, but he believed he felt,

just at the edge of his perception, that terrible buzzing drone that heralded the activity of the enemy. In any case, there was no doubt in his mind that Smith was now, once again, under the control of the thing from the cave. Their program called for his friend to consult both his map and his compass at some length before setting off, and then it was to have been in a more northerly direction—not directly toward the lair of the thing as he was heading now.

Pulling the small black transceiver from his belt, Collin pressed the transmit button in quick flashes, first twice in rapid succession, and then after a pause three times more slowly. That was the signal to Mason that the Shaktowi had taken the bait. He then pushed a button on the side of the device, and a continuous beeping began to sound in the earphone planted in his right ear. As Chris swung the small unit slowly to the right and left in front of him the signal alternately increased and decreased in volume. It appeared that the system was working properly; the tiny transmitter concealed in Smith's clothing was sending out its beacon, and both Collin and Mason (now somewhere just beyond the perimeter of the fenced-off area) could track him to his eventual destination.

Smith had almost reached the trees before Collin rose to a crouching stance and began to follow him. He endeavored to keep his friend always at the farthest limit of the nightscope's range.

The trek through the woods was not difficult. The body heat of the man ahead shone like a burning torch in the cold November night air when viewed through the infrared glasses. Further, anyone lying in concealment would also have been visible to him by means of the gadget, so Collin was spared the continual worry of looking out for hidden guards or watchers.

They had touched down within two miles of the abandoned mine, which they believed to be the new lair, and it was almost forty-five minutes after setting out that Smith broke free of the light woods and emerged into the dusty flat basin housing the new, half-constructed facilities of the supposed penal colony.

Collin, concealed at the edge of the trees, was not surprised to see two figures moving toward the African with the same measured pace. Without breaking Smith's stride, they took him by each arm and walked side by side into the lighted area bordered by a cave at the north end and the half-finished buildings at the south. Collin, by means of the glasses, could make out at least half a dozen watchers scattered in concealment at various points around the site, and didn't need the glasses to see several men standing motionless on sentry duty in full glare of the helium arc lamps.

Not wishing Smith to get too far ahead of him, Collin moved quickly along the edge of the trees to the point where they intersected with the jagged hillside that, a little farther on, housed the cave entrance. He scurried up the side of the small cliff and began to make his way along the top of the rise, moving on a course parallel to Smith and his captors' and yet out of the sight of the watchers below.

At a point where Collin estimated the cave entrance to be almost directly below him, the young man paused and watched carefully as the three moving through the lighted area walked directly through the center of the open ground, not stopping for even the briefest glance at the cave mouth. They proceeded toward the west section of the area, wherein stood a number of steamshovels, bulldozers, and other large earth-moving equipment.

Nodding to himself, Collin again thumbed the transmit button on his communication device, signalling to Mason that, indeed, the cave did not house their target, and that the path was leading to the west.

As he raised the glasses to scan the westward territory, Collin reviewed his mental map of the landscape. There was very little to remark out there, he realized. A storage place for the large trucks and machines, a latrine area, and at the very northwest corner, where the hill rose sharply enough and high enough to be considered a small mountain, a stone quarry had been carved, probably far back in the history of the land, undoubtedly predating the arrival of the Anansi Demon.

Collin's brow furrowed deeply as he tried to imagine where in that expanse the enemy could possibly be concealed. Then, he imagined he could see the faintest lines of heat rising from somewhere beyond his field of vision. He allowed the glasses to hang from the leather strap about his neck and began to work his way along the ridge once again. When he reached a point where it was too narrow to follow any longer, he pulled a thin but extremely durable nylon rope from his pack and secured it to a protruding tree root.

Taking a deep breath, he swung himself down the face of the rocky hillside and lowered himself slowly to the floor of the basin. At the bottom, he checked through the glasses to see if anyone had noticed him, then he checked on the position of Smith and his escort, who were by this time almost out of sight beyond the glow of the arc lamps.

Keeping to the shadows, Collin hugged the wall of the hillside and made after them at his best pace, unslinging his automatic rifle as he did so.

Several times during the next few minutes he sighted the telltale heat-beacons that heralded hidden watchers, and once he froze in terror as someone emerged from a deep shadow less than twenty feet in front of him and walked back toward the cave entrance, passing within barely a yard of the invader. Collin realized that the rock wall had effectively cut off whatever heat trail might otherwise have been visible from the man who had come so close to discovering him, and realized he had been relying too much on the glasses.

A minute passed before he dared to move, and even then he did so only because Smith was almost out of sight around the edge of the rock-face ahead. Collin exercised extreme care crossing the area from which the lone walker had emerged, and noted as he passed that the spot was a long-established sentry post, equipped with a canteen and rigged portable spotlight.

As he rounded a bend in the rock-face at this point, he came in sight of the massive three sided box-canyon that was the stone quarry. There was virtually no light here at all, and Collin could see with the naked eye neither the path ahead nor the three who preceded him, though he could still plainly hear their measured footfalls.

With the glasses to his forehead, he could make them out as perfectly as though they walked in the noon sunlight of the brightest day of the year. More importantly, the entire quarry was lit up through the eye of the infrared scope, even brighter than the area around the cave entrance had been.

At the apex where the walls of the quarry joined was a huge pile of rubble, dirt, and chips of stone, all leaning at a steep angle against the rock face. To all outward appearances it was the natural residue of whatever rock carving operations had once been carried out in the squared worksight.

In the light of day, Collin realized, it would be impossible, even with an infrared scope, to distinguish anything remotely suspicious about the enormous rubble pile. But at night, in air cold enough to sear the lungs, the center of the debris pile fairly glowed under the infrared, betraying some source of considerable heat, probably not far beneath the surface.

It was clear to Collin, though the three he trailed were still at least a hundred yards from the rubble mound at the end of the quarry, that this was indeed their destination.

Collin could see no sign of the entrance to the old mine. But he did not need to see it in order to know that it must be there somewhere.

He had his transceiver out without even realizing he had reached for it. He punched out the code, six long blasts, then six more. It was time for Mason to come—they had discovered the hiding place of the Shaktowi at last.

Collin knew that it would take at least several minutes for his friend to arrive, and he continued to trail Smith deeper into the quarry. He held the transmitter in his left hand, with his thumb over the talk button. In his right arm was cradled his automatic rifle, and in his right hand he held the nightglasses with which he never let Smith out of his sight.

The three ahead had traversed nearly half the distance to the shining rubble pile, and were scarcely fifty yards from it, when Collin began to notice a change in the waves of heat rising from the hidden source. In the very center of the affected area the radiation became more intense, more apparently concentrated, until Collin was sure he could make out a rectangular outline in the rocks. Then he could see a very regular opening in the cliff face, from which twin railway tracks emerged. It was the entrance to the old mine. Here, undoubtedly, was the Anansi's new lair.

This was it, he knew.

Fuck, he thought to himself savagely. Where the hell was Mason? In less than a minute, Smith and his zombie companions would reach that entrance. Collin began to run, as soundlessly and as well hidden as possible. In a matter of seconds he had closed to within thirty or forty feet of the three ahead and concealed himself behind a convenient boulder. He was a scant twenty-five yards from the opening in the rubble now, and Smith was close enough that the very small amount of visible light emanating from it made him and his escorting guards visible even without the glasses.

Collin, able to wait no longer, brought the transceiver to his lips and pressed the talk button. He took a deep breath and was about to speak when he heard from somewhere overhead the rather muted sound of Mason's small helicopter.

"Thank God," he murmured to himself. Then, he again pressed the talk button and said "Wagona ku moto noiye aona kut tentha," slowly and carefully. He waited a second and repeated it. It was an old saying in Ngbandi-Sango, which meant "He sits near the fire, he feels the burning." He set the radio to one side on the rock upon which he leaned and sighted in his rifle quickly and certainly upon the heart of the man to Smith's left. Before he had even tightened his finger upon the trigger an alarm began to sound somewhere back in the direction of the work camp, and he noticed the escorting guards seem to tense and begin to turn in an effort to look up at the helicopter, which was approaching in total darkness, but by now could plainly be heard overhead.

Collin squeezed the trigger in a smooth motion and the unfortunate man who held Smith dropped to the dirt floor. In a matter of seconds his companion to Smith's left joined him in tranquil oblivion. Collin's second bullet caught him in the side of the head as he was swinging around to look upward into the moonless night sky.

Collin's code word, transmitted to the earphone in Smith's right ear, had been the post-hypnotic cue to rouse Smith to full wakefulness, to remembrance of the fact that he wore upon his chest the medallion that had protected him in Africa. In that instant, he had been freed of the control of the enemy within the concealing quarry.

Regrettably, also in that instant the devil must have gained at least partial awareness of the deceit to which it had fallen prey. Action now had to be swift and immediate.

At the instant of firing his second shot, Collin was on his feet, running in long strides to his friend who had dropped to one knee. Just as he reached Smith, the entire interior of the quarry was suddenly illuminated as powerful lamps positioned high in the walls of the surrounding cliffs were switched on.

The siren was still wailing, and the sound of running men could plainly be heard from the direction of the work camp to the southeast.

Smith was just extracting a submachine pistol from his dummy parachute pack and assembling it. Collin, half-blinded by the glare, raised his rifle and fired it in the direction of one of the lights. He fired twice, then three times, and there was a crackling of broken glass as one of the lamps fizzled out.

"There are too many," Smith gasped, struggling to get his weapon ready to fire. "We'll never get them all."

"You're right." He looked around, debating whether they should run for cover or head for the gaping entrance, less than twenty yards away. As it was, they were fully revealed, completely in the open. "It's no good. We've got to call off the attack!"

Shots began to ring out as men flooded into the quarry entrance a hundred yards away.

Collin was sure they were doomed. Bullets ricocheted inches from their bodies as they huddled to the ground, but then the helicopter dropped beneath the level of the tops of the quarry walls and the flat, hammer-on-anvil cracks of exploding munitions heralded the blinding flashes of grenades and small bombs that rained down from the chopper onto the unsuspecting men below. It was Mason, his arrival timed to the second. Collin, with a precious instant to collect himself and take aim, let out brief bursts of rifle fire to provide cover as Mason set the chopper down between himself, Smith, and the bulk of the enemy force.

As planned, Mason had dropped incendiaries, so that a number of fires burned brightly and furiously among the ranks of the possessed. Strangely, there were no screams of agony to be heard above the whine of the alarm siren and the occasional chatter of gunfire.

Collin gestured toward Raymond and the helicopter. "Make a run for it and I'll cover you."

Smith nodded and turned away, sprinting through the hail of bullets to join Raymond behind the landing pontoon of the craft. Together, Smith and Raymond set up a barrage of covering fire while Collin made the dash.

But Collin was not to make the trip with the same good luck that Smith had enjoyed. A bullet creased his ankle and brought him down hard behind a small boulder.

Smith, watching his friend fall and fearing the worst, directed Raymond into the machine. Then, as the gunfire converging on them reached the frantic proportions of a hailstorm, the African regretfully turned away and boarded the craft himself, barely avoiding the whizzing bullets that came within inches of his body.

Smith pointed his submachine gun out of the cockpit and returned fire as Raymond coaxed the chopper up off the ground. They were already ten feet in the air when Collin recovered sufficiently to look up from behind his concealing boulder. Throwing his rifle away, he got up, ignoring the rain of lead all around him, and rushed limpingly across the open space to the ground beneath the helicopter. With a superhuman effort, he jumped up and grabbed the pontoon as Raymond, oblivious to Collin's presence, jerked the helicopter up and away from the conflagration.

Smith, whose efforts had been directed at keeping a steady stream of fire on the men lining the quarry, paused and looked down in search of Collin on the ground. His eyes widened in amazement when he saw his friend clinging helplessly to the landing pontoon. Smith turned and shouted something to Raymond, who responded by tilting the control stick and directing the craft toward the range of hills to the north. Within seconds they were clear of the quarry itself, though still within range of small arms fire.

Suddenly, there came a sharp crack and a shower of sparks from the engine powering the main rotor, and the smooth hum of the engine changed to an unhealthy, bone jarring clamor. The vehicle lost altitude suddenly, bouncing in the air with the gate of a bucking bronc.

Smith leaned down, reaching for Collin, who was losing his grip on the smooth metal pontoon. Smith reached out farther and farther, his hand almost contacting Collin's, and then Chris was gone. His tortured hands could endure the punishment no longer and almost with a sense of relief his fingers let go and he dropped away.

The helicopter, less than thirty feet above the hillside, canted over at a crazy angle as Raymond fought for control. Then, before Collin hit the ground, the vehicle exploded into a raging fireball.

EIGHT
Melville, Montana

It was late afternoon of the second day after the catastrophic raid when Collin recovered his senses and crawled out of the thicket that had saved his life. He found the remains of the helicopter and the bodies of his friends partially buried in the crater the chopper had created when it hit the ground. An attempt had been made to conceal the crash site, and Collin supposed that the wreckage would be very difficult to spot from the air.

He stumbled to the edge of the cliff overlooking the quarry and cautiously peered down. The job here had been much more thorough than that on the helicopter. Not a trace of the battle remained.

The rumble of an aircraft floated to him through the air, and he turned his head in time to see the same unmarked C-47 transport craft that had carried the demon out of Africa rising from a hidden runway several miles away. The demon was fleeing again.

His gaze shifted over to the eerie silhouette of Hotel Earth, framed in blood red against the setting sun. Tomorrow he would go back there, but he knew it would be deserted.

He began to limp slowly along the cliff, seeking a

way down to the road leading to Melville. The Guardian would have examined the charred remains within the chopper and discovered that Collin had somehow escaped. The hunt would be up, he knew. The Guardian would never rest now until Collin was found and destroyed.

No matter how long it would take, someday they would find him. There would be no safe place, and no living soul he could completely trust.

The sun disappeared and Collin was wrapped in darkness as he found the road. Sick, exhausted, and despairing, he limped along the road, realizing that the only course of action open to him was to find the demon again. Find it and somehow put an end to its terrible power.

He paused along the road for a moment, seized by an attack of the dry heaves. He looked up at the stars beginning to appear overhead and thought of the crushing losses he had suffered. Tears sprang from his bleary eyes as he forced himself to get up and continue the journey back to civilization.

Automatically, his pain-drugged brain began to plan his next moves. Collin found a stick to use as a crutch and smiled bitterly to himself. He would not have bet a nickel on his chances.

Sudan, North Africa
Four Days Later

Daniel Hunt was far too preoccupied with the photographs on the table to notice when Hesepti, one of the native diggers, slipped silently through the door behind him. The young Egyptian, clad in a dirty pair of shorts, moved forward soundlessly. When he was directly in back of the seated American he stopped and his left hand reached out hesitantly. His fingers nearly touched the shoulder of the Egyptologist before they paused and dropped away.

"Doctor?"

Hunt jumped as though he had received a high-voltage shock. "Hesepti!" Dan Hunt sighed in relief as he swung around to gaze at the digger. His hand had gone unconsciously to his chest as though to quiet his madly racing heart. "You scared the shit out of me!" Hunt breathed in Egyptian.

Hesepti had taken a quick step backward. "I'm sorry, Doctor," he answered in nearly perfect English. "You seemed so preoccupied I wasn't sure I should disturb you."

Hunt took several deep breaths. The things he had been working on left him profoundly uneasy. Once he had been a man devoid of anxiety, a man of iron nerve capable of venturing alone into the depths of an unexplored tomb in the darkest night. Now, after a year of study in the Ostium temple, he sometimes jumped at his own shadow.

"What is it?"

"A visitor, an American. He has just arrived by jeep from Flax."

"Hmmm." Hunt snorted. The team had made tremendous efforts to downplay the importance of the dig, to keep secret the things they had discovered. Part of Hunt's job as Project Director was to keep people away. "Did he come alone?"

"Yes. It's a strange thing, for him to have driven across desert he does not know, at night." Hesepti reached into his pocket and pulled out a brown manila envelope. "The visitor asked me to give you this."

Hunt accepted the envelope, tore open the seal and extracted a leaf of papers. On top of the stack was a letter of introduction from Mason Raymond. Hunt scanned the text in growing astonishment, then looked up at the Egyptian. "This man's name is Collin, Christopher Collin?"

"Yes. So he says."

"Have a look at his passport. If it checks, bring him to me at once."

Hesepti bowed slightly. "Yes, Doctor." He turned and left as silently as he had come.

As Hunt waited for the arrival of his uninvited guest, he reread Mason Raymond's letter.

Dan,
If you are reading this letter, I must assume that some disaster has overtaken me and I am unable to contact you myself. The gentleman bearing this to you is Christopher Arthur Collin. He is a white American, age twenty-five with dark hair and eyes. He has an identifying birthmark on the top of his left foot. This man has been working with me, and he knows everything about the Ostium dig. It is imperative that you give him your cooperation and assistance. You can trust him with your life. However incredible his story may seem to you, I can assure you that it is factual. I have enclosed a number of documents you will find useful in evaluating our discoveries. Dan, I deeply regret to tell you that as a result of my activities, there is reason to suspect that your life, and the

257

lives of everyone involved in the project, could now be in jeopardy. Collin could be your only hope. Good luck and God bless you; Mason Raymond.

Hunt scrutinized this remarkable letter carefully, realizing that the bold, precise handwriting was unmistakably that of his longtime friend and employer. He had just begun to flip through the rest of the papers when the door to the makeshift laboratory, located just a few hundred feet from the entrance to the Ostium Temple tunnel, swung open to admit Collin.

The two men stood in silence for a moment, examining each other warily under the stark glow of the desk lamps. Collin saw a man of perhaps thirty-five years, bronzed by the desert sun and with a lithe body even more muscular than his own. A touch of sarcastic confidence lurked in the depths of Hunt's now troubled eyes. He, like Doctor Raymond, had once been a military helicopter pilot.

To Daniel Hunt, Collin looked dangerous. He had the cold, menacing aura of a cat at bay. Hunt noted the single appraising glance the visitor had given the laboratory, as though checking it for hidden dangers. Collin was wearing Levi's and a waistcoat permeated with the gritty dust of the desert. He seemed a trifle underdressed for the chill of the desert night.

Hunt broke the silence. "Where is Doctor Raymond?"

Collin turned to be certain the door was closed and that they could not be overheard. "Mason is dead," he said simply. The cold emotionless quality of the voice sent a chill up Hunt's spine.

"How?"

Collin moved closer to Hunt. "He was murdered by the thing that once inhabited that temple out there." He nodded in the direction of the dig.

Hunt opened his mouth and closed it again without having uttered a word. He noticed for the first time that Collin seemed drained, exhausted. His eyes were red and strained. "Sit down, Mr. Collin." Hunt pulled his own chair out from the table.

Collin shook his head. "I would prefer to talk out in the desert. In here there's too much chance of being overheard."

The Egyptologist gazed at his visitor for a long moment, considering. Then he turned and grabbed an old khaki jacket from a peg on the wall. "Let's take a walk," he said.

Apart from the late Doctor Mason Raymond, there were two men on the executive board of the London Archaeological Society who knew the details of the discovery at Ostium. Both of them, Paul Sutcliffe and Merle McElroy, were at that very moment en route from New York City, where they had just attended a conference on ancient languages, to Miami, Florida, where they were scheduled to interview applicants for positions on a new expedition being planned for South America. For the occasion they had chartered a small executive jet, and they flew in the company of several colleagues from Harvard University. Midway through the flight, the four passengers drifted off to a comfortable sleep, each exhausted by their previous day's work.

At 4:05 A.M. the pilot caught his first glimpse of the lights of Miami International Airport through his cockpit window. He radioed for landing clearance and was granted permission for a routine approach to runway one seven, the east-west track. This radio transmission was the last word ever heard from the craft or its occupants. Bewildered flight controller A.J. West noticed suddenly that the small jet veered from its programmed approach and began climbing rapidly. It reached twenty thousand feet and settled into a course almost due east, directly out to sea.

West attempted repeatedly to contact the pilot of the jet, and became alarmed when he received no response. For twenty minutes he persisted in his efforts to communicate with the aircraft, then he contacted authorities at Pensacola Naval Air Station, who dispatched two fighter-interceptors to investigate.

Within thirty minutes, the pilots of the interceptors closed to within visual range of the small charter jet. The sun was just appearing at the horizon as they cruised alongside their target, and they could clearly see the pilot and co-pilot, oddly frozen and motionless at the controls. The passengers, also visible through the oval windows were equally entranced, as though mezmerized. For a full thirty minutes the two Navy jets accompanied the doomed aircraft as it sped ever farther from land. They signalled by dipping their wings, they closed to unsafe distances and attempted to attract the attention of the charter jet's crew, they examined the plane in minute detail. They drew no response from the passengers or crew, and learned nothing of value about the peculiar phenomenon they witnessed.

When the interceptors reached the safe limit of their fuel supply they turned back, leaving the Lear Jet to cruise on, farther and farther out to sea. At 8:14 that morning, the aircraft ran out of fuel and dropped into the chill, churning waters of the Atlantic Ocean, sinking in one hundred and forty fathoms of water. No trace of it, or its unfortunate passengers, was ever found.

"Farther down the passage is the lair itself, and the remains." Hunt remarked, motioning for Collin to look at some of the specimens of human remains that had been brought to the room for study. "We set up the lab here to do our preliminary cataloging and photography." Hunt picked up an open volume from the desk and offered it to Collin, who took it and glanced at pictures of an excavation near the Tigris and Euphrates River system. The two left the room and continued down the main tunnel.

They made their way through a great natural archway and stood before the enormous pit that had once contained the living beast. Collin and Hunt stood at the rim and looked down for several minutes.

A whispy formation of smooth, glassy substance filled most of the bottom of the pit. It resembled swirling formations of solidified volcanic lava. Dusty piles of rotted human bones littered the floor around it. Collin had seen such a lair before.

"What have you learned from the remains?" he asked.

"Very little, I'm afraid. What little is left of organic tissue seems to have undergone a process similar to petrification. It's almost like a fossil." They descended into the pit by means of concrete steps, which had been poured into the sloping wall of the pit, and walked up to confront the remains, illuminated by a battery of giant floodlamps, making it loom, unreal and forboding in the darkness around it.

"I've put together an extremely tentative picture of the animal, working on details with a Doctor Harve Neilson, the biologist assigned to us when we found the remains."

"He knows about this?"

"He regards it as the ancient remains of a long-extinct animal, heretofore unknown. He's tremendously excited about it."

"I should think he would be."

"When I need to bring myself back to the realm of the real world, I try to recall that there have been a number of exotic animals in the world that we have only discovered very recently. The gorilla, for instance, was just a scary rumour for hundreds of years before it was actually discovered at the end of the last century."

"And of course, there are other animals whose existence we have yet to confirm or disprove. Once, while backpacking, I came across an actual footprint of the so-called Bigfoot. I was thirty miles from the nearest road and it was just after a heavy rain. Yet, there was the track. I got a picture of it and found it to be identical to other prints found in California and Utah."

"There you go," nodded Hunt. "Other animals with highly developed camouflage instincts. A biological profile of our friend the Satan-beast would make him a parasite of a new order and genus, possessed of an incredibly long lifespan, probably warm-blooded. Its natural weapons seem to consist entirely of highly developed parapsychological powers; telepathy, image projection, and possession. It relies on camouflage to hide from its enemies and prey, and it seems to have no real natural enemies. It is obviously carnivorous, feeding on the brain cells of its victims. We have no idea whatsoever as to its manner of reproduction, or even if it *does* reproduce in the normal sense of the word. I suspect that a small fragment of the creature's body might have survived the flames in this instance, to be transported elsewhere and nurtured to a mature individual again."

"What makes you say that?"

"Wishful thinking, mostly. I'd like to believe that we're dealing with a single individual, a fluke of nature perhaps. The alternative—"

"Is to suppose that there are more of them around somewhere," Collin finished for him.

"Yes. A sobering thought."

"A very sobering thought, indeed, gentlemen." A voice came from the air behind them and they whirled about. Collin grabbed his automatic pistol from beneath his jacket as he spun, lining it up on the figure he could not see clearly beyond the glare of the bank of lights.

"Don't shoot!" The voice from beyond the floodlights came again as Collin lined up his pistol. He now detected the fact that it was the voice of a woman, speaking in clipped English; a Britisher.

"That voice sounds familiar," Hunt murmured

from beside Collin. "Who's there?" he said.

"It's me, Doctor Hunt, Samantha Egan."

Hunt looked over at Collin. "I know her. She's from the Archaeological Foundation. An anthropologist."

Collin looked over at Hunt skeptically, then looked back at the silhouette. "Come forward slowly, with your hands where I can see them."

The woman moved hesitantly forward into the light of the lamps, her hands held out before her. In one of them she held a manila envelope. Collin studied her carefully. She was rather pretty, in an understated way, with shoulder-length blond hair, tied back. She wore light brown shorts that tended to downplay trim, tanned legs, and a jacket that obscured the shape of her upper body effectively. Her mouth was set in an angry line and her eyes sparked in the lamp, betraying her fury at being held at gunpoint.

Collin looked at Hunt. "Is she a part of your team?"

"No. She's never been to the digs before. But we've worked together in the past. She's one of Mason's technical assistants."

"What are you doing here?" Collin asked coldly, still not lowering his pistol.

She looked at him with equal antagonism. "Put that thing away. You'll need it soon enough, Mister Collin. But not against me." She lowered her hands and stepped forward, despite the fact that Collin kept his pistol trained on her heart. She handed the envelope to Hunt and stepped back. "I've spent the last four months in a small village in Zaire on the instructions of Doctor Mason Raymond." She reached inside the neck of her shirt, a gesture that caused Collin to tighten his grip on the automatic, and then pulled out a chain, from which was suspended a silver medallion identical to the one Smith had carried, and Collin now wore. When he saw it, he instinctively relaxed. It was a talisman against possession.

"Where did you get that?"

She looked at him coolly. "Last August, I received a telephone call from Doctor Raymond. He relieved me of my duties at the institute and literally begged me to take on a rather bizarre assignment. At the time, I knew only the barest details of what had been found here, but Doctor Raymond told me just enough to make me take him seriously when he told me to quit my job and catch the next flight for Zaire." She smiled sadly. "He paid me well, sent me the airline tickets, and opened an account in my name in a Congolese bank. It was of critical importance, he told me, and it was top secret. At this point, I still didn't have any idea what it was all about. I thought we were investigating a new find of great significance, and that we were trying to prevent word getting out before we were sure of our facts."

Collin and Hunt exchanged glances. This was the first knowledge Collin had of any such action on the part of Raymond. "Go on."

"When I arrived at the river village of Gundji, a man met me, a black native ranger. He was a friend of your Ranger Smith's. This man had received a letter from Smith, instructing him to present me to the Chief of the Ngbandi, their tribe. Smith was quite specific. I was to be taken into the tribe fully, cared for and protected as one of them, and I was to be fully initiated into the Spider Cult, taught the secrets of their religious practices. A fascinating opportunity for an anthropologist, I assure you. But it was hard to see the connection between this little tribe in Zaire and the Ostium dig." She walked around and sat on a rock formation. "Fortunately, I had lived for a time in Central Africa while working on my master's thesis. I was able to pick up their language, Ngbgandi-Sango, fairly quickly."

Hunt began to unseal the envelope, without taking his eyes from the woman.

"I learned a very great deal," she went on, "a very great deal. But I did not realize what I was working with until one day they brought me to an old, old man. A man with no eyes." She watched Collin as she spoke this phrase, and smiled at the recognition in his eyes. "Yes, I saw Hasha. I heard his story. That and much more. But they showed me this only after I had been taught how to protect myself. After I had become what you might call a novice in their priesthood."

"Mason and Smith never told me," Collin said slowly.

"I know now that even Smith did not consciously know. Raymond induced Smith to write his letters while in a state of hypnosis. He wanted what you might call an ace in the hole, someone the Anansi couldn't trace, someone whose existence you could never be tortured into revealing. I thought you were dead, Mister Collin, along with Smith and Raymond."

266

"How do you know about us?"

She nodded at the papers Hunt was drawing out of the envelope. "Three days ago, I received that bundle of documents by special courier. As you can see, Dan, the writing is in the language of early Thebes. It's a dead language, not more than a few dozen people in the world can still speak it fluently. I am one of those people. Doctor Raymond was another. He told me everything, your story Mr. Collin, as well as his own. He included photographs of you, maps, and various supporting documents. And perhaps most important, a bankbook for an account set up in my name in a Swiss bank containing nearly half a million dollars, which he quietly diverted from the accounts of the Foundation, and that he augmented with money from his own personal estate, which was not insubstantial." She looked away for a moment. "You see, gentlemen, I worked for Mason Raymond for almost seven years." A tear glistened briefly in her eye. She wiped it savagely and went on. "He had arranged with a private mail service a weekly check-in schedule. If he failed to check in with them they were instructed to forward that package to me immediately in Zaire. Failure to check in, he told me in the letter, could only mean that he was dead."

"Yes," Collin said. "He is."

"Why did you come here?" Daniel Hunt asked.

"Probably for the same reasons Collin did. Doctor Raymond told me that you, Dan, were the only person in the world that I could trust with this."

Collin slowly lowered his pistol and moved over to stare at the papers in Hunt's hands. He looked at Samantha Egan consideringly.

Hunt, who had known and worked with her on several occasions, moved to break the suspicious silence that enveloped Collin and the young woman. "I can't tell you how glad I am to have you here, Sam." He handed the papers to Collin and stepped over to her, taking her two hands in his. "There's a great deal at stake here—it will be good to have you on the team."

Collin flipped through the papers, reassuring himself that the handwriting was Raymond's, then holstering his pistol.

"Oh!" Samantha turned away from Hunt as she focused her attention for the first time on the remains before them. "Is this . . . it?" She walked over to the swirled, shiny black formations that had once been the Satan animal.

"This doesn't bear much resemblance to the living animal," Collin commented sourly.

She ignored him for a few seconds, reaching out to run her fingers along the frozen ridges in subdued fascination. Then his words penetrated into her awareness and she turned toward him somberly. "I had forgotten. You've seen the thing, haven't you?" Her voice held a note of pity.

He didn't answer. Instead he began to move toward the concrete steps that would take him out. "I think I need some air," he said, not unkindly. "As you might imagine, I don't like caves, particularly caves that have been lairs."

Hunt and Egan exchanged resigned looks behind him and followed. "Between the three of us," Hunt remarked, "we ought to be able to come up with *something*."

* * *

After dinner that night, the trio reconvened in the small lab room within the labyrinth of the underground temple. They cleared the books and instruments off one of the large wooden tables and pulled chairs around it, so that they could sit facing each other. Hunt had spent most of the afternoon with Samantha Egan, briefing her on the discoveries at the dig, and just before dinner the two of them had prevailed upon Collin for an account of the circumstances of Doctor Raymond's death. Hunt and Egan had come away from the session deeply shaken by Collin's brief but unsparing narrative, and both of them looked at Collin with unabashed respect afterward. Neither could have conceived the details of his ordeals.

Collin eyed his two companions grimly as they sat down across from him at the table. "You know, Raymond's idea of sending Samantha to Chief Luba was brilliant. Those are the only people on Earth that seem to understand something about the Satan, and they are the only ones who seem to have any conception of how to deal with it." He shook his head and looked directly at the young woman. "It took a lot of guts coming here."

She looked at him expressionlessly. "I sense that now it's time for me to pay my dues to our little group and contribute my stock of knowledge to the collective pool." She picked up a glass of beer Hunt had poured for her and watched as Hunt poured glasses for Collin and himself. The dull metal armband on Hunt's wrist caught her eye. "I can start by explaining to you how these things work." She

269

reached out and touched the armband. "Magic, you see, *real* magic, is not a supernatural phenomenon. The force by which magic operates is supplied by human emotions. This is the core of the secret knowledge of the Ngbgandi-Sango, although I'm not sure they would phrase it like that.

"Doctor Raymond told me in his notes that you, he, and Smith carried out your discussions inside an active Faraday Cage." She smiled. "That may actually have worked for you simply because you believed that it would."

"In any case," Collin said, "I am increasingly convinced that it is dangerous to remain here. I think we ought to relocate. Immediately." He looked at Hunt. "Anything of significance here must already be known to you."

Hunt shook his head. "That's far from true, actually. But I must agree."

Samantha opened her mouth to speak, then paused as they heard the sound of slow, measured footfalls coming toward their chamber along the main passageway.

"Who's there?" Hunt called out.

They waited for several tense heartbeats. Collin was in the act of drawing his automatic and rising from his chair when Hesepti's tenor voice echoed to them. "It's me, Doctor."

Conversation ceased as the footfalls slowly drew closer. At last the trim form of the Egyptian appeared at the entrance to the lab room.

"What is it, Hesepti?" Hunt asked.

In the instant that Hunt asked this question, Collin swung his gaze to the newcomer's face and noted there the same peculiar, strained blankness he had seen on the features of victims of Anansi possession. His memory flashed back in an instant to the shuffling steps of Hesepti as he had approached, and he fit this memory to a mental image of the unnaturally stiff gait of a man under the control of the devil. But before he could act on his sudden certainty of demonic presence, Hesepti answered.

"Just this Doctor." A silenced revolver appeared as if by magic in Hesepti's left hand. Simultaneously Collin felt his ears filled with the dreaded buzzing sound that accompanied the psychic presence of the demon.

Collin sprang to the side at the precise instant that a bullet from the whispering handgun impacted with the arm of his chair. Hunt sat, too stunned to move, his mouth gaping open in astonishment as the Egyptian digger fired twice more at Collin, who rolled and dodged behind a filing cabinet.

Samantha, after a moment's hesitation, rushed at Hesepti from his left side and began to grapple with him for possession of the gun. This brief diversion gave Collin the time he needed to unholster his automatic and line it up.

With a careless, confident gesture, the possessed man flung the woman away from him into the shadows at the far corner of the earthen chamber. Casually, with no sign of outward concern at all, Hesepti turned his attention back to Collin, who crouched behind the cabinet. He sighted along the barrel of the silenced revolver.

At this instant, Collin fired. Once, twice, three times the blood-quenched bullets slammed into the

271

Egyptian's trim torso. The sound of the shots was virtually deafening in the confined space, and the flash of the muzzle was brilliant.

There was no sign in the Egyptian of the nerve shock that would normally have accompanied the impact of the bullets. Instead, death settled slowly upon him, awareness draining from the unnaturally calm features, the gun hand slowly lowering.

None of the three survivors could hear the clatter of the man's body hitting the floor when it finally sank down. Their ears still rang painfully from the gunshots. But Collin could plainly perceive the sudden increase in the intensity of the demonic buzzing in his head.

Suddenly, as he began to move forward from behind the filing cabinet, the lights that illuminated the bloody scene dimmed abruptly, flickered, and faded. The atmosphere grew heavy and chill. Within seconds, in the half-light, a freezing wind gathered from the shadows, swirling papers and bits of refuge from the tables and benches. The three human beings felt the air snatched from their lungs. Something was drawing energy from everything in the room.

Hunt had finally recovered from his shock. He rushed to the light switch and flicked it several times, accomplishing nothing. "What's happening?" he cried to Collin, struggling to keep his fear out of his voice.

Collin looked at him and said nothing. "We must have light. Do you have a lantern or some candles in here?"

Before Hunt could answer, he heard a gasp from

Samantha filter through his distorted hearing over the roar of the unearthly wind. The two men looked over at her, saw that she was staring in horrified fascination at the corpse lying on the floor directly in front of Collin. They looked at it, and felt their blood freeze in their veins.

NINE
Sudan, North Africa
December 2, 1970

The dead man was stirring slowly, methodically. His hands were reaching out, slowly pushing himself up off the floor. Collin fired several more shots into his back, and though this slowed his reanimation, it did not stop him. Slowly, the head lifted so that the face stared directly up at Collin. A horrible, demonic grin, almost unbearably inhuman, rendered the face unrecognizable.

The scene was ghastly beyond endurance, and Hunt backed away with a sharply bitten, "My God!" Hunt's face was as white as that of the zombie. Samantha remained where she was, in the corner of the chamber, and a corner of Collin's consciousness registered her voice mumbling a chant in an African tongue. It sounded like a prayer, a ritual, perhaps a curse. Collin himself did not back up, though he loathed the thing on the floor with all his being.

Fumblingly, with the eyes in that hideous face never leaving Collin's, the possessed creature extended its left hand and searched for the fallen revolver. The gloating, evil smile never faltered, though the face had turned a deep green in the dim, flickering half-light.

Collin kicked the fallen revolver away from the grasping fingers of the zombie, toward Hunt who stooped to pick it up. The thing struggled then to bring himself to an upright posture, but seemed pathetically unable to do this. Collin realized with a flash of insight that his blood-quenched bullets prevented the full revival of the corpse.

Samantha was chanting louder, more confidently, in that ancient tongue, and suddenly the evil face swung from Collin toward the girl, its grimacing grin was replaced in an instant with a contortion of evil hatred. He hissed and spat, causing Samantha to draw back involuntarily.

She faltered in her monologue for a heartbeat, then swallowed hard and gathered her courage. Holding out the medallion, she resumed the chant and slowly advanced toward the thing, which continued to snarl and spit. Plainly it was affected in some way by her actions, for it reacted with increasing violence as she approached.

Collin meanwhile had holstered his weapon and drawn his blood-quenched hunting knife. As the creature's superhuman gaze was locked on the advancing woman, Collin grabbed the hair on the chill, raging head and plunged his blade into the exposed neck. Blood boiled forth, the smell permeating every inch of the poorly ventilated chamber. The jaws continued to work hatefully as the human systematically sliced and hacked his way through the neck of the creature, not pausing until he had severed the head completely from the twitching body.

When the head was separated, the body dropped lifelessly to the stone floor. Collin turned the head around in his two hands and looked down at the face. The three survivors were transfixed in unimaginable horror as the eyes focused directly on Collin's face and the jaw continued to open and close. The severed head smiled once again its horrible smile of contemptuous evil, and the lips moved to form soundless words of revulsion and hate as blood dripped from the base of the skull onto the floor.

It was a moment no human being could experience and remain unaltered. But Collin had been through worse, and he did not release the head. He gazed down with a face that could have been carved from stone and said coldly and quietly, "Fuck you."

The buzzing in his ears reached a terrible crescendo as the lights flickered to near extinction. Then, as though a vacuum pump was suddenly turned off, air, warmth, and light suddenly flooded back into the chamber. The lights returned to their accustomed level of brightness. The three humans took deep breaths. Hunt supported himself against the wall to keep himself upright as he watched Collin calmly drop the motionless skull of the Egyptian digger into a pool of his own blood. Chris took a step, faltered, and grabbed the edge of the conference table, wiping the sweat from his eyes with the back of his right hand; the hand still unconsciously clutching the bloody knife.

He was breathing very deeply, in a state of shock, but he looked around with an unreadable expression to catch the unbelieving eyes of Samantha and

Hunt. Each was subconsciously and automatically evaluating the mental condition of the others.

"We've got to get out of here," Collin gasped.

Samantha looked at him with an ashen face. "Where will we go?"

Collin opened his mouth to answer, but he was cut off by Hunt, who staggered over and sat beside Collin on the table. He was staring down at the floor, seemingly unable to take his eyes from the head. "Zaire," Hunt said with firm certainty. "We'll go to Zaire."

Collin swung his gaze around to Hunt and considered for a moment. His breathing still showed no sign of returning to normal. "Yes. You're right. Maybe we'll have space to breath there. To plan. And to talk to Hasha."

Both men turned to look at Samantha Egan in unspoken inquiry.

She looked from one to the other, a myriad of confused emotions crossing her features. Hunt watched, fascinated in a detached way as she seemed to run the emotional gamut from terror to disbelief to curiosity, and finally to hesitant resolution. "All right," she said at last. She just wanted to get away. She didn't care where. "We'll go back to Zaire."

The three of them linked arms, reassuring each other by physical contact, and with guns at ready they moved slowly out of the dig and into the night air, never to return to the little chamber where the head still lay grinning up at the darkness around it.

It was nearly a week before Collin, Egan, and Hunt reached the river village of Gundji, from which Collin, Smith, and Terry McPhearson had set out on their fateful journey a year and a half earlier. From that point, it was a ten mile trip by jeep into the interior of the rain forest to the village of the Ngbandi tribe.

But when at last they reached the small, formerly tranquil settlement, they were greeted only by death and destruction. Most of the huts had been razed to the ground, and from the remnants tiny spires of smoke still rose lazily. The ground was littered with the bodies of the dead, some horribly mutilated, and try as they might Collin and Hunt could locate not a single survivor of the massacre.

Samantha sat sobbing at the edge of the village as Collin and Hunt returned from their grim survey.

"When did it happen?" she asked, careful not to look at the remains of the people she had come to love.

"Not long ago," Collin answered. "Yesterday morning perhaps."

"Who did this?" She rubbed her face with the sleeve of her shirt, pulling herself together.

Dan and Chris exchanged glances. "It looks as though they . . . they did it to each other," Hunt said slowly.

Egan looked at him uncomprehendingly.

Collin gently put a hand upon her shoulder. "I believe it was possession, on a massive scale. The whole village simply went berserk."

"The . . . the thing?"

Collin nodded.

"But how? Why?" she asked.

Collin pursed his lips. "Back at the dig, you used a chant or prayer. Did you learn it here?"

What blood was left in her trim face slowly drained away as she realized the implications of his question. "Oh my God!" She buried her face in her hands.

"What are you getting at?" Hunt asked.

"It must have recognized the chant, or the language." Collin looked at the destroyed village grimly. "The Satan always seems to move very quickly against anything or anyone demonstrating the power to resist. I think this was its vengeance."

"But how was it done? Do you think the creature has come back to Africa?"

Collin considered for a moment. "No. No, I don't. It took the demon as long to move against the village as it did for us to get here. I think that the Guardian, and perhaps some of the Guardian's people, can act as a relay station of sorts extending the power of the beast over great distances. I think it dispatched someone here, and through that person I think it channeled its power into the village."

"Perhaps we can trace whomever it was," Hunt said. "Check the boats and airlines."

"It's worth a try, but I doubt we'll find anything. Keep in mind that they can travel on any plane, boat, or train without being seen or remembered by *anyone*."

"Then what are we going to do?" Hunt felt the seething desire for vengeance coursing through him for the first time in his life.

Collin shook his head. "I don't know. We've got to find someplace, somewhere, where we can think, plan, sift the data we have. We need a base from which we can begin to search. It will take time to find the thing again." He looked at the girl beside him, who was sobbing quietly, overcome by her sense of guilt. "Think back, Samantha. Is there a clue somewhere among the knowledge you gained from the tribe? Where can we hide? Where can we think without being traced?"

She looked at him for a moment, but he could see that her awareness was directed inward. "There is one thing," she said dully. "It is said, or it *was* said, that in dealing with the Anansi there is safety in numbers. The more people around you, the more difficult it is for the devil to pick out any individual thought. It's as though the beast is deafened by the clamor of all those minds." She looked at Hunt. "The tribe always stayed close together at night. It was more dangerous to be alone."

Hunt and Collin began to guide the shaken woman away from the village and back toward their waiting jeep. They looked at each other as both came up with the same thought. "A big city," Hunt said. Collin nodded. "We'll hide in the middle of the biggest city we can find. And we'll not stay in any one place longer than a few days. That way, we may have a chance." They looked at each other for a moment longer in silence.

"How much money did Raymond leave you in the contingency account?" Collin asked Samantha suddenly.

She looked at him coldly. "Nearly five hundred thousand dollars. Why?"

"I've got about five thousand left over from the cash Raymond supplied to finance our last attack." Collin was speaking to himself, ignoring her question. He turned to Hunt and Samantha.

"I'll need free and unquestioned access to that

money," he said sharply.

"What do you mean?" Egan asked, her pale face was still streaked with tears.

Collin shrugged. "The job of preparing for our next venture is obviously going to fall on me, in terms of the technical details. And since I am the only one whose thoughts are reasonably secure, I want the freedom to procure whatever we need in total secrecy."

"Even from us?" Hunt questioned.

Collin gestured at Hunt's armband. "Those things protect you from possession, but not from telepathy."

Hunt nodded slowly. "So our job will be to find it, and yours will be to prepare for an assault of some kind against the Anansi."

Sam looked from one of them to the other. "I'll go along with it."

Hunt looked at Collin. "We're agreed then."

Collin swung his eyes across the remains of the native village. "Good." He started the jeep and shifted it into reverse, grinding the gears as he did so. He gunned the engine and the jeep lurched back in the direction of the river.

NEW YORK CITY
Three Weeks Later

Collin slid his magnetized passcard into the slot beside the door, then fit his key into the doorknob, calling out softly. "Hey, guys, it's me. Anybody there?"

"Come ahead." It was Samantha's cool voice from

the other side of the door.

Collin pushed it open and stood facing the young woman, who held a thirty-eight special pointed at his midsection. She scrutinized his face for a few seconds, probing for signs of possession, then sighed with relief and let the gun drop to her side. She stepped aside as Collin entered the room and tossed his suitcase into one of the several plush chairs within easy reach.

He was standing in the living room of a condominium unit, the third such accommodation they had occupied since arriving in New York three weeks earlier. Hunt did not even look up as Collin entered; he was sitting hunched over a small computer console, punching keys and studying readouts on a miniature TV monitor. The various components and software of a small computer system occupied haphazard positions on the table and floor around him.

A television set was on in another corner of the living room, and Collin could see the remains of a meal Samantha must have been eating just before he arrived. Her plates and coffee cup sat on top of a large stack of papers resting on the coffee table in front of the TV.

"You're two days late," she said accusingly.

Collin looked at her and shrugged.

"How did it go?"

"I've got a good start on collecting the stuff we'll need. Buying explosives and illegal weapons is a touchy business."

"Where is the stuff?" Hunt asked, still not

282

looking up.

Collin slumped onto the sofa and stared tiredly at the television. "I rented a couple of garages." He grabbed a potato chip from Samantha's dinner plate. "Hey, a vampire movie." He watched the television for a moment, drawn into the scene of a dark-cloaked Dracula being pursued across a fog-shrouded cemetery.

Samantha sat down in a chair across from him, brushing a lock of hair out of her eyes. Collin looked over at her as the movie broke for a commercial. New lines of worry had been added to her face during the last few weeks. He wondered what his own face revealed of his traumatic past. "What's he up to?" Collin nodded over at the preoccupied Egyptologist.

"While you were gone, we came up with a new idea." She pointed at the computer. "Since we already have the machine for the purpose of analyzing missing person data, Dan began to compile data on the past movements of the Satan animal. He's programming the computer with everything we know or can guess about the locations and characteristics of its hideouts. The idea is to find some sort of pattern that will enable us to predict its movements."

Collin shook his head. "Well, that's an idea." He did not sound overly enthusiastic about the prospects. He turned his attention back to the television, to images of the count being cornered in the ruins of a cathedral. After a moment or two, he rose and went into the kitchen, where he grabbed a can of beer from the refrigerator. As he came back to his seat he asked

Samantha, "How long have you been back?"

"I got back yesterday morning."

"Any luck?"

She exhaled slowly. "There are hundreds of demonic cults. It will take months just to get a complete list. As for tracing one particular cult for roots in Montana . . ." She looked as tired as Collin. "But the missing person data is easy to get. I went back through Doctor Raymond's sources."

"Discretely, I hope."

She glared at him for a moment. "The packages will come in to post boxes scattered all over the county."

Collin nodded his approval. "The animal has got to eat. People will disappear wherever it goes to ground."

"I just hope we're right about the animal still being in this country."

Collin watched, fascinated, as Doctor Van Helsing fought off the sinister vampire with a silver cross. "Well," he answered Samantha without looking up. "If it has left the country, it'll take years to find it."

Hunt had first concluded that the Satan animal was still in the United States by a careful check of transportation schedules. He had estimated the travel arrangements by which the Guardian or one of his followers could have made the trip to Zaire from America, and compared that to the elapsed time from the moment that Collin had beheaded the attacking digger in the Sudan. Since international flights into Zaire from America and the European continent are relatively infrequent, Collin had agreed that this method would give an indication that would carry at least some weight.

"Have you got the new alarm system installed?" Collin asked.

"Hunt had that finished before I got back." Samantha got up and stretched her trim body luxuriously, yawning as she did so. Collin paid no attention whatever as she walked across the cluttered living room and out onto the balcony that overlooked the pool. "Let's go for a swim," she said. "I really could use a break."

Neither of her companions appeared to have heard. "Hey," she called out more loudly. "Do either of you want to go swimming?"

Hunt shook his head absently as letters flashed across the blue computer monitor screen. Samantha looked at him in exasperation, then headed for her room. "Well," she said, "I'm going to go."

Collin looked up as she disappeared. "Swimming?" He thought back to the last time he had had any exercise. "Why not?" He rose tiredly from the sofa. "I'll go with you," he called to the woman. He picked up his suitcase and headed for the room he shared with Hunt. Then, as an after thought he returned to the television, watched the vampire for another few seconds, then reached down and clicked the set off.

In another apartment, on the other side of the city, another television displayed the image of the deadly Count Dracula. This dwelling was far more luxurious than the comfortable condominium that served

Collin, Hunt, and Egan as a headquarters-hideout. The motiff was ultramodern, the furniture comfortable beyond belief.

Seated in a plush blood red armchair in front of the television was the man Collin had come to know as the Guardian. He watched the vampire drama unfold on the screen with a boyish fascination equal to Collin's, though perhaps from a different point of view.

A young couple was making violent, sadomasochistic love on a bed in another room, visible through the open door, and others lounged about idly, watching and encouraging the couple. There were fifteen members of the Guardian's entourage with him in the flat, and they had abandoned themselves for the moment to whatever bizzare vices had first drawn them into his family. Sex was the most common, but a number of the disciples indulged in nameless, terribly potent drugs. For some, the panacea was violence. These members were the most valuable, but also the least controllable.

The Guardian had no interest whatsoever in the activities of those around him. Somewhere back in the centuries behind him he had lost the last remnants of sexual desire, and he now found the corrupt, perverted sexual practices of most of his followers mildly disgusting. Many lifetimes ago he had given up his humanity, but he had never lost his personal grace.

"Master?" The Guardian was interrupted by the arrival of a business-suited man in his thirties. The newcomer was slightly on the heavy side, with short hair but overly large sideburns. His name was Weston, and he was a relatively new member of the coven.

"Yes?" The Guardian swung his awesome concentration onto the man, who swallowed nervously. The Guardian had seldom seen such total self-interest in any human face.

"We found one of their hideouts, Master."

"Where?"

"In the suburbs. Across the Lincoln Tunnel."

"And you went there." It was not a question.

Weston gulped. Although he was supposed to have reported directly to the Guardian before taking direct action, he had felt that he could cull more favor with the Master if he could have presented the three cursed ones on a silver platter. "Yes. We went there."

"Obviously, you were too late."

Weston broke into a cold sweat. "They . . . they had moved out the week before. No forwarding address. We . . . interviewed . . . the neighbors. There is no doubt it was them, Master. The two men and the girl."

The Guardian favored the young follower with a glare of amused contempt. "And what did you discover?"

"They have acquired a lot of equipment. They came and went a lot. The Egyptologist, Hunt, is growing a beard."

"How did you locate this hideaway?"

"My team has been checking with the local real estate agents."

The Guardian caught and held the man's mind for

an instant, ready to squash him like a bug. Then, he relaxed. It was the type of show he needed to put on for these fools. "That was good work locating the unit. Continue checking. What is more, check the police stations and private detective agencies in the city. I will send you the power of the prince as before. He will conceal you. He will open the minds of those you question." The Guardian returned his attention to the television, and Weston, relief showing on his sweating features, began to turn away.

"Weston," the Guardian said softly without turning around.

"Master?" The man stopped.

"If ever again you fail to follow my instructions perfectly and to the letter, your blood will be mine. No power on Earth will save you. Do you understand?"

Weston's face was white. "Ye—yes, Master."

"Good. Now go."

Weston stepped around the sprawled, lounging forms of the other disciples of Satan and made his way to the door. He looked back once at the bizarre scene; couples copulating angrily, people disoriented and baying like sheep, small groups in conspiratorial discussions. In the midst of this madness the Guardian sat in withdrawn, almost uncomfortable silence, watching television. He did not seem to fit in. Weston was glad to make his exit, heading out to spread the contagion to the world.

Collin swam about slowly on his back, relaxing in the late afternoon warmth. He rolled over on his side and could not help but admire Samantha's trim figure, revealed nicely in her dark brown one-piece swimsuit, as she climbed out of the pool and walked quickly around to the diving board.

"Lookout," she called. Collin swam a few feet to his left and Samantha gracefully dove back into the pool. She surfaced beside Collin and shook the water out of her eyes. "This is great!" she said, her English accent very pronounced as she relaxed her usual firm control.

Collin smiled.

"I better mark this day on my calendar," Samantha said, swimming in a slow circle around him.

"Why?"

"You actually smiled," she said good-naturedly.

"Am I that bad?"

She pretended to consider for a moment, frowning. "Pretty bad."

He splashed water in her face and laughed. "So, I'm a cad, am I," he said with exaggerated dramatics. "Take that!" He splashed her again and dove under the water to escape her retaliation. In a flash she was after him, swimming as fast as she could as he dodged this way and that.

Finally she cornered him in the deep end, moving slowly in for the kill. "I surrender," he said, gasping for breath and laughing.

She moved her hand into position to splash him. "What will you give me to make me spare you?"

With sudden, lightning speed Collin launched himself through the water and caught the young woman around the waist, swinging her in a slow circle through the water. Her arms went round his neck as he pulled her luxuriously through the water. "What do you want?" he asked quietly. For her it was a surprise to see him so relaxed, so human. For the first time since she had known Collin, his mask seemed to have slipped.

She closed her eyes and relaxed as the water caressed her. "I want an end to all this," she murmured. She looked then at Collin's eyes and saw that the spell had been broken. He released her and swam to the side of the pool. With his arms he raised himself up and sat on the edge, letting his legs dangle into the warm water.

She swam over and pulled herself up beside him, grabbing a towel from one of the lounge chairs. Other than themselves there were only two or three other tenants in the pool area, all of them elderly.

"Are you still planning on going to your brother's wedding next week?" Collin asked her.

She nodded dreamily. "Yes. Life must go on."

He splashed with his foot. "Absolutely." He paused for a comfortable interlude of peaceful silence. "Just be careful."

She looked over at him with an amused smile. "Do you imagine that I won't be? I'm not one of those silly movie heroines who goes up the stairs of the haunted house alone, knowing there's something there waiting."

Collin laughed and lay back on his side, facing her. "Like the girl in the movie this afternoon."

She looked at him with a grimace of distaste. "Oh! That hideous monster movie. I don't know what people see in those things."

He shrugged contentedly. "I've always kinda' enjoyed those Dracula things. Hypnotic power over women . . . eternal life." He grinned.

She laughed with him. "Power over women indeed." She began to dry her hair. "You haven't exactly been out chasing skirts every night."

"Well," he said, "give me a break. I've been a bit preoccupied."

"Do you mean that beneath that cold, forbidding exterior there beats the heart of a lady killer?" Her eyes glinted mischievously.

"In the days of my youth—"

She hit him lightly on the shoulder. "Shut up, old man!" She got up and sat on one of the patio chairs. "How long has it been since you've even been on a date?"

He rolled over and began to get up, grabbing his towel. "Quite a while, I must admit." They began walking toward the elevator. "Seriously," his face took on a serious cast, "I haven't been on a date since the death of my fiancée."

"That was over a year ago, wasn't it?"

He thought a minute as the elevator door shut in front of them. She pushed the button for the third floor. "It hasn't been a year yet. I sort of lose track of the time."

The door opened and they walked down the hall. Samantha knocked on the door in their coded pattern and Hunt let them in. "Have a good swim?" he asked, returning to his computer keyboard.

"It was lovely," Samantha cooed. "You should

291

have come."

Hunt shot Collin an unreadable look, then returned to his work. Collin made his way to his room, thinking that as much as Dan tried to conceal it, he seemed to be in love with Samantha. The two spent a lot of time together, Collin realized. He, himself, was the odd man, the one who was separated from the other two. They knew that he was the only one whose thoughts were really secure from the prying mind of the Satan beast. As effective as their defenses seemed to be against possession, their minds could still be read, their presence sensed. They both realized that for this reason Collin never completely trusted them. The result of this was that he still felt alone in a way.

He had changed into a pair of clean blue jeans when a knock came at the door. "Come in," he said.

Samantha came in, dressed now in shorts and a halter top. She had a bottle of beer in one hand and a backgammon game in the other. "Let's play a game or two." She sat crosslegged on the floor in front of the bed and began to set up the board. There was another television on a dresser nearby, and Collin turned it to a news station.

Samantha looked at him quizzically.

"I just want to see what's going on in the world," he explained sheepishly.

She shook her head. "It's your night off, for God's sake. Forget that and let's play. Here." She handed him her beer and Collin took a drink.

"Okay. Who goes first?" He sat down opposite her.

"We roll, dummy. Don't you know how to play?" She was trying to goad him good-naturedly; he had beaten her the last four times they played.

Collin grumbled and rolled the dice. "Okay, okay. You go first."

She rolled, considered, and moved several of her markers. "You know, we ought to go out to a really great restaurant tomorrow night. We deserve a little enjoyment, after all."

Collin rolled. "Sounds great. There must be hundreds of great places around here."

She rolled again. "Let's go to an Italian place."

Collin took another drink of beer. "Dan hates Italian food."

Samantha moved her markers, counting under her breath. "Then he can stay home." She put down the dice cup and looked up at him. Her hand reached out slowly and rested on his. "We don't have to do everything as a trio, you know."

Collin looked at her for a moment. "Are you asking me for a date?" His eyes twinkled.

She smiled slyly. "I'm just desperate, that's all. I'm dying for an Italian meal. Come on. I've been out with Dan several times, and I'm getting sick of his damn French food."

"Well, with an invitation like that, how can I resist. Are you paying?"

She laughed. "We'll right it off as a tax deduction."

Collin grinned at this. "Very good. Entertainment expenses for the monster hunters."

Samantha reacted unthinkingly to something in his expression. She leaned across the table, knocking the markers helter-skelter, and kissed him on the lips.

For an instant Collin did not move, then he slowly responded, gathering her into a close and passionate embrace. He kissed her again, tenderly but with the pent-up force of his long suppressed emotions. She was overwhelmed by the sheer energy she felt emanating from him.

Hunt's voice came to them excitedly from the living room. "Hey, Chris, Sam, I think I've got something. Look. at this I—" He charged into the room and stopped suddenly, his mouth open in shocked surprise.

The two turned and looked up at him guiltily, as though they had been caught in the act of some unthinkable crime. The look of hurt and rejection in his face was unmistakable. If Collin had needed any confirmation of Hunt's feelings about Samantha, he had it now.

Dan began to speak, closed his mouth and swallowed as Samantha pulled away from Collin. "So," he said, his face reddening. "While I've been in there sweating my brains out over this shit you two have been in here grab-assing!" Dan exclaimed angrily. He threw his collection of computer print-outs across the room and began to pace back and forth, raving as he did so.

"When I think of the hours and hours I've been sitting out there like a dumb shit, beating my head against the wall! You two damn well know how critical all this is. We haven't got any business wasting time on that kind of childish nonsense. Goddamn, I'm surprised at you two!"

Collin and Samantha exchanged looks, both of

them astonished at this bizarre outburst. Dan Hunt had never been other than completely calm and stable throughout their efforts. As Collin and the girl locked eyes, an unspoken message passed between them. Dan was reacting to the terrible stresses they were all being subjected to. Unlike the other two, he had had no outlet. Samantha knew that Dan had barely slept at all for the last four nights.

"Come on now, Dan," Collin said placatingly. "It was nothing to get worked up about." Collin stood up.

This only seemed to arouse more anger in the Egyptologist. He glared at Collin, his strained eyes bloodshot and wild. "I'm not going to have you take advantage of this girl, Goddammit. I know what kind of man you are! A killer! A man with no roots and no hope, nothing left but hate in you. You can't love, and you can't trust, and by heaven I'm not going to let you use this woman, not Samantha. She's too good for that." Hunt was gesturing violently, and Collin could only watch him in shocked disbelief.

Samantha moved toward him, but he hastily backed away. "Can't you see that he just wants to use you?" Hunt asked her desperately, beseechingly.

The girl opened her mouth to answer, but there was no reasoning with him.

Collin had stiffened at Hunt's verbal onslaught. "I don't think you are yourself right now, Dan, so I'll forget you ever said that." He began to move toward the door, trying to edge past the irate Hunt.

"No you don't," Dan grabbed Collin's arm. "I'm

not through yet, Goddammit! I'm telling you that if I catch you near her again—"

Collin shook his arm free easily despite Hunt's best efforts to hold him. "I said you're through!" Collin shouted unexpectedly, his own composure vanishing. "You stupid, blind sonofabitch! Who the fuck do you think you are?" Collin turned away to step through the door, but Hunt abruptly raised his fist and took a wild swing at Chris's face.

The blow never landed. Out of sheer reflex, Collin raised one arm to block the punch and simultaneously struck out with the other arm, landing a perfectly executed counterpunch to his assailant's jaw. Hunt pitched backward over the bed and collapsed in a heap on the carpet.

Samantha stifled a cry, and for an instant she and Chris simply stood dumbfounded, staring down at their friend's bloodied chin.

Then, Collin shook himself out of his shock and cursed. "Goddammit!" He ran to Hunt's side and cradled his head up, wiping at the blood with a handkerchief. "Dan, Dan, I'm sorry," he nearly wailed. "I didn't mean to . . . you took me by surprise. Dan?" Collin gently rocked Hunt's head from side to side, exploring for signs of serious injury.

Hunt moaned and his eyes rolled in his head. "Jesus!" Collin looked over helplessly at Samantha. "I hope to God I didn't hurt him." In a strangely childlike gesture he began to rock his semiconscious friend slowly back and forth, like a mother comforting an infant. "You'll be alright, you'll be alright," he repeated, his eyes closed.

As stunned as Samantha had been to see the confrontation between Hunt and Collin, she was even more astonished to see tears began to roll down Collin's rough cheeks. He was sobbing pathetically, helplessly.

Samantha could not take her eyes off the unbelievable scene, Hunt groaning and stirring slightly, blood dripping slowly from a split lower lip, and Collin completely unmanned.

"You were right in a way, Dan," Collin muttered, still with eyes closed and wet cheeks. "Ever since they got Sandra, my fiancée ... I haven't been ... I haven't been—" He broke down into uncontrollable sobbing.

In that instant, Samantha realized for the first time that she was in love with Collin. In his moment of weakness, when the terrors of his past finally overwhelmed him emotionally, she felt she could glimpse who and what he really was. But in the same instant she perceived that he had not yet really faced the loss of his dead fiancée. He was a man not yet free to love again as he must once have loved. He was not yet free of the devil's curse. She moved to the two men and knelt down beside them. Gently she removed the bloodstained handkerchief from Collin's hand and began to dab at Hunt's face.

"I think he'll be alright," she said patiently, tenderly. She helped Collin stand, and together they lifted Dan and laid him on the bed.

"What, what happened?" Hunt looked up at them uncomprehendingly.

"It's okay," Samantha said.

Dan rubbed his chin and groaned. "God, I sure had that one coming."

Collin pulled himself together. "I can't tell you how sorry I am, Dan. You've worked too hard, I knew that. As for the kiss—" he looked over at Samantha, "that's all it was. I didn't plan it. We've all been working too hard."

"Yeah." Dan worked his jaw and sat up on the bed. "I'm sorry for the things I said. Don't know what got into me." He looked over at Samantha Egan, the remnants of his pain at seeing them together overshadowed by the shame he felt at his behavior. "It was none of my business." He swung his gaze over to Collin. "After everything you've been through, I wouldn't have blamed you for killing me for the things I said."

Another tear flowed down Collin's cheek. The floodgates, once opened, were not easily resealed. He sniffed and tried to smile. "I don't seem to be myself, either, just now Dan." He glanced at Samantha. "Neither of us males put on a very good performance for the lady this evening."

Samantha moved over to Hunt and leaned down, embracing him. "I'm sorry Dan. I've known how you felt and I didn't mean to hurt you. There's too much at stake here to let personal feelings get out of hand." She kissed him on the cheek. "I don't want you to feel that I've rejected you, just because I kissed our grumpy partner, here. But don't ask me to choose between the two of you." She looked at him gently. "Not now."

Hunt smiled somberly. "Hey, I almost forgot what

I came in here for." He twisted around to look for the papers he had scattered all over the floor. "I think I've found something important. When I programmed the computer with every fact and supposition about the known historical movements of the Satan beast; the position of every site tht might possibly have been a diabolical lair, I came up with a pattern to its travels. I can't explain it yet—why it moves according to a set series of distances. But I think I can predict where it went, in a broad sense. You see, it always seems to move in a pattern of two long-distance relocations, say in excess of three thousand miles, followed by a short move, generally not more than a few hundred miles. The next two moves tend to be long ones, followed by a short relocation. This pattern seems to have been repeated four or five times over the last six or eight thousand years. Of course, there are a lot of gaps in the data."

Collin wiped his face with the back of his hand and sat down on the bed beside the other two. "What does it mean?"

"The thing has tendencies, habits. If it is behaving in a manner consistent with its past actions, it will not have moved more than a thousand miles from its previous location. For some reason, it will probably have moved eastward. And I can give you a collective profile of the type of site it will have selected. Its choices of lairs are remarkably consistent, wherever it goes."

"That's fantastic," Collin said.

"You've narrowed the field down to a target area within which to search." Samantha said. "Now it'll just be a matter of time and research."

"Of course, it's based on a lot of speculation. I've read a lot in between the lines of the history books."

"Well," Collin said, "I can't think of anyone better qualified for the job."

"I'll get you an aspirin," Samantha said, getting up and heading for the kitchen.

When she was gone, Hunt looked at Collin. For a split second he was certain that despite the things Samantha had said, she was lost forever to him. Dan found himself wishing that Collin would not survive the inevitable confrontation with the demon. But Daniel Hunt was a fundamentally decent man, and he hated himself for this emotion and quickly set it aside as unacceptable.

Collin set his hand tentatively on Hunt's arm. "I'm sorry, Dan." Hunt realized with a shock that Collin's shame and despair were greater even than his own. Dan reminded himself that Collin had already lost the woman of his dreams to the Satan creature, as well as all of his best friends. Hunt nodded to Collin and returned the strong grip of hands. The wounds remained, but the two men rose above them by force of will and mutual respect.

Samantha returned with a glass of water and a pill. "Take this." She handed them to Dan and watched as he drank it down.

"I've got a whale of a headache," Hunt said after downing the water. He lay back and relaxed against the pillow. "Guess I'm pretty beat." He was fading before their eyes.

"That's damn great work, Dan. I've got most of

300

what we need when we finally find the thing. Guns, gas, explosives, and most of the radio stuff."

Hunt's eyes dropped shut of their own accord. "Good, Chris, good." His voice sounded far away.

Samantha ran a soothing hand over his brow. "We all need rest," she said. "It's tiring work, hunting the world's biggest game."

Collin nodded, mulling her phrase over in his mind. "The world's biggest game," he repeated. "Man's only current natural predator."

Samantha reached down and checked Dan's eyes. "He's asleep," she whispered. She picked up the blanket folded at the end of the bed and covered him with it. Then the two of them quietly rose and left the room, turning off the television and the lights before closing the door.

In the living room Collin slumped into an armchair and sighed heavily. He felt as exhausted as Hunt. He looked at Samantha, who had seated herself on the sofa, and tried to think of something to say. He failed, then turned to look at the time. Still only a little after eight o'clock.

"Are you all right?" Samantha asked, looking at him with concern.

"Me? Of course."

"Don't give me that. You're as human as the rest of us. And you're hurting. I saw that. Before, I thought you were impervious, that you had ice water for blood. I don't know what I thought exactly."

"We've talked about the animal," Collin said slowly. "You know what it is and what it does. You've even seen some pretty terrible manifestations.

301

But you haven't *seen* the thing. you can't really know what I feel."

"I want to try. Tell me."

He looked at her, almost with resentment for a moment. Then he shook his head as though in surrender. "You won't like it."

"I don't care."

"Okay. I feel hate. I hate the thing. Even more than it hates me. And I'm afraid. Twenty-four hours a day I can taste it in my mouth. Sheer terror. I trust no person and no thing, not even you and Dan, completely. I can't. I've seen my best friends corrupted, possessed. I killed a man once who was my best friend, after he had tried to shoot me." Collin shook his head with the memory.

Samantha watched him grimly.

"It's even in my dreams," Collin went on. "Every night of my life it haunts me. My dreams are even worse than the things I've seen in reality, although that scarcely seems possible. And more than anything else, I want revenge. I want to pay it back for all of them, in spades. I want it to know me when I come for it, and I want it to know why when it dies."

"But I know that's not all you feel. You grieve, you grieve for them all. But you never let yourself deal with these feelings."

Collin glared at her. "Oh, I didn't know you were a psychologist, too, Ms. Egan." He caught himself, then smiled apologetically. "I'm sorry. That was unfair and uncalled for. I'm afraid I'm out of the habit of talking to people. Particularly about these things."

She nodded. "I know. Have you ever thought of walking away from all this, while you still can? With your immunity it would probably never find you."

His brow furrowed as he considered this. "No. I have nothing else to live for, I suppose." He smiled to himself. "And to tell you the truth, I suppose that at times I actually enjoy the hunt."

She looked at him silently.

"That must seem strange to you."

Samantha got up and crossed the room, kneeling down beside his chair. "I think you are the most courageous man I've ever known." She spoke simply and honestly.

He looked down at her as though seeing her for the first time. "No," he said sadly. "Just the luckiest to have survived this long."

"Suppose you found something else to live for, Chris? Would you walk away then?"

He ran his hand through his already unruly hair. "You don't have much hope that we're going to kill it, do you?"

She looked up at him and rested her hand on his. "Do you?"

He studied the lines of her face for a moment, unconsciously breathing in the subtle interplay of the scents and sounds of her. "If there's a chance in ten thousand, I'm still going to try," he said softly. "I owe a lot of people. People who aren't here any more to act for themselves."

She leaned up and, for the second time that night, she kissed him passionately, fervently, putting her arms tightly around his neck. He stirred in her arms, returning her kiss with gentle fire. After a moment he pulled away enough to look into her eyes.

"Don't make me fall in love with you, Samantha. Please." Deep in his eyes she could see powerful, nameless forces stirring.

"Why not?" She tried to fathom this mysterious individual, to find the touchstone that would be the key to understanding his strength and his loneliness.

"Because, when the moment comes, I will sacrifice myself, Dan in there, anyone—even you, to get that thing. It's bigger than all of us, this project. You've got to understand that."

She did not pull back as he spoke. "I do understand it," she snapped a trifle irritably. "I know what's at stake. But we've got to live. We've got to maintain our own humanity while we fight it." She reached up and caressed his cheek. "We must take care of each other." She kissed him again and his resistance crumbled. He lifted her gently into the chair with him, kissing her lips, her forehead, running his gentle hands up and down her spine.

"I could love you," he whispered painfully as he held her tightly against him, "if I had the courage."

"You don't have to," she replied. "Just know me for what I am, and let me know you." She kissed him again, running her hands up and down his chest, across the medallion he wore there.

Unbidden by his conscious mind, his hand went to her firm breast, caressing it through the fabric of her shirt. Instincts and emotions he had thought long dead throbbed to life within him and he kissed her again, ardently, feeling her melt into him. He knew he was past the point of no return, and to hell with the consequences. Just as he was about to speak, she stirred in his arms and whispered, "Please, take me to bed, Chris."

He looked at her wordlessly, then they stood up and made their way hand in hand to her bedroom.

TEN
New York City

That night in his dreams, Collin sat once more with Raymond and Smith in a council of war. They all huddled poised over a complex map of the area around the mine outside of Melville, Montana. Smith kept pointing a black finger at the mine entrance and repeating to Collin, "Chris, you are a fool. You have let the demon deceive you like a magician fools a child watching his sleight of hand." Smith's voice was gentle but sad.

"Go back, Collin, go back." Raymond would always add.

"Where?" Collin would ask. But they just kept pointing to the map and repeating the same sentences.

In the morning, when Samantha and Hunt awoke, Collin was long gone. He had caught the 6:45 plane to Montana.

Louisville, Kentucky
Three Weeks Later

Collin brushed the dust from his clothes as he

climbed the steps leading up to the run-down apartment. At the landing he kicked a few old newspapers out of the way and tried the doorbell, which failed to work. He knocked tentatively on the wooden door panel.

A faint stirring reached him from beyond the faded paint of the door, and the knob turned. A variety of old smells rushed out at Chris as the door swung inward, revealing an elderly gentleman dressed in a tee shirt, trousers, and house slippers.

"Yes?" The old man's alert eyes belied the age of his slightly stooped body.

"My name is Collin, Christopher Collin. We spoke on the phone."

"Oh yes." The old man smiled. "You're the young fellow who wants to hire my expertise." He backed away from the door to allow Collin's entrance. "There hasn't been much demand for it lately."

Collin stepped into the house. "I appreciate your taking the time to talk to me."

"Well, young fella'," said the old man, pausing at a worn dining-room table to light a large wooden pipe, "time is something I seem to have on my hands the last few years. Had a lot of time to think since I retired, ten years ago."

Collin noticed several pictures of tall, rugged young men resting on the hearth of an artificial fireplace. "These your sons?"

The old man nodded proudly. "Yep. The one on the left is Michael. He's married. Got two sons of his own. Lives in Buffalo. Gets down to see me once or twice a year. He's in ceramics; didn't want to be a miner like me and my father before me. Now, Chris, that's the one on the right, he was a born mining engineer. He followed my footsteps damn well. Was one of the best in the business."

"Was?"

The old man settled into an old but comfortable easy chair as the pain of an old hurt flashed briefly across his features. "He was killed in the Newhope Mine disaster back in sixty-four. You might remember it. Thirty men died when a section of mine they were working on flooded out suddenly, unexpectedly. He looked sad. "The Newhope was in southern Montana."

Collin nodded. "I know about the accident. I'm sorry, I don't mean to rake up bad memories. I didn't realize that your son was one of the men killed in that accident. But as a matter of fact, it's about the Newhope Mine that I've come to see you. I'm told that you know as much about that mine and the series of caves adjoining it as any man alive."

The old man nodded thoughtfully. "Yep. I guess you could say that's true, now that old Jake's gone; he was the owner of the Newhope. Jake and I worked on that mine for damn close to ten years, extracted almost ten thousand tons of copper before the accident."

"Was the damage to the mine so great that the mine couldn't be operated?"

"Well," the old man lounged back and considered, chewing on the stem of his pipe. "You couldn't say that the flood itself was the direct cause of the closing of the mine. It was the insurance problems afterward that caused Jake's company to go belly up. He was underinsured to begin with, it turned out. The claims just about wiped him out. We were forced to close it down about six months after the disaster."

Collin unrolled a large blueprint he had brought in with him. He spread this out on the coffee table. "Did you ever pump out the flood waters after the accident."

"No, no I don't believe we ever did. Didn't seem to be no point. It was an exploratory shaft, and the water level stabilized before it rose to the upper levels, where it would have been a problem." The old man leaned over and picked up a pair of glasses and a magnifying glass, with which he studied the blueprint. "You really do your homework, don't you young fella'?" He grunted with interest as he studied the drawing. "Yep. This is the Newhope all right. Here's the spur we dug in fifty-six. That's pretty damn complete. Most of the old prints don't even show that. Where'd you get this?"

"Let's just say I had to dig for it." He produced another large blueprint. "Here is a map of the area around the mine. Now when I compared the two, it looked to me like the entrance to this exploratory spur here is located about here. But that can't be because there's a small lake there now." Collin pointed to the matching coordinates on the two documents. The spot was west of a dot marked "Hotel Earth."

The old man studied them for several minutes, chuckling to himself. "Yes, young fella'. You figured right. I used to warn them about this. You see, there were several other companies working these same hills in the sixties. One of them, Columbine, is prob'ly still there now. The other went under a couple years ago when they got caught skimpy on their safety expenditures and environmental controls. Anyway, what happened here is this. You see this large lake up in the high ravine above the Newhope Mine?" It was several miles north of the old hotel.

Collin nodded. "Yes."

"That dam was put in about, oh, twenty-five years ago for the purpose of forming this reservoir as a water source for strip mining. Dangerous as hell, I always thought. Look at what could happen if that old earthen dam were to give way. The water would flood down this ravine, completely drown and flood the Newhope and several other mines along the track, and probably destroy this little town, uh, Melville, which is down somewhere around here." The old man indicated a position just off the paper.

"Yeah," Collin said. "I know about that town."

"Anyway," the other man went on, "I remember when we first started to work the Newhope vein, we used this area here as a slag dump. Anyway, about two years before the accident, we were dynamiting a new core area, right adjacent to one of the most magnificent natural cave sites I've ever seen. It's roughly here in this leg." The old man pointed again. "Anyway, we had a slide on the hill above. Quite a bad one actually. A man was killed as I recall. It filled up the west end of this ravine here, where the small lake is today. You see, it blocked drainage for that section and formed an accidental earthwork. Old Jake just decided to leave it as it was. We couldn't afford to move all those tons of debris. That was a bad mistake, it turned out. Cost my boy his life, and the lives of all those other men."

"You think it was water from this little reservoir that flooded the mine?"

"No doubt about it in my mind. Of course in them days it wasn't quite as obvious as it is today. The water level in this pond wasn't nearly up to the entrance to the secondary leg—we called it shaft forty-three B. I'll never forget that destination. Forty-three B. Where my son died."

Collin paused for a moment, sensing that the old man had withdrawn into himself. Finally, he pointed to another spot on the old mine blueprint. "Now this tunnel here, this is beyond the flooded section. Did it actually connect with the main passage, uh, two A? That's what this shows."

After another moment's reflection the old man nodded. "Yes, I recall that it did go through. In fact, that's how we finally got through to recover the bodies." His face was pinched, bleak. "We never did get them all though. My son's still down there, along with four other good men."

Collin did not let the old man lapse into his grim memories. "So theoretically a man could still get from one tunnel into the other?"

"Well, yes. Although before we closed the mine we took the trouble to board up that junction. We didn't want some poor kid to wander in and drown."

Collin studied the map and blueprint once more, searching his mind for any questions he may have overlooked. "Shaft two A did intersect with the natural cavern shown here, didn't it?"

The old man did not even bother to glance at the

311

blueprint. "Oh, yes. Large, majestic cavern. Miners used to climb in there to eat lunch, sometimes."

"Would you say that these dimensions are correct?"

"Undoubtedly. If my memory serves me rightly."

Collin leaned forward. "Now I'm going to ask you two more questions, that's all. Think carefully, because they're critical. First, would you examine this blueprint as carefully as possible, and mark any errors or omissions with this pencil?"

"Mmmm." The old man bent over the paper and studied it with serious attention. From time to time he'd mutter to himself and amend the lines he saw. Collin watched carefully and noticed that none of the corrections involved sections of the mine that were of critical interest. When the old man had finished Collin leaned back.

"Now, this last question is the most critical. What in your opinion is the present condition of these submerged sections of tunnel?" Collin pointed to the flooded sections in which the old man's son had died.

The old man sat back for a long moment, staring off into space. His pipe had gone out, but he did not seem to notice as he chewed the stem absently. "You know, young fella', I've thought a lot about that over the years. What with my son's body lying there still." He shook his head. "Most of that was dug through contiguous layers of rock, and shored up damn well as I recall. My son did that, and with him safety was the first concern. 'Course I can't be certain, what with the presence of all that water over the years. But barring any major geological activity in the area, I'd say the tunnel is probably intact. It might even be passable, if you was a fish. It'd be dark and dirty as hell, though."

Collin rolled up the two maps, his face not betraying the pleasure he found in the old man's answers.

"Now young fella', you said you was a writer. Are you gon'a tell me why you're interested in all this?"

Collin extracted a manila envelope from his coat pocket. "This should answer all your questions." He handed it to the old man, who slowly opened it and removed a wad of hundred dollar bills.

"There's five thousand dollars there," Collin said, smiling.

The old man was flabbergasted.

"I only ask that for the next thirty days you stick that in the bank or wherever you keep your cash, and keep your mouth shut about this little interview."

The old man looked at him, his eyes sparkling. "You plannin' to reopen the mine? Is that it?"

Collin stood up to leave. "No. As a matter of fact, I'm planning to close it. Forever."

As Collin interviewed the old man in Louisville, in New York Samantha met a short, hyper little man who called himself Denver McGhee. He was one of dozens of contacts she had acquired during the months of investigation that stretched behind her, months spent prying into the secrets of the Satan cults and devil worshipers that existed in the United States as a quiet subculture.

They met at a tacky bar on Fifth Street, and talked for a time over a couple of weak martinis. Underneath her demure expression she found him amusing. He asked the usual questions with even less tact or sincerity than most of the other recruiters she had met. His obvious mocking lust for her was poorly concealed, and her cover story—that she was an amateur witch and occultist seeking initiation into the greater mysteries—was received by Denver without even the barest cross-examination. He obviously thought that she would be a great addition to whatever orgiastic rites of worship this particular cult enjoyed.

The very unprofessionalism of his manner made her tend to think that this was just another blind alley, another group of pathetic hedonists using the name of Satan as an excuse for their own vices. When her obviously eager escort suggested that they drive downtown to the "temple," she sighed inwardly and collected her purse, expecting the evening to progress into the usual scene, with herself firmly bowing out before things got out of hand.

The temple turned out to be a large, country estate located on a small, tree-covered hill on the outskirts of the city. Driving her rented Toyota, she pulled into the long driveway behind Denver's multicolored Cadillac and parked beside a garage containing a variety of expensive and elegant automobiles.

With a degree of gallantry she could never have foreseen, Denver hurried over to her car and opened her door for her, helping her to step out into the well-lit walkway. His manner was far more serious, more controlled than it had been earlier. Even his speech was less affected.

"This is our temple for the time being," Denver was saying. "We've only moved into the area recently and have yet to really find a permanent scene, you know?"

Samantha looked around. "It's lovely, really. I never expected anything like this."

He looked at her self-importantly. "The master does alright by his people." His look was significant. "In the coven, you can have anything you want. Literally anything."

They were up to the door. "The master?" Samantha asked.

The little man nodded definitly. "You'll see." He opened the door and led her inside to one of the most beautifully decorated houses the young anthropologist had ever seen. A long, shiny black Steinway piano occupied an alcove that appeared to be specifically designed for it. The furnishings were uniformly splendid antiques of a period Samantha could not immediately identify. A garden with a beautiful, black bottomed pool could be seen fleetingly through crystal-clear picture windows.

The house was full of people, people who moved slowly and purposefully about. Samantha had seldom seen such a diversity of types, ages, and styles of dress. They were at ease; some reading, some speaking on telephones, and some simply lounging with drinks or books. The scene bore no resemblance to the tacky settings of other covens Samantha had visited.

Denver called to a beautiful black girl, clad in the skimpiest possible bathing suit. "Hey, Jenny, honey, is there any of that left?" He gestured to the liqueur glass in her hand.

She brightened at the sight of him. "Sure is, Denver." She walked up to them, looked cheerily at Samantha. "Who's this?"

Denver smiled. "A newcomer. Jenny Johnson, meet Carol Cooper."

Jenny smiled even more openly. "A pleasure Carol." Her voice was as sensuous and seductive as her body.

"Thank you." Samantha looked around. "This place is certainly . . . magnificent."

Jenny looked around. "It's nice." Her tone implied that it did not measure up to the accommodations the group had grown accustomed to.

Denver had stepped to a lavish wet bar and returned with two full glasses. "Come on." He led her throughout the group, performing introductions. She noted the almost beastial sexual appraisals made of her by most of the male members she met, and indeed by a number of the females.

After a period of small talk during which she described the fictional background that served as her cover in seeking contact with Satan worshipers, Denver led her to an ornate wooden double door.

"What's this?" Samantha asked.

"You're doing real well, babe. Everybody seems to agree you've got potential." He looked her up and down. "Real potential." He leered at her, holding his glass unsteadily. "But now there's someone special I want you to meet." A look of something resembling fear flashed briefly into his eyes.

Samantha swallowed, thinking that perhaps she had finally struck pay dirt. "Who is it?"

"Him." The voice accented the single word emphatically.

"Who? The master?"

Denver shook his head. "No. Not the master. No, the prophet. The master's guardian."

A chill ran up and down the length of Samantha's spine. She made a great effort to retain her composure as Denver reached up and tentatively knocked on the door. A deep, carefully modulated voice said, "Come in."

Denver handed his glass to Samantha and said "Wait here a minute, babe." He appeared to be bracing for an ordeal. He mustered his courage and disappeared through the door.

Samantha found her hands shaking as she evaluated everything she had seen and heard. So much about this particular group was different from the others she had seen. And his reference to the master's guardian!

The great door swung open and Denver appeared, obviously relieved that his brief interview was over. He smiled transparently at Samantha and lifted the glasses from her hands. "Go on in," he said. Then he bent over for a brief, conspiratorial whisper. "Be nice to him. If he likes you, then you're in." He winked at her and walked away, leaving her to move through the doorway and into the room alone.

She braced herself and looked around as she entered the chamber. She found it to be a library, lined with carefully bound books on ornate shelves from floor to ceiling.

The room's only occupant sat in a large leather chair behind an immense oak desk, upon which were scattered a number of books and papers; as though the man had been engaged in deep and careful study before the interruption.

Samantha stepped hesitantly into the glow of a skylight through which the moon shone brightly. The library was otherwise illuminated only by a desk lamp shining on the Guardian's work. Nevertheless the man was clearly visible, and Samantha found herself forming sharp emotional impressions.

He was tall and thin boned, with eyes that betrayed deep intelligence and curiosity but not the faintest trace of evil or malice. She realized with something of a shock that this man was handsome, profoundly so, and there was something in the way he idly held the pen in his hand that bespoke elegance and breeding. In their first instant of eye contact she knew beyond a doubt that he was indeed Collin's mortal enemy, but in that same instant she knew that there was far more beneath the surface of this individual than a perverted, sadistic intellect.

The Guardian meanwhile had watched her carefully as she entered the room. He always watched the new arrivals in this manner, and had acquired the habit of mentally catagorizing them within the first few heartbeats.

Most were so shallow and oblivious that the usual telepathic probings were rendered superfluous. Some, like the psychopath Weston, required a careful weighing of the pros and cons before being admitted

318

to the order.

But this girl, brought in by the ludicrous expimp who called himself Denver, was different. A thousand minutia in her walk and facial expression betrayed her as an impostor. It was obvious to the Guardian, without the use of the extrasensory abilities he had come to rely upon so steadily over the centuries, that this woman knew who and what he was.

He allowed her to stand silently before him for a few moments, noting with hidden approval that she was not goaded by this into premature speech. "Good evening," he said at last.

She almost jumped imperceptibly at the sound of his voice, then swallowed. "Hello."

"My friend Mr. McGhee tells me that you're interested in joining our little family." His voice was soothing, cultivated. The Guardian smiled an unassuming smile.

"Well," she stammered for a moment. "That is, I think so. I'd like to know more about you, of course. But I . . . I certainly am interested."

The Guardian indicated a plush armchair close to the desk. "Please sit down. Since we have no formal rules with respect to who can join us, these little interviews are not much more than formalities. Actually," he said, toying with his pen, "they are more for the purpose of allowing prospective members the opportunity to ask questions than for anything else."

"I see," Samantha said. Despite herself, she found him charming, and found herself relaxing slightly.

She was certain that he had no idea who she really was.

The Guardian picked up a carved cigarette box and offered it out. "Do you wish to smoke?"

She shook her head. "No thanks, I quit some years ago."

"Very wise." He set the box back down on the desk. "You may be wondering who I am." The Guardian smiled again. "I have noticed that my associate Mr. McGhee seems to like to leave me in the roll of a mysterious guru, and he seldom offers proper introductions."

She smiled now in turn. "Well, as a matter of fact, I was wondering—"

"My name is Maximillian Grey." He folded his hands in front of his chest. "During the course of my own highly personal religious pursuits, I seem to have acquired a small following over the years, as you seem to be aware."

"Yes."

"We are informal, lacking any rigid structure such as you find in more conventional religious organizations. Just a group of people united by a common interest and belief in a common idea."

She nodded as he spoke, trying to fit the urbane figure to the image Collin had conveyed of a monstrous, superhuman creature.

"You see Miss . . . I'm sorry, I seem to have forgotten your name—"

She was so at ease that she almost blurted out "Samantha Egan." But she caught herself and said, "Carol Cooper."

"Miss Cooper. You see, the idea of Satan is a very real, very viable one to us. Through the worship of the master, as we know him, the ordinary problems of life are swept away, and the rewards are great, very great." The being who called himself Grey found himself intrigued by the girl. She was far more complex and powerful than the hollow females who usually found their way to his dens. For an instant, he reflected again on the disadvantage that had constantly plagued him: Most of those who were capable of giving themselves to pure and true evil were flawed in some fundamental way. Individuals such as this one crossed his path only as victims. He tried to brush this thought aside as he continued the charade.

"You see Miss . . . Cooper, alliance with the master brings with it real, tangible rewards. Gratification is instant, we do not subsist on promises of a cloudy future existence in some unknowable 'hereafter.'"

"I know something of magic," she said, feeling for direction. "It is the promise of power, real power, which draws me."

As she spoke, the Guardian gently probed her aura, and found her presence awakening responses he had thought long dead. Here was someone who, if he were still mortal, he could have loved. He found himself pleading his case with far more than his usual sincerity. If such a person could join them! How it would magnify the spiritual power of the coven. And he could explore his own inexplicable attraction to her.

"Think of it, Carol. Worlds and powers you have

never conceived in your wildest fantasies lie open to you. Good and evil; these are relative terms. Nothing in this universe is black and white, I assure you. The greatest reward of all is not beyond your grasp if you are willing to reach for it."

She leaned forward, at once frightened and fascinated. "And what is that?"

He looked at her gravely, yet somehow beseechingly. "Immortality. Life. Awareness without limit. This is possible through union with the master."

"Do all your . . . followers . . . receive this gift?"

He laughed gently and shook his head. "No. I'm afraid most human beings are far too flawed to partake of this treasure." He looked at her almost sadly. "But you, if you had the will and heart for it, you might be one of the special ones."

An awkward moment of silence followed. She looked at him searchingly, and for a fleeting instant Maximillian Grey felt that somehow the tables had been turned and it was she who was toying with him.

"What form does your worship take?" she asked at last.

He smiled. "I conduct brief . . . ceremonies . . . whereby the initiated give of their own energies and allegiances to the master. They feel a moment of, uh, contact, shall we say. In return they are given a form of nourishment. And they are given purpose."

"Specifically, what do you do at these ceremonies?"

The Guardian paused, recognizing the tremendous courage required to voice so direct a question under the circumstances. It amused him to wonder what she would do if he told her the truth. He considered this for a moment, then sighed and reminded himself of his duties. "I seldom discuss the details of our rituals with individuals who are not initiates."

She nodded, retaining her composure in a way he had to admire. He was glad his plans did not call for drawing her to the ceremony that night. She interested him more than any person now living, excepting only the enigmatic Collin, and he did not savor the thought of killing her merely for her blood.

Finally she spoke again. "How do I go about becoming an initiate?"

"So you have decided you are interested in pursuing our humble beliefs at greater length?" He smiled yet again. "How splendid." He wrote an address on a pad of paper and tore off the page. "Be at this address next Wednesday, the fourteenth."

"Not here?" she asked, leaning forward to accept the paper.

"We will be moving on to a new accommodation tomorrow, something more private."

"I see." For some reason, a chill ran up her back at these words.

The Guardian stood up, and at his cue Samantha did also. She took his hand and he reached to guide her gracefully to the door. He had kept her only long enough to be certain that she had seen the maps lying openly across his desk top, and had had ample time to read the name stamped plainly on them—"Newhope Mine."

"I can't tell you how much I've enjoyed chatting with you, Carol. I'm pleased and flattered that you might be joining us." He opened the door and beckoned to Denver, who had been waiting just outside. "See Miss Cooper to her car," he said as one would command a dog to fetch.

She turned to the Guardian. His hand, cold but not repellent, still held hers lightly. "Thank you," she said. "Meeting you has been an experience I will never forget."

The Guardian saw that she meant this revealing phrase in many ways, and he smiled. "Until we meet again. Good night." The door was shut and his powerful presence was blocked away from them with the suddenness of a candle being extinguished. It was then that she became aware of an intriguing truth about the Guardian: His presence was most acutely sensed when it was withdrawn.

Six hours after his interview with the old miner, Collin sat alone in a filthy garage he had rented in the outskirts of New York City. A huge truck loomed at rest in the shadows behind him, and his attention was absorbed by a complex jumble of electronic equipment lying in pieces on a wooden workbench. He cursed suddenly, made an adjustment on a partially assembled switch panel, then touched a button on its face. He was rewarded with the sound of an electric motor whirring somewhere on the body of the mammoth truck. Stacks of technical books littered the area around him, and he rummaged for one hurriedly, flipping the pages as he continued the adjustment process.

"Shit!" he exclaimed softly. He picked up a

smouldering soldering iron and completed a circuit connection. Then, after another test, he began securing the switch panel to the briefcase-sized control box.

As he drove in the phillips-head screws he reflected upon the weeks it had taken him to assemble this mass of gear, the incredible expense, and the complexity of his plan.

Collin had staked everything on the apparent dependence of the Guardian on telepathic powers. But in so doing, he realized, he was stretching his technical capabilities far beyond their reasonable limits.

He picked up the grease-smeared receiver of a phone beside him and dialed a number. As the phone at the other end of the line was ringing he continued to fiddle with the circuitboard in his hands. Finally, there was a click and Dan Hunt's voice said, "Hello."

"Dan, this is Chris. You sound tired."

"I am."

"Any results?"

"I'm getting close."

"Good." Collin sighed tiredly. "Things are just about ready on my end. Another few days and all the gear will be finished." He paused and took a swig of beer. "Is Samantha around? Why don't we have dinner out tonight?"

Hunt's jaw dropped. "What? She's on her way to meet you right now in Montana. She left six hours ago!"

Collin set the beer bottle down and gripped the phone tightly. "What the hell are you talking about, Dan?"

Hunt picked up the phone and carried it over to the sofa, where he sat down. He felt his stomach doing flip-flops. Taking a deep breath to calm himself, he asked, "Chris, you *did* call here earlier this afternoon, didn't you?"

Collin frowned. "Dan, believe me I haven't spoken with a living soul for twenty-four hours. What happened?"

Pale-faced, Hunt said, "Wait a minute." With a trembling hand he set the receiver down and walked to the dining-room table. There came a click and a high-pitched squeal as he wound back the cassette tape in the machine into which he had been dictating his notes. He stopped the tape and listened, then rewound for another few seconds. He set the machine to "play" and listened to the metallic reproduction of his own voice droning terse comments about the material under study. After a few moments, he could hear in the background the sound of Samantha opening the front door. His own voice stopped, then a few seconds later said, "I'll get it." Next came the sound of Samantha's books hitting the floor as she accidentally dropped them when the phone rang, followed by Hunt's voice again, saying, "Hello."

Hunt rewound it and played the sequence again, the chill of horror running up and down his spine. No question about it, the sound of the phone ringing was missing from the tape. The first call from Collin had never come through. It had been an illusion.

Quickly, and with growing fear, Hunt fast-forwarded the tape, then played it to check for the ring of the phone he had heard a few moments ago on Collin's second call. It was there plainly on the tape. Hunt breathed a sigh of relief. He returned to the phone.

"Chris, listen to me."

"Dan, what the hell—"

"Just shut up, will you!" Hunt shouted. He wiped the sweat from his forehead. "Sorry, but hear me out. We received a call from you about six hours ago, or at least we thought we did. You tried to convince both of us to meet you in Melville, at that old hotel. You said you'd found something important there, and that you needed Samantha's help. Something about telepathy or some such thing."

"Go on." Collin's voice sounded choked.

"When I told you I was close to a breakthrough with my research, you asked if Samantha would go alone."

"So you actually took the call?"

"I heard the voice at the other end of the phone, if that's what you're getting at. But it makes no difference. You see, there was no call, actually. It was some kind of illusion. My recorder was running and I just listened back. The phone never really rang."

"I see." Collin's mind was racing in despair. "Can we catch her at the airport?"

"Her flight took off hours ago. She's probably already in Montana, somewhere on the highway going north."

"Maybe her flight was delayed. Find out. And check with the car-rental agencies. Maybe we can catch her there. We've got to stop her."

"I'll try." In his heart, he knew it was hopeles. "Why would they want to lure her to Melville?"

"Dan, I found out two weeks ago that the demon has been there all along. Its flight away from the lair after Smith and Raymond died was a trick, a precaution."

Hunt raged, "You fucking bastard! You've known for two goddamn weeks where the thing is, and you never told us?"

"I know how you feel, but there's no time to argue about that now. Cool off and listen, there still may be time to save Samantha."

Hunt fought the anger within him. "Go on."

"Dan, open the back panel on the television. Inside, you'll find an envelope with instructions that were meant for you and Samantha in the event that anything happened to me. They detail a plan of attack I've worked out. Everything you need to know is in that letter."

Collin's thoughts were going a mile a minute. He fought to keep from vomiting as he realized how hopelessly premature this action was going to be. Key pieces of equipment vital to his intricate plans were still unfinished. He kept his terror out of his voice. "Now listen, Dan. The fact that they were able to induce that illusion in you means that they know where you are. You've got to get out of there as soon as possible. Don't stop to destroy anything, don't take anything with you except a gun and some money. Use the escape route we worked out, the condo might be surrounded by now. Everything you need has been set up for you, and the letter will tell you where. But don't even read it until you're safe in a crowd somewhere, where there's less chance of the demon picking up your thoughts."

Hunt was already fumbling with the back of the TV set, the receiver of the phone held against his ear by his shoulder. "I've got the envelope," he said hurriedly, infected by Collin's urgent desperation. "Will we meet—"

"Wait!" Collin hissed. "I hear something. I think someone's outside the door." His voice had dropped to a whisper. "Wait a minute. It could mean trouble." Dan heard the sound of the receiver being gently set down, then a vague fumbling noise barely perceptible over the hum of the phone line.

Seconds passed, then Hunt was stunned by the roar of gunshots, and then a single, bloodcurdling scream of death agony. Even through the distorted medium of the telephone, Hunt had no difficulty identifying the voice as Collin's.

"Chris, Chris!" he called desperately into the phone. There came one final gunshot, which cut the screaming off in mid-cry, and the line went dead in his hand.

Hunt wasted no further time, certain that he was now on his own. He tucked Collin's last instructions into his pocket and moved to the coffee table, upon which rested a thirty-eight caliber revolver. Seizing this, and some extra ammunition, he moved into his room and grabbed his wallet and a black leather jacket.

Finally, he moved to the back of the living room, by the drapes that concealed the sliding glass door leading to the third-story balcony. He reached for the light switch, but before he could touch it he was plunged into pitch blackness; every light in the building seemed to be out, as though someone had pulled the main circuit breaker. Hunt grinned bleakly. It was all to the better for his purposes.

Within seconds he was out the glass door and over the guardrail, shinnying down a thin rope to the cement of the patio below. He made it to the alley before the first of his attackers crashed noisily through the locked condominium door.

Miles away, Collin sat quietly at his bench in the hidden workshop. His automatic was still in his hand, a thin stream of acrid smoke trailing upward from the end of the barrel. The wooden cabinet into which he had fired the shots was a splintered ruin, but his mind failed to register this fact; it was already far away from the convincing performance he had just put on for Hunt's benefit.

Collin was mentally tracing Dan's route through the city to a rented garage on the East Side, a garage containing the carefully prepared array of equipment Hunt would need in order to carry out a frontal assault on the entrance to the lair in the quarry beneath Hotel Earth. Collin tried to calculate whether or not Dan would stick to the instructions. Hunt was in love with Samantha, and he could easily move against the hotel instead of the lair, on the chance that she would still be held in the ominous wooden structure.

Collin shook his head. It was problematical, but it was out of his hands. His gaze took in the mass of equipment around him, alot of which had just been rendered useless. The fact that Samantha was now in the Guardian's hands changed everything.

He stood up and holstered his gun. It would all be improvisation from here. Glancing at his watch, he began to pack. There was so much to do in the few hours he had left.

The sun had long since disappeared when Samantha pulled up the long driveway to the hotel. No lights burned within, and from what little she could see as she got out of her car the place was as deserted as Collin had said it would be. She saw the yellow sedan that Collin said he had rented parked on the other side of the dirt lot. Leaving the headlights of her own vehicle on, she took a flashlight from her purse and walked over to the yellow car. She saw the passenger door was open as she approached.

Something felt wrong in the atmosphere, a kind of spiritual chill that her Africa-trained senses recognized as a sign of demonic presence.

The wind blowing up from the plains moaned and whispered in the unnatural stillness of the shrubs, and the loneliness of her position was almost overwhelming. Unbidden, her hand went to her purse and extracted the pistol she had concealed in her suitcase during the flight.

Her flashlight beam played back and forth over the car, which was unoccupied. But she could not stifle a sudden gasp as she sighted a small puddle of some dried liquid on the front seat. Almost certainly blood, she realized.

She leaned over and aimed her light into the back, and drew back in horror at the sight revealed then. The body of a little girl, not more than four or five years old, lay stretched out on the back seat. She was nude, and in the space where her chest should have been a great cavity had been opened up, revealing rows of cracked ribs. The little girl's living heart had been torn out, and her throat cut from ear to ear.

Samantha turned away and vomited immediately, her composure totally shattered. She backed away from the death-car, breathing raggedly. The wind had stopped completely, and the stillness was more threatening than any sound could possibly have been.

Somewhere in the night an animal howled. She spun to face the darkness to the north of the massive, looming walls of the old hotel. Her flashlight beam was a puny weapon against the impenetrable darkness.

The next sound she heard came from her right. It was the sound of her rented car being started. The engine turned over twice and the headlights dimmed, then the motor began to run smoothly.

Paralyzed with fear, she stood watching as the vehicle backed up and turned, shining its headlights directly into her eyes. When she heard the gears being shifted out of reverse, she raised her pistol with unnatural calm, sighted on the blackness behind the windshield, and began to fire.

Once, twice, and the engine was gunned viciously. The car squealed and leapt forward, straight for the girl. Samantha held her ground for an instant, letting off one last shot that she was sure shattered the windscreen directly in the face of whomever was driving the car.

She dove to one side as the car rushed by her, her beaten mind frozen with a new agony. She had glimpsed, for one brief instant, the face of the driver, glaringly illuminated by some chance reflection of the headlights. Sitting with a mocking, demonic grin behind the wheel she had seen the moldering corpse of Mason Raymond, most of the flesh decayed but still horribly recognizable.

The car was coming around again for another run at her. She scrambled to her feet, clutching the gun and flashlight, and made a dash for the hotel. The rented car swerved as she ran to evade it, and almost hit her. But this time the corpse behind the wheel had extended its rigored arm out the driver's window.

Samantha felt something clutch her behind the neck as the car whooshed by, and she reached around in panic to dislodge whatever it was that was gripping her so tightly. She managed to knock it loose and trained her light on it. There, writhing toward her in the light, was the decayed forearm and hand of the corpse.

Samantha was beyond screaming. She turned and fled in the only direction open to her, toward the great black shadow of the desolate hotel.

Her footsteps echoed hollowly on the creaky steps as she approached the doors. One was slightly ajar, but she paused, repelled by the presence she could sense lurking somewhere within. She turned around to look at the maniacal car, still running in crazed circles in front of the hotel, and determined to stay exactly where she was. Sooner or later, either daylight would come, or the vehicle would run out of gas.

At that moment, a terrible scream echoed out from somewhere inside the hotel. It was the sound of a man in agony, begging for help, tormented past any sane endurance.

In shock and horror she recognized the voice as Collin's. He must have come before she arrived and been captured by the Anansi's sadistic cultists.

The screams continued and Samantha could not ignore them. Mustering every reserve of courage, she raised her pistol and stepped through the doorway into the lobby of the old hotel.

There was a strong wind blowing inside the place, a wind far stronger than the breezes that had prevailed outside. It ruffled the dusty, rotting curtains that writhed out from the windowsills. Her wandering flashlight beam exposed the huddled shapes of sofas, chairs, and marble tables littered with old newspapers.

She took one step, then another, while all the while the screaming continued. The screams were coming from upstairs, so she directed her steps toward the velvet carpet of the wide stairway that curved upward. Around her, the house shifted and groaned, as though some incredibly heavy creature stalked the halls.

As she neared the top of the staircase, Collin's screams were so racked with agony that she could scarcely bear to hear them, and the effect on her nervous system was so devastating that she found herself on the verge of blacking out.

Samantha counted the times she had fired her pistol in the lot outside, vowing to herself that she would save one bullet for herself.

She moved along the hallway, passed dark rooms with doors half-open, guided only by the tiny circle of light provided by her small flashlight. Nothing could have been more agonizing than the nightmare journey she made through the blackness toward the sound of Collin's dying cries, through the passages of the macabre structure that she knew was infected with the most hideous evil.

She passed the open doors of three silent rooms and neared a fourth when the screaming suddenly stopped. She halted her shaking steps, pointing her light beam ahead of her at the seemingly endless row of gaping doorways.

From somewhere deep inside her came a sudden insight, the knowledge that even if she were to miraculously survive this night, her life could never be the same. She was too close to evil to emerge unchanged.

She took a step, then another, and the wind resumed, streaming at her from the unseen depths of the hallway. Samantha was approaching another doorway, this one with its door open no more than a few inches, revealing only blackness beyond the threshold. Though she was on the third floor, the number on the door panel appeared to be 666, the number of the devil.

She paused in her advance and played the light around the opening, distrusting this room instinctively.

Taking a deep breath, she placed her palm against

the door and slowly pushed.

With a groaning creak, the door swung away from her hand, and there, revealed in the white glow of her flashlight, stood the most horrible sight she had ever seen in her life. Fangs protruded from the deformed upper lip of the thing, its rotten flesh puffed and putrified. Its skull was a boney ridge from which decayed flaps of skin dangled. The humanoid thing hissed at her like a snake and sprang forth out of the shadows with clawed hands upraised.

Samantha screamed and sank back, firing her pistol in a reflex action as she ran unthinkingly farther down the hall. She reached the end of the hallway before she even realized she was running, and she paused at the open door to the room in which the screams must have originated.

She scanned the area behind her with the light, but there was no sign of the nightmare apparition that had attacked. She recalled that the bullets in her gun had been heated and quenched in human blood, and speculated with a part of her mind that they might therefore have been effective against such a monstrous being.

Feeling compelled to act, Samantha burst into the terrible room at the end of the hall, shining her light frantically in all directions and waving her pistol threateningly.

She had expected to find some horrible scene of torture and depravity, but the room was empty. A bed, carefully made up, rested in one corner, and a breeze blew in from an open window. A door leading to a bathroom was open and she walked across the room with quivering steps.

"Chris?" she called softly. Taking a deep breath, she moved into the bathroom and looked around. It was empty.

She moved back into the unoccupied room and made one more sweeping circle with her light. Still nothing.

For a heartbeat, she pondered her situation. It was possible she had been mistaken about the source of the screaming. Possible, but not that likely. Samantha realized that her mind would not stand the strain of searching the entire hotel. Further, since the cries had stopped, Chris was probably dead and there was nothing she could do for him in that event. A detached part of her deep inside began to wail at this realization. She was in love with Christopher Collin.

Her decision was to get out of the hotel, back to the relative safety of the open air.

She had taken her first steps back toward the hall when she heard the faint shuffling noise. It was coming from the closet.

"Chris?" she called again.

This time she heard a faint murmur of pain and she was convinced that she had finally found him. "Chris!" she hissed. Samantha took three quick paces across the room and grasped the handle of the closet door. Tightening her grip on the gun, she slowly turned the handle and pulled the heavy door outward.

She gasped at the sight revealed to her then, for it was her own mother, a women twelve years dead from cancer, which huddled in the darkness, impaled on a sharp metal pole that had been forced into her body at the anus and ran up the length of her spine, protruding out beside her collarbone.

Samantha's mother looked much younger than she had during the months before she died, but her skin was virtually chalk white in the flashlight's beam. Except for her face; that was deep green. The expression in her eyes was truly evil; demonic. Her mouth, which was twisted into a hideous smile, was rimmed with bright scarlet. The apparition looked up at Samantha and smiled even more widely, showing no sign of squinting at the bright light shining into her inhuman eyes. A sharply pointed tongue flicked out to lick the moist bloody lips.

"Hello, my daughter." Her voice was a rough, masculine rasp with overtones that spoke of sadistic cruelty.

Samantha drew away in horror, and the thing impaled in the closet suddenly drew back its head and vomited a gushing stream of steaming blood across the room, striking Samantha full in the face and soaking the front of her jacket.

She turned then, mindlessly, to run from the thing she could not bear to see, but the light on the nightstand by the bed sprang on, emitting a pale but adequate light, and she was confronted by the monster from the hall, blocking the doorway. It hissed again, as it had the instant she'd confronted it in the doorway. Then it raised its clawed hands and advanced. She slowly backed into the one corner from which nothing threatened her.

She dropped the now useless flashlight and brought the gun up, aware that she had just two bullets left, and that one must be saved for herself. There would be no time to reload.

Samantha sighted shakily on the chest of the nightmare figure and forced herself to take a slow breath in order to be sure of her aim. She fired, but to her horror the shot had no effect.

Samantha brought the barrel of the pistol up to her head, tears springing from the bright eyes that had once seen the good things of the earth. Then, as her finger tightened on the trigger, her left hand went unbidden to the silver medallion she had been given by the village priestess in Africa, and her lips began to form the words of the chant designed to break the power of evil sendings. Her mind reacted to the words, seized upon them as she began to rebuild her shattered will.

It dawned on her for the first time that what she was seeing and had seen could not possibly be real, that she was dealing with a creature known to be able to induce hallucinations in its victims as a matter of course. She had foolishly thought herself immune to its power by virtue of her priestess training, but now she realized that she was going to have to fight for reality if she was to save her life.

With a spark of defiance she began the ritual chant, moving with her body and drawing symbols in the air. She stood up proudly and disdainfully, giving no ground at all as the fanged half-man from the hall closed to within a few feet from her corner.

A huge roaring sound filled the room, and she realized that it was the cry of the demon she was hearing; not with her ears but with her mind. The wind became a hurricane, whirling the furniture around the room and threatening to tear the clothes from her body.

340

Still she chanted, weaving a spell of magic that had power because of her committed belief.

A clawed hand raised to strike her and fangs poised to spring. Samantha knew that if it struck before she finished the spell she would die horribly. The mocking laugh of the thing in the closet shattered every bit of glass in the room.

Ignoring them, she completed the ritual, feeling a power within herself unlike anything she had experienced before. As she uttered the last words and drew the last symbols, her enemy struck.

But in the striking, it vanished, as did the creature in the closet, evaporated into the night like the phantoms they were. Samantha stood alone, exhausted but defiant, gasping for air to fill her starved lungs.

"So," a gentle voice floated to her from the doorway and she turned to see the Guardin leaning against the jamb. "Very well done, Samantha Egan."

She looked over at him, her composure unruffled. She was tasting for the first time a sense of personal power unlike anything she had ever imagined. Even the Guardian could not strike fear into her heart in that moment.

"You have been in the crucible and survived." The Guardian spoke again, overtones of respect apparent in his voice. "I would not have imagined that the training of the priestesses could have been so effective. We were right to destroy the tribe."

"Why did you do this to me?"

The Guardian smiled peacefully, no remote hint of malice or mockery in his tone. "I myself underwent such a trial, many centuries ago. I know how it felt, and what you are feeling now."

"You went through this?"

He nodded. "When I was human. It was the first of many steps to becoming what I am now."

She considered this, and he read her racing thoughts. "No," he said, "we do not intend to make a Guardian of you. You have the power, but not the . . . detachment for it."

She looked puzzled but still not threatened. "Then why?"

Maximillian Grey sighed. "Several reasons. With you here, your friends will be forced to move before they are ready. Also, we truly wanted to test the powers of the human race to resist the master." The Guardian looked at her with genuine sympathy in his eyes. "And also, we wanted to strengthen you, to awake the psychic force buried beneath the surface. The stronger the mind, the greater the—shall we say—delicacy provided to the master. You will be a rare pleasure for him."

This time horror showed on her features. "But—"

The Guardian stepped aside and allowed a shorter, stocky man to step into the room. "This is Weston, one of my followers. He is a psychopathic killer, and his job for the next few hours will be to see that you do not leave this room for any reason. He is instructed to kill you only if it is unavoidable. But if he is forced to take action, he has been told to destroy you by methods even more unpleasant than those employed by the master." The Guardian looked with distaste at Weston. "He is also a sexual deviant, but he has been forbidden to touch you unless you try to escape, or attempt suicide."

She looked at Weston, armed as he was with a long knife, and shuddered. Her bladder, which had held fast throughout her inhuman ordeal, suddenly gave way and warm urine flooded her Levi jeans. She looked at the Guardian defiantly, but his look conveyed neither derision nor amusement.

"What about Chris?" she asked suddenly.

"Collin?" The Guardian frowned. "That devious creature was never here, my dear. Your friend Hunt seems to be certain that Collin is dead, but the circumstances of his passing are obscure, particularly so since none of my operatives have reported locating him. A puzzle, for the moment." The Guardian went to the window and looked out. "Your friend Hunt is on his way to the quarry." He laughed softly. "The supposedly late Chris Collin has cleverly laid out a plan the details of which even Hunt doesn't know. He just follows instructions as he goes along. Brilliant." He turned and smiled again at Samantha. "There is a passage leading down through the cliff to the tunnels of the lair below. I'd best go and prepare things. It will be an exciting night, my dear." The Guardian turned gracefully and left the room.

Samantha stood, shuddering in the delayed reaction that was inevitable after her ordeal. She looked for an instant into the lust-filled, murderous eyes of the monstrous Weston, then sat down heavily on the bed and began to weep.

At that very moment, Daniel Hunt crouched behind the concealment of a large tree and studied a map with the aid of a hooded penlight flash. It had been nearly an hour since he had set the helicopter down at the hillside landing site Collin had specified in his detailed instructions. Ever since, Hunt had been skulking steadily through the nearly pitch black night toward another point, several miles from the quarry, beneath Hotel Earth, which housed the lair of the Anansi.

Since he read and implemented his instructions sequentially, with no knowledge of what he was going to be doing next, Hunt had no idea what awaited him at his destination. He calculated that he must be very close to it, but he did not know what to look for.

With a last look at the map, Hunt extinguished the light, took up his automatic rifle and headed out into the night, trying to move as soundlessly as possible. Within several minutes, he literally stumbled onto his goal.

It was a very large truck, camouflaged on all four sides with dense brush, so that it would have been invisible from the road that ran a few hundred yards to the south even in broad daylight. Before taking any action, Hunt crouched down and dug out Collin's instructions, which informed him that the cab of the vehicle had been reinforced with bullet-proof steel plates, and that the windshield had been replaced with bulletproof glass. In short, the massive armored flatbed had been converted into an assault vehicle.

In accordance with Chris Collin's step by step plan, Hunt tore away enough of the concealing foliage to allow him to swing open the massive door. He stepped up into the cab and sat behind the wheel. His instructions from this point were simple.

Hunt started the engine with a brief touch of the starter switch, and was impressed with the smooth and silent operation of the engine. Collin had mentioned that the motor had been carefully muffled, but Hunt had not expected the silencing equipment to work so well. From this point, he had only to drive the truck along the mine's access road, crash through the barbed wire gate at the entrance of the quarry, and run the truck through any opposition, directly into the mouth of the mine entrance. There were three toggle switches Hunt was to throw at various stages of the invasion, but as yet Dan had no idea what their functions might be.

He put the truck in gear and drove forward, plowing through the massed protective underbrush surrounding the vehicle as if it did not exist. In a matter of seconds, it seemed, he was on the access road, where he brought the speed up to thirty-five miles an hour; as fast as he dared travel without the use of headlights.

As he neared the area of the mine, Hunt wondered what provisions, if any, Collin had made for the escape of the truck driver once the truck was delivered to its target.

Suddenly, the road ahead was illuminated and Hunt could see the outline of a large gate, with a guardhouse to one side. Small red flashes appeared from the guardhouse, followed by the sound of bullets bouncing harmlessly off the skin of the truck. Hunt leaned down and pulled the headlight switch; there was no longer any need to travel in darkness.

The truck was through the gate with no apparent break in its smooth momentum. The road continued at an uphill slant, leading directly to the gaping tunnel entrance leading to the demon's lair, but midway up the slight hill a line of oil drums had been set up, and Hunt could make out the forms of armed men lurking behind them. He pressed the accelerator to the floor.

Bullets were impacting on the windscreen and cab walls constantly now, making a ringing sound like metallic popcorn. Hunt leaned over and flipped the first of the three jury-rigged toggle switches, and a cassette machine on the seat beside him began to play. Collin's voice was barely audible over the sound of the gunfire.

"There are two gas masks in the glove compartment," the recording stated. "Put them on."

Hunt realized that when Collin had set up his elaborate scheme he had anticipated that both Hunt and Samantha would be in the cab. Dan had difficulty driving the truck and leaning across to grab the masks. The vehicle swerved as he fought to get one of them over his head. The line of oil drums was within a hundred feet now, and Hunt could see the faces of the bizarre group of defenders who huddled behind them, their eyes squinting in the glare of his headlights.

They were a cadaverous lot, some of them obviously moving with the stiff gate of demonic possession, while others seemed more lively. Hunt guessed correctly that they were a mixture of the cultists and the possessed legions of the Anansi.

With a crunching, jarring impact, the truck collided with the oil drums, crushing some and scattering others wildly. Hunt immediately leaned over and flipped the second toggle switch. From somewhere on the shielded flatbed space four make-shift bombs were flung in four directions, wreaking havoc on the groups of possessed men and women who were converging on the path of the invading truck.

A final group of a dozen of the enemy stood directly in front of the tunnel entrance, firing steadily with rifles at the cab. Hunt drove right over them when they refused to give way, watching in fascinated horror as their skulls ruptured under the advancing wheels.

Within a few seconds, he was inside the wide tunnel, driving over the rail lines that had once served the mining company responsible for having dug the labyrinth.

To his terror he perceived, lined up like a waiting army, scores of possessed figures—a mixture of races and cultures ranging from African tribesmen to men in the uniforms of state police. They moved slowly but threateningly toward the still moving truck, as though by their puny efforts they would halt it. Sickened, Dan drove over the first rows, having been instructed by Collin to be certain the entire body of the vehicle was well inside the mine.

He stopped at last, his glaring headlights illuminating the frightful sight of the emaciated army that swarmed over the truck. Several of them sneered and hissed at him, climbing up to press their faces against the bullet-scarred glass of the windshield.

He pressed the third switch quickly, and braced himself for whatever might follow. At first, nothing happened, and Hunt wondered if the mechanism of the truck had been damaged in the assault. But then, he perceived a cloud of heavy white vapor billowing out from the rear portion of the flatbed.

The gas enveloped everything in the tunnel, flooding out in an incredible torrent. Those it enclosed gasped painfully, convulsed, then collapsed. Whatever the gas was, Hunt thought, it killed very quickly.

In a matter of seconds, the high-pressure streams of gas completely filled the passage, obscuring everything from Hunt's eyes. It would be like driving through a very dense fog.

He did not know how long he waited there, but after a time the gas settled close to the ground and hung there, at knee level, writhing in the air currents like a living ocean of death.

Hunt read Collin's final page of instructions. A pack of gas grenades had been provided. Dan was directed to leave the truck and proceed on foot to make sure the gas had done its job on the demon.

Hunt grabbed the pack of grenades and opened the door. Very cautiously he stepped down and surveyed his surroundings, afraid of a trap. Standing in the death fog he saw only the huddled forms of the fallen legion protruding here and there from the white mist.

Acting on Collin's last direction, Hunt turned and locked the door of the cab, pocketing the key.

The headlights stabbed out like twin laser beams in a science fiction film, pointing the way deeper into the labyrinth. With a trembling breath, Hunt raised his automatic rifle and set out alone toward the horror that awaited in the darkness beyond.

*　　*　　*

From its position on the hilltop overlooking the quarry and mine entrance a half-mile away, the delapidated upper floors of Hotel Earth offered a spectacular view of the fiery assault affected by Hunt. Spellbound, Samantha stood side by side with the psychopath Weston, and both of them stared out the window at the conflagration below.

When the flames of the explosions had died away and the truck disappeared into the mountainside, the area below was too dark to allow the two watchers to determine the outcome of the struggle. She realized he was standing close beside her, and she quickly backed away from the window.

Weston followed her with his eyes, but said nothing. He had not spoken at all since having first -been stationed in the room. But his sadistic hunger for her radiated from him in waves that sent chills of horror running through her body like electric shocks. Mustering her courage, she made her only play for escape, having come to the conclusion that she would surely die if she did nothing to save herself.

"I know I'm going to die soon," she said softly, looking straight into Weston's two-dimensional eyes. She sat back on the bed. "I . . . I don't know how to say this, but," she gave him a shy look, "I'm a virgin, you know. All these years saving myself for the right man, the special man. Someone I'll never meet, now." She stretched out in a subtly provocative, vulnerable posture. "I never wanted to die a virgin . . . never to know what it is like to . . . to make love," she said the last words in a husky, ashamed whisper, glancing at him sidewise like a frightened little girl.

Weston smiled for the first time. Looking down through the window, he tried to calculate how fully the Guardian's attention would be engaged in the lair below. It was tempting, he thought, so very tempting. Still undecided, he took a step closer to the girl, then another.

She sat still, totally so, as he moved up to her. She could not risk looking up at him lest her eyes betray her disgust and loathing.

She felt the warmth of his approaching hand as it reached out to roughly unfasten the top button of her shirt. She barely repressed an involuntary shudder as his trembling fingers moved down to the next, exposing the smooth skin of her left breast.

He began to reach for it, roughly, and she exploded into desperate action, striking with all her strength at his crotch. She ducked just in time to avoid the savage swing of Weston's knife, then rolled away, grabbing her own discarded gun.

The man was doubled up in agony, eyeing her with a terrible hatred. She wasted no time trying to further immobilize him. Samantha was out the door and into the pitch blackness of the hall in less than a heartbeat.

Heedless of anything that might lurk in the darkness, she careened down the passage way, tripped once, then raced down the wide staircase to the lobby, operating on memory alone to guide her through the total darkness.

To her dismay, the great front doors were securely locked, and try as she might she could not get them to open. She heard the sound of running feet on the landing above and turned away, racing across the lobby to a door she had noticed on her way in. She eased through the door and shut it soundlessly, relieved to find there was a small amount of light here, provided by a candle somewhere beyond.

She was in a descending passage traversed by wooden steps that led to a wine cellar. She moved quickly into it, unaware that she was in the spot where Collin and Raymond had first confronted the Guardian. She moved past the rows of bottle racks, out into the floorspace that still harbored the five-pointed star of the Guardian's ceremonies. Picking up the candle that burned at the nearest point of the star, she explored the room, which she calculated to be underground. In one obscure corner, she came upon yet another descending passage, one that appeared to be freshly dug. Samantha was certain this was the connecting tunnel the Guardian had mentioned, linking the hotel to the lair far below. She hefted her pistol and realized she had only one shot left.

Despite the constant shaking of her hands, she quickly reloaded the weapon with spare cartridges from her pockets. Then, she plunged down into the depths, determined to help Hunt if he were still alive.

The passage was featureless and seemingly without end. Obviously it had very recently been carved from the rock of the mountainside. As she made her way down quickly but carefully, she wondered how the work had been accomplished.

The smell of the air around her began to thicken unpleasantly, and with every downward step her feeling of fear increased as she sensed the presence somewhere ahead of the demon Anansi.

The light cast by her small, flickering candle was so weak that she could not see more than five or six feet in either direction. But suddenly she became aware of a dull glow coming from somewhere beyond the reach of her candle flame. The glow was intermittent, but as she watched it became brighter. Someone was coming up, someone with a flashlight in his hand.

Instantly she pinched the wick of the candle and the fire hissed out, plunging her into darkness. She flattened herself against a depression in one wall and waited as the figure advanced. Trying to still her ragged breathing, she lined her pistol up on the form behind the blinding light.

When it was twenty-five feet away, moving furtively and quietly, she glimpsed the monstrous face of the man; large reflecting eyes and a corrugated snout that hung down across his chest like an elephant's trunk. She did not want to see the thing in any greater detail.

Any second now the light would expose her. She slowly tightened her finger on the trigger.

Then, an instant before the gun would have discharged, the figure slipped on a loose rock and the flashlight slipped from its grasp.

"Shit," the figure hissed almost inaudibly. A long arm reached for the flashlight, and for an instant the entire body was clearly illuminated as it picked the tool up. Samantha saw the gas mask and Dan Hunt's familiar black jacket. Her gun dropped to her side and she cried out in agonized relief.

"Dan!"

Hunt looked up quickly and extinguished the light. His voice came from a different point a second later. "Samantha? Is that you?"

"Here," she called softly, her caution returning. The light stabbed directly into her eyes, and she squinted blindly. A second later she was weeping softly in Hunt's arms, overcome with the joy of companionship. She had not realized how desperate she had become for someone to lean upon.

"Thank God," Hunt whispered. "What happened to you?"

"It was a trap. Collin was never here."

He stroked her sweat-soaked hair. "I know." He gestured up the way he was heading. "Is there a way out up there?"

She looked at him and shook her head.

He frowned inside the gas mask. "Then it's back down." Hunt fumbled inside his pack and came up with an additional mask. As she slipped it on, he briefly described Collin's death, and his own implementation of Collin's plan.

"Is it dead?"

He stood up and helped her to her feet. "I don't know. I've been looking for you. But I haven't seen a living thing since I left the truck." He did not describe any of the horrors he had seen in the side tunnels and caverns he had explored; the moldering heaps of victims, the traces of torture and suffering.

They moved down, retracing Hunt's path, and within a few minutes they encountered the first whisping traces of poison gas. If Hunt had not found Samantha, she would have died a victim of the vapor

353

before she reached the lower levels of the lair.

They came upon a flat side tunnel, running horizontally, and Hunt eased Samantha into it, both of them holding their guns at ready. Digging into his pack, Hunt produced a red emergency flare that he ignited and tossed into the tunnel ahead of him. Then he switched off his flashlight and proceeded to lead Samantha through the tunnel by the dull red illumination the flare provided. The bodies of the dead were everywhere, and Hunt was afraid to travel with a light in his hand; it made him much too obvious a target.

"Are we going out?" Samantha asked, her voice muffled by the mask.

Hunt looked over at her. "Collin came up with a map of this mine. He has marked some possible sites for the inner chamber." He paused. "We've got to make sure, Sam."

She looked back at him, wide-eyed, then nodded.

As they negotiated a gradual curve in the tunnel, passing several boarded-up accessways to other areas of the mine and several vertical shafts leading to deeper levels, they verified for themselves the penetrative action of the gas Collin had chosen for the job. It seemed to have seeped everywhere, filling every nook and cranny of the passages like a dense fog. The red glow of their flares reflected eerily in the transluscent whisps of gas.

Everywhere they went they found evidence of the occupation of the underground labyrinth by the demon. Some side tunnels had been opened, machinery had been brought in and set up, new reinforcing beams had been brought in to shore up uncertain sections of passageway. And everywhere, they found the bodies of those who, either willingly or unwillingly, had been a part of Satan's legion.

At last, after several more terrifying turns and junctions, they came to the section of mine that intersected with a vast network of natural caverns. Hunt waved for Samantha to pause, then he turned to her and spoke carefully. "I think it's just ahead." Even his voice, muffled by the gas mask, sounded unearthly.

They had taken barely three more steps before they began to distinguish a motionless human form standing peacefully in the middle of the passage ahead of them. From nowhere a chill breeze swept through the tunnel, brushing the veil of deadly gas away from the waiting figure. Samantha froze in horror as she recognized the waiting specter as the Guardian. He stood statue still, with no gas mask to conceal his handsome, placid features. When she had last seen him he had been wearing a perfectly tailored European-styled suit. Now, he wore a dark cloak or robe that obscured the details of his physique. No sight on earth could have more unnerved Samantha and Hunt than this image of Satanic power, standing alone and unperterbed by the mists of death that washed around it like an evil tide.

He smiled at them. "I've been expecting you." His voice had the hollow ring of the crypt. Dan raised his rifle then, but hands gripped him from behind and spun him around, tearing his weapon from his grasp effortlessly. Hunt was terrified to face the thing that

355

had disarmed him. It was one of the corpses he had just passed in the tunnel, reanimated by the demon.

The Guardian noted Hunt's revulsion and sighed sympathetically. "It's a pity we can't revive them all," he said. "It would save so much time."

Samantha felt the bitter taste of defeat in her mouth and battled an urge to vomit. She lowered her rifle as another ghastly shape moved toward her from the shadows cast by Hunt's last flare. "What's going to happen to us, Mr. Grey?" she asked.

The zombies began to push them forward as the Guardian spoke. "It was a brilliant plan. Magnificent."

"Why did it fail?" Hunt asked, his voice catching as he was shoved violently by the dead man behind him.

"We were prepared for you," the Guardian said. "From the moment Miss Egan contacted us at the coven, I've followed your thoughts." He smiled. "Except for the lapses during which you vanished into the city. You were right in your supposition that we cannot easily track you through the interference generated by masses of pathetic, unworthy brains."

"But you couldn't have known it would be gas!" Hunt challenged. He was now level with the Guardian and being pushed ahead, farther into the tunnel. "We didn't know that ourselves."

The Guardian turned to Hunt as he staggered by. "True. We had to improvise at the last moment. Collin was a truly brilliant man." He paused as Samantha was led roughly past him. "We sealed the inner chamber with rock and earth. The master exercises a certain . . . control . . . over air currents as a byproduct of his influence. He was able to stave off the flow of gas for the critical moments we required."

Hunt remembered the chill, pounding winds inside the Ostium dig when Collin had beheaded the dead Egyptian digger. He nodded his understanding.

Samantha had registered almost none of this conversation. Defeat washed over her in waves, and her emotional control was nearly shattered by the terrifying prospect of the fate that awaited them. "You haven't answered my question yet," she said coldly. "What are you going to do with us?"

He looked at her with compassion in his eyes. Yes, there was definitely something of great value in that creature, he thought. He felt again the stirrings of long dead human responses. He sighed. "You have expended a great deal of energy to reach the inner chamber," he said gravely. "There is nothing I can do for either of you." He looked first at Hunt, who tried futilely to strike at him, before being viciously subdued by the animated corpse beside the imprisoned Egyptologist. Then he turned and looked directly into Samantha's fear-clouded eyes. "I'm really sorry."

Despite herself, Samantha found herself believing in the sympathy he extended. His eyes, though displaying cool knowledge of personal power and ruthless intent, contained no trace of cruelty. He was truly alien.

She shivered as at last the Guardian looked away from her. Then she was struck from behind and forced to walk ahead into the tunnel. A part of her

357

consciousness was aware of the Guardian's light footsteps behind her. Oh, God help us! she prayed desperately to herself. Then, from behind, the Guardian's voice answered her.

"There is no God to help you, Samantha. Better to pray to the devil, whom you will meet shortly."

They disappeared into the tunnel maze.

TWELVE
Melville, Montana

Collin shifted position as he lay upon the freezing ridge. From his vantage point on the north side of the canyon he had followed the action as Hunt guided the truck up the valley and into the cave. Collin had tracked Dan after he landed in the helicopter and watched as he exchanged gunfire with the remnants of the Guardian's force. With his infrared nightscope he had seen the truck approach the tunnel mouth and vanish inside.

He waited for several seconds after they disappeared, monitoring the area around the tunnel mouth. The slight signs of movement around it were all he needed to confirm his guess about what was happening.

He slid carefully down to the path behind him and walked uphill, toward the snow-covered ruins of a concrete structure that had once been a pump station in the days when strip mining had been practiced in the area. From this location, atop the mountain into which the Newhope Mine had been dug, he could see both the large man-made reservoir at the top of the immense valley, and the smaller body of water which had been accidently formed just above the Newhope's main entrance.

Collin returned to the inside of the open concrete-walled building and gathered up several heavy duffel bags full of gear. He paused to kick his rumpled sleeping bag into a corner and to check a large detonator. Wires from this black box led off down the mountainside in the direction of the great reservoir at the top of the valley.

He grunted under the weight of his burden and set off in a different direction, down the west side of the mountain toward the smaller lake just above the Newhope. The Hotel Earth was visible, a mile to the southwest.

Five minutes later he arrived at the water's edge. He pulled painfully at a deep thicket, exposing a cache of equipment he had concealed there several days earlier. He hauled a large cylindrical object directly to the water and left it sitting in the mud. Then he began to peel off his heavy overcoat, gloves, and trousers, exposing a thick wet suit he wore beneath his clothes. After pausing to stuff his hand-guns and ammunition into waterproof plastic bags, he dragged a complete set of scuba equipment out of hiding and fit it swiftly to his body. When he had completed this, Collin attached the two gear bags he had carried down the mountain to lanyards hanging from the large cylinder he had left in the mud. This was a powerful underwater scooter that he had painted jet black.

When his preparations were complete, he eased into the pitch dark, icy water and pulled his gear-laden scooter in after him. His booted feet sank unpleasantly into the muddy silt on the bottom as he adjusted his mask, fins, and regulator. He pushed a lever on the scooter and activated its built-in buoyancy compensator, adjusting it until the scooter and its burden were neutral in the stagnant water.

Collin looked around one last time before submerging, checking for landmarks by which to establish his exact position. Then, with a minimum of splashing, he sank beneath the surface and pulled the triggerlike switch that turned the scooter's powerful electric motor on. It pulled him forward effortlessly, and he guided it down to the bottom, where the blunt nose impacted with a barely perceptible thud. Collin could see virtually nothing but a pitch blackness so complete that it was almost physically painful.

The depth gauge on his wrist told him that he was in twenty-five feet of water. The murky liquid was so dirty that he doubted whether even the slightest glow of a light could possibly be seen from the surface. In any event, he had no choice.

With the flick of a thumb switch he activated the scooter's headlight. Even with the aid of this he could not see more than a few feet directly in front of him.

Using the light as a blind man would use a cane, he headed out in the direction he had predetermined a week earlier, using his underwater compass to guide him. There was no sign of life whatsoever in the filthy water, and despite the aid of his full wet suit, he was rapidly getting dangerously cold.

He reached the point where the side of the lake sloped up rapidly, then followed the sloping wall around. The only sounds he heard were the faint whir of the scooter and the gurgle of his own escaping bubbles.

As he followed the unearthly lake bottom, he came suddenly and unexpectedly upon a gaping chasm, a well of utter blackness that led directly into the side of the mountain. This was what he had been searching for, and he unhesitatingly angled the scooter to draw him into the opening.

For the next fifteen interminable minutes, as Hunt and Samantha Egan approached their terrifying confrontation with the Anansi in the mine, Collin wove his way in and out among the obstacles that over the years had accumulated in what had once been mine shaft 43-B. Collin could not help but recall that thirty men had choked and sputtered out their lives in this filthy passage eight years earlier. He came at one point to a solid, massive wall of silt that had somehow gathered at a sharp turn in the tunnel. With his very small field of vision he searched up and down, to and fro, terrified that the tunnel was completely blocked and the way impassable.

But finally, on his third pass, he found an opening just large enough for him to squeeze through. He discovered a streak of claustrophobia he had hitherto been unaware of as he negotiated the next strip of flooded tunnel. This was choked with the debris of construction: old helmets and shovels. He saw what might have been a human bone protruding from the silt.

After this, the way cleared and he found the passage widening, heading definitely upward. Thirty seconds later he broke the surface in darkness, save only for the glow of his scooter's headlamp.

He activated the buoyancy regulator on the scooter

and glided along the surface for a few feet until he came to a ledge. With an effort he pulled himself out of the water onto a tunnel floor of firm dirt. Then he turned and hauled his scooter out of the water, dragging the gear bags after it. From his belt he produced a flashlight with which he examined his surroundings. He was in a fair-sized passage, blasted from some type of rock. It extended deep into the mountain for as far as his light would penetrate.

Collin set the light on a niche in the wall and set to work. Five minutes later, just seconds before Hunt and Samantha were fated to confront the demon, he had shed his scuba gear and donned a set of black coveralls over his wetsuit. His tank and scooter were laid out carefully, awaiting his return, and beside them were two other scuba outfits. The additional tanks were single thirty-eights, much smaller than his seventy-two inch air cylinder.

Collin wore a gas mask tied to his neck, but not yet fitted to his face. A set of nearly opaque goggles also dangled by an elastic strap from his throat. His pistols were strapped to his belt, one still enclosed in a waterproof bag, and a submachine pistol was cradled in one arm. A large, heavy backpack was strapped to his shoulders.

Looking at his watch and cursing, he picked up his flashlight and set off hastily down the tunnel. In thirty seconds he reached the intersection where tunnel 43-B joined one of the main arteries, 2-C. It was boarded tightly shut. With another muttered curse, Collin attacked the rotted wood, desperately afraid that he would be too late.

The scene that confronted Samantha and Hunt when they arrived at the inner chamber, the lair of the beast they had tried to destroy, was truly sinister.

The cavern was enormous, a natural underground cathedral with an inverted bowl-shaped ceiling from which stalactites hung threateningly. Light was supplied to the scene by small lichenlike creatures, which glowed in various unlikely colors. They wriggled and crawled slowly across the vast walls of the dank cavern.

By the light of these weird creatures, small piles of rotting corpses could be seen scattered randomly across the floor. Hunt, after his year spent studying the Ostium lair, found his mind automatically noting and classifying the objects around him. There was no question that this was a much larger lair than the one at Ostium. But it was much newer. His brain simply refused to contemplate the creature itself.

The Satan animal lumbered in the center of the great cavern, quivering and pulsating. The mass of light sparkled and arced, giving off the same pastel colors as the lichens emitted from the walls of the chamber. It was fully aroused, vibrating with rage and hunger, and a chill wind swept around it constantly, as though its intellect searched furiously back and forth for fresh prey.

The Guardian had marched them into the cavern with no more discussion, his face placid. He paid no attention to the revitalized corpses that served as guards for the two prisoners, and when they reached the lair itself, possessed human beings, some of them black Africans in tribal dress, stepped forward from the shadows to accept custodianship of the terrified man and woman. As they did so, the zombies collapsed quietly to the floor, discarded and lifeless again.

A psychic roar louder than any verbal cry echoed through the minds of the prisoners, and the pitch of the furious wind increased. The Guardian accompanied them midway across the rubble-strewn floor of the cavern and then he stopped. He seemed unperterbed by the behemoth they confronted. He paid it no overt respect, but he did not share the horror and revulsion that showed in the faces of Hunt and Egan.

The two prisoners were positioned on either side of the Guardian. A feeling of raw, unbridled power permeated the atmosphere around them. Their hair and clothes snapped and sparked with static electricity, and the roaring wind grew to a fever intensity.

"I have watched the human race through much of its history," the Guardian said. "The mind of man has tended to assign phenomena it does not comprehend to the realm of a supernatural existence." He shook his head. "We live in a universe of living things. A great many of them are as yet beyond the reach of your limited senses, as bacteria have been until very recently. You talk of gods and devils, angels and evil spirits." He smiled ironically. "But there are only animals. There are an infinite variety of predators and prey. You see before you the greatest power in existence, the ultranatural, a creature that has persisted in its present form for untold thousands of years, and that will survive for thousands more.''

Hunt and Samantha stood mutely. Both still wore their amulets. Collin had provided them with devices that, in the event an attempt was made to remove the protective charms, would detonate high-explosive charges Hunt carried in his pack. These kept them free from demonic possession.

"All that you are will be absorbed into the master," the Guardian said. "He has expended a great deal of energy as a result of your activities. It is time now that he be repaid." He spoke dispassionately; a neutral observer verbalizing a reality that could not be altered.

An unspoken order was transmitted, and two strong hands gripped Samantha's upper arms. The Guardian turned to her. "It is a mercy," he said quietly, "that you will be the first."

"No!" she screamed frantically, struggling against the hands that gripped her with unnatural strength. "No!" Her iron control had finally shattered.

"Damn you!" Hunt lunged forward unexpectedly. He was dragged back to his place by the two attendants who flanked him, fuming and cursing. In this final extremity his inate courage and spirit surfaced in the form of this hopeless physical resistance. He was no longer terrified for himself. Instead, he raged inside, his whole being filled with anger such as he had never before known. The scholar had been transformed at last into a warrior. The Guardian recognized this as he watched his aids subdue the man. He granted the Egyptologist a grudging respect and reflected briefly that the quality of those who resisted the master had reached a new high in this trio.

Meanwhile, Samantha had been dragged, kicking and screaming every step of the way, through the tracks of dried blood and decayed flesh that led to the beast. Her guards held her immobile as the writhing monster began to extend its tentacle appendages toward her face. Although she and Hunt were only partially susceptible to its projected hallucinations, it began to force horrifying images into her brain, seeking to maximize her horror before it fed.

Closer, closer the tendrils came, lines of smoke or steam rising slowly from them as they writhed. Hunt wanted to close his eyes, but found he could not abandon her even in this small way. "Samantha!" he called to her desperately, in agony. He could not tell if his cry penetrated the terror-fogged awareness of the woman he loved.

Then, as the tendrils were at the point of touching her face, a new voice echoed through the cavern. "Wait!"

Such was the commanding power of this voice that the demon itself paused, bewildered, and the Guardian whirled in shocked amazement to face the newcomer.

Collin stood as still as a rock just inside the cavern, directly in front of one of the side tunnels that led into the mine. His gas mask had been pulled free of his face and the goggles rested on the patch of forehead above his eyes. One hand trained a submachine gun on the crowd of the more than thirty possessed servants of the creature. In the other he held a small metal box with several pushbuttons on its face. "If I lift my finger from this switch, Guardian," Collin said with the deadly force of absolute truth in his voice, "the explosives in Hunt's backpack will detonate." He was lying, but he prayed the Guardian wouldn't see it.

The Guardian stared at Collin for several seconds, evaluating this wholly unexpected new threat. Collin's eyes showed only his unqualified willingness to sacrifice them all, if need be, to triumph over the master.

The raging wail of the beast washed over the cavern like a tidal wave, bringing with it the icy force of the demon winds. Collin stood unmoved by the display of insane anger. He gestured to Hunt and Samantha. "Release them." When no one moved he took a threatening step forward. "Release them, I said, or by God I'll blow us all to hell!" His voice was a growl as menacing in its way as the demon's cry had been. "I mean it."

The Guardian believed him; Collin had nothing to lose at this point. The slaves guarding Hunt and Samantha released their holds and stepped away. Hunt ran to the weeping, distraught woman and snatched her out of the reach of those horrible, writhing tendrils. With his arm around her shoulders he all but carried her swiftly across the cavern to Collin.

"So, you survived after all," the Guardian said calmly. "What was the point of all this? You surely didn't let them wander in here just so you could rescue them."

Collin turned to Hunt. "Get out of that pack. Quick." Turning back to the Guardian he said, "I had hoped that the gas would do the job. But I wasn't certain. I was watching from the old pumphouse at the top of the mountain while Dan guided the truck in. I saw him land, saw him enter the cavern to check on what had happened." Hunt had eased out of his own pack and now had Collin's on the floor as well.

"Unfortunately for you," Collin went on to the Guardian, "I also saw your people closing in behind them. I knew we had failed. I was pretty sure we would. After last time, when Smith and Raymond died, I knew a direct approach against you would be all but impossible. This attempt was merely a diversion, a cover up." Hunt was looking over at him in angry amazement. "My main plan will destroy you and everything else in this valley."

The Guardian had long since analyzed the memories of Hunt and Samantha for every scrap of information on Collin's plans. "The dam!" he whispered to himself. It was an incredibly adept analysis.

"Yes," Collin said. "Tonight, while you were occupied with this, I mined it. I'm going to blow it before you can possibly drag that filthy creature out of here." He gestured with disgust at the enormous animal.

"Why are you telling me this?"

"Because you can't possibly stop me now. I'm telling you so you and that . . . that demon will know why and how it's being destroyed. So it will remember Sandra and Raymond and Smith and Mc-Phearson and all the others it has murdered." Collin

369

literally sputtered in rage.

The Guardian turned suddenly to Hunt and directed a question at him as a man would throw a knife. "Where would he put this detonator?"

An image arose unbidden into Hunt's mind, a picture of a marking on Collin's worn map showing a spot marked with an "X" and labeled "detonator." It was the abandoned pump station on the mountain!

The Guardian showed no sign of the knowledge he now possessed. "How will you escape from here?"

Collin motioned for Samantha and Hunt to proceed him into the passageway at his back. "That's my problem." He nodded. "Good-bye, Guardian."

The Guardian nodded in return. "Until we meet again, Collin." He retained his imperterbable calm.

Collin considered firing a burst into the tall figure of the demon's messiah, but regretfully decided that such a move would bring the slaves down on them regardless of his explosives. He backed toward the tunnel, then he pulled a large flare from his belt. It was a special magnesium flare and its glare in the confines of the cavern would be blinding even to the Guardian's superhuman eyes. Collin struck the fuse and tossed it out to the center of the floor. Slowly the magnesium began to ignite, and he slipped his goggles down prematurely. The Guardian sensed his mistake instantly and realized that there was not yet enough light for Collin to see through the welder's goggles.

He launched himself across the open floor with superhuman speed, striking with the energy of a jungle cat. Collin had been backing toward the cave in which Hunt and Samantha awaited him, and in the sudden blindness of the goggles he saw only a blur approach him before the Guardian collided with him, snatching the remote detonator from his hand before he could release the switch. It was an incredible display of strength, speed, and dexterity. The Guardian crossed the thirty feet separating the two of them, struck Collin down, and grabbed the transmitter without allowing its push-button switch to be depressed. Only a desperate man would have attempted it.

With his free hand the Guardian enclosed Collin's throat, bringing his great strength to bear to choke his enemy, or break his neck. Collin struggled and writhed desperately. He knew that he would already have been dead if the Guardian had free use of both hands.

The two struggled as the slaves moved haltingly forward, and the flare burned more and more brightly, filling the cavern with an unbearably intense light.

Collin felt himself going under as the light flooded the cave, the last of his strength was slipping away from him. But the light enveloped them completely, blinding the legions of possessed and thereby blinding the demon who watched through their eyes. It blinded the Guardian as well, who released Collin and raised his free arm up to shield his eyes, crying out as he did so.

Collin was up and away in a heartbeat, shoving the Guardian aside. The goggles protected his own eyes from the worst of the terrible glare, and he could see reasonably well as he staggered toward the tunnel where Hunt and Samantha waited.

The two had shielded their eyes with their arms and so escaped being totally blinded. The shadows of the tunnel walls had saved them. They caught Collin as he staggered in.

"You both all right?" he gasped. They nodded. He was pleased to see that Samantha had recovered at least enough awareness to respond. "Let's go!" He began to run down the narrow, winding passage. As he did so, he groped for the two gas masks he had brought for his friends, tore them free of their clips and handed them out without breaking stride. He reached then for his own and realized that it was gone. It had been torn off during his struggle with the Guardian. He kept running. He could only hope that the worst of the gas had dissipated. Collin glanced at his watch. Over an hour had passed since it had been released. It was possible that by this time the gas had dispersed to nonlethal levels.

They approached the most dangerous of the up-coming intersections and he tossed another flare out, holding his friends back while the flare sputtered to full life. He could see struggling, blinded figures staggering within the glare and he brought his sub-machine gun to bear for the first time, mowing down the helpless figures. With a click his automatic weapon stopped firing. He realized it was empty and he urged his friends to link hands and shut their eyes as tightly as possible.

Ramming a new magazine into his gun, he hooked Hunt's fingers in his backpack and led the two of them through the open intersection. They reached the other side and Collin turned down a smaller tunnel. The fact that Hunt and Samantha were now effectively blinded did not disturb him. If they did not know where they went, the demon would not be able to track them by reading their minds.

At last they came to the boarded-up side passage that led to the flooded length of tunnel. Collin guided his two friends inside and then eased through the small opening he had made in the wooden barrier. When he was safely through he made an effort to close up the barrier in such a way that it would appear unbreached from the other side. This done, he slung his submachine gun over his shoulder and disgarded the goggles and pack. He felt they were now safe from immediate pursuit. But this thought did nothing to diminish his sense of urgency. "Come on." He led the other two, whose vision was slowly clearing, down the narrow tunnel by the light of his flashlight.

"Where are we going?" Samantha asked.

Collin had no time to answer her. He hurried them down the tunnel and was infinitely relieved to come into sight of the water-filled entrance to their escape route. Hunt's vision had cleared to a point that he could distinguish the scuba gear. "So that's how you did it?"

Collin nodded. He knew that Hunt was a certified diver, but that Samantha was not. "Help her get into this, will you?" Chris was still too exhausted from his struggle with the Guardian to have the energy to assist the girl. He barely managed to get his own tank and mask on by the time the other two were ready. Hunt was giving quick, breathless instructions to Samantha.

"You just breathe normally, through your mouth. Keep breathing freely and constantly, and don't hold your breath. You got that?"

She nodded uncertainly as Collin handed them a length of line. "You both hang onto that. I'll go first." He slipped into the water and manhandled the scooter in with him.

As Hunt and Egan eased down into the icy water Dan asked, "Are you really going to blow the dam?"

Collin looked up at him and nodded. "You better believe it."

Hunt shook his head. "Think of all those people."

"That's why you and Samantha have got to get out of here. You've got to warn the town and the mines."

Hunt nodded, seeing the sense of Collin's urgency.

They ducked under the surface, leaving a trail of bubbles on the top of the filthy pool to mark their exit.

Ten minutes later they broke the surface of the lake. Collin immediately scanned the terrain for signs of ambush and Samantha began to cough and sputter, having spat out her regulator mouthpiece too soon and swallowed some of the stagnant, scummy water.

Collin had extinguished the light on the scooter before they had headed for the surface, and they made their way to the bank in almost total darkness. Gasping, the three hauled themselves out of the water, abandoning the scooter in the shallows.

"What happens now?" Hunt asked, slipping out of his oxygen tank where he lay, exhausted and shivering from the icy water.

Collin turned to the others. "You two have got to get to the chopper. You've got to warn the town about the dam." He handed Dan a sealed, waterproof envelope. "When you're airborne over the mine, open that."

Hunt nodded and said nothing more.

"The Guardian knows by now that we've escaped," Samantha said, her voice little more than a harsh croak.

"Right," Collin said. "He'll be doing two things at once, unless I miss my guess. He'll be having his people breaking their backs to get that damned beast out of that lair as fast as possible. He'll try to outrace me. And second, he'll send someone to try to get to the detonator before I do."

"What if they beat you there?" Samantha asked.

"I've got a good lead," Collin said. He had planned his route with care. He wriggled out of his tank and stood up. From the bushes he picked up two more submachine guns. "You better get going. Your chopper is that way." He pointed to the southwest.

Hunt evaluated their present position with respect to the helicopter and realized for the first time the care that Collin had put into the planning of the operation. Collin had specified a landing site that gave Hunt and Samantha an advantage on this return journey. They, also, would probably have a fair head start on the Guardian's forces.

Collin unwrapped his dry pistol from its water-proof bag and took his first steps up the mountain. "Get going," he said. "It's vital that you make it." He turned back toward them as he spoke.

Samantha and Hunt stood up unsteadily and slung their weapons on their shoulders. Both were shivering violently with the cold.

"Oh," Collin said suddenly. "I almost forgot." He gestured toward the brush where he had hidden the guns. "There's a couple of dry jackets in there." He turned once more to go.

"Chris?" Samantha called softly.

He turned again. "What?"

"If this works, and we survive, I'll never forgive you for deceiving us like this, for making us think you were dead." She tried to smile.

He smiled tiredly back at her. She was going to be all right. "We'll talk about it in a few hours. Now get going." He turned his back on them and stalked away into the darkness.

Hunt helped Samantha into her jacket, then looked at his watch. "Four-thirty A.M. It'll be daylight in an hour."

Samantha glanced once more in the direction in which Collin had vanished, then she followed Dan down the sloping side of the mountain, toward the helicopter that awaited them just over a mile away.

Collin's guess as to the actions of the Guardian was almost exactly correct, save for one detail only. The demon's force of slaves was indeed hard at work preparing the beast for transport out of the lair.

Teams were at that very instant dragging in the huge sledlike apparatus by which the animal was hauled in and out of its lairs. Others were clearing and opening the way, while still others were breaking the Satan beast's transport plane out of camouflage in the valley below. These latter were chosen members of the Guardian's willing followers.

But the Guardian had reserved for himself and a handful of his cultists the task of pursuing Collin to the mountaintop in an all-out attempt to prevent him from blowing the dam.

Collin could not have anticipated that the Guardian would have an all-terrain vehicle by which he and his force of five armed men would motor nearly a mile up the mountainside before being forced to continue on foot. He did not know that his precious lead had been cut down to bare minutes as he slogged tiredly up the wooded, snow-dotted mountainside.

His first indication that he was being overtaken came when a shot rang out, echoing loudly. The bullet struck a tree ahead of him and to his left. He dodged behind a granite boulder as another bullet struck where he had been walking.

He pulled his pistol from his holster and looked back. There was enough light now for him to see the approaching party, swarming madly up the mountainside after him. He judged that they were still perhaps a hundred yards behind him. Too far, really, for an accurate pistol shot. He loosed off a couple of shots anyway, and had the satisfaction of seeing them dive for cover as he had done. He crawled on his belly into the line of timber running up the ridge and got to his feet, resuming his dogged progress toward the ruined cement pumphouse above.

The Guardian turned to his lieutenant, the young psychopath Weston, and saw that he had taken one of Collin's bullets in his left biceps. "Ignore the bullets," the Guardian commanded sternly. "He can't get all of us."

Weston nodded, more afraid of the Guardian than of Collin, and anxious to please the master by this proof of bravery in tracking down and destroying the sacrilegious enemy, Collin.

The team broke into the open and resumed their running, panting progress up the wooded, snowy slope.

Collin waited in the bough of a great pine that hung out over the ravine and looked down on his backtrail. When his pursuers closed to less than fifty yards, he carefully sighted and squeezed off a round that struck the lead man neatly in the heart, dropping him like a butchered steer. "Let's see you bring that one back to life," Collin muttered to himself as he sighted and fired again, this time at the second man in the line.

He missed, then ducked and rolled as a bullet skillfully aimed by the fearless Weston impacted on the branch of his concealing pine tree.

More shots rang out as Collin staggered up the rise, toward the gathering light of dawn. A demonic wind beat down upon him, and the buzzing of attempted possession grew in his ears to a maddening pitch. He ignored, as best he could, the awful, agonized howl of the raging creature as it pounded down upon him waves of energy; furious screaming torrents of force combined with the icy winds of death.

He slipped and struggled, fighting for every precious inch of ground he gained. The demon was doing its best to slow him down until the Guardian caught up with him.

Collin cried out in defiance and pain and lunged forward a long step at a time. With the worst of the storm upon him he tripped and fell hard on a boulder, feeling a terrible pain lance through his left leg.

New shots reverberated across the terrain. He had no idea where the bullets struck, and he was too terrified to turn around and look. Ignoring the agony in his leg, he got to his feet and sprinted several yards to the shelter of an immense outcropping of rock. Here he fell, unable to go farther, and turned to face his pursuers again. The trees were thicker here, and he could not see them. But he could hear them as they crashed through thickets on their way up the slope. Collin looked around behind him. He was now a mere twenty or thirty yards from the concrete pump-house.

Those tracking him were desperate. As Collin watched, the first man up the hill broke free from the trees and charged into the open, straight at Collin's hiding place. When Collin had a clear shot his pistol bucked in his hand and the running man clutched his side and fell. He was wounded but not dead.

Chris pumped several more shots into the struggling man, then ejected his expended magazine and slammed a fresh one home. No sooner was he reloaded than the next runner broke into the open. But this one saw his dead comrade and dove at once for cover, just as Collin fired.

He missed the diving man and swore savagely. Shots began to ring out from the trees below and Collin ducked back behind the rock. His breathing was so heavy and his ears so abused that he almost missed the sound of running feet as one of the remaining four enemies rushed at his position. Collin rolled into the open and fired at point blank range directly into the torso of the charging attacker, who fell directly beside Collin's hiding place.

More gunfire spat from positions in the trees below as Collin crawled quickly out of the line of fire. A bullet nicked his forearm and blood spurted thickly along the sleeve of his coveralls.

The Guardian, standing in the concealment of the trees thirty feet down the slope, caught the scent of the blood and unconsciously licked his lips. He knew the smell of Collin's blood from previous encounters, and he knew his quarry had been wounded.

"He's hit," the Guardian hissed to Weston, who had been firing from a position of concealment beside him.

Weston turned questioningly to the Guardian.

"You go up that way, send Trovsky there," the Guardian pointed. Even his own chill breath condensed into mist in the early morning cold.

"Right." He waved for the attention of his only surviving companion, then indicated the Guardian's orders by handsignals.

As Trovsky, a former psychiatric inmate at Atuscadera Prison in California, began to move around the right side of the massive rock obstruction ahead, Weston took off around the left, favoring his bleeding left arm. Guardian was glad when the psychopath was gone; the warm smell of his fresh blood was an irritating distraction.

The Guardian stood still for a moment behind the shelter of the trees, peering up through the branches at the spot where Collin had disappeared. He could still catch a faint whiff of his enemy's blood on the demon wind, which had now subsided to a breeze.

As he waited impatiently for his men to move into position, the Guardian probed with his thoughts into the progress in the mine below. The slaves had nearly finished removing the earth and rock barrier they had set up against the gas, while another group was still in the midst of the laborious process of heaving the master's huge body upon the long rolling platform that would bear it to safety. Not for the first time the Guardian reflected upon the irony of his master's form. This being, of superior intelligence and power, had no physical senses or musculature of its own. The master was wholly dependent upon the labor of its victims for every physical need.

He probed outward, checking the progress of the team working on the plane in the valley beneath the mine. Progress there, too, was acceptable.

A sudden biting impression reached him from the work party clearing the escape tunnel. The great invading truck could not be moved. Its brakes were firmly locked and the cab doors had been welded shut. The windshield had been replaced by some transparent pane that so far had resisted the efforts of the team to shatter it. The Guardian saw in this instant another dimension in Collin's insidious plan. What an adversary, the Guardian thought. With a mental command he dispatched one of the members of his coven from the plane to the tunnel entrance, instructing him to bring an oxyacetyline torch.

Swiftly, the Guardian estimated the amount of time required for the master to be removed to safety. Then, he measured with his eye the scant distance between Collin and the abandoned pump station on the summit. Unless the cunning man were delayed somehow, the Master would die in the inevitable flood.

Shots rang out from the left, and the Guardian's head snapped around, his nostrils expanding. He dared not contact the mind of his servant Trovsky, for fear of distracting him at a crucial moment, so he fought down his desperate curiosity and headed around the left side of the clearing ahead.

As the Guardian moved around, Trovsky lay a hundred feet above, behind a hollow log with a bullet in his leg. Collin had been circling around in search of a less exposed path upward, and unfortunately for Trovsky, he had chanced to check his back trail just as the coven member stealthily climbed into the open, a bare twenty feet away.

Trovsky leaned up over the tree trunk and snapped a quick shot off with his carbine at the tree behind which Collin had taken cover. Trovsky's leg was bleeding badly, but he had no time for more than a glance at it.

He fired once more into the tree trunk, seeing no reaction as the bullet knocked a clump of slushy snow and bark loose from a low branch. Trovsky chewed on his lower lip. The pain in his leg goaded him for revenge. And further, if Collin had escaped him and was now on his way to the top of the slope . . .

The wounded man laboriously pulled himself to his feet and sprang at his best speed for the line of trees at the edge of the small clearing directly ahead of him. He dragged his bloody, useless leg in a limp, grunting involuntarily with each ragged step. The sky was getting lighter each second, and he could see quite clearly into the shadows as he struggled up the slope. With one last lunge, he threw himself beyond the trunk of the tree behind which Collin had hidden, his carbine spitting fire and bullets. But there was no one there.

Trovsky searched the ground for tracks and saw the traces Collin had left when he had dived for cover. But there were no tracks leading away from the tree in any direction. Suddenly, from the air around him, he heard a tense voice. "Up here."

Trovsky jerked his head around in panic, firing wildly in an arc around him, again seeing no one. The truth dawned on him too late, and he looked up at the branches of the tree just as Collin shot him cleanly between the eyes.

Collin dropped heavily onto the snow-dotted ground, grabbed the carbine and slung it over his shoulder. He knew it would be no use against the Guardian—only his blood quenched forty-five caliber bullets would be effective against that being. But the carbine might be a help against the other man, the last of the Guardian's party. Collin did not know where he was.

He glanced at his watch and then up at the brightening sky. Soon, now, he thought. He wondered if Hunt and Samantha had reached the helicopter yet, then dismissed this and all other distractions from his weary mind.

After looking and listening carefully, he set off stealthily up the wooded mountainside and moved off out of sight of the clearing beside which the dead man lay. Thirty seconds later the Guardian glided silently into the shadow of the fatal tree and looked down emotionlessly at his fallen minion. Another failed, he thought. Only Weston remained, but Weston was the most dangerous of them all, a born assassin. Collin's trail, dotted here and there with traces of his blood, was easy to follow. The Guardian could track him easily now by scent alone. He continued up the slope.

Two miles away, Hunt and Samantha staggered into the clearing where their helicopter awaited them, just as Hunt had left it. They had heard the intermittent crackling of gunfire behind them, heard it and dreaded the events it bespoke. But they maintained hope that Collin would somehow reach the detonater and blow the dam, and they hurried in order to bring warning to the townspeople in the valley below.

The Guardian, picking the details of their mission from their minds, had not troubled himself with them; they could be tracked down later. But the master, searching for targets in its hatred and fear, dispatched its possessed to intercept them; a group of four former policemen armed with rifles. Samantha had caught sight of them far down the hillside several minutes before they had reached the clearing.

Hunt helped her up when she stumbled over a boulder, still a hundred feet from the chopper. "Hurry," he breathed, "it's going to be close."

With their last reserves of energy they put on a burst of speed and reached the aircraft before their pursuers came into view beyond the canyon rim. Hunt threw his submachine gun down between the seats and strapped on his headset. Muttering to himself he leaned down, primed the engines and threw the starter switch. With a muffled bang the engines began to rev. Slowly, ever so slowly, the rotors began to turn and Hunt flicked several more switches in succession. "Strap yourself in," he ordered. "And keep your gun ready."

Samantha obeyed, keeping her eyes glued to the canyon rim at the point where the enemy must soon appear.

Several seconds passed as the rotors came up to speed. Hunt gripped the control stick and the helicopter hesitantly lifted a few feet off the ground.

"There they are!" Samantha shouted into her throat mike. Heads had appeared at the rim line.

"Hang on!" Hunt began to guide the craft

upward, as a volley of shots rang out over the roar of the motors. Samantha poked the muzzle of her automatic out into the open air and released a burst of bullets that impacted on the ground in the general vicinity of the four armed men. To her dismay, they ignored the mortal danger and continued to aim their rifles at the slowly rising helicopter. Bullets tore several silver-veined holes in the cockpit, and sparks suddenly escaped from a corner of the control panel with which Hunt flew the craft. The helicopter swerved for a second, and dropped a dozen feet before Dan regained control, struggling to compensate for a disabled stabilizer.

One of the four men had dropped his rifle and was running at amazing speed across the clearing while his companions continued to fire. Samantha regained her balance and took careful aim with the gun. She squeezed off an amazing line of bullets that started at the left of the three riflemen, then swept with precision across the first two in line, dropping them twitching to the ground. The third man lept out of the way.

Meanwhile, as the craft rose to a bare eight feet off the ground, the running man beneath them reached the ground directly under the slowly rising craft and jumped, grabbing on to the left pontoon, the one directly beneath Samantha's seat. The helicopter dipped and dropped again, until Dan applied more power and drew it aloft once more.

Up higher, higher they lifted, and the clinging madman slowly drew himself up over the pontoon. Samantha pointed the submachine gun directly into his face and squeezed the trigger, horrified to find she was out of ammunition. Using the weapon as a club, she began to beat and pound at him, hoping to drive him loose. But though she jabbed and slashed, he continued to pull himself up, reaching to get a firm grip on her.

His possessed face was deep blue, and blood had begun to seep from his pores as the muscles in the body were driven far beyond human tolerance. The evil hatred that poured out of the maniacal eyes was recognizibly that of the beast she had faced in the cave, and this knowledge nearly drove her to madness.

Finally, one of the cold blue hands found a grip on her leg as tight and strong as a band of steel. She cried out, kicking and screaming as she felt herself being dragged slowly, inch by inch out of her seat. She felt the straps that secured her to her seat slowly beginning to part, incredibly. In the last seconds before she knew she would be swept out and down to death she raked the face of the thing with her fingernails, gouging the eyes, tearing the eyes, struggling to dislodge herself, all in vain.

And then, the chopper bucked and twirled as Hunt took his hands from the controls in a gamble that could have proven fatal to them both. He picked up his own submachine gun, and emptied it into the head and upper torso of the zombielike creature looming in from the pontoon.

The sound was deafening, the flash in the confined space blinding, but the next thing Samantha knew, the creature was gone and Hunt was one handedly pulling her back into the cockpit. His other hand fought with the controls, stabilizing the flight of the chopper.

At the instant Collin heard the echo of the helicopter's engines, a sound that assured him that at least one of his friends had reached it safely, he was making his way into the cleared area directly below the cement walls of the abandoned structure inside of which he had concealed the detonator.

In the dawn light the patches of snow piled in the cracks at the base of the cement walls glistened clearly as he flattened himself against the freezing slab of the south wall.

With all his being he listened, knowing that somewhere nearby someone was waiting, stalking. Several seconds passed, and again he heard nothing. Then, he edged forward and eased around the corner, facing the west wall where the gaping entrance awaited him. He took a silent step, then another, his heart pounding in fear. His third step brought the sound of a snapping branch and he froze. Nothing.

As he was about to take his next step, a figure flashed out of the opening with incredible speed, launching into the open directly in front of Collin. It was Weston, who had reached the entrance ahead of him after all. His carbine was chattering even as the psychopath flew through the air, and only by a miracle did Collin escape that initial barrage. He dropped to one knee by reflex, thus avoiding Weston's next shot, which bounced off the cement wall behind him.

With the cold, resigned calmness of a man who believes himself lost, Collin resisted the temptation to loose off a series of wild shots. Instead, he took the extra heartbeat he needed to take careful aim, allowing Weston to squeeze off several more poorly aimed bullets at him, one of which took some flesh from his left side, just above the hip.

Collin's clean single bullet caught Weston high in the torso, above the heart, and the shock of its impact threw him back and over the edge of an embankment. Collin heard the man fall farther and farther down the hill.

Some part of his mind noted that the carbine was empty and he dropped it limply into the snow, turning slowly toward the door.

His dazed mind had barely grasped the fact that he was still alive when the black-coated figure of the Guardian swung down from the overhang above the rectangular opening in the cement wall.

They stood facing each other, Collin's automatic having come into his hand seemingly of its own accord. In the silence that followed, they absorbed each other's presence, each noting the animal energy flaring in the other, the even rhythm of breaths condensing into mist and escaping on the mountain wind. Collin remembered a samurai saying to the effect that a fight was already won or lost before a sword was drawn, in the battle of wills preceding actual combat.

"So it's down to the two of us," Collin said.

"It always has been." The Guardian's calm was not shaken.

"How fast can you move?" Collin asked, keeping his weapon trained on the enemy's heart. "Fast enough to dodge a bullet?"

The Guardian had gone into a state of controlled tension, floating easily on his feet, responding minutely to changes in Collin's stance. They circled for several seconds, during which Collin reached to his belt and came up with the same blood-quenched knife that he had used to behead the digger in the Sudan.

The Guardian showed no sign of fear as he fluidly shifted around his prey. "You are one of the best opponents I have faced," the Guardian spoke calmly, seriously, "across thousands of years."

Collin kept his eyes on the Guardian, straining for the moment when violence would erupt. "What are you, that you can live so long."

"I was once—" in midsentence the Guardian lunged with superhuman speed for the man, almost reaching him before Collin could pull the trigger. The blast of the gun rocked the Guardian back. His face reflected shock and his hand went to his right shoulder where the bullet had penetrated. Blood seeped slowly onto his cloak, and he backed up to his former distance of about ten feet.

"I was once a man," the Guardian continued as though nothing had happened. It had been so long since he had been truly harmed that he had trouble believing it had really happened, even though intellectually he had known it was possible. He continued to circle. "I was born into a civilization so far removed from this place and time that not even the slightest trace or memory exists."

"How did you become . . . what you are?"

"Like you, I was different. And the master was young then. I desired life; life eternal and unchanging. And so, back before the dawn of history, the pact was struck between us. And the terms: life everlasting for me—"

"In exchange for the guardianship," Collin finished. He backed toward the gaping doorway and the Guardian's eyes narrowed. "Symbiotic," Collin went on. "As long as it lives, you live, and vice versa."

The Guardian nodded. "Yes. My humanity was a high price to pay, but I have seen much." He lunged again, slightly more slowly this time as his wound sapped his strength, but Collin fended him off by whipping the pistol in his direction.

The Guardian backed off, then with a flash of his old blinding speed he ripped a branch from a tree behind him and lashed it swordlike at Collin, who loosed off a wild shot and dodged as the branch struck the cement wall behind him. He whirled and fired again as the Guardian advanced, slashing with the branch in such a way as to keep the man off balance and without a clear line of fire.

Collin backed, firing a third and fourth shot, one of which creased the side of the Guardian's neck and drew more thick blood.

With a cry of rage, the being lunged forward again, driving the man up the north side of the summit and away from the waiting cement pumphouse.

The Guardian grabbed a softball-sized stone and hurled it the few feet between them, striking Collin's right wrist and jarring the pistol loose. It clattered back down toward the cement structure and the Guardian closed in, swinging sledgehammer blows at Collin, who had backed up against an embankment leading to the cliff at the very top of the mountain.

Collin slashed back with his knife in defensive terror, cutting long deep slices in the forearms of the creature. But not before the Guardian had dealt him several bone-jarring punches to the head.

The Guardian backed up as Collin shinnied around a tree trunk, then the creature turned and rushed back toward the waiting cement structure. Collin cried out, "No!" and rushed after him, staggering with the last of his energy.

In triumph the Guardian burst into the darkness of the pumphouse and searched among the scattering of debris for the detonator. He found it just as Collin appeared behind him in the doorway.

With a totally human cry of victory, the Guardian savagely tore loose the cables that were connected to the poles of the detonator. With the device in his arms, he whirled and plunged right through Collin, ignoring the slashing of the knife across his back, heading for the cliff above the pumphouse, beyond the spot where Collin had lost his pistol.

Staggering and crying out in anger, Collin ran after the fleet-footed servant of Satan. He reached him just as the Guardian stood up at the ledge that looked down on the small lake just above the mine entrance, the lake through which Collin had gained access to the mine.

In triumph, like an ancient priest casting a sacrifice to some terrible demon-god, the Guardian lifted the detonator high above his head and cast it down, down, farther than a human arm could have flung it. It hit the surface of the lake far below, shattering on impact, and sank from sight in the center of the body of water.

Slowly, gathering energy from the beast being moved from the cave below, the Guardian turned on Collin, who shrank away from him, his back against the embankment. He held his pitiful knife in front of him like a silver cross before a vampire.

"And, now, my worthy friend," the Guardian began. He was interrupted then by the sound of the helicopter approaching from the west, and he glanced up.

In the cockpit, a very dazed Samantha was searching the mountainside for signs of Collin at the pumphouse. Hunt had insisted that they swing up before heading down to the town. "Do you see them?" Hunt asked.

She shook her head. "No, I . . . wait!" She got her binoculars and looked down. "I think I see what looks like a body lying in the snow. I can't be sure." Her emotions were too overworked for her to react even to Collin's death.

Hunt pulled the envelope that Collin had given him from a shirt pocket. "He said that after we were airborne, we were to read this." He handed it to Samantha, who tore open the waterproof plastic seal.

"My God!" She looked over at Hunt with wide eyes.

"What is it?"

"Never mind," she said. "There's no time to explain." She dropped the paper and searched frantically for a control panel that Collin's note described. "Take us back over the mine!" she screamed. "Hurry!"

Hunt immediately altered his course, swinging westward and slightly down, as Samantha took the control box across her knees and activated it.

Far below, the body of the Satan beast was being borne on its rolling platform toward the front of the tunnel. It was propelled by the labor of dozens of straining slaves, moving it in exactly the manner in which it had been transported from lairs thousands of years ago.

It was within a few yards of the gigantic truck that stood blocking its escape when the terrified coven member finally melted the welds by which Collin had sealed the door on the driver's side of the cab. The coven member, when he looked at the advancing monster, did not see the true form of the thing. He saw only the image of demonic, glowing presence, his own mind's conception of the devil he worshiped. Terrified, he pulled open the door and climbed behind the wheel. At this instant, Samantha looked out the window at the quarry, gauging the action in the tunnel below, lit by the headlights that still blazed, and by the sunlight beginning to filter in.

"What's happening?" Hunt asked desperately, watching the scurrying figures on the ground below. The distant crackle of small-arms fire filtered up to him as sharpshooters tried vainly to shoot the helicopter down.

"It's escaping," Samantha said slowly, her mind concentrating on Collin's note. "They're going to try to back the truck out," Samantha said. Her finger hovered again over a red button. "I'm going to press it twice this time." She repeated Collin's written instructions to herself. "Press it once, then wait until the truck is moving."

On the mountain below, the Guardian's searching mind had picked Samantha's thoughts from the air. "No!" he raged, screaming with true demonic fury. He raised his fist to the air and torrents of fury, devil winds of incredible violence, rocked the helicopter in the sky. "Damn you, damn you!" screamed the Guardian, glancing down with hatred at Collin. "You never meant to blow the dam!" It was an accusation.

"No," Collin said, overcome by the spectacle of the Guardian aroused to his full wrath. "There are no charges."

The Guardian screamed again and clutched his head with his hands, framed against the rising sun. The howl of the beast filled the air around him, and around the teetering helicopter in which Samantha and Hunt fought for their lives.

A burst of lightning flashed from nowhere, striking the plexiglass windshield directly in front of Samantha. Involuntarily she drew back within the bouncing, gyrating craft and the control box slipped from her knees onto the floor.

As she struggled to retrieve it, the welder in the tunnel below scrambled into the driver's seat and turned on the ignition, setting the vehicle to a gentle vibration as the engine turned again.

As the Guardian raged and the helicopter danced across the sky overhead, the welder slammed the gear-shift lever into reverse, grinding the gears unmercifully, then slowly let out the clutch.

In that instant, the helicopter banked steeply in an impossible wind that threatened to smash the craft in midair, as the full power of the demon was unleashed upon it. Thrown against the pilot, Samantha was unable to stop the control box from sliding out of the cockpit and careening downward.

The Guardian's cries of rage mingled with those of the beast he served as his fist continued to pound the air at the helicopter. And then, as the control box plummeted earthward, the driver of the truck in the mouth of the mineshaft eased the clutch all the way out and the wheels did a complete revolution, activating the detonator of the massive charge of explosives Collin had concealed within the gas canisters.

A mushroom cloud of flame and debris erupted from the mine, and the earth shook as hundreds of thousands of tons of dirt and rock shifted. In the seismic shock that followed, quaking and shaking the mountain on which Collin and the Guardian stood, the insanely raging Guardian, staring flabber-gastedly at the helicopter and then down at the total destruction of the mine below, toppled slightly, losing his balance for an instant as the ground shifted and danced beneath his feet.

In this instant, which offered Collin's only remote

hope of survival, he threw his knife, which buried itself to the hilt in the Guardian's shoulder, then he lunged forward after it, hitting the creature with a flying tackle at knee level, pushing the Guardian off the cliff and into space.

To the bitter end, Collin had played his game of deception, gambling on the Guardian's deeply ingrained reliance on reading the minds of others. Samantha's control box could in fact have detonated the truck's explosive cargo. But he had not relied on it. Everything had been designed to lure the creature into the open, into the close proximity of the truck, and convince the Guardian of the desperate need to get the truck out of the way. The charge had been set to go off as soon as the truck began to roll backward.

Collin did not look down over the rim of the ridge. Instead, he collapsed, breathing deeply, frantically, his cheek pressed lovingly against the frosty ground. Never had he felt so wonderfully grateful to be alive, never had the Earth seemed so sweet and welcoming.

He half walked, half crawled to the stability of the embankment against which he had almost died, and here he curled up in a pile of leaves, exhausted. From where he lay he could see the helicopter glinting in the light of the rising sun as it slowly flew westward, and a trail of smoke rising from the mine out of his view.

His breathing had subsided now, and his mind began to retreat into a dreamworld of peace and serenity, of comfort and love, as it cut the cords of consciousness that connected him with his bruised and battered body.

A gentle wind caressed his cheek as he dreamed, unable to move, or worry, or even wonder at the extent of his victory. Later there would be time, he thought to himself. Later. His eyes closed and he was untroubled by conscious thought for the rest of the day.